OUTCASTS OF TIME

EDGE OF TIME BOOK 1

JEFF MILLS

LONG STORY PUBLISHING, LLC

For Mr. Webb.
His passion for history was more infectious than he ever realized; I think he would have appreciated what he inspired.

CONTENTS

CHAPTER 1

RUDE AWAKENING

When Simon Foxx met Catalina Carabresa, he unwittingly set into motion a sequence of events that would, in a relatively short time, lead to the complete annihilation of the Earth—twice. Granted, one could make the argument that if his parents had not been introduced to each other on a double date one stormy summer evening; and if Simon's future father had not insulted his future mother; and if his future mother had not, in a fit of fury, slapped his future father, immediately realized her error, and overcompensated in her effort to make amends; then they might not have married the next summer and Simon Foxx might very well not have been born on another stormy night three years later—and the Earth might have continued undisturbed in its natural celestial course.

But they were, he did, she did, they did, and he was.

Naturally, Simon Foxx never intended to cause any harm, let alone destroy all life on the planet; his was a kind and gentle soul, compassionate, understanding, generous, naïve to the point of absurdity. He saw good in people, even when they themselves didn't know it existed; always with him people received the benefit of the doubt, as he rationalized their actions and words, saw deeper meaning in their behaviors. He rarely got angry, even when he had reason for it. Though at heart a happy person, he grew up lonely and depressed, primarily because the people in his life rarely took him seriously—which ultimately manifested as an appalling lack of confidence when it came to social skills, particularly those pertaining to women. So he turned to books as his one great solace. Dumas and Hugo, Dickens and Scott, Twain and Melville all taught him that life held a higher purpose, and he gladly lost himself in their pages, always hoping that one day things would change and he would ultimately make a difference in the world.

So, to say that Simon Foxx intentionally obliterated his home planet—twice—would be a complete misrepresentation of his character, an injustice of cosmic proportions, and an unconscionable perversion of the facts.

The truth is he only meant to do it once.

Simon Foxx didn't hear the sharp crack of breaking glass as he slept soundly after a long night of trying to decide what to do on the last day of the weekend. In six weeks of college the weekends had all gone pretty much the same: after class on Friday you make plans with the guys concerning what to do on Saturday; you continue this into the wee hours of the morning and consequently oversleep; you lounge about all day, continuing to make plans, with no real prospects for the evening; as evening approaches, you go to dinner at the campus center, see that most people are in your same situation, and end up watching some bad action movie by yourself in the dorm; you stay up late again, trying to decide what to do on the last day of the weekend; and on Sunday evening, if you remember in time, you stay up past midnight writing the 5-page paper you should have spent the weekend composing for your 8am class on Monday. Simon had, of course watched a fairly awful movie until the extreme hours when night and morning are essentially the same, and at some point before dawn had crawled into his upper bunk with the prospect of snoozing most of Sunday away—at least until the double digits of late morning.

So when a river of icy water poured across his body in the moments before dawn he jolted awake with a gasp.

As he tried to sit up, the unexpectedly harsh current washed him out of bed, depositing his half-naked body onto the floor in an ungainly heap, his head throbbing from an unfortunate encounter with a well-stocked bookcase. A second, more successful attempt at sitting up cleared the fog from his head and brought him to full consciousness, a state he immediately regretted. In the dim light radiating from a small lamp across the room he ascertained several important facts in a single glance. First, his roommate had not come back; a social genius who always ended up someplace better than a basement dorm with what he called his Eccentric Cellmate, he usually landed in the arms, if not the bed, of his current conquest. That suited Simon; he preferred to have the room to himself. Still, it irked him that this sleazy, fake, morally deficient cad could bed nearly anyone he chose, while Simon struggled to speak to a girl, usually with embarrassing results.

He noticed also, in that glance, a powerful waterfall pouring furiously through the opening above his bed, as though his room had become the bathtub drain for the world. He sat with his arms out behind him, taking in the scene, attempting to make some sense of it. He expected the torrent to subside, but it showed no such indication; if anything, the volume increased as he watched.

"Great," he muttered. "The place floods when it rains. I should have asked for the third floor."

Simon slowly pulled himself up and took a painful step toward the foot of the bed, away from the gushing surge of water that poured across his mattress. Water splashed up to his ankles. He should have anticipated the danger of remaining in his room, five feet below ground level, but his coffee-deficient brain could not make such rational decisions. Not, that is, until a ragged, waterlogged tree limb, almost entirely stripped of its branches and leaves, launched through the opening like a spear chucked by some angry native in the heart of Africa. A few seconds earlier the same trajectory would have carried the thing through

Simon's bare and unprotected chest, pinning him to the bookcase.

There are times in life when a healthy surge of adrenalin out-performs even the most heavily caffeinated cup of coffee; unfortunately, those times usually also require unhealthy levels of fear and desperation. Simon experienced that moment of clarity when he realized the imminent danger into which he had been thrust, and which had just been thrust at him. As quickly as the adrenalin of desperation could allow, Simon sloshed through the water toward the door at the other side of the room, grasping articles of clothing as he went. By the time he reached the hallway he realized this was not just some freak storm spawned by a hurricane.

"What's going on?" he and the guy across the hall asked each other at the same time. Joe Sperry's proficiency at tackling people on the football field had earned him the nickname "Fearless Joe" his freshman year, for reasons as yet unknown to Simon—frankly, he didn't care—but Joe would have lost it handily in the basement corridor if anyone but Simon had seen the sheer panic on the guy's face.

"We need to get out of here," Simon said with more authority than he felt.

Just then a beautiful young freshman girl that Simon had seen around campus poked her head through the doorway, trembling with cold and fear. She barely wore an absurdly oversized football jersey, her long blond hair soaked and matted, clinging to her face and neck. Simon didn't know her name, but made a mental note not to ask her to Homecoming.

Joe Sperry, wearing a tee shirt and shorts, raced barefooted down the hallway and up the stairs, leaving Simon and the girl staring at each other. She blushed. Simon nodded. And then she sloshed after the brute who had abandoned her to a watery fate.

Simon turned to follow, but suddenly wondered how many guys in the dorm remained asleep. College boys maintained a well-earned reputation for drinking themselves into a stupor, regardless of campus rules, and could sleep through a nuclear blast. He normally avoided them, but he couldn't let them drown.

He splashed along the corridor, pounding on doors left and right, opening ones that weren't locked and called out to everyone to wake up. Swears and oaths emanated from the rooms, mostly directed at him until feet splashed into cold water. Then the swearing took a different turn. He heard more than a few high-pitched screams and shrieks, and by the time he reached the stairway at least a dozen young women had emerged, trembling and shaking, in various states of undress, swearing and cursing as vociferously as their half- naked men.

"Jeez! Am I the only one around here who can't get a date?" he muttered under his breath.

He was.

The water splashed around his knees as he grasped the handrail and rushed up the stairs to the first floor. Shivering from the cold, Simon stood in the stairwell and quickly put on the clothes he had grabbed on his way out of the room, including shoes, all of which had landed on a mercifully dry chair the night before. He scampered out to the main lobby as the lights flickered and died.

Dozens of people gathered around the doorway and spilled onto the expansive columned portico that looked out across the campus. Modeled on a classical Greco-Roman design, each building, residential and educational alike, consisted of large Doric columns, pediments, friezes, pilasters, and the occasional dome. They bordered a meticulously landscaped open grassy area, called the Commons, adorned with trees and walkways, the occasional fountain, stone benches, a gently babbling brook, several small gazebos, and a variety of statues cast and carved by former art students. Simon had visited numerous colleges during high school, but this one had stood out because of the classic beauty and sense of history that he felt when he strolled along the winding paths. This was where he could learn and study and meet girls. Well, two out of three.

Simon Foxx slunk through the trembling, dripping, murmuring crowd of men and women, conscious to avoid accidentally brushing against something he shouldn't or to make eye contact with anyone that might get him thrashed. He stepped on a bare female foot, but in her half-frozen state she barely felt the transgression. The crowd scattered onto the portico, but Simon found plenty of room in the early predawn light to make his way to a rail, from where he expected to see the tastefully lit campus spreading out before him.

He did not anticipate a vast unbroken sea where the Commons had existed the night before.

Chapter 2

Art Department

Simon gaped in awe at the sight before him. An expanse of rippling water separated the buildings from one another, punctuated by the occasional tree or tall shrub. Currents and eddies swirled like an abstract painting, on the surface of which floated the detritus of both man and nature. Limbs, branches, and foliage coursed between the structures, as did newspapers, drink bottles, and overwhelmed trash cans. Small animals struggled to stay above water.

In the early predawn light Simon discovered a cloudless sky: no rain. In fact, above the waterline the buildings appeared perfectly dry, as they had all week. What could have caused a flood of this magnitude other than a huge storm?

"This is weird," he said.

"You think?" a guy next to him said as he held up his phone to record the scene for posterity. The half-naked girl clinging to his arm did the same.

"I mean it's weird to have a flood with no rain," Simon clarified. "We're not close to a river."

"Who cares what happened?" the young woman whimpered. "Who's going to save us?"

Standing among them as the only one wearing all of his clothes, he saw panic in their eyes, fear etched into their features; he felt it as well, but more than that he experienced a kind of vigor previously unknown to him, as though the moment of truth had finally arrived and it was time to prove his worth. Add to the mix insatiable curiosity, and suddenly he felt more powerful and vital than he could ever remember.

The feeling lasted about six seconds.

"Out of my way," a deep voice boomed from behind, accompanying an unexpected and unfortunate shove. Simon sprawled onto the floor for the second time that morning, but without a soft bookcase to break his fall; his head scraped the brick façade as his bottom plopped onto the concrete portico. Towering above him loomed the shirtless form of the school's star football player, a veritable mountain of a man—a volcanic mountain ready to blow at any moment; not the serene, peaceful mountains from The Sound of Music.

As a registered and licensed coward, Simon dutifully slunk back through the doorway and into the main lobby, where by now close to a hundred people had gathered, pressing toward the opening, straining to see outside, phones raised in unison to capture images of the devastation that would undoubtedly result in an extremely rare cancellation of classes, the last of which had occurred 30 years ago, during a blizzard, when the grounds crew could not shovel snow quickly enough to allow the campus center doors to open. That lasted all of one day, initiating make-up classes the following Saturday. This disaster might prove slightly more troublesome, not that the guys playfully splashing water on their strained girlfriends cared at the moment.

It occurred to Simon that he could make a name for himself—perhaps even entice the interest of a girl or two—if he could somehow document the events of the morning. After all, as a staff photographer for the campus newspaper, The Monitor (which he initially took to be a lizard), with a weekly circulation of nearly 800, he felt compelled to gather as much information as possible for what might amount to the most important story in the school's history. But he needed his camera....

He started back toward the stairwell, weighing his life against an attempt to retrieve his camera from the rapidly flooding basement; with water chest-deep, and the thing probably destroyed by now anyway, he decided his cell phone camera would have to suffice. And then he realized something that would ultimately save his life.

"Great. I left it in the art studio. Idiot!"

The human brain is a strange and inexplicable mass of mystery. When you try to think of something, like the name of an actor in a movie or the right equation on an algebra test, you can almost see the letters and numbers, as though a dim light needs only a slight surge in power to make it visible; and then there are times when for absolutely no reason at all you see everything as clearly as if the universe made perfect sense. Some people call it an epiphany, others inspiration, and some might say divine intervention. Whatever the case, Simon suddenly knew what he had to do—in spite of the fact that the school's biggest and meanest bully would probably pound him into the ground for it. But it served him right for knocking him down a moment ago.

Chris Hobson, the largest player on the school's football team, and the oldest junior in the school's history, enjoyed precisely three things: beating up players on the field, terrorizing freshmen, and enticing women into his canoe. He came from a rural area where people spent much of their time fishing and boating, and he learned long ago that once he got a girl into his canoe and far enough from shore she could not escape his enormous pawing hands. Freshman girls learned the hard way.

Hobson kept the canoe locked away in a storage room on the first floor, where no one could get to it. No one, that is, except a young freshman who knew where the dorm's Resident Assistant kept the key. And since everyone in the building had by this time squeezed out onto the portico to marvel at the flood, Simon met with no objection when he lifted the key from the RA's apartment, unlocked the storage room door, and dragged the slender but surprisingly heavy boat out the back entrance and into the water.

Never having sat in a canoe before, Simon wondered if he had perhaps gotten in over his head. But how hard could it be? The flat parts of the oars go into the water, right? He gave it a try and collided with the top of a mostly submerged car.

His new vantage on the other side of the building revealed more expansive flooding than he imagined—not simply a localized event in the vicinity of the college. Houses and businesses jutted from the water for as far as he could see in every direction. What could have caused this? No substantial rivers flowed within five miles of campus, and the ocean remained at least that far to the east—and dozens of feet below the school's elevation. A sizeable dam existed twenty miles away, but certainly that couldn't affect this region. Not to mention that it would take a major earthquake to bring it down—and a tremor that size would have brought down more than just the dam.

Simon angled the canoe around the building, and by the time he rounded another corner he started to get the feel for the small craft. He aimed for the Art Building on the other side of campus.

"Dude, isn't that your canoe?" he heard someone call out from the portico. A few people laughed.

Chris Hobson screamed with rage. Simon cringed at the thought of the guy turning green, ripping out of his shirt, and throwing a column at him. But even that muscle-headed dunce knew better than to rush into the current to get his boat back. Instead, he swore profusely and made some promises Simon hoped he would not have the opportunity to carry out.

Simon approached the Art Building, his second home for the past six weeks, where he delved into art and photography, subjects about which he felt intensely passionate. Most people took an art class as an elective to fulfill one of the many maddeningly unnecessary requirements for graduation; but Simon intended to take them all—not only because he wanted to major in art, but because he longed to follow in the footsteps of his heroes: Michelangelo, Bernini, Rembrandt, Canaletto, and a dozen others. Mostly he had the place to himself, particularly in the evenings, when he worked on drawings and played around with his camera. Few girls ever visited the art department, except when they got lost and needed directions; still, he looked forward to his time there every day.

He found it deserted, as expected. The canoe scraped along the portico and came to rest near the top step, six feet above ground level. Simon stumbled out and raced to the main entrance, which remained locked. Fortunately, as a staff photographer who could need the dark room at any time, his professor had given him a key to the building. It only unlocked the front door and the Art Department, but that was all he needed at the moment.

He fumbled for the keys, dropped them twice, and then succeeded in opening the old, creaking door. The power had flickered off the same time as that in the dorm, but he could have made the trip blindfolded, as many times as he had traversed the corridors and stairwells in the darkness of night. Down the long corridor, into the stairwell, and finally arriving in the basement, Simon discovered that the Art Department had not yet flooded. That boded well because his old Canon Rebel T1i might not react well to submersion.

Usually, in the middle of the night, after locking up the studios and classrooms, emergency lighting from the exit signs provided enough illumination to see the dim passageways and an assortment of half-completed sculptures eerily cloaked in shadowy darkness. But in this instance tables and work stations became obstacles in the blackness. He knocked over an amorphous mass of marble the size of a table lamp that might have had a human arm sticking out of it, though he couldn't be certain; perhaps the professor could teach the class how to repair damaged sculptures. If Michelangelo could repair his David after the 1527 invasion of Florence, then there was hope for this hunk of rock.

Stumbling around in pitch blackness, Simon regained his bearings and located the small office in which he spent the majority of his work-study time. As part of his financial aid package, he worked as an art assistant 15 hours a week, which really meant that he got paid to do his homework while waiting for the phone to ring—which happened about five times a month, since no one in their right mind ever called the Art Department. Occasionally, he straightened up the studios, organized supplies, emptied the trash, and cleaned paint brushes, but such chores required mere minutes of his time; the rest he spent reading whatever novel or history book struck his fancy. Many an hour he wiled away in this tiny cubby hole, filling his brain with uselessly fascinating trivia that appealed to no one. He might have felt lonely, but the adventures of D'Artagnon and Frodo and Huck Finn kept his mind pleasantly occupied and unconcerned with the obvious deficiencies of his own life.

He pulled open the desk drawer and found his backpack perfectly intact. His grandparents had given it to him for graduation last spring, to go with the camera his parents had gotten him; designed specifically to hold a DSLR and several lenses, filters, memory cards, spare batteries, and any other accessories necessary for the photography enthusiast, he could sling it over his back to keep both hands free for the art he loved. A quick examination of the contents revealed everything in perfect order: one mostly charged iPhone, two fully-charged camera batteries, half a dozen memory cards, a battery charger, a small satchel of fine art pencils, and a Moleskin sketch book in case of an emergency—one never knew when one might drop the camera, rendering all but the most basic tools useless.

"Okay," he muttered. "Where to first?"

A couple of good shots from the portico might be nice, but what he really needed was elevation... a trip to the roof, where he could capture the carnage in relative safety, get the Big Picture.

He reached for his tripod, a solid piece of equipment that folded up small enough to strap to his backpack, just as the unmistakable sound of shattering glass exploded somewhere close by. His heart skipped a beat, his pulse raced, and every hair stood on end. Then the roar of water filled the silence of the Art Department, and his next step splashed disturbingly.

"Great. Here we go again."

Simon raced to the stairwell, and by the time he got there the water in the corridor had risen to his ankles—four inches in about ten seconds. He emerged onto the portico, where the canoe remained exactly where he had parked it; thank goodness no one ever purposely visited the Art Department!

The scene remained as he had left it, though the sun had risen a few degrees higher; the air felt slightly warmer and the wisp of a breeze had developed from the direction of the coast. He turned to go back inside, to venture onto the roof, but something froze him in mid-step, entirely changing the course of his life.

From the next building, a shrill scream pierced the quiet morning air, chilling him to the bone.

CHAPTER 3

STORM VICTIMS

Simon snapped a quick shot of the Science Building before settling back into the canoe. The scream had projected from one of its upper floors, from the side facing the Art Department; what could have elicited such a sound: a cry for help? A passionate moment with a boyfriend? A sudden fall into unexpectedly chilly water? Never the heroic type—he avoided conflict at all costs, including at times the cost of his dignity—his almost fanatical curiosity, stemming from his love of knowledge, spurred him forward. He rowed quickly in his clumsy fashion toward the next building.

"Probably some wasted chick woke up and fell into a puddle," Simon mused as he approached his destination. Still, he might get a good picture of this "storm victim" and enough of a story to justify a column in the next Monitor.

Or worse: suppose he found his damsel in distress, saved her life, and had to deal with the undying affection of Jabba the Hutt's big sister? That could end poorly. He still had time to turn back....

A second scream, muffled and abruptly cut off by a slapping sound, reinvigorated Simon's quest for truth. He heard the desperation in her cry, the violent response, and the overwhelming need for help. Any help. Even his help. But what could he do? His puny, gaunt, unremarkable frame held little in the way of musculature, and his lack of reflexes had thwarted his sporting endeavors early in elementary school.

He needed a plan, and perhaps the element of surprise.

The canoe scraped against the portico of the Science Building. The water here lapped at the door frame, inches above the top step. Either this building stood lower than the previous one—and he knew by the almost imperceptible slope of the Commons that it didn't—or the flood waters had risen since sunrise. That couldn't be good.

His shoes sloshed in an inch of water, but he moved almost soundlessly toward the door, which fortunately remained unlocked; breaking a window certainly would not have aided in his attempt at stealth. Swirling currents poured through some of the lower windows, indicating massive basement flooding: nothing but trouble there. He silently opened the door and stepped into the main lobby.

Like the Art Department, few people purposely visited the Science Building if they could help it, especially on a Sunday morning. Even dedicated nerds spent little time here, which made Simon wonder who on Earth could have gotten in, and why. Couples desiring some quality "alone time" might take advantage of the empty rooms, but certainly they could find a more enticing place in which to stage a rendezvous, especially with dorms apparently designed for such encounters. Plus, campus police made their occasional rounds, though evading them didn't require much effort even on the part of third-year sophomores.

Simon moved like a ninja up the stairwell, cloaked in blackness, occasionally stumbling over a step. He continued past the second floor, moving on to the third, where he was certain the scream had originated. It might have been the fourth, but—

Shattering glass on the third floor redirected his attention. It sounded different from the heavy window panes, like a beaker or a test tube—something small and thin—the kind of noise you hear in the grocery store when the spaghetti sauce hits the floor. He knew that sound all too well.

The stairwell door creaked open and Simon silently glided down the dim corridor, illuminated by ambient light emanating from windows on the other side of the classroom doors, each of which held a narrow vertical pane that allowed him to see into the rooms. Carefully peering through each one as he passed by, halfway along the corridor he discovered the scene he had hoped not to find.

"Great," he sighed. Acting the hero, saving the damsel in distress, could end in only one way: his destruction.

He looked into the science lab, where two people struggled with each other; at first glance the casual observer might have assumed two lovers throwing caution to the wind in the midst of a natural disaster that neither might survive; but Simon's careful eye saw fear on the young woman's surprisingly beautiful face, anger in her eyes, the trembling of her lithe body as it sprawled across the nearest work table. A monstrous, hulking Himalayan peak of a man leaned into her, his beefy hands locked around her wrists, holding them above her head, the weight of his torso pinning her to the table. She writhed in protest but could not squirm free.

A thin trickle of blood dripped from the corner of her mouth, the result, no doubt, of the slap that had ended her last scream.

The beast uttered something Simon could not hear, an obvious threat; but the time for talking had ended. Her screams and protests would go unanswered, and in another moment this lowly depraved lout would do something so unspeakable that his sudden death would not even begin to answer for his crime.

Only Simon Foxx stood between this terrified young woman and the violent destruction of her body and soul.

She might have wished for a better hero.

Simon quietly removed his backpack and retrieved the tripod; gripping it firmly in his right hand, he carefully opened the science lab door which, to his surprise, made no sound at all. But not so with the slight squishing of his shoes.

After two steps the campus rapist stood up, turned around, and spied his attacker. The man's eyes widened in the instant before the end of the camera accessory caught him across the temple with a resulting thud that sickened Simon and rendered the larger man instantly unconscious. The student, one Simon had occasionally seen on campus, usually in the company of beautiful freshmen girls, dropped to the floor in an awkward heap, not unlike the common sack of potatoes.

Simon looked at the end of his tripod and discovered the camera mount had broken in half. Perfect.

"Are you okay?" he asked the trembling young woman who still lay sprawled across the table, disoriented and unsure of what had happened. Simon could scarcely believe it himself; he had saved her! Him! With just one swing of the tripod! And she turned out to be quite lovely. Not at all what he had expected....

"Do I look okay?" she snapped. She sat up abruptly and glared at Simon with the contempt of a viper before it plunges its fangs into your neck. He realized that her body trembled not with fear but with rage, and for a moment he wondered if he had done such a good thing after all.

She got to her feet, adjusted her disheveled clothing, and glanced down at the body piled on the floor. "I don't have time for this crap," she said as she kicked him in the face. Then, returning her attention to her astonished rescuer: "Who the hell are you?"

"Uh...."

"Out of my way." She stormed across the room to a table strewn with assorted papers, a laptop, and equipment Simon could not identify.

He watched in awe as she settled into her chair and clicked away at her computer as though nothing out of the ordinary had just occurred. He moseyed over to her table, set his broken tripod near her papers, and stared at her.

"Did you know that guy?" he asked.

She promptly ignored him.

"I mean, the guy who attacked you," he continued.

Nothing.

"The one I just saved you from."

An annoyed nothing.

"Excuse me," Simon said, feeling a different kind of annoyance, "but could I have just one moment of your time?"

Her sudden gaze of pure hate burned a pair of holes in his head and made the hairs on the back of his neck stand at attention.

"Go away," she demanded in a seething voice that could have emanated from the Devil himself.

"Jeez," he muttered. "I'm not looking for your undying gratitude, but maybe a slight acknowledgment."

The rage in her eyes softened infinitesimally as she burned another pair of holes in his cranium. "You're not going to leave me alone until I thank you for saving me, is that right?"

Simon's mouth gaped in stunned silence.

"Do you want a hug?" she demanded. "A kiss? Maybe a hundred dollar bill?"

"Well... I could use another tripod," he said rather sheepishly.

"Why are you here?" she asked. "Actually, I don't care. Just lock the door behind you when you leave. And that should be now."

"So, no hug?"

He thought for a moment her head might explode: a shame, because it was such a lovely head, beneath the simmering layer of rage. He wondered what she might look like if she smiled. On second thought, he didn't want to know.

Simon took a step toward the door, but thought better of it. He looked at her again, her strikingly beautiful face bathed in the unnatural glow of her laptop screen. He simply had to know more about this intriguing young woman, and why he had never seen her on campus before.

"Must be some project you're working on," he observed.

Her shoulders slumped as she sighed almost violently.

"What do I have to do to get rid of you?"

"Look, I understand how you must feel," he said. "An attack like that has to be pretty devastating. I just came to help."

"I don't care," she replied, the coldness of her voice almost creating a visible frost in her breath. "About him, about you, or about anything else. I just want to be left alone. I can't be any clearer than that."

"Fine," he said. "But what about when he wakes up? I bet you'll care then."

She muttered something vulgar that Simon couldn't quite make out. Then she got to her feet and stalked over to the unconscious mound of muscle heaped against the side of the work table. She kicked him in the side of the head and looked back at Simon.

"Satisfied?" she demanded.

Simon stood in stunned silence.

He jumped nearly out of his shoes when the massive meaty hand suddenly grasped her ankle and dragged her to the floor.

CHAPTER 4

THE SCIENCE BUILDING

It happened so quickly that he reacted before he could even think about what he was doing. One moment the formerly unconscious rapist had grabbed the girl's ankle and knocked her down, and the next Simon had the tripod in his grip again, pounding away at the guy's arm. He kept up the brutal attack until the tripod bent out of shape, rendering it largely useless; but those few seconds made all the difference.

The young woman wrenched free of the brute's grasp and clambered to the relative safety of the next table.

Then the guy stood up to his full height and Simon suddenly wished he had turned the canoe around when he had the chance. He peered up into the bloody and distorted face of a guy who towered at least a foot above average, just dripping with muscles. Simon might have rendered himself unconscious scrambling to get away, had his body not frozen in abject fear. Some hero.

"Uh, can I get your picture for the Monitor?" he asked rather lamely.

Something grabbed his arm and pulled him briskly toward the door—all the incentive he needed to decide between fight or flight. The young woman half-dragged him into the corridor, slamming the door behind them as the thug collided with it.

"Not the sharpest knife in the drawer," she commented.

"I thought you didn't care," Simon pointed out.

"I don't," she confirmed. "But I can't have you guys displaying your primitive manhood in my lab. I want you both out of here!"

They raced down the corridor toward the stairwell as the lab door opened and one angry earthquake of a man stepped out behind them. He screamed something indecipherable that Simon felt lucky not to understand, and then followed with the speed of an Olympic athlete. The inevitable collision occurred as Simon opened the stairwell door, and the impact flung him down the first flight of stairs. The girl unexpectedly slammed the door in her attacker's face, effectively breaking his nose and eliciting a cry of rage that made her attitude seem saintly by contrast. She followed Simon down to the first floor.

"Come on," he urged as he opened the door. "I have a canoe."

The non sequitur caught her off guard, but she shrugged it off.

"I can't leave without my stuff," she said.

"We'll come back for it later," he assured her. "Right now we have to get out of here!"

Unfortunately, as a certified Master of Poor Timing, his urging proved too little too late. An avalanche of muscle and sinew poured down the stairwell, sending them flying toward the basement. But instead of breaking their arms and legs and necks on the hard steps at the bottom, they splashed into a dark pool that completely enveloped them.

Simon thrashed and kicked until he hit something solid, then propelled himself toward what he hoped was the surface. He nearly made it. His head hit a wall about the time he inhaled, and only part of the pool flooded his lungs. He coughed and sputtered, but before he could find a good hold on something—anything—something found a hold on him. It dragged him under the water and pulled him down into the darkness, deep into the basement, against harsh currents and eddies, like a mermaid tugging him to his doom. He fought as well as he could, but in his terrified state he found resistance entirely futile.

He broke the surface as his lungs exploded and discovered the disgusted form of the woman he had saved glaring at him and wiping her face as he coughed on her. That would undoubtedly cost him later.

"What happened?" he spluttered.

"We're in the Lecture Hall," she spat, "no thanks to you."

"Sorry."

"I can get back to the lab from here without him seeing me," she said. "It opens onto the second floor."

Simon realized the soundness of her plan. The Lecture Hall, situated in the center of the building, rose three levels to accommodate stadium seating, with rows upon rows of chairs all arced in a semi-circle around a stage at the front of the high-ceilinged auditorium. Hundreds of students routinely sat here for freshman-level lectures in biology, astronomy, philosophy, and mathematics. He never thought he'd be happy to see the place.

"Brilliant," he said, starting to recover his senses.

"What did you expect?" she retorted.

"What is it with you?" he said, suddenly irrationally angry. "Is this how you—"

She held the palm of her hand up to his face in a gesture that abruptly cut him short.

"Look," she said in her most sincere and civil tone, which he found hardly convincing, "I don't care what you have to say. I don't know you. I don't want to know you. If you want me to say thank you for knocking out that creep, then thank you. If a hug or a kiss will get you the hell out of my life, then so be it. You tell me. And then just leave."

How should a man respond to a woman like this? Perhaps he had knocked out the wrong person in the science lab.

"I left my camera in your lab," was all he could manage to say.

"We'll get your camera," she sighed. "Then will you get out of my life?"

"Fine," he agreed.

They worked their way up the rows of stadium chairs to the uppermost level of the hall, moving inexorably closer to the second floor entrance. Neither knew their assailant's location, but they felt beyond imminent danger.

"Why is the basement flooded?" she suddenly wanted to know.

"It's not just the basement," he informed her. "The whole campus is underwater, and the town too, as far as you can see."

"That's not possible," she retorted.

"You're dripping with the evidence," he pointed out.

"That would explain your canoe," she muttered. "If everything is flooded, what are you doing here?"

"I was in the Art Department getting my camera when I heard your scream," Simon explained. "I came to see what was going on."

"Oh," she said. "You're one of them."

"One of what?"

"An Art Major."

"What's that supposed to mean?" he complained.

"It's not a real major," she stated with apparent authority.

"That's not true."

"It is. You sit around all day drawing things. That's not real work."

Simon shook his head in disgust. "Look, this probably isn't the right time for an argument," he observed. "We need to get out of this place."

He glimpsed an evil grin on her face and decided he did not like it. Not at all.

They reached her lab unmolested and Simon picked up his backpack. Before he could sling it over his shoulder, however, the young woman broke the relative silence with an oath he had not expected.

"What is it?" he asked, suddenly alarmed.

"My phone is missing," she said. "I must have lost it in the water."

"I'm sure your insurance will cover it," Simon said in as comforting a manner as he could manage under the circumstances.

"You don't understand," she said firmly. "I have to have it."

"If you lost it in the water it's destroyed by now anyway," Simon said.

"Hardly," she replied. "It's in a waterproof case that's supposed to float.

"It could be anywhere."

"We have to find it."

"We?"

"Do whatever you want," she said. He couldn't tell if she was more irritated or exasperated. He decided it didn't matter. "I'm going back for my phone."

He watched intently as she packed up her computer, her papers, her external drive, all the cords and accessories, and a few other things the purpose of which he could not fathom. What kind of school project weighed so heavily on her mind that nothing else— neither a campus rapist nor the worst flood of modern times—could distract her from it?

"I'll help you find it," he said as she zipped up her backpack.

"Joy."

He followed her into the corridor and they both nearly collided with the now insanely angry junior they had left in the stairwell. But now the guy had a weapon: a rather familiar-looking oar he had lifted from an unlikely canoe parked out front.

"Don't count on getting out the way you got here," the man spat. He didn't really need the oar; he could have pulverized Simon out of existence without it.

"Look, we can talk about this," Simon said as he carefully reached into the backpack and pulled out his camera.

"You won't talk," the monster assured him. "And they'll blame it on the flood."

"Get ready to run," Simon muttered to the woman who instinctively clutched his arm.

"You aren't serious?" she replied. "He'll tear you apart!"

"You don't care."

"I—"

As quick as a flash, Simon snapped a picture of his assailant—and the resulting explosion of light momentarily blinded him. The disorientation lasted only an instant, but that instant allowed the two sopping students time to reach the stairwell and descend to the second floor. The madman followed, much more slowly, rubbing his eyes and feeling his way along the corridor.

"Talk about brilliant," the girl said once they returned to the Lecture Hall.

"Actually, Hitchcock gets the credit," Simon replied.

"Who?"

She never ceased to amaze him.

"Alfred Hitchcock?" he said. "One of the greatest directors of all time?" Her blank look spoke volumes.

"Jeez...."

"I don't have time for this," she suddenly snapped. "I have to have my phone. Set your stuff down and help me look."

"Yes, Your Highness," he replied.

She stepped into the water and waded up to her waist, preparing to submerge. Then she looked back at Simon, who simply stood watching her.

"Well?" she demanded. "Are you coming?"

"Here's the thing," he started. "You see, uh, the truth is... well...."

"Don't tell me you can't swim."

"I swim like a rock," Simon admitted. "And not an igneous rock—some of those can float. I'm more like a sedimentary rock, straight to the bottom every time. In fact, I've nearly drowned in almost every kind of water you can imagine: pools, lakes, rivers—"

"Just leave," she said, clearly exasperated. Then she disappeared beneath the surface.

About the time she vanished Simon heard the door open on the upper end of the chamber. Very quickly he gathered the two backpacks and hid behind a table at one side of the room, where he hoped the brute could not see him.

Through a crack in the table he watched as the rapist stumbled along the rows of chairs, methodically searching every one. He moved slowly, purposefully, his oar held at the ready. This time no unexpected flash of light would catch him unawares. Simon marveled at the fiend's sheer height and bulk. Not an ounce of fat marred his flawless physique, and his once handsome face—now broken and smeared with blood—had no doubt charmed many an unwary freshman girl. But Simon also recognized insanity in the man's eyes, rage—an irrational need for violent revenge. By helping the damsel in distress, Simon had literally awakened the proverbial sleeping giant.

The beastly man covered half the distance to the main floor when the young woman suddenly emerged from the water, an unexpectedly satisfied smile on her hard face. "I found it," she announced. When Simon didn't respond, she looked around and discovered her attacker glaring at her. The smile faded as quickly as it had appeared.

"You might as well come out of there," the man said as he stepped onto the floor, his shoes sloshing ankle-deep in cool water. "Your boyfriend has abandoned you and there is no way out. I'm going to win."

Simon watched in fascination as the bully crept toward the now frightened young woman, with every step approaching the desk under which Simon hid.

"I promise I won't hurt you," the man sneered. "Not at first, anyway. Besides, you know you'll like it. It's what every woman really wants. You'll beg me not to stop."

The young woman stood frozen in place, waist-deep in water, clutching her phone. She could swim back the way she and Simon had come, but he would only meet her there. She felt trapped.

The burly junior took another step, which brought him very near the edge of the stage, his back to the desk beneath which Simon cringed. But Simon didn't cringe for very long. An overdue surge of adrenaline pulsed through his veins as he placed his hands on the underside of the desk and heaved with all his might. The force of his motion hurled the desk squarely into the rapist's back, flattening him solidly to the floor in an explosion of breath and water.

The young woman splashed past his unmoving form and rejoined Simon on the stage, dripping and shivering, astonished to see him in one piece.

"H-he said you abandoned me," she stammered.

"Never believe the bad guys," Simon said. "You think a rapist would have second thoughts about lying?"

She looked at him as if for the first time and for an instant her features softened. But they froze again the moment her gaze drifted to the dripping phone in her right hand.

"I don't have time for this," she snapped. "What the hell is going on here?"

"A flood," he replied. "No rain, no storm, no river, just a flood."

"A saltwater flood," she spat.

"Hey, that's right," he suddenly realized. "It must be coming from the ocean."

But that didn't make sense either. What could cause the ocean to rise overnight without warning? A hurricane? But there would have been plenty of warning. An earth- quake? Could this be the result of a tsunami spawned by deep-sea tectonic activity thousands of miles away? It would explain some of what he had seen this morning. But that answer seemed less than satisfying.

"I don't know what it's all about," Simon admitted. "I'm just a photographer for the school newspaper. I'm only trying to help."

"Yes, you've said that."

He could understand why someone would want to attack her.

"I guess you lost your canoe," she pointed out.

"Maybe," he replied. "If you believe what he said. I really don't think he would get rid of his only way out of this place."

"Well, we should get out of this place," she said. "That's odd...."

Simon followed her gaze and discovered that the stage had become completely visible, as had part of the ramp that led down to the corridor from which she had recently emerged. The limp form of their attacker no longer lay mostly submerged. Muddy stains smeared the chamber walls several inches above the waterline, and the swath of brown widened as they watched.

"The water's going down," Simon said.

"You think?"

The receding water filled him with dread. For most people it might have come as a relief, the end of the flood, the danger past—time for a massive cleanup. But a nagging memory gnawed at him, and suddenly he knew what to do.

"We have to get to the roof," he announced, seemingly out of the blue.

"But what about your boat?"

"That won't do us any good now," he said. "Come on!"

He led her up the rows of chairs to the second floor as the body behind them began to stir.

"Why the roof?" she asked as they climbed beyond the fourth floor to the door that led out onto the roof of the Science Building. It was, of course, locked.

The young woman pulled a pin from her hair and pressed it into the lock; in a matter of seconds the door swung open.

"You mean that really works?"

"I come up here all the time when I need to think," she said.

The door closed solidly behind them.

"If it wouldn't be too much of a bother," Simon said, "can I at least know your name? For my article, I mean?"

"You're never going to leave me alone, are you?"

"My name's Simon," he said. "Simon Foxx."

"I don't care," she replied.

His shoulders slumped.

He followed her to the east side of the building, from where they could see much of the town and the coast a few miles away.

"Some flood," she said. "Where's all the water?"

Simon peered out at the muddy desolation, the carnage wreaked by six feet of water—deeper closer to shore. Toppled trees had followed wending currents into the sides of buildings, where they had broken windows and scraped foundations with their stripped branches and exposed roots. Automobiles caked in mud lay strewn across campus. The commons, once the jewel of the college, had entirely vanished beneath dunes of silt.

But the water had receded, leaving only the occasional puddle.

People ventured out of the buildings to investigate the horrific damage. Simon retrieved his camera and snapped a few pictures. Only then did he notice a freshening of the morning breeze. But it was too strong and blowing from the wrong direction.

"Strange...," Simon said, but the girl did not answer. Her gaze remained fixed on the horizon, in the direction of the sunrise, and so he turned to see what had captured her attention.

He regretted that decision.

"This is impossible...," she muttered. He could barely hear her over the now howling wind.

Behind them a crashing sound drew his attention; an instinctive glance revealed their attacker standing on the roof, the door hanging by one angry hinge. But it didn't matter. Nothing mattered. The thug took a few steps before he saw what had petrified his victims, and even he stood frozen in place, powerless to act.

Far off on the horizon, a wall of foaming, frothing water grew impossibly higher as it approached the coast. Traveling at hundreds of miles per hour and blocking out the morning sun, it already towered a thousand feet above sea level, poised to annihilate everything in its path. Simon looked left and right and saw that it extended to the horizon in both directions, with the power to wipe out a sizeable portion of the east coast in a matter of seconds—millions of lives, countless cities and towns, an entire civilization.

The building shook as the approaching roar howled over the gale-force wind; the combination of forces made standing a dubious proposition, but he remained by the side of the woman he had saved, only so that he could die with her.

But then he noticed that she no longer stared out in terror at her imminent fate, which had already covered half the distance to shore. Instead, she concentrated on her phone, furiously pressing buttons, her fingers blurred against the glowing screen.

"It won't do any good," he called over the shrieking gale. "There's no service!"

"Kasey," she replied, not taking her eyes off the screen.

"What?"

"My name is Kasey."

The wall of water loomed over the town and bore down on the campus before it ever started to crest. Simon looked up at the swirling green expanse of seawater that now blocked the entire sky, frothing white peaks ready to spill over at any second. The Science Building groaned and rumbled as the ground beneath it turned to quivering mud.

The campus rapist screamed at the top of his lungs.

Kasey clutched Simon's arm just as the world ended.

She pressed a button on her phone and everything vanished.

CHAPTER 5

WHEAT

Simon felt the sensation of falling an instant before his tired body smacked into the ground.

He lay on his back gasping for breath, staring up at blue sky through gently waving stalks of tall wheat. Dazed, his clouded mind grasped at reality, failed, and refused to focus on anything—his name, his college, the town in which he lived, even the girl who had fretted the life out of him. Long seconds crept by while his pulse settled and his mind cleared.

A flood. A campus rapist. The end of the world?

No. A bad dream. An intensely vivid nightmare. Nothing more. He opened his eyes again and stared up at the deep blue midday sky. Had he fallen asleep outside? Him? He blinked forcefully, but the bleariness of sleep had long since faded.

Kasey.

He remembered her name. His weary brain must have imagined her in the dream; no real woman could be that annoying. But why would he dream of someone he had never met before? And what about all this wheat?

Slowly and with great effort, Simon sat up until his head rose above the grain. He saw only more wheat. Acres and acres of it, stretching to the horizon, waving quietly in the gentle afternoon breeze. Huh? He must still be asleep. He pinched his arm, for all the good it did.

He distinctly remembered an impossible wall of water surging above, crumbling the building atop which he stood. A dream analyst would have a field day with that one. He knew he couldn't die in a dream, so obviously he hadn't. Or had he?

Suppose he and a few million other people had simply ended their existence in an unexpectedly violent splash? At least he hadn't felt any pain. Except for landing on his back in this wheat field. How could a spirit get winded? And why a wheat field? True, Richard Dreyfuss had landed in a wheat field with Audrey Hepburn, and that hadn't made much sense either; but neither had the haircut.

"Great," Simon finally muttered. "Either I'm dead or completely insane."

"You're not dead." A lovely but disheveled head popped up from the tall grass a few yards away; several broken strands of wheat clung to her hair.

"So, you're insane too?"

"We're not insane," she assured him. "I think."

"You're a real comfort."

He looked around; not even an occasional tree or knoll broke the monotony of the amber waves of landscape.

"Damn," Kasey groaned. She tapped her phone hopelessly.

"Problem?" Simon inquired.

"It doesn't work," she said, only half paying attention to him. That was progress; usually women paid him no attention. "If I had my computer I might be able to fix it."

Simon felt behind him and found the two backpacks he had rescued from the lecture hall. He held hers up. "You mean this?"

He saw something that made the morning's devastating adventure worthwhile: the most breathtaking and glorious smile he had ever had the pleasure of witnessing. The fleeting moment vanished as the cold, hard features returned to her young face. Still... long, golden brown tresses framed a lean and lovely countenance that contained the most piercing and frosty steel gray eyes Simon had ever imagined. If only she could use her powers for good....

He watched as she hastily opened her backpack, started up her computer, and plugged in her still wet phone. She worked furiously, oblivious of her surroundings. Simon considered a feeble attempt to draw his companion's attention, to request some explanation for the obvious delusion he had just suffered—and was likely still suffering—but decided to delay the derision with which she would pierce him if he dared to bother her at the moment. In truth, those eyes frightened him; they might yet bore holes in his head.

Simon snapped a few pictures of the beautiful young woman sitting in the wheat field, and then he spent an hour drawing her as she worked, studying her features, every line and curve, each wisp of hair that brushed her cheek, even the slight dimple in the center of her chin. She never moved, never looked up, never noticed anything but the computer in front of her. Only when he started shading the storm clouds behind her did she begin to stir, her legs numb after so much time in one position.

"You've been uncharacteristically quiet," she eventually said, still not looking at him.

"I didn't want to bother you."

"That's a first."

"So… can you explain any of this?" he asked. "I mean, why we're here, what just happened to us, where our campus is?"

"You wouldn't understand," she said with her characteristically authoritative tone.

"Look, I'm not exactly stupid," he retorted. "I do go to college."

"Not a strong argument for intelligence," she sighed. "They let anybody in, you know."

He wanted so badly to hate her, but somehow he found her more intriguing than before. Her intensely negative attitude made him want to know what made her tick. No one could be this arrogant without good reason.

"After all we've been through this morning, you owe me an explanation," Simon insisted.

That irked her. The level gaze that penetrated his head might well have melted lead; he made a mental note to test that sometime.

"I don't owe you anything," she seethed. "Not you or anyone else. What I do is my business, understand? I let you tag along because you helped me in the lab. My mistake. But that's all. I don't need you, I don't want you, and I really don't give a crap what you do from here on. As long as you leave me the hell alone!"

And with that, she packed up her belongings and stormed across the wheat field.

"Was it something I said?" Simon muttered.

He sat staring at the freshly completed drawing. Such a lovely face, but so cold and full of anger. What had happened to her? An attempted rape had not fazed her; a massive tsunami had scarcely rattled her resolve. Even this strange surrounding did not upset her in the least. Only his interest had thrown her over the edge. Fascinating. Simon pressed his thumb to the page, holding it against the freshening breeze. He liked her features. That brief smile had deeply affected him. Something had gone very wrong with her and he had to know what. Her softly-drawn face against the dark sky pleased him—a very good drawing if he did say so. He closed it up and placed it back in his bag.

Dark sky? Storm clouds?

He hadn't noticed, so engrossed had he become in his work. He packed up his belongings and raced across the field toward the intriguing young woman and caught up to her as the first bolt of lightning split the atmosphere beyond the horizon.

"That's about right for us," she sighed.

"Sorry," Simon said.

"You don't control the weather."

They found a narrow dirt road that ambled to the horizon in both directions. Deciding that any direction they chose would be the wrong one, Simon flipped a coin and consequently turned to the left. They covered perhaps a mile in silence before the rain started pelting them with impossibly huge drops. The first ones stung when they hit, but soon soaked clothing absorbed the impacts. Strong winds lashed them and loud cracks of thunder accompanied every frequent flash.

With no shelter in sight the travelers saw no recourse but to keep hurrying forward, bent over against the storm, hoping to eventually locate something of use—a barn, a decrepit old shack, an abandoned automobile, a highway overpass. For the better part of an eternity they spotted nothing.

But upon cresting a knoll they spied a small farmhouse in the distance. With renewed vigor Simon and Kasey half ran and half dragged themselves toward it, splashing in mud up to their knees. By the time they reached the front porch they looked frightful: hair matted, mud and grime dripping from their clothing, their eyes tired and defeated.

Nevertheless, Simon knocked on the door.

He didn't expect to get greeted by a shotgun.

CHAPTER 6

JIM AND MARTHA

"What do you want?" a gruff and decidedly malevolent voice boomed from the other side of the door. The shotgun barrels looked about ten feet across. "Well?"

"We, uh, just wanted shelter from the storm," he said in as manly a voice as he could manage. He failed utterly.

"We don't take in strangers," the voice replied. "Move along."

"It's kind of pouring out there," Simon insisted. "Could we at least just sit on your porch until the storm's over?"

A long pause ensued, during which Simon and Kasey set their backpacks on the floor and shared a frightful glance.

"Jim!" a voice shouted from further back in the house. Simon had never heard the name pronounced with two distinct syllables before—Jeeum—which did not fill him with confidence concerning the mental capacities of the people in the house, especially the one holding the gun. "Who's at the door?"

"Two mean-lookin' folk," Jim replied. "Up to no good, if ya asked me."

The door swung inward, revealing the stately form of an older woman, easily in her sixties, with soft features on her work-lined face. Bright eyes complemented an otherwise dull, rounded countenance. Gray hair streaked with silver, pulled back in a tight bun, a few strands escaping confinement, rested unnaturally atop her ancient head. But Simon saw kindness in her eyes and knew she would not let the unseen man shoot him. He hoped.

"Jim, you put that thing away before you hurt a body," she scoffed.

"What if they're bank robbers?" he protested.

"They ain't no banks for a hunnert miles," she chided. She peered intently at the dripping young college students standing silently on her front porch, her big blue eyes taking in every detail with a grandmotherly sweep. "Just look at you, all sopped up like a wet towel."

A flash of light punctuated the need to get indoors, and the resulting boom of thunder, a fraction of a second behind, insisted that the storm had no intention of letting them off the hook. It might rage for hours.

"Jim, git 'em some towels," the woman said, "and put another log on the fire. They're gonna need it."

She ushered them into the house, which somehow seemed smaller on the inside than it had appeared from the outside. Comprised of only a couple of rooms, an attic, a kitchen, and a pantry off to one side, the house stood unevenly, possessing no straight lines or right angles; the main room took up almost the entire front of the house, on the far side of which the fireplace glowed warmly in the near darkness. An antique sewing machine occupied one corner, and against the adjacent wall stood an old hutch very much like the one passed down for countless generations in Simon's family. A pair of rocking chairs and a small table completed the furnishings. A single oval-shaped rug of brightly colored yarn stretched across uneven wood floor planks. Naked walls lacked even the smallest art or photographs, and a large black family Bible represented the only reading material in the house, with the exception of a fresh newspaper folded haphazardly on the table. Simon felt odd, as though he didn't belong here; his skin crawled and his stomach fluttered.

Jim arrived with the towels, which Simon found unexpectedly coarse. He had grown up with thick, plush towels that soaked up water and left him feeling dry in seconds; this towel, as thin as a sheet, absorbed very little and served only to trap in heat as he and Kasey moved close to the fire.

In the dim, flickering light Simon caught a shadowy look at the man of the house, a tall, lanky, solid old cuss who had no doubt spent his life toiling in the fields, raising crop after crop of wheat and corn. Hard lines etched deeply into his vertical face, and squinting eyes peered out from behind wrinkles of darkly tanned flesh. Simon saw intelligence, but limited knowledge—at least, of the kind familiar to him.

"You two just look affright," the old woman said. "But we can fix that. Nothin' a hot bowl of rabbit stew won't cure!"

"Thank you, ma'am," Simon replied as he settled next to Kasey by the fire. Jim employed large cast-iron tongs to place another log into the fireplace. Simon saw the look of disgust on Kasey's face at the thought of consuming a bunny rabbit. It didn't appeal to him either, but he could not in good conscience turn down this woman's hospitality. The poor old couple felt no qualms about sharing what little they had with strangers in need, and Simon had no intention of insulting them.

"Please, call me Martha," she replied. "And this here's my husband Jim."

"Nice to meet you," Simon said. "Thank you for taking us in."

Kasey remained silent.

"Once you warm up and have a bit of stew, we'll get you out of those wet things and into a nice hot bath," Martha continued. "And we insist that you stay the night. The road won't be worth traveling 'til tomorra no ways."

"We got room in the barn," Jim spoke up. "Don't mind the pigs none."

Time basically stopped while Simon and Kasey warmed themselves by the gently roaring fire and forced down a most unsavory helping of rabbit chunks swimming in a greasy mass of half-congealed goo. Simon bit into what he hoped was a carrot, but thought it unwise to pursue the matter. The storm abated as the sun touched the horizon; it would take until the next day for the road to dry out sufficiently for travel. And since the travelers had no place else to go, this remained their best option.

A multitude of questions formed in Simon's mind, but he dared not ask them in the presence of his hosts. For some inexplicable reason he sensed they would not understand any of what he had to say. They seemed confused when he asked about the location of the bathroom, and Jim mentioned that he had heard of people having such things inside the home, but thought it a fad that would pass when people came to their senses. The mention of a car left them with blank stares. Electricity? Simon had simply inquired if the power went out often during storms, but they had no idea what he was talking about.

Kasey contributed nothing to the conversation.

Before sunset, Simon and Kasey found themselves wearing only the towels Martha draped over them, for she had confiscated their clothes in order to wash away the mud and grime. Kasey ended up in the barn, in an embarrassingly small wooden tub of lukewarm water. Martha scrubbed her back and washed her hair, then poured cold water over her head—a sight Simon really wished he could have seen. When his turn came, Jim poured the water, but Simon, thankfully, was on his own for the scrubbing.

Strangely refreshed and clean, their stomachs full, and still wrapped in towels, Simon and Kasey spent the night together in the hay loft above the horses and pigs in the barn. Martha had given them each a thick, warm quilt to keep out the chilly predawn air, and Simon had made a mental note of the outhouse's location. He knew that would come in handy. Jim kindly lent Simon his newspaper, but not without warning him to be careful about burning down his barn. The reference went over Simon's head.

"I still can't figure it," he said once they had settled in. He lay on his back in a mound of hay near the wall, while Kasey sat a few feet away in the corner, staring intently at her computer screen, occasionally typing. "You know something about all this, but you've hardly said a word all day."

She ignored him.

"I think I've been pretty patient," he continued. "I didn't want to say anything in front of Jim and Martha, because they don't seem to know about the flood—or much of anything, for that matter—but you have to understand that I have a few important questions that I think only you can answer."

Nothing.

"What do I have to do to get through to you?" he demanded. His extraordinary patience wore thin.

"Just read your paper," she said and resumed ignoring him. "Fine."

He glanced at the headline:

OLYMPIC GAMES OPEN IN ATHENS

"I didn't know the Olympics were this year," Simon muttered. He glanced through the article and moved on to stories about a devastating drought, the upcoming election in the fall, and the plunging price of wheat. Things were tough here in Kansas. Thousands of farms had failed in the last couple of years owing to extremes of heat and cold and a catastrophic lack of rain. The occasional thunderstorm dumped huge amounts of water in localized areas, but more often than not the lightning started fires that damaged already dry crops. With some luck, McKinley would win the election and do something to help the poor farmers of Kansas.

McKinley?

Simon turned back to the first page and stared at the date: Friday, April 10th, 1896.

"This is weird," he muttered. "The guy gave me an antique newspaper. Must be some kind of joke."

"It's no joke," Kasey said without looking up from her computer.

"He must have gotten it mixed up with the real one."

"It is the real one."

Simon glanced over the paper and found her eyes gazing intently at him. What was the joke? He didn't find it at all funny.

"I don't understand," he admitted.

"I know," she replied. Then she resumed her work.

"That's it?" Simon demanded. "That's all the explanation I get? I want to know what's going on here! Stop stringing me along and tell me something before I throw that blasted computer down to the pigs!"

Simon rarely shouted; in his agitated state he got to his feet and took a menacing step toward the most infuriating woman on the planet. He fully intended to carry out his threat if she didn't give him immediate satisfaction.

"Please close your towel," was all she said.

That took the fire out of his charge; he settled back beneath his blanket.

"How can I help you if you won't tell me what's going on?" he finally said, now entirely beyond exasperation.

"I don't need your help," she replied. "You will only get in my way."

"What happened to our school?" he asked. "Why are we in the middle of nowhere, sleeping in the Clampets' barn, with a brand new paper talking about the Athens Olympics of 1896? You know what this is all about. And I will keep pestering you until you let me in on your Deep Dark Secret."

Her shoulders slumped and she sighed in the exasperated defeat of an annoyed mother giving in to her relentless child. "It says 1896 because that's where we are," she finally said. "Or when we are, more accurately."

"That's...," Simon tried to reply.

"Impossible?" she finished for him. "Everything's impossible, until someone does it."

"I...," but for once he could not find any suitable words to fit the occasion.

"Yes, I built a time machine," she said. "It saved our lives this morning when some unknown force destroyed our world. No, it wasn't supposed to bring us to Kansas in the nineteenth century. And yes, you were better off not knowing the truth."

She resumed her work.

Simon sat in silence, trying desperately to wrap his numbed brain around the few short sentences she had just uttered. Time machine? In a cell phone? Totally absurd. This woman was crazy, an unfortunate redundancy of words! Still... it would explain a great many things....

"Why Kansas?" he asked. It remained the one flaw in her story.

"I don't know," she answered simply. "It malfunctioned. Maybe it got wet, or my software was corrupted, or a random neutrino surge from a solar flare interfered the moment we shifted through time. I'm trying to figure it out."

"Where were we supposed to land?"

"On the roof of the science building, but in the middle of the previous night—when I knew no one would be there."

"Oh. That makes more sense."

Simon pinched himself once more, just to be certain.

He asked her questions for a good part of the night, but she frustratingly offered no more answers. Eventually he drifted into a very unsatisfying sleep filled with the most bizarre dreams he had ever experienced, and his subconscious mind looked very forward to waking up in the morning.

Sunrise came early and bright, poking harshly through the many cracks in the barn wall, robbing him of the sleep he needed just when it felt like he was getting comfortable. He hated that. His towel had shifted embarrassingly during the night, and the warm blanket covered only the barest essentials, a situation he rectified immediately, hoping he had awakened first. He lay in silence, but decided that he and Kasey really needed to talk. No more Mr. Nice Guy.

"Kasey," he called to her. But she ignored him, as usual. "Kasey."

He sat up and peered into her corner.

But she had left sometime during the night, without a trace.

She didn't even leave a note.

Chapter 7

Farming

"That girl's really starting to annoy me," Simon sighed as he flopped back into the hay.

Kansas. 1896. He knew the impossibility of her words. How could a college student build a time machine out of a cell phone? Talk about an expensive app! She must think him dense as a post to believe such nonsense, and yet—he could not explain the sudden wheat field, the old couple in the farm house, the antique newspaper....

A time machine?

No way! Obviously someone had dragged him to a party, gotten him sloshed until he blacked out, and then left him naked in a barn dreaming the wildest dreams of his life. Yes. That could have happened.

No, it couldn't have. He didn't drink. And him at a party? Unlikely.

Simon looked at the newspaper again. It felt real. The ink left faint smudges on his fingertips when he rubbed it. The Titanic wouldn't sink for another sixteen years; World War I remained eighteen years off. His own birth wouldn't happen for more than a century. The Wright brothers still operated a bicycle shop in Dayton, Ohio, with no idea of the impact they would have on the rest of history.

Simon's brain strained almost to its limit. He prided himself on his calm demeanor, his ability to examine a stressful situation from every angle and then rationally decide on the proper course of action. That had kept him out of trouble during all four years of high school, as well as his often stressful after school job working with an irate public.

But the skill failed him here.

A leathery old face poked above the rickety ladder that connected the hay loft to the straw-strewn floor of the barn.

"Mother's got breakfast," Jim said simply. "Here's yer clothes." He flopped them over the edge of the loft and disappeared from sight. Simon heard him tinkering in the barn for a few moments before finally going back out into the morning sunshine.

He donned the clothes, now stiff and clean and smelling like old people, and descended the ladder, leaving his belongings in the loft, deciding not to pollute the timeline with technology from the future—assuming, of course, Kasey had told him the truth. And that he could trust his senses.

The sagging barn looked as dreary in the bright light of the morning sun as it had in the moonlight the night before. Uneven planks of rough, faded wood provided minimal protection from the elements, which he guessed was all that animals really needed. The drooping house appeared only slightly more carefully crafted. Both structures might have stood in this spot for a hundred years, slowly warping and twisting in the alternating forces of heat and cold, sun and rain, gradually deteriorating even as their occupants did the same. It depressed Simon more than he could express.

He sat down to breakfast alone in a rocking chair and ate overcooked bacon, slimy eggs, and something he might have described as a pancake based on the shape and texture. Jim and Martha had long since consumed their morning meal, opting to allow their guests the rare privilege of sleeping in. Martha had spent the morning—which, for her had begun an hour before sunrise—scrubbing clothes and hanging them out to dry before starting on breakfast. Jim had already fed the animals, milked the cow, and gathered eggs from what passed for a small chicken coop out back.

"Too bad 'bout yer wife," Martha said as she lit another candle and settled into her rocking chair, holding a needle and thread, a torn pair of overalls resting in her lap.

"She's not my—" Simon began, not sure how to finish. Anything he said would require an explanation, and he simply didn't have one.

"Jim said he thought she might be yer sister," Martha suddenly understood. "Runaways, I s'pose."

"Something like that," Simon said.

"Well, she's a'runnin' without ya," Martha said, shaking her head. "Took off before sunup, clothes still wet. Nary a word spoke. Poor girl got problems, no doubt."

"No doubt."

"Young man like you, strong, fulla energy, should be able to catch up to her without much trouble," Martha pointed out. "Ain't no place really for her t'go. Kirchner farm's closest place, and that's a three hour walk. They won't have no use for a skinny thing like her."

"I'll never catch up to her," Simon sighed. "Not unless she wants to be caught. And she doesn't."

He suddenly realized the predicament in which that frustrating little wench had left him: trapped and alone in the official middle of nowhere with people who could never understand him, and with no hope of returning to his own time and place. His grandparents didn't exist yet. His college wouldn't be built for another quarter of a century. If he could get his hands on that girl he would strangle the life out of her. How dare she!

"Where ya plannin' t'go?" Martha asked. "Ya got work some place?"

"I have no place," Simon replied. "No family, no home, no hope." His shoulders slumped and his chin might well have scraped the floor.

"Jim could use some help in the field," she offered. "Always use a strong back. Can't pay you nothin' but ya can sleep in the barn and share our meals, jest 'til ya figger out what yer gonna do. Yer sister won't stay lost forever."

"I'm not so sure about that," Simon muttered. He smiled weakly at Martha. "I appreciate your offer. I could use a few days to get my thoughts in order. Thank you."

Unfortunately for Simon, Jim needed help plowing the south field, a career path for which neither high school nor college had prepared him. Jim showed him the basics, with more than a little frustration on his deeply shadowed face, and suspected trouble when Simon shied away from the horse, as though he had never seen one up close. With some effort they led the beast and the plow out into the field, the younger man stumbling and slipping.

Simon started a row that a drunken sailor on shore leave could have followed with no difficulty.

"Boy, ain't you never seen a field before?" Jim inquired, scratching his head before replacing his worn out old wide-brimmed hat.

He had... from the air, while flying out west once. He felt like Abbot and Costello meet Little House on the Prairie, a reference that arced completely over his friend's head.

Nevertheless, in a couple of very uncomfortable hours Simon started to get the hang of the operation, though he had to admit that the horse did the lion's share of the work. His rows got marginally straighter, and Jim left him alone to work in another part of the field. Simon expended a terrible amount of energy and suffered all the deprivations of hard work—sweat, sore muscles, dehydration, a clear head—while the sun inched higher in the morning sky. The temperature climbed into the sixties.

The intense labor of farming—a skill that yesterday he would never have considered—had the miraculous effect of focusing his mind on the situation into which Fate had so suddenly thrust him. The fog cleared as the hot sunlight of truth beat down on him, and he saw things as clearly as he ever had. It all made perfect logical sense. The more he concentrated on the horse and the plow, the less he worried about the future—a future in which he knew most of the major events that would take place for the next century.

A plan developed in his freshening mind, a way to make the best of this dreary existence. Knowing the future would allow him to live comfortably, for he could easily amass a fortune if he put his knowledge to proper use. Assuming his survival—people still died of horrific diseases and infections in this century—he could quietly live out his days in peace and comfort, well away from the civilization that would soon tear itself apart.

He felt bitterness where Kasey was concerned. She had no right to abandon him to this unexpected fate, regardless of her motives. What had inspired her to make a time machine in the first place? Impossible as it sounded, he could no longer deny the truth. No drunken party. No drug-induced nightmare. No hallucination. Still... she had saved him from the destruction of the world. But even that was no credit to her humanitarian nature: he just happened to be the guy standing next to her when the wave hit.

If he hadn't left his phone in the Art Department he would have died in that natural disaster, along with everyone else, never knowing what had happened: one moment standing on the portico staring out at the flooded campus, the next total oblivion. Just like that. As much as Kasey and her time machine, his own disorganized nature had saved his life. He found that difficult to swallow. And his parents said his forgetfulness would be the end of him!

His parents. All those college students. Family, friends, acquaintances. The inhabitants of all the towns and cities on the East Coast. The nice lady in the book store. The strangely pleasant girl in the coffee shop that always gave him an extra squirt of raspberry syrup in his mocha. The old woman in the toy store who never raised an eyebrow at his frequent LEGO purchases. Even the grizzled old man who bagged his groceries every Saturday.

All dead. Suddenly, violently, unexpectedly. An entire civilization wiped clean, as though it had never existed. No one could have survived that colossal wave. He had seen footage of the 2004 tsunami originating in Indonesia the day after Christmas, with waves dozens of feet high that rippled across the Indian Ocean, inundating coastlines and killing hundreds of thousands of people on two continents. That paled next to what he had witnessed.

What had caused it? A meteor impact? He had read that scientists predicted a one percent probability of a major impact sometime in the 21st century—not a huge risk, but in cosmic terms quite significant. Could that explain the end of his world?

More importantly, what could he do to influence the outcome? He knew the exact time and date that the world would end. Should he devote the remainder of his life preparing humanity for the impending devastation? No one would believe him, of course, and he would die of extremely old age long before the catastrophe proved him right. But he had to do something.

Suppose he amassed a huge fortune and left it all to his future self, with a detailed note of explanation telling him exactly what to do and when, citing specific pieces of knowledge that only he could know, proving the authenticity of the information? That could work... but to what end? What possible instructions could he give to his as yet unborn self that would be of any worth? He might survive the devastation, only to die miserably in the aftermath. Better to escape with a beautiful woman... sort of.

By midday, Simon's busy mind had developed a detailed plan of how to survive the future, starting with a way to build a fortune. He knew where to live, how to avoid the conflicts of the looming twentieth century, and more importantly what to say to his future self and the best means of imparting his unnatural wisdom.

Simon paused to wipe sweat from his face in the now blistering heat of the noon sun. The horse stirred uncomfortably while he leaned on the plow, his body coated with moisture, his clothes soaked, his heart racing. This was no life for him. A few days at best, and then he would have to move on.

The temperature on this early April day easily approached 80 by now, but the thermometer may as well have read 110 for all the shelter and comfort his ill-fitting clothing provided. He would sleep well tonight, barn or no barn.

All his plans faded to nothingness when he heard a rustling sound behind him, turned, and saw Kasey standing there alone, looking as though she had suffered through a second Armageddon.

She collapsed at his feet and he knew he could never hate her again.

CHAPTER 8

MENDING

Simon pulled her into a sitting position in the slim shadow of the horse. He retrieved a canteen of warm, stale water that provided little in the way of refreshment but would at least stave off dehydration. An ugly bruise marred her left eye and torn clothing indicated participation in a fight in which the opponent had proven victorious. A puffy, swollen lower lip offered testimony to his assessment.

But more important than her physical condition, which would heal in a few days, her attitude had changed.

"I'm fine," she finally said as she pushed away the battered and slightly rusty canteen.

"You don't look fine," Simon replied. "What happened to you?"

"I don't want to talk about it," she said.

"Then why did you come back?"

She didn't have an answer, so she ignored the question. But her hard-edged demeanor softened and her tone indicated total exhaustion instead of contempt. Progress.

"We'll deal with that later," Simon sighed. "Right now we need to get you back to the house so Martha can clean you up and mend your clothes."

"Mend?"

One day on a farm and he had already started picking up the jargon.

"You don't look like a farmer," she said. An almost imperceptible smile turned to a grimace as her lip cracked and started to bleed again. Somehow Simon found the attempt endearing.

Kasey recovered for three days, most of which she spent in various stages of unconsciousness, occasionally moaning from within an escape-proof nightmare. Simon remained by her side as much as discretion allowed, when not attempting to help Jim in the fields—help that Jim reluctantly accepted in light of crooked rows and irritated livestock.

But Martha, the hero of the day, attended to Kasey as a mother would have done: comforting her, cleaning cuts and scrapes, filling her with warm soup, holding her when she needed it. Simon marveled at the change in the younger woman, saw helplessness through her fierce façade, loneliness that had gnawed at her soul, and realized that this girl, more than anyone he had ever known, remained entirely alone in the universe.

No wonder she had returned to him.

Kasey spoke little during her recovery, with one notable exception: on three occasions, during her most intense nightmares, she screamed a single word, "Carista," before collapsing back into a fitful sleep. Simon didn't know what it meant, or if she would ever tell him, but he knew the word retained some vital significance. Otherwise she said essentially nothing beyond the pleasantries of "thank you," "good morning," and "I'm going to be sick,"—a warning he appreciated more than she could know.

By the third evening her lip healed and the bruise around her eye faded to a shadow of its former self, leaving her cold hard face as lovely as the day he had first seen it. Simon had purposely avoided asking uncomfortable questions until she regained her strength, and now the time had come. He sensed her restlessness, the urge to get away from this miserable little farm in the middle of nowhere that had meant so much to them; he felt it as well, but for perhaps different reasons.

"You look better," Simon started, the chill night air penetrating his blanket. April weather reached uncomfortable extremes out here on the prairie. "How do you feel?"

"Better," she said simply from her mound of hay in the corner. She hadn't touched her computer since her return. That worried him.

"I thought you were gone for good."

No response.

"I had this strange feeling that you were going to leave me here in the nineteenth century," he continued. "Alone, helpless, at the mercy of Fate."

"I did," she replied after a significant pause. "I had no intention of returning."

Her frank honesty caught him off guard. But at least he had her talking.

"Was it something I said?"

"It's not you," she assured him. But he didn't feel assured.

"So… you have a problem and I get to live out my days on the old frontier with the nearest Starbucks eighty years in the future," he sighed. "Glad it's not me."

"Actually, you didn't make it that far," she said softly.

Simon sat up and stared at her across the loft, dizziness momentarily overcoming him. He glared at her until she elaborated.

"The Spanish Flu," she explained. "You made it until 1919, but once you caught it you were gone in two days."

How could she possibly know that?

As if in answer to his unasked question, "I tracked you down on ancestry.com and figured out what happened. You lived a pretty miserable life out west, and once you came east and started to find success, the flu nailed you."

Simon flopped back into the hay. "Not exactly part of my plan," he said. "But I thought you didn't care."

That left her quiet for a long while. When it became obvious that she would not break the silence he decided to go for broke:

"What happened to you?"

At first he assumed she had ignored his question, but a glance at her face in the flickering light of the oil lamp indicated otherwise; she needed time to compose her thoughts and tell the story in the most effective manner possible.

"I failed," she finally said. And that was it. She turned out the lamp and settled in for another fitful night's sleep.

Simon's body trembled with uncontrollable rage. He had known this arrogant, condescending, sharp-tongued shrew for less than a week, and already she had gotten under his skin like no one else ever had, including members of his own family. He had rescued her, put up with her attitude, and gotten stranded in a really bad made-for-TV drama that ended in his own untimely demise, and for what? Because she didn't feel like talking?

Tough!

In the darkness he launched to his feet, stormed across the loft and relit the lamp. He crouched in the hay, his face hovering inches from hers, though she remained facing away from him. Grasping her shoulder, he pulled her around, startling them both. She lashed out, but in his excited state his heightened reflexes allowed him to grasp her wrists before she could hit him. After a brief struggle her sore body went limp and she gave up the fight.

"I have shown you the patience of Job," he seethed. "I have no intention of hurting you, but I deserve some answers. Like it or not, we're in this together, and the more I know the better off we'll both be. Now, start talking or I will hound you 'til the cows come home."

She forced a sad smile. "The cows are already here," she said. "Can't you smell them?"

He released his hold on her wrists and she slapped him hard enough to flay the skin from his cheek. The impact sent him reeling backward into the wall, where his head collided into a pine plank with enough force to crack the thin slat. He actually saw stars.

"Next time you put your hands on me I swear I will break something," she promised with all the venom of the Kasey he remembered from the science lab. The cold hate on her deceptively attractive face lowered the temperature in the barn. Simon thought he heard a gust of wind blowing up against the structure from somewhere in the night.

"Sorry," he said, rubbing his sore head, rage replaced with pain and regret. He lived by a solid principle: never touch a woman without her permission. Of course, that could explain why he always remained single. Women wanted to be touched, sometimes. "But you have to understand my frustration," he said. "You have answers and all I have are guesses."

"I don't have anything," she said quietly, now sitting with her legs crossed, her chin resting in one hand.

Strands of hay tangled in her hair, and in the rejuvenated flame of the lantern Simon saw perhaps the most beautiful woman in all of Creation. The most frustrating, to be sure, but physically flawless. And obviously brilliant.

"You know what's going on and I don't" Simon said. "You built a time machine! Out of a cell phone!"

"It didn't work," she lamented. "I failed and now it's over."

"Just like that?"

"Just like that."

"What about the end of the world?"

"I don't care."

"How can you not care about that?"

"Because nothing matters," she replied.

"Because whatever secret mission you had in your head didn't work out the way you planned?"

"Something like that."

"And... you're not going to tell me about it?"

"I don't want to talk about it."

"Okay," he said, forcing back the ire. Beautiful or not, he wanted to punch her in the face. It worked for Paul Newman in The Verdict—maybe the most satisfying scene in the movie—but somehow he suspected that Kasey would tear him limb from limb. "Maybe you can answer one question for me."

"We'll see."

"What is Carista?"

Her face turned to stone. The color drained and for a moment he thought she might actually crack and crumble to dust. Tears welled in her glassy gray eyes, threatening an uncharacteristically warm show of emotion. She successfully fought them back.

"Where did you hear that name?" she demanded. An edge of anger tinted her voice.

"From you," he replied. "It's the only thing you said during your nightmares. Is it a person?"

"That's none of your business," she snapped.

"You still haven't told me why you came back here," he persisted. "Your phone could have taken you anywhere in history; you could have lived your life in any setting you desired, from the dawn of humanity to the twentieth century. Yet you picked this tiny swath of nothingness. Why?"

She stared into his blue eyes and looked away, down at the floor, fixated on a single strand of wheat. "I had nowhere else to go," she admitted quietly.

A wave of pity overtook him, but he dared not show it for fear of embarrassing her and shutting her off completely.

"Strange as it might sound, you are the only person in my life," she said.

He found that difficult to believe.

"I have no friends, no family, no one who cares about me; and there isn't anyone I care about," she continued. "So I guess that evens things out."

"You've only known me a few days," Simon observed. "And we haven't exactly been on the best of terms."

"Still… you're the only anchor I have," she said. "And besides, it wasn't fair to leave you here to die."

"I'll buy that. But if I had lived and become successful, would you have come back?"

"I don't know," she replied. "Maybe."

"Then, I guess it's good that I died horribly when I did," he sighed. "Otherwise we wouldn't be having this conversation."

She smiled slightly, and this time it was the genuine thing. He liked it.

"I visited the future," she said in a faraway voice that sounded hollow and delicate. "I know what happened to our world."

Simon remained quiet, giving her time to compose her thoughts.

"It was a meteor," she continued, "a planet killer."

"Like the one that wiped out the dinosaurs?" He barely contained his excitement; alarmists and crackpots had warned for decades that something big lurked out there, and in fact Earth saw some very near misses from time to time.

"I tapped into news satellites and pieced together what happened," she said. "It came from the direction of the sun, so ground-based telescopes never saw it coming; even the Hubble and the James Webb were too close to us to be able to see it. The world had about three hours' notice and decided to launch all their nuclear missiles in a Hail Mary pass to hit the meteor."

"It works in the movies," Simon lamented.

"It might have worked this time, too," she replied, surprising him.

"What do you mean?"

"Last minute calculations showed that it would miss the Earth, barely," she explained. "But something happened in Ukraine and they unexpectedly launched a rocket; it split the rock into three enormous chunks that circled back and hit the planet in three different parts of the world: the Atlantic Ocean, the Indian Ocean, and Siberia. Smaller pieces wiped out cities all over the planet."

"So, that's what happened," Simon said breathlessly, hanging on her every word.

"But it was a malfunction," she insisted. "Something happened in Ukraine that set it off; they sent distress calls saying they were under attack and it was an accident. Not that there was anyone left to blame them."

"I can't believe something like this could happen...."

"The impacts spawned massive tsunamis. I think every coastline got wiped away—a few billion people in a few hours. The rest of them died more slowly of starvation and exposure during the long winter. I don't know how long it lasted, but when I was there, about five years after the event, I saw no signs of life."

"You mean... everybody?"

"Maybe a few people survived somewhere, someplace too remote for me to detect," she said somberly. "All I know is that civilization was gone, instantly, and I couldn't find a trace of recent human activity."

"So, our only future lies in the past," he observed.

"I guess so," she replied. "I didn't have anywhere else to go, so I came back here."

He knew she had left out substantial portions of her story, like where she had gotten those bruises and cuts, the real reason she had left him here in this wasteland of history, and why she had built the time machine in the first place—though he already had an idea about that. He opted not to press the matter tonight. She had spoken more to him in these few moments than in all the days he had known her put together, and he certainly had no wish to quell this progress. Her volatile personality made probing a dangerous activity at best, and at worst she could simply leave him again to the whims of Fate.

A crazy notion entered his mind and spilled out before he could stop it.

"You have a time machine," he reminded her. "Suppose we could figure out what happened—exactly what and how—and stop it from happening?"

"And just how would we do that?" she demanded.

"I don't know," he replied rather lamely. "Yet."

"You're forgetting one thing," she said. "It doesn't work."

"Of course it works," he scoffed. "Just... not well. Maybe you should have used an iPhone."

She flopped back into her hay and doused the lamp.

"Some genius you turned out to be," he chided.

"Super genius," she corrected him.

He could almost hear the grin on her face.

CHAPTER 9

LONG WALKS

S he called it Spatial Displacement.

Obviously the name meant nothing to him, requiring a lengthy explanation that made no sense, though he nodded and pretended to understand. They took long morning walks on the dirt road before breakfast, and in those rare and beautiful times Kasey eased through the barrier that separated her from the rest of humanity. She talked to Simon about the Secret Project and the sometimes fascinating details that had consumed her last four years.

"Everything is in constant motion," she explained, her voice animated with the passion she felt for her subject, "from the smallest subatomic particle to the most massive super galaxy in the universe."

Simon nodded. So far so good.

"Right now the Earth is rotating on its axis at about a thousand miles per hour," she continued. "We can't feel it because all motion is relative. And while it's rotating, the Earth is also speeding around the sun at 65,000 miles per hour. The entire solar system is orbiting the galaxy at 486,000 miles per hour—about 150 miles every second—and the galaxy is moving through space at 360 miles per second—or 1.3 million miles per hour—so you can see why I had so much difficulty with my calculations and why it took so long to build."

Simon had never seen her so excited, but he had absolutely no idea how to connect the motions of celestial bodies to a time-traveling cell phone. The leap made no sense, yet. But he hoped it would.

"You'll have to build a bridge to span that gap," he told her. "I'm an Art Major, remember?"

She almost smiled. He wondered how a frappucino might affect her.

"The important thing is that you know all things are constantly in motion," she said. "I had to compensate for that motion."

She sensed his continuing confusion.

"You've read Einstein's work, right?" she asked.

"I once saw Eisenstein's Battleship Potempkin," he replied. "But I bet that's a different thing, huh?"

She returned his confused look. "Anyway, you can't travel faster than light," she continued. "But if you did, which you can't, you could theoretically reach your destination before you left your starting point. That's when I started reading Hawking and his ideas about multiple curled-up dimensions, and suddenly it all made sense."

"I'm glad...."

"Time and motion are intrinsically linked," she said. "You can't have one without the other. And gravity is what makes both possible. Now do you get it?"

"Should I yet?"

She sighed. He tried to feel stupid, but failed. Maybe if he concentrated he might work his way up to moron.

"Okay...," she tried again. "At the beginning of the universe nothing existed, not even time. That's because there was no motion, no light, no gravity, no anything. Just a void. The absolute definition of nothing. And then came the Big Bang, a sudden expansion of matter that formed our universe and everything in it. Time started at that moment because suddenly there was matter and motion. The two have to have each other. The result of their union is gravity."

"I'm with you so far," he lied.

"But I discovered the truth," she said in her most intriguing voice. And then, in almost a whisper, "They are the result of gravity, not the other way around. Once you control gravity, you control motion, and consequently time itself. Now does it make sense?"

"Does it to you?"

He felt the pained expression on her face without even looking at her.

"My app manipulates gravity, giving me control of time," she continued. "But motion is the most difficult variable, because there is just so much of it, and in every conceivable direction. Both have constancy, of course, but—well, it gets complicated from there. My app allows us to shift through time, but I have to compensate for the relative motion of the universe and everything in it so that we don't end up in the wrong place."

A light suddenly flashed on inside Simon's head. He got it. Not the technical minutiae, but the practical idea of it.

"In other words," he said, "when we jump through time we have to also move relative to the universe so that when we reappear we don't end up either ahead of or behind our destination. Kind of like jumping onto a moving train—you have to time your jump just right or you land on the tracks."

She smiled beautifully, surprised at his sudden comprehension, primitive though it remained. "Yes, basically that's right," she said. "When we shift through time we stop for an instant—but the universe is always in motion, so my calculation is what prevents us from reappearing in outer space either in front of or behind the Earth. The greater the time shift the greater the likelihood of landing in the wrong place."

"You should try to speak in metaphors," Simon suggested. "Art Majors are visual and need the imagery in order to grasp difficult concepts."

"I'll try to remember that."

"So what happened?" he asked her. "Why didn't we end up where you wanted?"

"Because with all my calculations and careful planning," she replied, "I failed to compensate for the most obvious factor."

He didn't find it all that obvious.

"I allowed for the motion of all the bodies in the universe," she said. "But not for the universe itself. It moves as well, but as there is no way to measure that movement—because there is nothing to measure it against—it never occurred to me to compensate for it."

"So… we're lucky to still exist at all," Simon realized. "We could have landed anywhere, from outer space to a few miles above the ground."

"Or a few miles under it," she said grimly.

He suddenly felt weak.

"But you made it back here in one piece," he pointed out.

"I rebuilt my operating system," she said, "using data from the previous jumps. It's not perfect, but the risk is minimal now. It only took a few tries to get here."

Somehow he didn't look forward to using her device to escape this period of time. Maybe the flu wouldn't be so bad….

"My first phone never reappeared," she admitted with a wry grin.

"Should have used an iPhone," Simon chided.

"That's a child's toy," she scoffed, "designed for those of limited cognitive means. Besides, they aren't compatible with anything, especially custom-built operating systems and software."

"But they always work."

She sighed. "Anyway, the first time I tested it nothing happened," she recalled wistfully. "It made me angry."

"You? Angry? I find that hard to believe."

"So after a few months' work I tried it again and the thing disappeared," she said. "Never saw it again."

"What do you suppose happened to it?"

"My calculations put it in lunar orbit," she sighed. "If we ever get back to the moon, some astronaut is going to make the find of the century when he uncovers a smashed cell phone lying in a crater."

Simon couldn't help but laugh at the absurd image. "Talk about long distance!"

"By that time Verizon will have lunar coverage," she quipped. "Heck, with the case it's in, the thing might still work!"

"That's a sobering thought," Simon realized.

"What? Lunar roaming fees?"

"A government agency getting its hands on your time machine," he said. "There's no telling what mischief they could manage with one of those."

"I never thought of that," she suddenly said, her face turning white. "Suppose a time machine is illegal?"

"You think?"

"Who cares?" she said lightly. "It's over, anyway."

"Why?" he asked. "Don't you think we can stop the catastrophe?"

"No, I don't," she said matter-of-factly. "And it's really not worth saving."

They walked in silence, ambling peacefully along the dry dirt road, oblivious of the world around them, eventually reaching a second road that intersected the first at right angles. They stopped and stared at the quiet, barren intersection, lightly rutted by the occasional wagon wheel. A gentle morning breeze stirred some dust and rustled the wheat in lazy patterns. Somewhere a crow cawed.

"I think we've reached a crossroads," Simon observed.

"Are we speaking in metaphors again?" she asked.

"Yes and no," he replied with a silly grin, the symbolism lost on neither of them. "We have to do something. We can't stay here, as kind as our hosts have been. The world needs us. And we need it. You think it isn't worth saving, and after some of the stuff I've seen I might agree with you. I mean, I worked in a grocery store for four years. But there are good people out there, friends and family, history and civilization to think of. We—you and I—are the only ones in a position to do anything about it. Maybe the task is too big. Maybe we will fail. But our souls depend on us to at least make the attempt."

"Souls?"

"What?"

"You're not one of those too, are you?"

"One of what?"

"One of those deluded Bible-toting idiots who think some all-powerful God gives a crap about what they do in their petty, meaningless little lives," she spat. "Please don't let me be trapped in time with a Jesus freak."

"Uh... maybe we should save that argument for another day," he wisely suggested.

She shook her head in disgust. "An Art Major and a Jesus freak," she muttered.

It turned out to be a long walk back to the farm house.

CHAPTER 10

THE TRIP

Simon and Kasey spent two more days in Kansas with Jim and Martha. Kasey grew stronger with each sunrise, though she remained tight-lipped about the ordeal which had weakened her in the first place; Simon, now thoroughly put off by ornery horses and difficult farming equipment, finally plowed a straight row on his last day, much to Jim's amazement. Simon broke the news of their departure to the kind old couple over dinner, and while Martha felt sad to see them go, she and Jim both knew their strange guests could not stay forever.

"D'ya need a lift in the wagon?" Jim inquired as he slurped the last of his rabbit stew, an acquired taste that Simon had yet to acquire. "I can getcha as far as the Hicks place, and then it's jest a day's walk to the train station."

"Thank you," Simon replied. "But we, uh, have a mode of transportation."

"Suit yerself."

That mode of transportation, four legs and a time machine, carried them just beyond sight of the farm house the next morning, after several handshakes and surprisingly affectionate hugs. Childless and largely friendless, Jim and Martha's only contact with the world occurred at church on Sundays when they made the ten-mile trip to what constituted the nearest town. Theirs was a lonely existence, but they had each other and that sufficed. Still, they had enjoyed the unexpected company of this mysterious young couple, brother and sister runaways from back east, and felt sad for them to go.

"I wonder if we'll ever see them again?" Simon sighed as they crested the knoll a mile from the house. Waving fields of golden wheat spread to the horizon in every direction, an unbroken sea of gently rippling grain, making him feel insignificant.

"I wouldn't think so," Kasey replied.

"What will become of them?"

"You don't want to know."

"Why?" He asked suddenly. "Do you know something?"

"I researched them when I looked for you," she explained. "Two years from now Jim will have a stroke; he'll survive it, but while he's recovering a tornado will decimate their house. Because of their remoteness no one will find them for weeks. You will have left them about a month before his stroke."

Simon felt sick.

"We have to do something," he finally said. "They've been so good to us!"

"Simon, we don't know what kind of impact our interference would have on the future," she pointed out. "The consequences of any action on our part could have devastating results—"

"More devastating than the end of the world?" he blurted. "There won't be a future, so what does it matter? And besides, I thought you didn't care."

"There's no telling what influence our presence here has already had on the way history will unfold," she replied. "Maybe leaving now instead of you staying two years will alter things. When we get back to our own time we can check up on them and see what happened. If things went poorly, maybe we can go back and tweak something to make it right."

Simon took some comfort in the idea. But it surprised him that she would suggest it. She cared little about anything, even her own failed project. He had spent two days convincing her to return to the future and find a way to prevent the cataclysm that had wiped out civilization. She still felt reluctant to make the attempt—her heart, if she had one, simply was not in it.

"Okay," he said with some measure of authority once the farm house had vanished from sight. "I guess this is as good a place as any."

"I suppose," she sighed. She reached into her pocket and retrieved the seemingly normal cell phone, a gadget that literally tens of millions of people used every day of their lives in the twenty-first century. No one would have thought twice about her typing into it; Simon doubted anyone would even notice if two people simply vanished from sight.

"A year before the Incident," Simon breathed, hoping all would proceed according to plan. His hands felt cold with anxiety at the thought of reappearing in solid rock miles beneath the surface; or worse, rematerializing in the molten mantle deep beneath the Earth's crust. That would have to be worse than outer space or high in the atmosphere. Kasey assured him that her recent modifications would minimize those risks, but her voice lacked the confidence he wanted to hear.

Watching in silence as she typed the coordinates into her phone, Simon checked to make certain he had all of their gear, including the sandwiches Martha had packed for them. Along the way he had stopped to take a few pictures of the farm house, but regretted not getting portraits of the couple who had meant so much to them; whipping out a sophisticated piece of twenty-first century photographic technology four years before George Eastman's first brownie appeared might have required more explanation than Simon could offer: some form of sorcery to people who did not even have electricity or running water. So, Simon had to make do with long shots of the fields and hazy images of the house and barn with his digital zoom.

"Ready?" Kasey finally asked him.

"Ready as I'll ever be," he replied nervously. "We're not going to die, right?"

"Who cares?" she breathed as she pressed the last button in the sequence.

Simon felt a cold blast of air that he did not remember from their last jump through time; the sensation of falling, however, remained exactly as he remembered it—sort of. He braced himself for the inevitable impact with the ground, eyes clenched shut, breath sucked in, his trembling body tight and rigid. But for some reason he missed the ground.

He opened his eyes and cursed the instinctive reaction.

Undulating tracts of endless farmland spread out before him, a patchwork of greens, browns, reds, and yellows, punctuated by occasional sharp-edged smears of blue. Shadows of mountains hinted at snow, muddy rivers snaking out from them and into the flattened landscape. But what bothered him about the breathtaking scene were the puffed, billowing clouds that drifted like lazy cotton swabs in the morning sun—between him and the ground.

Simon turned his head and saw what looked like a 737 descending somewhere off to his left, aiming for an airport miles away; he wondered how many passengers now glanced out the windows to see the unlikely shapes of a person or two plunging toward death.

On his other side, Kasey clutched her phone, desperately tapping the touch screen. Her long hair trailed out behind her like a sail, and for all that Simon could tell she appeared totally unaware of her surroundings. Typical. But he realized his error when he angled his body to move closer and saw that she could barely get her hand close enough to the screen to type the commands. Dropping through the atmosphere at a couple of hundred miles per hour proved too much for her strength. Simon knew they would form matching craters long before she could press the necessary buttons.

"Kasey!" he screamed at the top of his lungs. But he could not hear his own voice.

She looked up at his approach, sensing his nearness, and grasped the phone tighter as he reached for her arm. After a couple of bumbling tries he grasped onto her like a drowning man clinging to a buoy. He climbed onto her back, shifting his body until he could press her arms closer together while still clinging tightly to her with his legs. His strength added to hers allowed Kasey to get her fingers in contact with the phone.

While she worked, Simon couldn't help but notice how close the clouds had gotten. They looked so different from above. He had often fantasized about strapping on a jet pack and zooming among the clouds, speeding through the aerial foam and playing like a child of the heavens. He decided it would make him sick.

Kasey worked furiously as they plunged through a cottony white puff of mist, which had no more sub-stance than a common fog on the ground. Somehow Simon found that disappointing. They emerged from beneath it a few seconds later, moistened but un-harmed, and Simon suddenly realized just how little time they had left. He discerned cars on country roads creeping along between the fields; farmhouses dot-ting the landscape; a neighborhood somewhere off to his right; a copse of trees, the remnant of a flowing green forest that had once spilled down from the nearby mountains; the faint forms of people craning their necks and shielding their eyes with their hands in order to see the strange pair of skydivers who had yet to open their chutes....

Then all he could see was the grass moving clos-er at impossible speed, the horizon disappearing all around, wind whistling in his ears as his third-worst nightmare came barreling up at him—

—and then he plunged through water that hadn't existed an instant earlier. He lost his grip on Kasey, torn free by the sudden and unexpected change in motion, and drifted helplessly in the blackness. Was this death? At least he hadn't felt the impact that cer-tainly would have made the six o'clock news... some-where.

Simon felt his lungs burning for oxygen. Disori-ented, submerged, panicked, he realized his second-worst nightmare had come to pass, and that very soon he would truly expel his last earthly breath. His rotting corpse might wash ashore someplace without explanation, and he would lie in an anonymous grave for all eternity. And to think that just minutes ago he had stood in a Kansas wheat field at the end of the nineteenth century.

He opened his eyes and saw a faint glow, and for a moment he thought it was The Light. He instinctively moved toward it, anticipating the greeting of Death. Cold arms reached out to him, grasped his hands, pulled him close—

—his lungs exploded and when he convulsively gasped for air he found it clean and fresh and abundant. The sky had brightened, the air had warmed, and for a long and disorienting moment he honestly could not tell if he was alive or dead. But he breathed, and for now that was really all that concerned him.

That, and the fact that he could not move his arms and legs. Or his head. Or his fingers. Or anything else, for that matter.

He opened his eyes and peered into those of a small lizard before it scampered away in fright. In its place he saw only a mound of hot, golden sand the color of Kasey's hair. He had never seen the ground from this perspective before: as part of it.

"This can't be good," he muttered. His head, buried up to his ears, but angled so that his mouth remained exposed, turned slightly to left and right, carving enough of a channel to move more freely. But that only reinforced his growing dread of the predicament in which he had landed.

Simon strained and heaved and struggled in a vain attempt to get free, his efforts resulting in nothing but panic and frustration. Sweat soaked his forehead as he closed his eyes tightly, forcing panic from his mind. Relax, he told himself. Stay calm. People who panic get eaten first. Was it possible to experience claustrophobia in a wide open space? For him, no doubt.

"Simon, can you hear me?" a familiar voice whispered from a few feet away. His fear subsided when he realized she had survived. But she had landed behind him, where he could not see her.

"I'm here," he replied. "You okay?"

"I've been better," she answered. "Can you move?"

"My lips and my eyes," he replied. "That's about it. You?"

"I'm not as deep as you are," she said. "One of my shoulders is almost free. I think —" she grunted and strained, a colossal effort that he could not witness, "—I can almost... get my arm... free!" With the last word Simon heard the sounds of shifting sand.

In another second he felt something crawling in his hair; if not for the earth trapping his body like cement he might literally have jumped out of his shoes. He did, however, manage a most unmanly, high-pitched shriek that startled him as much as Kasey.

"Relax, will you?" she snapped. "I'm just trying to get hold of something so I can pull myself out."

"I'd rather you didn't pull my hair out in the process," he said, relieved that it was not something trying to eat him.

She pulled until the pain in his scalp nearly blinded him, but it didn't help her situation. Even with one arm free she remained stuck. She gave up the effort, much to Simon's relief.

"Can't you dig yourself out?" he asked her.

"I'm trying," she said gruffly. "It's no easy thing."

"So, now what?"

"Now we wait," she replied, obviously frustrated.

"For how long?"

"Until someone finds us."

"And if no one does?"

"Then we're already buried," she pointed out.

And he didn't think she had a sense of humor.

Time crept by as the hot sun beat down on them. They waited patiently, mostly in silence, for someone—anyone—to come along and dig them out. Simon wished he could see Kasey's face; cold and filled with hate, it was still beautiful and would have made a much more pleasant final sight than the shallow mound of sand a few inches from his nose. Of course, all she could see was the back of his head.

"That was terrifying," he said after a while.

"What?" she answered after a lengthy pause.

"The trip here," he said. "Did that happen to you before?"

"No," she admitted. "I'm not sure what happened. Maybe it was the extra mass. I'll have to factor that into the next upgrade."

"Next upgrade?"

"Every time we jump I learn something new," she said. "You wouldn't believe the variables I have to account for. But once I write them into the program they should minimize future risks."

"That's a comfort," he sighed.

"At least we learned something significant this time," she said.

"Which is?"

"What would happen if we materialized inside something solid," she explained. "I didn't know if our molecules would merge with those of the surrounding matter or if they would get bumped to someplace less dense."

"Huh?"

"Our arriving forms displace the surrounding material, which is good news for us," she said.

"If you say so."

"It means we don't become part of the material into which we appear," she explained. "We displace it... like a ship moving through water."

"Okay, now that makes sense. Nice metaphor."

They remained quiet for a moment.

"But that still doesn't help us to dig out of here," Simon said.

"Not so much."

"We're going to have to do something about this," he observed.

"About what?"

"About being helpless," he replied. "We've been at the mercy of Fate ever since we met, and it's time we did something about it."

"I'm not sure I follow you," she admitted.

That was a first.

"What I mean is, when we get free we need to rethink our strategy," he started. "We'll need protective gear, in the event that we reappear someplace dangerous, like what just happened. Suppose we materialized fifty thousand feet up and couldn't breathe? Or in space? Pressure suits are a good idea."

"Sounds expensive," she pointed out.

"Kasey, you have a time machine," he reminded her. "Making money to fund our mission will not be a problem. Trust me."

"Is that ethical?"

"What do you care about ethics?" he snapped. "You built a time machine. How ethical is that?"

Score a point for the Art Major.

"All I'm saying is that we have all the resources of history at our disposal," he continued. "We should utilize them in order to make time travel safer and more effective. We are limited only by our knowledge and creativity."

"Creativity isn't my strongest area," she admitted.

"That's okay," he smiled weakly. "I've got that part covered. Daydreaming is one of my best things. Just ask any of my teachers. I can come up with all kinds of possibilities."

"Then dream up a way to get us out of this mess," she said, effectively ending the conversation.

He tried to think of a witty come-back, but never got the chance.

A heavy shadow fell over them, entirely blocking the harsh sun, and Simon knew as the blood turned cold in his veins that something was about to eat him.

CHAPTER 11

A GRAVE SITUATION

Simon craned his neck in a largely futile effort to see what manner of beast had come to claim him. He fully expected a wild tawny feline to swipe at his face, ripping out his eyes and cheeks, before chomping on his head and yanking his body free of the earth. He cringed in anticipation of the fateful blow.

But instead, a long, spindly brown leg ending in a cloven foot clomped down in the sand inches from his face. Whorls of short curly fur clung to the limb in haphazard patches. Startled half out of his wits, Simon might have wet himself; he couldn't be sure, since his buried clothing had yet to dry from his brief undersea experience.

A deep male voice boomed from high above, though he could not make out the words. Masculine tones thundered with an air of authority, followed by the rustling of leather and fabric in quiet response. No other voices broke the afternoon stillness, but he got the impression that several people scampered about, frantic to obey the command of this overpoweringly dominant force.

"What's going on?" Simon asked Kasey, who had yet to speak.

"I don't know," she replied. "I can't see any more than you can. Everything is happening behind us."

"Story of my life," he muttered.

Soft, swishing footsteps moved rapidly nearer from behind, and in a moment small, delicate hands pawed at Simon's face. He quickly realized that they did not intend him any harm; they dug out the sand from around his neck, freeing his shoulders, working close around his chest and back. He caught fleeting glimpses of shimmering fabric, flashing eyes behind mysterious veils, but no one spoke as they methodically heaved mounds of sand away from his body.

He heard a commotion behind him, and then saw Kasey step into the shadow above. Sand clung to her damp clothing, but her lithe form appeared no worse for wear. Somehow she seemed taller than he remembered.

"You're not going to believe this," she said when their gazes met.

"Quite a statement coming from a time traveler," Simon smirked.

Three women dug furiously to free Simon, and once his arms came loose—somewhat numb from hours of immobility—he aided in the rescue effort. Soon the women extricated him from what could have become a rather grave situation indeed.

He wobbled, regained his balance, and turned around to see what had impressed Kasey.

To his utter bewilderment, he came face to face with a rather large and imposing camel, its thick lips curling and smacking as it chewed lazily on a cud. The thing paid him little heed, eyeing him halfheartedly as a rhinoceros might eye a housecat, more from amused curiosity than anything else.

Astride the great dromedary sat an imposing figure of a man, clad in bright red and gold robes, his head covered with a flowing white headscarf tied around the temples by a single loop of leather. Ponderous brown eyes peered out from an intelligent, inquisitive face—the face of benevolent authority, a powerful and capable leader who inspired his followers and intimidated his enemies, or so Simon imagined. A strong Arabic nose gave a slightly haughty air to this sheik of the desert, and a curl of black hair protruding from the headscarf on one side of the forehead gave a slightly carefree appearance to what might have otherwise seemed a stern and solemn countenance.

It was a good face: strong, confident, intelligent, and kind; slight lines at the corners of the mouth indicated frequent laughter. Simon hoped this master of the sands did not take joy in the cruel punishment of others. Still, those warm, intelligent eyes did not look like the eyes of a monster....

The man spoke sharply and the women—four of them—set to work brushing dirt and sand from the strange clothing of the mysterious foreigners. Small, strong hands patted Simon's back and chest, his arms and legs, and soon he stood in the sun as clean and dry as when he had left nineteenth century Kansas—only a few hours ago. He and Kasey looked uncertainly at each other.

"This is weird," Simon breathed.

The four women stood quietly on either side of them, waiting for the next command, while the mysterious Arab gazed down at the unexpected travelers, taking in every detail of their foreign accoutrements. Simon and Kasey still wore their thankfully waterproof backpacks, and Kasey clung ever more tightly to her singularly valuable cell phone. Simon's faded jeans and green flannel shirt seemed suddenly out of place here in the middle of— nowhere. Again.

Kasey, in tighter jeans and a simple gray blouse, drew the man's lengthy gaze, as though he had never seen anything like her before. It was not a leering, creepy, salacious look, like the rapist on campus, but rather one of barely constrained incredulity. The women, under the same spell, made Kasey uncomfortable.

"Why are they all staring at me?" she asked Simon, barely moving her lips as she spoke.

"Got me," he admitted.

He looked around at the wide expanse of cream-colored desert, long rolling dunes with wind-whipped ripples decorating their smooth surfaces; occasional brave foliage eked out a scant living in the extreme environment. A cloudless sky stretched from horizon to horizon in every direction, not even the speck of a bird breaking its monotony. He suddenly missed the wheat field.

Eleven camels made up the caravan, each draped with bright, colorful fabrics and tassels, most fitted out for riders and some laden with bundles of supplies. They stood in a straight line, pendulous necks swaying, absurd heads turning slowly from side to side, comical lips curling while broad teeth ground their cuds. It was something out of an old Middle Eastern travel poster.

Another sharp command from the Arab trader and the women moved to attend him as he gracefully descended from his regal steed. If Simon had thought him imposing atop his beast, his heart almost stopped when the formidable mountain of a man stood towering in front of him. Simon craned his neck to gaze up at the statuesque form draped in exquisite robes that brushed the sand when he walked. Kasey, no less impressed, inched slightly closer to her fellow time traveler as the mysterious man approached them.

"How's your Arabic?" Simon asked her.

The Arab paused at the sound of Simon's voice, his ears perked and his eyes trained on the fantastic young man who might as well have arrived from another planet. He said something incomprehensible, in a low tone intended only for Simon to hear; when Simon could not answer, or even feign comprehension, a slight scowl darkened the larger man's face. He moved on to the young woman, uttered a few syllables, and took hold of her thin, delicate hand, a hand longer and far more supple than those of the women in his caravan. In fact, Kasey stood taller than any of the other women, by at least half a head, and that impressed the trader. He touched her golden brown hair, mussed but shimmering in the hard light of the desert sun; holding a lock between his fingers and thumb, he smiled appreciatively.

"Simon, what do I do?" she asked quietly.

"I think you're doing it," he whispered.

The Arab stared at them uncomprehendingly before speaking in what sounded like a friendly tone. But they could not understand any of the words.

"We speak English," Simon said slowly, realizing that most people at least recognized it when they heard it, whether they spoke it or not. Perhaps he knew of a translator.

But Simon's words dumbfounded the trader. Could they have landed someplace so remote that no one spoke the language? Kasey had aimed for the early 21 st century, a mark that seemed surprisingly difficult to hit.

"This could prove tricky," Simon said.

"You think?" Kasey retorted.

"They didn't exactly offer Arabic in high school," he said. "What did you take?"

"Latin, of course."

"Well, my three years of Spanish won't do us much good."

The Arab trader smiled as the two strangers completed their brief exchange. For a moment Simon thought that meant some level of comprehension, but the feeling quickly passed. The Arab spoke a few more soft syllables and then shouted a sharp command to the women, who snapped into action.

Soon Simon and Kasey sat atop adjacent camels, encouraged rather vigorously—but gently—by the four veiled women, each of whom wore a different set of colors, the two helping Simon draped predominantly in greens and blues, while those assisting Kasey displayed reds and yellows. None of them showed any portions of their bodies save for those penetrating eyes peering out from their veils and strong, work-hardened hands that easily manipulated camels, supplies, and guests.

"Sure beats Jim's ornery horse," Simon observed as he settled into his saddle, an ornate affair complete with arm rests, a cushioned back, and a frilly red shade that extended over his head to block out the sun's glaring rays.

"Just don't run into the back of mine," Kasey chided. Simon could barely see her though the back of her own saddle, but occasionally the steed's jostling, swaying motion shook her hair loose, especially when a gentle desert breeze gusted through it.

Neither of them knew the first thing about driving or steering one of these great ships of the desert, but to their good fortune—and perhaps owing to the foresight of their new host—all of the beasts were tied together, end to end, forming a long line that stretched across the dunes. The Arab led the way, with Simon and Kasey near the middle, and the women both before and after them.

With a command from the front of the caravan, the beasts loped forward, their gentle swishing motion soothing and calming, not unlike that of a ship at sea. For as far as he could see Simon did not detect another living thing moving anywhere for miles around. They had been fortunate indeed for this caravan to venture close enough to have heard their conversation.

"Where do you suppose we are?" Simon asked, trying to start a conversation.

"Norway," Kasey replied, killing the idea.

He figured they had to have landed somewhere in North Africa or the Middle East, which seemed perfectly obvious, but he could not pin down the time frame. A lack of contrails in the sky might indicate a pre-aviation era, but that could mean any time before the mid-twentieth century. And since traditional Middle Eastern garb had changed little in many centuries, he had as yet too little information on which to base a solid judgment.

"Maybe we'll see something to give us a sense of timing," Simon tried again. "A building or a monument of some kind."

"What good would those do?" she asked.

"Seeing the local architecture might give us a clue as to when we are."

"What are you now, some kind of historian?"

"I read a lot," he defended. "I know my history."

"Great," Kasey sighed. "An artsy Jesus freak who wants to bore me with useless trivia. However did I ever get so lucky?"

He didn't try again for the rest of the day.

Chapter 12

Oasis

They traveled in relative ease for the first time since the day Fate had thrown them together. The gentle swaying of the camels took some getting used to, but Simon at least enjoyed it; he found it relaxing.

Kasey, on the other hand, paid little attention to her surroundings. She rigged a support across the saddle armrests and strapped her computer to it; swaths of fabric draped from the small canopy above provided ample shade to block the glaring sunlight, enabling her to see the glowing screen. She swore occasionally as the jostling beast of burden slipped in the sand, the resulting lurch interrupting her delicate work. It was all the sound Simon heard out of her for hours.

His iPhone, which still worked, though largely useless except for measuring the passage of time, indicated five hours of travel before he noticed something in the distance other than endlessly rolling hills of rippled sand. Initially a dark smudge of green separating the golden yellow landscape from the washed-out blue above, as the caravan drew nearer he discerned broad leaves and fronds jutting from the tops of date palms, dozens of them—hundreds, per- haps—and smaller foliage he did not recognize. Short grasses grew in patches near the bases of trees, and soon he heard the distinct noises of civilization: snort- ing animals, clanging metal, creaking wood, snapping leather—and the unmistakable voices of men carrying on conversations, shouting out orders, laughing. He heard the higher tones of children as they called out to each other, running and playing without a care in the world.

"Kasey, wake up!" Simon called. "We're here!"

"What!" she snapped, the annoyed tone heavy in her voice. "I'm not asleep." She had spent the last hour dozing, but would never admit it.

Simon had watched Ben-Hur more times than he could count—it was his favorite movie—and so he recognized an oasis when he saw one. He recalled the scene when an aging Balthazar cast his shadow over Judah, hoping him to be the One for whom he had returned to Judea in order to follow: "He would be about your age now," he had said. But he saw only Charlton Heston lying lazily in the sand, fresh from his adventures in Rome, determined to rescue his mother and sister; nevertheless, the two struck up an immediate friendship, and the old man had then taken young Judah to meet his host, the Sheik Ilderun.

"I'm not setting foot in a chariot," Simon muttered as they approached this center of life and activity in the middle of the deadly wasteland on a well-beaten path that might have existed unchanged for thousands of years.

People displayed the garb of various tribes, nationalities, cultures, and backgrounds. Simon saw turbans atop some heads, others adorned with simple headscarves, while several wore more complex keffiyehs that covered virtually the entire face. Most men dressed in long robes, or tobs that flowed from the shoulders to the ground, covering sarongs; over their tobs some wore striped abas, or sleeveless coats. Wood and leather sandals protected their feet from the hot sand. Simon noticed with some dismay that a few men, wearing simple headgear and not much else, attended with diligence the other men in the oasis—carrying water, brushing camels, feeding horses. Naked to the waist, displaying hard muscles, they toiled in the sun while their masters relaxed in the shade.

No one matched the richness and ostentation of the trader who had rescued the hapless young time travelers from the desert.

"Where are the women?" Kasey inquired as their caravan marched through the center of the oasis, accompanied by the longing and appreciative stares of Bedouins on either side.

"Indoors, I guess," he replied.

Elaborate tents sprouted from the ground throughout the oasis, forming a community of nomads, each of differing size and shape and color, but all of a common ancestry. Some nearly the size of modern houses, richly woven wool and cotton stretched into enormous walls, dyed in bright reds and blues, their patterns ornate and traditional, no doubt dating back to the very beginning of time. Simon studied them intently, and through the broad folds of their openings he saw dark eyes peering out from behind silken veils.

The long train of desert beasts halted at the far end of the oasis, near the grandest, most richly detailed and imposing series of dwellings in the region. The tent peaks towered a dozen feet in the air and each easily encompassed a thousand square feet or more, the interiors subdivided by woolen walls that could be moved or extended in any configuration the inhabitant wished. One tent had its walls rolled up, allowing a comfortable place for people to gather out of the sun but unhindered by interior dimness.

A sharp command from the powerful Arab and half a dozen veiled women emerged from the tents to take control of the camels and their burdens. Small children accompanied them, helping out as much as their tiny bodies could manage. Other men greeted the imposing trader, and while a few stood as tall, no one matched his broadness of shoulder, girth of chest, and commanding gaze. Nor did their attire appear half as regal.

Once on the ground the Arab engaged in brief conversation with his subordinates, occasionally pointing at Simon and Kasey. The other men turned their heads to see, and gasped in amazement at the unlikely discovery.

"I wish I knew what they were saying," Simon said.

"With any luck it won't matter," Kasey replied. "Once we get inside one of those tents we can be out of here—I think."

"You think?"

"I've tried to compensate for every variable," she explained. "But that's only half the problem."

"What's the other half?"

"Power."

That didn't sound good at all.

"Shifting through time requires a lot of battery power—especially when it has to transport two of us. Today's journey nearly drained the battery."

"Can't you recharge it?"

"Gee, I wish I had thought of that," she said, her look of scorn thankfully hidden by the fabric blocking out the sun. "Of course I charged it. But once my laptop power dies we're going to be in trouble."

"Don't you have a spare battery for that?" Simon asked.

Her resulting sigh of exasperation might actually have left a bruise. "The spare is dead," she said. "It has a five-hour working life. The other one has four hours to go. I have at least a couple of hours of work ahead of me if we are going to get out of this place without dealing with what happened this morning, or afternoon, or whatever the hell time of day it was."

"So, it's going to be tight," he said carefully.

"You could say that."

She closed up her computer and replaced it into her backpack as the women arrived to help her from the saddle. One of them tried to take the backpack, but Kasey refused to give it up. A commanding glance from the trader and the woman released her hold on the bag; she bowed submissively and left Kasey alone.

No one bothered Simon's gear after that. He walked closer to Kasey and stood next to her, unsure of what to do next.

"I guess our sandwiches have gotten mashed by now," he said simply. "How can you think of food?" she snapped.

"My stomach's doing that thinking for me," he admitted. A growl of abdominal displeasure emphasized the point.

"Tonight we escape," she told him.

"Escape?" he replied. "I don't feel like a prisoner."

"You don't honestly think they'll keep us as guests?" she looked at him as though he were the densest idiot in all of history. "How naive can you be?"

"Well... what do you think they're going to do with us?"

"They'll probably kill you," she said. "And put me in a harem."

"He wouldn't want you in a harem," Simon smiled, amused by the absurdity of such a notion.

Her look of hate could have melted rock.

"I'm just saying," Simon grinned. "You're not exactly the demur, servile type."

Her hard silence amused him further.

"Still, you'd look pretty amazing in one of those sarongs with all the veils," he chided, "doing one of those dances, with castanets on your fingers, men howling and clapping...."

Kasey turned abruptly and folded her arms in contempt, drawing the unwanted attention of the men still no doubt discussing her fate. Simon barely stifled a laugh.

The Arab spoke sharply; several women approached the strangers and gingerly ushered them inside a tent. Simon wondered if he would ever emerge from it again.

But he needn't have worried... yet. Three women maneuvered him into a private chamber the size of his college dorm room and proceeded to strip him of every stitch of clothing. He fought them off as best he could, but their steadfast determination easily overpowered him. Accepting that they had the upper hand—and lower hand and mid-range hand—he finally gave into their ministrations, soon realizing their practical intentions. They rubbed him with scented oil, coating his chest and back, arms and legs, until he felt very much like a sardine about to spend some quality time with a dozen of his closest friends. The women rarely looked him in the eye, and when one of them did she giggled and quickly looked away. That filled him with confidence.

Once they had him shined like a banker's shoe, they wrapped him in endless yards of cotton fabric, looping and tucking until he felt like an Egyptian mummy. Over this they pulled on a sarong, followed by an elaborately woven aba, a sleeveless coat similar to one the Arab had worn, though far less ostentatious. They completed the ensemble with a simple headscarf and leather sandals, entirely obscuring the pale and pasty frame of the puny college student from the twenty-first century.

They bowed and filed from the flimsy chamber, leaving him feeling foolish and unsure of what to do next. He waited in awkward silence before venturing out of the darkened room, expecting someone to accost him with threats he could not understand. He felt no wish to die violently at the hands of these primitive Bedouins. What would become of Kasey? Despite a fierce attitude, he suspected that beneath her cold, hard façade resided a scared little girl desperate for love and comfort. He could not allow her to suffer a lifetime of slow death in this inhospitable climate.

Outside he discovered a darkening sky as the harsh desert sun slowly settled into the western sands, casting long and mysterious shadows across the lonely oasis. Fires sprung up in the shallow dusk, combating the approaching darkness. Voices elevated in song broke the stillness of the encroaching night.

A strong but gentle hand on his shoulder startled him out of his light trance. He turned and found the towering Arab standing near, smiling, his eyes conveying no sense of threat. Warmness on the face reassured Simon that this man meant him no harm, that Kasey's assessment of the situation had no basis in reality. The Arab motioned for Simon to proceed along the path between tents, out into the open, where he could see all that the oasis had to offer.

Tents glowed in the dimming light, illuminated by roaring, crackling fires, many burning beneath spits containing pigs and lambs that slowly rotated over the heat. His grumbling stomach could not take it. He needed food, and fast. Nor was he disappointed. The Arab, after a brief tour of the surroundings, led him inside the main tent, which featured a long, low table covered with food.

Succulent ham and veal dripping in glaze drew his attention first, followed by grapes and melons and pomegranates, accented by a variety of olives and figs and dates. His mouth watered at the sight. For a moment he seriously entertained the possibility of diving into the table and swimming through its exquisite array of gustatory delights.

And then something unexpected caught his wary eye.

He glanced toward movement to his left and discovered a sight that drove him to speechlessness and made him forget about the hunger that had consumed him for most of the day.

At first he almost didn't recognize her; such was the transformation that had turned a brilliant college student into a stunning jewel of the desert. She wore bright red shimmering silks woven with sparkling gold and silver threads; her unmarried status compelled her to display her torso and arms in ways that nearly bugged Simon's eyes out of his head. An elaborately decorated headdress flowed from her temples, framing her lovely face, and draped down her shoulders and onto her back. Silken robes brushed the ground when she moved, a melodic swirl of fabric and grace that took Simon's breath away. He wished he could pull out his camera and snap a few dozen pictures of her.

"Don't say a word," she warned as she flowed nearer to him.

He raised both hands in defense, shaking his head. "Whatever you say," he said. "But that word would be... WOW!"

She flashed a look that might have killed ten ordinary men.

Contrary to Kasey's paranoia, the Arab trader treated them as guests, sharing his exquisite meal with them, followed by the entertainment of his sinuously dancing wives and concubines: colorful, wispy veils waved well into the night. Simon enjoyed the distractions, though he had no idea what was going on most of the time; occasionally someone told a joke—no doubt at his expense—and all the men in the tent erupted in boisterous laughter.

Kasey spent the evening looking bored and embarrassed, her stern features unchanging from the moment she had entered the tent. Simon took note, however, that she ate at least as much of everything as he did. She would never admit it, but her human needs remained every bit as strong as his.

His belly full and the bleariness in his eyes overtaking him, Simon felt a great sense of relief when the Arab finally dismissed his wives and stood to his feet. A few sharp syllables and the guests all exited the tent. And just like that the revelry ended.

"I wonder if this is a special occasion or if they eat like this every night?" Simon said as he and Kasey unsteadily rose from the table.

"What does it matter?" she snapped. "We're leaving in a little while."

"True...."

"Meet me behind my tent in one hour," she commanded. "Don't fall asleep."

Simon, of course, fell asleep. He couldn't really help it—after a meal like that, and the excitement of dancing women, the exotic environment, the fatigue of the day—his weary mind and body left him no alternative but to rest, if only for a few minutes. Those minutes stretched into hours.

His first hint of consciousness arrived in the blackness of night. He ignored it. Pressure on his shoulder roused him from the depths of slumber, and then he felt something gently jostling him awake. Before he could say anything, complain about this untimely interruption, a cold, strong hand clamped over his mouth.

Bleariness instantly faded from his eyes, replaced by sudden panic, as he realized that she had been right all along. They had come for him, in the cold desert night, to slit his throat and leave his body to dry in the morning sun.

But the frosty gray eyes glaring at him from the darkness, inches from his face, told an altogether different story. Kasey held a finger to her lips, indicating silence, and then she released her grip on him. As quiet as shadows, they crept through the stillness, stepping around mounds of furs and wool blankets beneath which other men slept. The Arab trader, the wealthiest and most powerful man in the oasis, slept in a private tent, attended by one or more of his wives, their bare bodies staving off the chill desert night air. Simon supposed this nomadic life could have its advantages....

"I thought I told you not to fall asleep!" Kasey seethed in her quietest but equally venomous tone once they reached the safety of the nearest copse of tall date palms. A full moon provided ample illumination, casting cold shadows across the sand. A slight breeze rustled the bushes and palm fronds, and goose flesh appeared on Simon's arms and chest. He shivered.

"Sorry," he whispered. "I did my best."

"You're just lucky they were all asleep," she snapped.

"I said I was sorry," he replied, increasingly annoyed by her attitude. "I don't know what your problem is but—"

She held up her hand, palm outward, in that frustrating and insulting way of cutting his sentence short.

It meant that whatever he had to say was either entirely unimportant or that she was just not interested. It annoyed him almost to the point of insanity. But to his intense anger, it worked every time she did it. He immediately stopped speaking.

"This is no time for an argument," she scolded, the hate in her voice chilling him almost as effectively as the cool breeze wafting across the sands.

It frustrated him even more that she was right.

They stood in deep shadow amidst the thick growth of desert shrubs; stalks and leaves extended well above their heads, providing deep cover. Simon noticed that Kasey wore her jeans and blouse again, which disappointed him; but he understood her feelings. He wished he had changed as well; it wouldn't do for them to appear in the middle of a giant modern metropolis dressed like characters from the 1001 Arabian Nights. That would turn a few heads.

A sharp cry pierced the night, turning the blood cold in Simon's veins. It emanated from Kasey's tent; a similar cry rang out from his tent seconds later, followed by shouting and rustling fabric, swords clanking in sheaths, feet pounding rapidly across packed sand.

"Uh, you might want to hurry," Simon whispered as Kasey typed the commands that would turn her cell phone into the most important device in all of human history.

He reconsidered his notion that he and Kasey were guests of the Arab trader; guests would not incur a frantic search in the middle of the night the moment they went missing.

Footsteps drew closer, many of them, attracted by the mysterious light emanating from Kasey's cell phone. Simon heard shouting from every direction, crushing foliage, snapping limbs, the scraping of metal on metal as swords slid from scabbards....

"Any time you're ready," Simon insisted. He grasped onto her arm, suddenly aware of everything in their vicinity: the shadows of men rapidly approaching, the cold light of the moon exposing their location, the backpacks strapped to their trembling bodies, the strength of will and determination of the young woman that had become the most important person in his life. He knew so little about her, and even though she treated him horribly he had the nagging feeling that deep down she didn't really mean it. They might die in the next instant, by sword or the vacuum of space—or worse—and he felt it strange that his last thoughts would be of this cold, hard, unfeeling, emotionally unstable young shrew instead of his family and friends back home.

He wondered what her last thoughts would be.

Swords flashed in the moonlight, and then Kasey pressed the final button in the sequence.

CHAPTER 13

THE COWARD

S imon held his breath, his adrenaline-infused body tensed and ready for anything— with one exception.

Nothing happened.

Kasey pressed the button again, but the screen flickered once and died. No amount of cursing and swearing on her part shocked it back to life.

A dozen swarthy and half naked Bedouins surrounded them, moonlight gleaming from eyes and blades, and for a very long second Simon expected one of those curved swords to separate his head from his shoulders.

But once again nothing happened.

The men stood motionless and menacing, tight-lipped and silent as the cold shadows they cast in the compromising light of the full moon. Interminably awkward silence preyed upon the pair of 21st century college students trembling from cold and fear. Kasey's useless phone now resided out of sight in her back pocket, safe from her captors' prying eyes.

The towering Arab trader arrived in a whirl of flowing white robes, an air of authority preceding him as it always did. The men cleared a path, until he stood before the cowering young couple. But Simon noticed that of the two only he cowered. Kasey stood tall and defiant.

"Kasey, what are you doing?" he demanded. "He will kill you!"

"Man up," she snapped, peering at him with disgust.

Shame replaced fear, but only by a slight margin. He still trembled.

The Arab shouted quick commands and several men disappeared into the night. Then he reached his hand out to Kasey, touching her hair as he had earlier. But she smacked his hand away, startling everyone within sight. Swords flashed and gasps erupted. But no one dared to move without their master's authorization. Kasey glared with fury into her host's warm face, little expecting him to smile back at her, perfect white teeth glinting in the moonlight. He looked at Simon, who could barely maintain eye contact, and shook his head, amused.

Simon thought for a moment he might let them live—until the Arab unexpectedly grasped Kasey by the throat, squeezing until she could barely breathe; her hands clawed in desperation at his impossibly powerful arm. Simon, overcoming his terror, tried to intervene, but unseen hands held him back. The towering trader raised his arm until Kasey's feet dangled inches above the dark sand, her eyes bugging out from the intense pressure on her face.

Then the Arab released his grip and Kasey's trembling form collapsed in a desperately heaving, gasping, coughing pile. The trader uttered something unintelligible before turning and walking briskly back to his tent. Feminine hands reached from out of nowhere, attending to the shaking young woman, and soon she disappeared from sight, leaving Simon alone in the company of six armed Bedouins. He braced himself for the inevitable, closed his eyes, and waited.

Laughter spread across the oasis, echoing into the night, and then they all disappeared.

Simon slept fitfully on his mound of furs, beneath a warm wool blanket, undisturbed by anyone else in the tent. Unremembered nightmares left him in a state of agitation, and his head ached from a now noticeable lack of coffee. Dim illumination softened the impact of awakening, and when he opened his eyes he discovered the tent empty of the night's occupants. He had not heard them leave, nor had anyone roused him. He lay quietly while his weary brain attempted to organize the events of the previous day into a sequence that made sense. He remembered the terrifying trip through time, getting trapped up to his cheeks in the

ground, the long caravan, the oasis, dinner and entertainment, escape—

—but they hadn't escaped. Something had gone
horribly wrong. The mercifully brief encounter—when
the Arab had hefted Kasey into the air—had inspired
fear in Simon unlike anything he had ever experienced—surpassing even the wall of water that had
loomed over campus, tearing a swath of destruction
like nothing else in human history.

They were lucky to be alive.

Simon gathered himself together, mentally and
physically, slowly got to his feet, and stepped out of
the tent. The sun approached zenith, surprising him;
he had slept half the day, and yet he felt anything
but refreshed. Slaves toiled in the hot sun, carrying
water and attending to their masters; animals stirred
restlessly, eating and grazing; children laughed and
played silly games; Arabs talked and lounged, discussing everything from the care of livestock to the
meaning of the stars, or so Simon imagined. It looked
like a peaceful place to live, with ample water and
food, a comfortable climate as long as one knew when
to stay in the shade, and the company of jovial men
and mysteriously beautiful women—although, Simon
could only make that last assessment based on flashing brown eyes peering from behind colorful veils.

The tranquility lasted a moment before an Arab
spotted him, elicited an amused cry, drawing the attention of other nearby men; they all laughed, then
ignored him completely.

"Great," Simon sighed. "Even they know not to take me seriously."

"You bring it on yourself," a deceptively soft feminine voice said from somewhere behind him.

Simon turned and saw Kasey leaning against a tree, wearing her gray blouse and tight jeans, eating a fruit of some kind. A headscarf barely contained her flowing golden brown tresses. She looked amazing, obviously refreshed from a better night of sleep than he had experienced, marred only by a red mark on her neck that would fade in a day or two.

"How is that?" he asked her. "All I ever do is try to help."

"You're a wuss," she said, tossing him a fruit. "A cowardly, puny, self-deprecating sheep hiding behind your natural shyness as an excuse to avoid relationships. People sense that immediately. No one will ever respect you until you show a little backbone."

"Thanks for pulling your punches," Simon muttered. He already knew all of that about himself. "Why aren't you decked out in your harem gear?"

"Because I don't want to wear it," she said simply. "It's silly. I think I made my point last night."

"So did he," Simon observed. "He could have killed you."

"But he didn't," she reminded him. "No thanks to you."

"Hey, I tried."

"Trying isn't the same as succeeding," she said harshly. "No one remembers the guy who tried to fly a plane before the Wright brothers, or the guy who stumbled upon America before Columbus, or the guy who almost went to the moon before Armstrong. People who succeed are rewarded and the ones who just tried are forgotten."

"Is that why you built it?" he asked. "So you wouldn't be forgotten?"

"I don't give a crap about fame or fortune," she snapped. "I have my reasons for what I did."

"Like what?"

"Like none of your business."

"Uh, I think it kind of is my business," he said. "We're sort of in this thing together now, so I have a right to know what's going on."

"I never asked you to come along," she snapped as she spat a seed from her mouth.

He marveled that such a beautiful form could contain so cold and callous a soul—assuming, of course, she had a soul.

"That's not exactly fair," he said, his temperature rising and his hands trembling. "You never would have gotten out of the science lab if I hadn't shown up. And then where would you be?"

"I would have gotten out on my own."

"What? After he raped you?"

"If necessary," she said.

"What about your self-respect, your dignity, your soul?"

She grimaced. "None of those things are important. You wouldn't understand."

"Did you come out here just to pick a fight?" Simon demanded.

"I came out here to eat this fruit," she replied. "You're the one who started this droll excuse for a conversation."

"Shouldn't you be working on your problem?"

"Too many people," she reminded him. "Besides, there's the matter of the low battery. I only have a few hours left, and I have to put them to good use."

"Do you know what happened when we tried to escape?" he asked.

"We overloaded the processor," she sighed. "I may have to replace it."

"There's not exactly a Radio Shack in this neighborhood."

"You think I haven't noticed that?" she spat. "I don't want to get stuck here anymore than you do, but until I find a way to repair it, we don't have a choice."

"Sorry."

"There you go again...."

"What?"

"Apologizing." She shook her head in disgust.

"So?"

"You didn't do anything to apologize for." She sounded angry now, not just cold. "It's no wonder you have no confidence, always apologizing for everything, cowering in fear, afraid someone is going to hurt you. I'm wearing my own clothes and showing my face in this oasis because I want to. Who gives a damn what they think of it?"

"Kasey, these people are dangerous," Simon told her. "There's no telling what they might do."

"I'm not the one they're laughing at," she observed. "And they leave me the hell alone."

And so their conversations went: Kasey getting the upper hand and Simon feeling like the most foolish person on the planet. She delighted in their frequent arguments, emasculating him at every opportunity, inspiring laughter and amusing looks from people in the oasis who readily identified her tone and his discomfort. They left the quarreling couple alone, especially since the newcomers knew they had nowhere to escape to. The oasis became as much a prison as a home, offering plenty in the way of food, water, entertainment, and comfort, while denying them the one thing that really mattered: freedom.

Kasey pored over her computer at night, eking out as much battery life as she could manage; her mind and her fingers worked at blinding speed in a race against the clock. Each day she reported her progress, or lack thereof, before finding some new way to humiliate him.

Simon, in the meantime, continued to wear his Bedouin clothing, not just out of respect (or fear) for his host, but because the clothing remained infinitely more suitable to the climate, a fact that did not go unnoticed by his companion, who constantly complained of chafing as a result of sand getting into everything. He spent his days drawing pictures of the oasis, capturing the faces of the Arabs when he thought they weren't looking, detailing the tents and trees and the vibrant, close-knit community that had grown up in this miraculous garden in the middle of nowhere. Occasionally he risked snapping a few pictures with his smallest and most unobtrusive camera, one he could hide in his robes at a moment's notice.

People left him alone, except for the Arab's wives who attended to him for basic grooming, a time of the day he actually enjoyed once the awkwardness wore off. Men kept their distance, grinning and looking away whenever he approached, as though something about him struck a chord of humor that would never go away. It reminded him of the time in high school, as a freshman, when he developed a crush on a spectacularly beautiful sophomore so far out of his league that she might as well have been royalty. He kept his secret for months until, on the advice of a friend, he wrote her a letter spilling his guts. Her public reading of his letter in the cafeteria robbed Simon of his dignity, denying him peace anywhere in school, from the library to the art studio; people hounded him for months, and even after spring break constant ribbing only subsided into smirks and barbs. Classmates reminded him of the incident all the way to graduation. At least here, in the Arabian desert, lost in time, he could not understand the jokes and jabs that so amused the people around him. Of course, that didn't make him feel any better about it.

Sometimes he despised women. The fairer sex indeed. They ruled the world through their own subversive means and they all knew it.

The wealthy trader kept his distance from Simon; but to Simon's irrational annoyance, the man frequently approached Kasey, careful not to make any offensive moves that would force him to take unpleasant action against her. He felt drawn to the intriguing, pale young woman he had found mysteriously buried in the desert.

Simon lingered in the shadows as the Arab attempted communication, smiling with amusement at her petty show of stubbornness. He no doubt knew he would break her eventually, though he had never encountered anyone like her before. Simon guessed that fair-skinned light-haired people rarely showed up in this part of the world, and they were looked upon as sort of a novelty.

Kasey and the tall dark Arab strolled through the oasis, the Arab doing most of the talking, not that it mattered much; Kasey replied with such sneering comments as "Your friends must think you a fool to waste so much time with me," and "You may as well give it up because I'm not joining your stinking harem." She employed civil tones, of course, even when she called him a repulsive representative of a backward race that she regarded no higher than dried camel dung. Simon cringed, but the Arab only smiled in blissful ignorance.

The host typically left her at midday, allowing Simon opportunity to communicate with the only person capable of understanding anything he had to say. The fact that she did not respect him—or even like him—made their encounters challenging at best. He obviously needed her far more than she needed him. And they both knew it.

"Your boyfriend has taken an interest in you," Simon observed a week into their stay in this remote paradise.

"Whatever," she replied.

"He's definitely attracted to you," he insisted.

"Big deal," she spat with disgust. "He'll never miss me when I'm gone."

"Will that be soon?" Hope glimmered in his eyes.

"Soon enough," she said. "A few more days and we should be ready to give it a try. Unless you'd rather stay here. It might be dangerous to go with me."

"I'll take the chance."

They strolled in silence, wandering among tall palms, shaded by wide fronds. People paid them little attention as their curiosity wore off, replaced by the familiarity of prolonged proximity; but Simon knew that if they attempted escape again the reaction would be swift and harsh.

"You don't have to be angry all the time," Simon finally said. "I'm not your enemy, even though I think you want me to be."

Kasey flashed him a hateful look, but left her insult unspoken.

"I know I'm not the best company in the world," he continued, "and I'll never win marks for bravery; but a little civility goes a long way. Whatever is bothering you, I can help." He couldn't be any more reasonable than that.

"I'll be angry if I want to be," she said, rather lamely he thought. But she didn't storm away in a fit of rage this time. Progress. "Some things are personal and I don't feel comfortable sharing them with someone I barely know."

"I don't think you share with anyone," he bravely replied. "I think you're so used to being alone that you can't recognize when someone else might actually care. It's easier to keep everything bottled up, so you don't have to take the chance on a friendship. And you call me a coward."

This time she did storm off in a rage, ultimately settling in a lonely corner of the oasis, pouting in the shade, her hard cold features making her the only chunk of ice in the middle of the burning desert.

CHAPTER 14

CARAVAN

The next day their world changed again.

Simon hoped Kasey would complete her repairs before anything else dramatic happened, but she informed him too late that she needed one more good day of uninterrupted work. Utilizing pencil and paper—generously offered by the Art Major— preserved her depleting battery; but it came at the price of time. She possessed ample spare parts, components, tools, and supplies; but she lacked sufficient time and power to implement her changes.

Simon's first indication of alarm arrived in the form of camel herders leading twenty magnificently ungainly beasts into the oasis toward the grand tent occupied by the Arab trader. The trader met them with pleasure, paid them handsomely, and issued a series of sharp commands that resulted in a flurry of activity. Men, women, and slaves set to work fitting out this new caravan with the comforts and supplies necessary for a long voyage across the vast ocean of sand that surrounded the island of sanctuary. Slaves hefted saddles onto bulbous, humped backs while harnesses of brightly colored leather and silk extended from comic animal faces to the hands of trainers. Rolls of fabric and sturdy posts hung from the sides of steeds, while others carried food and water for the journey.

In the space of an hour the tawny, spindly, awkward-looking creatures transformed from naked, lumbering beasts with bare patches of rubbed-off fur into magnificently appointed, richly decorated regal steeds of Arabian royalty, their bodies adorned with fine, elaborately woven cotton cloth. Simon scarcely believed what he witnessed, and in so short a time.

He didn't notice when Kasey stopped beside him to watch the spectacle.

"We better hope he's not planning to take us with him," she eventually said, drawing his attention away from the brilliant parade.

"Maybe he'll take us to civilization," Simon replied, "where someone might speak English."

"And maybe he'll kill us in the desert."

"I can't believe that," he retorted. "He's been good to us, and asked for nothing in return."

"Simon, he doesn't speak our language. Of course he can't ask for anything in return."

"There are other ways of communicating," he muttered. "I'm not stupid."

"Let's not get back on that again," she sighed.

"You know, it seems like all we do is argue," he said. "We'll never accomplish anything if we fight all the time."

"Then let's not fight today," she suggested.

It was a good idea. But it kept them quiet for hours.

The caravan ambled out of the oasis at midmorning, carrying five wives, four slaves, three Bedouins, Simon, Kasey, and the wealthy Arab trader, whose name Simon had yet to learn. Twenty beasts of burden, adorned in the best desert finery, carried their ponderous loads atop absurdly knobby legs that moved at awkward angles in the loosely packed sand. Ungainly and perilously top-heavy, the great ships of the desert moved sinuously and steadily across the dunes at a gait no horse could match. And camels never tired; they maintained their monotonous pace hour after hour, requiring neither food nor drink, oblivious of the harsh midday sun and the fine grains of dusty silicon blowing in the intermittent breeze. Thick woolly fur protected their tawny bodies from both heat and cold, while extra eyelashes filtered out the most stubborn windblown sand; colossal humps of fat provided ample energy for long stretches between oases, days or weeks at a time, which separated the camel from a drying carcass. God had put a lot of thought into these majestic vessels, even taming them for domestic use. Simon admired them a great deal.

Kasey spent hours in deep thought, contemplating her notes, struggling to focus on the work that had consumed the last four years of her life. Nothing had gone according to plan, and now she doubted her ability to find a way out of this miserable place. Her mission had failed, with a finality that made a second attempt impossible. Add to that the destruction of the world from which she had barely escaped, the compounding problems with her software, the unwanted attention of an Arab prince, and the sniveling righteousness of the guy she had inadvertently brought along for the ride, and it felt overwhelming.

But something about Simon nagged at the back of her mind, like an annoying puppy that required too much attention. How could she take him seriously? He lacked drive, motivation, and courage. This average, small-minded sheep, one of the masses, this puny, primitive little man, could never understand the way her mind or the rest of the universe worked. She looked upon him with pitiful contempt, as one might look upon a strange little bug, too harmless and inoffensive to squash, and just unusual enough to taunt and study until something more interesting happened along.

She looked forward to depositing him in some relatively safe time and place before deciding what to do with the rest of her life. She certainly did not want any harm to befall him, hence her return to Kansas;

he had, after all, saved her life. But she could not see wasting more effort on this witless, pathetic, sickeningly polite young clod, this artist, this God-fearing dunce who probably still thought the flat Earth remained at the center of a very tiny universe.

Simon, on the other hand, spent his morning carefully snapping pictures of the desert and the caravan, occasionally sneaking a good shot of Kasey atop her steed. Then he settled back in the shade of his protected saddle and worked on a series of rough sketches, made rougher by the gentle swaying of his desert yacht. He intended to clean them up later, hopefully in the college art studio, once he and Kasey found a way to save the world from annihilation.

The careful and deliberate process of drawing a picture freed his mind from the stresses of life: the inattention of girls, the over-attention of harsh professors, the occasional bully, an impending English paper—even the destruction of all life on the planet. His skillful hand swept across the page, holding the pencil at the perfect angle, shading and blending, depositing smears of graphite into fine cotton fibers; the motions sent him into another plane of existence. He saw the world through the eyes of an artist, focusing on details most people never noticed. The universe comprised infinite invisible lines and curves, filled with merging colors and shadows, the most relevant of which he reproduced on paper; this way of seeing, of reducing every person and object to its basic elemental components, allowed him to understand how things worked, the way everything fit into the universe in relation to everything else. Studying those shapes and forms forced his mind to see beyond them in ways that altered his perceptions: he got occasional epiphanies. For glorious moments the universe actually made sense. He felt sorry for people who lived their lives without the divine gift of inspiration, without the joy and happiness and sense of accomplishment that comes with completing a work of art. He, the artist, strived to communicate the flash of insight to them in ways that positively impacted their souls.

He wondered if the sharp, coldly scientific, harshly critical young woman behind him in the caravan had ever experienced a creative thought in her life. Of course, she had turned a cell phone into a time machine....

The caravan plodded through loose sand, over high rolling dunes, across the expansive golden wasteland for most of the day. The sun climbed high overhead, heating the ground so that the air shimmered when Simon peered at the horizon. He saw frequent mirages during the hottest part of the afternoon: cool refreshing lakes where none existed, multiple horizons, another caravan in the distance that he thought might be some desert reflection of his own.

The sun began its descent, inching toward the horizon on his left, indicating that he and his companions traveled roughly north and somewhat west, although at the moment that meant very little. He knew they had to be in the Middle East or North Africa, at any time in the last 3,000 years, but he could not narrow the scope. Yet.

The powerful and commanding Arab trader halted the caravan at the base of an enormous dune an hour before sunset, and in a flurry of chaotic activity his wives and slaves quickly erected four travel tents from the materials rolled up on the backs of the camels. Smaller and less ornate than the ones in the oasis, they still made imposing dwellings in the middle of nowhere, casting long shadows across the hot sand. Simon marveled at the efficiency with which everyone worked, as though they had completed the same tasks thousands of times and could do it in their sleep.

By the time the deep orange sun scorched the horizon with intense purples, reds, and pinks, the camp stood regally intact, ready for the travelers to retire for the night. A large fire in the middle of camp served the multiple purposes of heat, protection, and the roasting of a lamb stretched across it on a spit. Several such creatures milled about, tied to camels, awaiting their turns at consumption. Simon felt bad for them, wished for a nice garden salad, but knew that under the circumstances he could neither complain nor refuse the meals offered to him. Kasey sat quietly and nibbled on her food, lost in thought, barely conscious of her surroundings.

The wives danced in their seductive fashion as an Arab strummed a primitive stringed instrument, and afterward the trader spoke a few words in his deep, authoritative voice. Then a woman gently urged Kasey to her feet and led her inside a tent. Another did the same to Simon, and so the young college students retired for the night, in the same tent but separated by a wall of fabric.

"Kasey, can you hear me?" Simon whispered as he settled onto his mound of furs.

"I'm here," she replied in a few seconds, her voice coming from only a few inches away through the cotton barrier.

"Have you made any progress?"

"Nothing substantial," she admitted. "A few calculations, but without my computer it's slow going."

"At least we don't seem to be in any immediate danger," he said.

"So far."

"My guess is we're headed to a trading center, a town or village," Simon continued, "where someone might speak English. Maybe there we can get a good idea of where we are and when."

"You mean the history buff hasn't figured it out yet?" she scoffed.

"Not enough information," he replied, ignoring her mocking tone. "I can put us after the Bronze Age, based on the quality of their weapons."

"That helps."

"Kasey, we may be stuck together for a long time," he sighed, trying to overcome his irritation. "I don't know why you hate me, but it's not very constructive."

She didn't know why, either. At first she dismissed him as irrelevant, an innocent bystander caught up in her rapidly unraveling plan; and then he had become important to her, a circumstance on which she had not counted. To some extent she now relied on him, much to her dismay. She had not relied on anyone for anything in so many years that she found the whole concept offensive. She obviously had a psychological need to be rid of him, and to that end her subconscious mind continually prodded and provoked him, encouraging him to leave of his own volition. That seemed to always work when someone tried to get close to her. But not this time. He clung like gum on the bottom of her shoe. Certainly circumstances added to the difficulty, but she could not deny his natural tenacity—and the fact that without him she would have died, probably a couple of times. Plus, no one else in this part of the world could understand her; without Simon she would be completely alone . She thought that was what she wanted, but somehow she had gotten used to his presence and knew she could not easily be rid of him. Nor could she allow him to get close enough to hurt her.

"I don't hate you," she admitted, surprising him. "Sorry."

Had he been standing, a grain of sand blown on a gentle desert breeze could have toppled him to the ground.

"I know this has been a difficult time for you," he said after a pause. "It's been no picnic for me, either—all the terror and frustration and weirdness—but you have to know that I'm not your enemy—never have been—and I will do my best to not let you down."

A long silence ensued, at the end of which Kasey said: "Simon, why are you so nice? I give you no reason for it, and yet—why?"

"Why not?" he replied. "It really doesn't require any special effort, and it makes you feel good."

"I don't get that," she breathed. "Everybody wants something; no one is just nice for no reason: either they want you to help them with a school project, or borrow something they'll never return, or they want to coax you into a compromising position in the back of a car. Everyone has a motive, an angle, a desire of some kind, and when they say otherwise they're lying. And if they're not lying, there is something very wrong with them."

Simon lay silent, processing her words—perhaps the most she had spoken to him, outside of an angry tirade, since they had landed in the desert.

"That's kind of a pessimistic view of the world," he said carefully.

"Realistic," she corrected him. "Once you accept what people really are, then you can more easily deal with them."

He thought about that before composing his response: "I think you deal with people by not dealing with them," he said. "You dismiss them, avoid them, circumvent them, and in the process you miss out on the best parts of life."

"Like lame parties where people get too drunk to stand up?" she retorted, but the anger had slipped out of her voice. "Girls who ramble about clothing and nails and which actor is dating whom? Boys who think memorizing sports statistics has some transcendental quality that will make them appear intelligent to anyone but others of their kind? Science majors who don't know an electron from a gamma ray? Simon, I have professors who don't realize the Earth revolves around the sun! I've seen math majors use a calculator to solve the cube root of 27 —and get it wrong. My high school physics teacher said 'nucular,' and no one knew to correct him. Sure, I dismiss people, but only because they deserve it!"

"I understand," he replied. "But not everyone is on the fringe like that. And some of them who are... well they can have a positive impact."

"People are revolting sacks of filth who overcome their mutual disgust long enough to create little sacks of filth that grow up to do the same thing."

"I always kind of thought procreation would be more attractive than that," he said. "A man and a woman fall in love, and Nature sighs a breath of profound relief when a beautiful new life emerges from their union."

"More like a gasp of unrestrained horror," she said.

"I've never encountered anyone so bitter," Simon sighed. "Are you sure you never worked in a grocery store?"

She didn't laugh, but he thought he almost heard a smile.

"Not everyone has an ulterior motive."

"What's yours?" she wanted to know.

"I don't have one." But he hardly sounded convincing.

"Why did you come to the science building?" she asked. "I'd never seen you there before."

"I came to help," he replied. "When I heard you scream."

"You could have left me alone and no one would have ever known."

"I'd also be dead right now."

"You couldn't know that."

"I couldn't let him hurt you."

"Why not?"

"It wouldn't have been right."

"You did it so you could be a hero and get some attention," she accused.

"That's not exactly fair," he replied, mildly offended.

"Suppose I had been fat or stupid? Would you have stayed with me? Or would you have left the moment he was unconscious?"

"Well, under those circumstances he probably wouldn't have attacked you in the first place."

"Nice. But you haven't answered the question."

"Okay, maybe something along those lines crossed my mind—briefly—but a lot of things cross my mind; they don't really influence the decisions I make. I stayed with you because I found you intriguing, and later I just thought you needed a friend."

"And what did you need?"

"I—I... don't know what you mean."

"Everybody has an angle," she emphasized. "You wanted to rescue the damsel in distress and win her gratitude."

"Is that what you really think?" he scoffed.

"I don't know what to think. You tell me."

A significant pause ensued.

"When I was twelve I went on an overnight retreat to a lake with the church youth group," Simon started, seemingly without purpose. "I didn't really know anyone, and even though the other kids were friendly it felt obvious that I didn't fit in. They swam and played and did all the stuff kids do in a place like that. I wandered around and looked at the flora and fauna, drew pictures, and pretty much kept to myself, always looking on as the outsider, watching the other kids have fun and wishing I could be like them.

"On the second day I wandered too far from the lodge, found a river that looked interesting, and followed it for too long, studying and exploring. I didn't know the terrain, or very much about tromping through the wild. So, when I lost my footing and fell into the river I knew I was going to die. I couldn't swim. I swallowed half the river. I've never experienced panic like that, before or since. But I remember every second like it was in slow motion. I'll never forget it.

"And I'll never forget the face of the man who pulled me out of that river. I have no doubt that he saved my life."

"You must have been scared," Kasey said softly.

"Terrified," he admitted.

"What did he do then?"

"Nothing," Simon replied. "He was an old man, maybe just out fishing, and he told me to watch out for those slippery rocks. Then he was gone and I never saw him again. I walked back to the lodge, dripping wet, afraid someone had found out and that I would get in trouble. But no one had missed me. They were used to me wandering off. A stranger that had been in my life for all of one minute had more of an impact on me than just about any friend or relative before or since. I would have died that day if not for him. Since then I have tried to live my life so that I can be there when someone needs me.

"That was why I came to the science building. Because of that old man by the river who saved my life. And because of him I was able to save your life. And because of me you were able to save us both. And now we are the only hope for a lot of other lives. He didn't stick around for a reward, or for glory or gratitude. He simply did the right thing for the right reason. And we're both alive because of it."

"You've given me a lot to think about," Kasey said in an uncharacteristically subdued tone. "Maybe there's more to you than I thought."

He smiled faintly in the darkness.

"Of course, you could have made all that up just to impress me," she said coldly as she shifted away from the flimsy wall to the other side of the tent.

God! She could be maddening!

CHAPTER 15

DESERT VOYAGE

At dawn the tents came down and the caravan continued its trek across the cold desert sand. A pre-dawn chill made Simon shudder, so he wrapped himself in a wool blanket atop his camel, as did the other people in the entourage. It struck him as odd that the temperature could fluctuate so wildly in the desert, from triple digits during the day to near freezing at night; such was the nature of this inhospitable domain, and why so little lived or grew here.

A cloudless sky brightened in the east, glorious pinks and oranges splashing through the heavens, washing away the last remaining stars, brilliant Venus the last to go. Long, deep shadows spread out from the caravan, undulating across low dunes as the camels plodded in their straight line toward a destination the young time travelers could only imagine. Simon still hoped that in a day or two a translator would assist them, and he would have the opportunity to thank the Arab for his generosity before setting off for more familiar territory. Kasey certainly would have an easier time working in a place where the language and the customs took on a more familiar feel. Perhaps they had, in fact, arrived in a part of history in which they could find the supplies necessary to continue their journey through time—particularly a way to recharge the batteries in Kasey's devices. Still, he had seen nothing to indicate a modern time period—no Coke bottles, jeans, pens or paper; no chocolate, coffee, electronic devices, telephone or telegraph poles; no train tracks, or contrails in the sky. Even so, he knew that as late as the twenty-first century parts of the world had never encountered such foreign concepts.

No coffee. That bothered him. He hadn't sipped a cup of coffee since his last morning in Kansas—hadn't enjoyed a good cup since the day before the end of the world. By his time coffee had spread to every corner of the globe, become the second most traded commodity behind petroleum, and defined the economy of many a nation. If coffee hadn't reached this part of the desert, that could mean only one thing: they had arrived in a time that predated the most wonderful substance in all of human discovery. An Ethiopian shepherd boy had discovered the coffee plant about a thousand years ago (he still thought of time in relation to his own place in the 21st century) when his sheep ran off and got the first coffee high from eating the cherries. The boy tried it as well, and then told the people of his village, who took great pleasure in the discovery. Over the ensuing hundreds of years coffee beans spread across the region, eventually becoming the beverage that would shape the world, more so than any other item of consumption, with the possible exceptions of sugar and salt.

If coffee did not exist in this time, then they might have landed centuries or even millennia before their destination. That could easily preclude the possibility of locating a translator, not to mention finding a place in which to more comfortably live while Kasey implemented her repairs. Suppose this world into which she had thrust them predated the English language? Or European civilization in general? The thought made him distinctly uncomfortable.

He pondered at great length as the sun arced ever higher toward its zenith. The sky deepened and the air warmed, eliminating the need for his now sweltering blanket. He had the strange sensation that this day might turn out to be the hottest one yet, and that did not fill him with joy.

Kasey rode behind him in the caravan, allowing him to sneak a few discreet shots of her atop the gently swaying camel; with his digital zoom he captured some close-ups of her face in the gloomy shadows of her saddle's canopy. His own shadows shielded him from prying Bedouin eyes, preventing the need for awkward explanations. He watched as she rode lithely in her saddle, cut off from the world around her, lost in thought, occasionally peering out at the barren landscape. She kept her lovely steel-gray eyes closed much of the time, and Simon realized that when she wasn't angry—which seemed to be most of the time—she became one of the most remarkably beautiful women he had ever encountered.

Maybe she was right about him. Had he stuck around after her rescue in hope of a reward, in the form of fame or money? Or perhaps even physical attention? She had quashed those ideas at the time, before they could form in his mind; but on a subconscious level had that actually been his motivation? He hated to think so. But he couldn't be certain. He did crave the attention of the opposite sex, which seemed perfectly normal and natural; but just as often he preferred solitude. And what if he did find her attractive? Was that so bad? How could she hold that against him? The odds of her finding him at all desirable remained nil at best, so he put no stock in that scenario. He doubted she would ever take him seriously, even if he were the last man on Earth. Of course, from a certain perspective, he actually was the last man on Earth. No wonder she looked at him with such disappointment.

Last night represented progress. She had opened up to him, at least for a few minutes; no, that wasn't exactly accurate: he had opened up to her and she had not belittled him. Okay, definite progress. He had gone to sleep angry over her cold dismissal, but the more he thought about it the more he realized that her last comment was a manifestation of her deeply rooted defense mechanism hard at work. Perhaps he actually had gotten through, and that scared her. She could not risk getting close to anyone, and so her defenses kicked him away. Someone must have hurt her very badly for her to live in such a heavily guarded shell.

At midday the caravan stopped by a high dune long enough for the slaves to carry a light lunch to the travelers, who ate atop their steeds rather than dismount into the hot, arid sand. Simon glanced back at Kasey and he thought he saw her turn away very suddenly, as though she did not want him to know she was studying him. Interesting. Of course, he did possess a fairly active imagination.

Lunch consisted of figs and dates, the freshest he had ever tried—not like the dried ones in the grocery store—and flat bread that lacked both flavor and texture. A skin of watered-down wine complemented the sparse meal, but it served its purpose. His rumbling stomach settled down for a few hours.

The caravan resumed its trudging march across the desert toward destinations unknown to the young passengers from the future. Or were they from the future? Suppose Kasey's time machine had inadvertently thrust them hundreds or even thousands of years into their own future, and these were the remnants of humanity, nomads wandering through the wasted remains of a once thriving world? Suppose these primitive tribes represented the last vestiges of the human race clinging to existence as the world died around them? Simon could scarcely comprehend the thought.

An hour after lunch a freshening breeze from the east whipped through the caravan, swirling fabric and forcing people to cover their faces. The camels plodded on, unperturbed. Soon Simon heard the first shrieking sounds of high winds screaming across the dunes, chilling his blood and forcing him to wonder if this was an ordinary occurrence. A glance back at Kasey revealed uneasiness in her eyes, but she remained steady, her hands clinging more tightly to the crosspieces of her saddle.

With any luck the squall would blow itself out and leave the travelers unmolested.

But Simon knew better than to trust his own luck.

He didn't know what to make of it at first—a roiling black cloud on the horizon, hugging the ground, with clear blue sky above—but as it rapidly approached, his heart pounded and his body numbed. It reminded him very much of the impossibly destructive and overwhelming wall of water that had decimated the east coast of the United States a short time ago. But this towering wall, moving at a fraction of the tsunami's speed but still swirling along at a powerful clip, consisted of stinging, pelting bits of sand, from the finest powder to chunks large enough to put out an eye. It coursed like an ocean wave across the desert floor, pulsing and flowing, hundreds of feet thick, obscuring everything in its path.

Simon watched in awe as it raced nearer, and almost too late did he notice the other people in the caravan pulling their garments over their heads and bracing for the sudden impact. The camels stopped and angled toward the looming cloud of destruction. Simon quickly followed suit, and glanced back to see that Kasey did the same. And just in time.

It hit with the force of an ocean wave, but instead of water it felt more like an all encompassing blanket of sandpaper, pelting and scratching and irritating. He closed his eyes, and when he opened them he saw only the dim brown shadowy figure of the camel immediately in front of him, its rider hunkered low in the saddle. He looked back and discovered that Kasey had survived the impact as well as he had, and that filled him with hope.

Then the caravan started moving again, much to his surprise. With all the beasts connected by stout ropes, none of them could get separated in the storm, and Simon suddenly realized that storms such as this had to occur on a regular basis. He found it terrifying and exhilarating, but to everyone else it remained an an-noyance—like a summer thunderstorm that disrupts a cookout.

His camel lurched forward, swaying unsteadily in the hard wind that swept from every direction at once. He hoped the trader could see better than he could! Simon double checked the zippers and Velcro closures that tightly sealed his camera gear against the brutal weather. He did not want his drawings to get dam-aged, especially the one of Kasey in the wheat field, the very first portrait he had drawn of her—and his favorite. As he felt for the slight bulge in his pack that represented the sketchbook, he glanced back at Kasey to see how she was handling the ferocious storm. Wind howled in his ears and particles stung his exposed forehead, but he knew it could be worse. His camel lurched and lost its footing as it slid across an exposed rock, but the beast quickly recovered and lumbered ever onward.

Simon grasped his saddle to steady himself and turned back to see Kasey.

But her saddle was empty.

CHAPTER 16

SANDSTORM

K asey's vacant saddle wobbled atop her stumbling steed, and in the murky brown swirl of air behind it Simon glimpsed a shadowy motion, the flash of an arm before it disappeared into the vortex.

Simon prided himself on his ability to step back from difficult situations, to analyze the details, and then to carefully plan a meaningful strategy: that trait had kept him out of trouble for most of his young life. In this case, however, he quite literally threw caution to the wind. Reacting on instinct, though he often convinced himself he didn't have any, Simon grasped his backpack and leapt from the camel into the raging, stinging storm.

He landed hard on the side of a low rippling dune, lost his balance, and toppled into the sand. Struggling to his feet, attacked by the very air he tried to breathe, Simon plowed forward in the direction of the young woman who had fallen from her unsteady mount. She could not have landed far away; visibility extended no more than twenty feet in any direction, and his steed had covered no more than half that in the time he had taken to react. But he also knew that in the midst of the destructive and debilitating tempest he might step directly over her and never know it.

As dumb luck dictated, he stepped on her, specifically on her left leg, and the sudden shift in ground texture sent him sprawling into the sand on his face. Rising to his knees, he felt around for her body as a gust of whipping sand rippled through buried fabric, uncovering her senseless form. He lunged into the dune and dug out her prostrate frame; freeing her head and shoulders, he pulled her into a sitting position, using his own body to shield her from as much of the storm as he could manage.

He found a strong pulse when he pressed his finger to her neck, but he could not rouse her to consciousness. Turning back, he found no trace of the caravan that crept slowly through the pulsing, shrieking murk. They couldn't have traveled far in the short time it had taken him to locate Kasey's body; and yet second after second ticked by as his numb legs stumbled and staggered, his painfully sand-caked eyes searching the ever- swirling vortex for some shadowy movement, a flash of metal, anything to lead him to safety.

He saw nothing but angry sand.

Panic seeped into his weary mind, clouding his brain as effectively as the storm cloaked the desert. He fought it, cognizant of the knowledge that people who panicked got eaten first; what happened to his coolness under pressure, his iron constitution, his unique ability to think through a situation without reacting on raw emotion? Of course, in his eighteen years of life, fate rarely hurled him into a situation in which abject panic remained a viable and appropriate option. Usually he dealt with angry customers over missing fuel points; malfunctioning cash registers; system-wide network outages that disrupted people's ability to use credit or debit cards; faulty equipment that crashed and needed rebooting (his definition of which involved a swift kick followed by another); and the occasional screaming child that had fallen from a shopping cart and landed on its head (stickers cured crying, but not inattentive parenting). Nothing in the grocery industry had ever prepared him for a desert tempest in a strange time with a woman who couldn't stand him.

Panic seemed the right way to go.

But Simon retained one life-saving trait that never failed to aid in his survival, for better or worse: cowardice. It came in many forms and took on a host of shades and degrees, cloaking everything he did in a yellow veil of fear. Brave people, he understood, fought valiantly, defied impossible odds, leapt into fearful situations, and battled the forces around them with abandon. They took chances, made leaps of faith, and changed the world. But it was the cowards who recovered their beaten and mangled bodies and lived to see the next brave hero stand up for something intangible.

It was that fear, that resistance to death, that overwhelming sense of self- preservation that ruled Simon's intellect and emotions. It prevented him from asking out the young art student who sat next to him in his freshman drawing class; it kept him from going to parties off campus for fear that a police raid—which occasionally did occur—would get him kicked out of college, whether he had been drinking or not; it kept him from defending himself against the hatefully venomous words of the irrationally angry customer who blamed him personally for the fact that his store had not ordered enough diet caffeine- free sugar-free gluten-free taste-free kiwi-lime soda in the twelve-pack cans that were on special this week. It also prevented him from curling over the top of his unconscious companion to wait for slow and agonizing death to claim him.

With cowardice came a fierce determination to avoid conflict, and consequently to avoid injury and death; and to that end Simon's instincts demanded that he heft Kasey over his shoulder and trudge through the raging tempest until he found some safe haven in which to hide.

He never thought of himself as brave. He simply accepted a crisis for what it was and adapted to it in the least threatening manner available. Dragging Kasey across the rolling dunes, with sand swirling up to his thighs in winds gusting above one hundred miles per hour, made perfect sense in his fear-induced state:

only she could get him out of this godforsaken world, provided he could get her out of this wrathful storm.

And so the duly registered, card-carrying coward labored under the increasingly burdensome weight of the delirious young woman draped awkwardly over his shoulder, like the huge bag of dog food that he routinely carried to Mrs. Peterson's car every Thursday. He dared not stop to rest for fear of succumbing to the overwhelming forces of Nature, realizing that a pause of only a few seconds might turn his numbing form into a tiny dune indistinguishable from millions of other motionless waves in the solid sea of sand.

Simon trudged for what felt like hours in the murky brownness, hard winds tearing at his flesh through the thin protection of his clothing, any exposed skin rubbed raw as from the constant scraping of sandpaper. His legs felt the burden of his labors, not only the weight of two people but the constant sloshing through loose earth, like walking on an oceanless beach in the fiery depths of hell. The effort might have carried them a few miles or a few yards, so little could he judge distance or direction; for all he knew he might have walked in tight circles as the ground undulated beneath him, tricking him into thinking that he followed a straight line. The caravan had long since faded away, both from his sight and from his mind, now no longer the objective of his desperate journey. He sought only a cave, a building, a copse of trees, a dead camel, anything that might provide some barricade against the shrieking wind and pelting sand.

His shadowy destination loomed out of the murk as unexpectedly as a ghost in the night, a mysterious specter, haunting and inviting, filling him with a strange mixture of relief and dread. It meant refuge and survival, but he could not know what magnitude of horror lay on the other side of the broken and abandoned opening.

A stone structure, mostly submerged, jutted from the side of a colossal dune; barely more than a façade, like the great temple of Khasneh hewn from the side of a cliff in Jordan's Petra, it beckoned Simon and the heavy load beneath which he staggered. In the constantly moving shadows and waves of airborne sand he discerned few features other than the sloped pediment reminiscent of ancient Greek temples and some cracked and partially crumbled columns that looked older than time itself. The peak of the classical roof rose perhaps twenty feet above the desert floor, indicating a relatively small temple, but it appeared different from anything he had ever studied. It reminded him of something Greek, but only in the vaguest sense; it remained foreign and unfamiliar, small in scale, and strangely located in the middle of nowhere. He just hoped it stayed standing for the duration of the storm.

At the top stone step Simon heaved with a final burst of adrenalin-induced strength and collapsed through the threshold into the darkness beyond. Kasey tumbled in a half- controlled fall onto a soft windblown sand drift, uninjured but still unconscious.

With most of his strength ebbed, his arms and legs now made of stiff rubber, Simon grasped onto Kasey's hands and dragged her further into the temple, around the wall that blocked the entrance from the main room, and settled into a corner; here they could rest for as long as it might take to wait out the howling tempest, now muffled and toothless beyond the stone walls.

He brushed sand from Kasey's dusty clothing and propped her in a more comfortable position, using his backpack as a pillow to ease her suffering. Her breathing became erratic and she mumbled frequently; in a moment of intensity she screamed out the same mysterious word, "Carista," that she had spoken in her disturbed sleep in Kansas, and then a frighteningly deep sleep consumed her. Simon kept watch over her, protecting her with his thoughts and prayers, willing her to stay alive, until eventually the sheer exhaustion of the afternoon took its toll and rendered him unwillingly unconscious.

CHAPTER 17

MOONLIGHT

When Simon woke, he became aware of two things: near total darkness and silence as absolute as a tomb. He could not know how long he had slept—hours or days—but it had done him a world of good. His arms and legs felt stiff but not painful, previously atrophied muscles reawakening to the new stresses of his cowardly heroic life. Bleary eyes adjusted to the gloom, revealing a soft and subdued glow of ambient light almost indistinguishable from the blackness of night, but enough that he could make out shadowy shapes and forms.

His sturdy backpack leaned in the corner, the sum total of his personal belongings. He yawned. Maybe random temples sprouted up all over the desert and he had just stumbled onto one of them. Possibly the caravan had taken refuge in a similar one along the path.

He looked around for Kasey, last seen resting like a corpse against the wall. Had she left him again, this time in a place to which she could never return? But even she, in spite of her callous attitude and obvious contempt, could not leave him here to die a slow and miserable death.

Simon slowly got to his feet, steadying himself against the wall, and peered intently into the darkness for some indication of the woman he had rescued. He saw only dark walls and shallow alcoves, supporting columns and ominous shadows in the temple's spooky interior. He discovered drifts of sand piled in the corners and spread across the stone floor, an inch-thick carpet that obscured details as effectively as the darkness.

But the storm had ended. Through the grace of God he had survived the worst ordeal of his life. Nothing could ever compare to the hell he had crossed to get to this place; he wondered if he would have to cross it again to get out.

He found Kasey leaning against the doorway, staring across the clear desert, the cold light of a full moon illuminating fresh dunes like ice flows in an arctic sea. Sensing his noiseless approach, she chose not to acknowledge him. She still wore her jeans and gray blouse, the rest of her protective clothes piled in a heap behind her. The pale light of the moon hardened her features, turning her into a colorless statue carved from frosted ice, still and frozen, incapable of the warmth of humanity.

But closer examination revealed ruddy stains of dried tears streaking the powdered sand on her cheeks.

He studied intently the delicate, lithe form leaning casually against the hard stone opening. Her soft hair glowed in the light of the moon, strands of it tangled and matted, but most of the sand now brushed out by dry fingers. Her left arm dangled lifelessly by her side, her wrist loosely brushing the faded denim covering her hip; the other hand rested on the simply carved stone door frame, partly supporting her own cold frame. In sharp, crisp profile he recognized vulnerability in her gentle curves, the sudden roundness of her face, the smooth white mounds of her cheeks, the softness of her nose, the fullness of her thin lips, the firmness of her feminine chin. He noticed as if for the first time the length of her neck, the shape of her head, the slenderness of her tall body, a perfect model for the most beautiful Botticelli masterpiece. But her cold gray eyes commanded his attention as the most striking feature of this physically flawless young woman. They were bright, intelligent eyes, shimmering with life and pain, the depths of which Simon could scarcely imagine: turbid oceans surging with mystery and feeling cloaked by a calm and placid surface.

Kasey stared into the barren wasteland, now the color of white cream, and barely blinked in all the time that Simon watched her. He glanced at the rolling dunes and cold shadows, then took a step back toward the interior. He had seen enough desert for one day.

"Wait," a strangely soft and distant voice emanated from the night. "Please don't go."

Simon turned and found Kasey staring intently at him, her expression one of wonder and surprise, tinged with suppressed suffering. He had never seen her so weak and vulnerable, even after her return to Kansas.

"I'm here," Simon assured her. His voice sounded loud in the stillness of the night, inducing him to speak in whispered tones.

"I have some vague recollection of being carried through maybe the worst storm of all time," she said softly.

"I thought I lost you," he replied.

She smiled, a treat she only rarely shared with him, and suddenly the pain and suffering and terror became worthwhile. "I have a feeling that as long as you're close by I'll never be lost."

It was the kindest thing she had ever said to him.

"I'll never know how you did it," she admitted. "You're not exactly the heroic type— but I have to admire your determination."

"We got lucky," he said. "The storm uncovered a temple, in the right place at the right time—almost like someone was looking out for us."

She ignored the primitive reference. "We're still lost," she pointed out.

"I'm sure that once they discover what happened they will come back for us," Simon said, the words sounding hollow and desperate even to his own ears.

"Always the optimist," she said coldly. "You only prolonged the inevitable; we're going to die here—either in this building or out there trying to find some-place equally as useless. You should have stayed on your camel."

"You know better than that."

"At least one of us would be alive."

"We're not going to die," he told her with an author-ity that for a moment he actually felt.

"No food, no water, no supplies," she sighed, "and all my gear is still on the back of that stupid camel."

Simon slumped against the door frame, the heavy wooden door long since deteriorated, leaving the temple's interior unprotected from the ravages of Nature. He slid to a sitting position, resting his chin on his palm. To his surprise, Kasey sat next to him, inches away, closer than she had ever purposely ap-proached. Every fiber of his being became suddenly and awkwardly aware of her nearness, and he fought desperately to remain calm even as his pulse quick-ened and his face reddened. Fortunately, in the cold light of the full moon, color became largely irrelevant.

"I know I've been hard on you," she said in a tone she had never used before, one that startled him—one that frightened him. "It's just that... things have not gone the way I planned, and it's all been for nothing."

It was the tone of utter defeat. Kasey had given up, lost all hope, and had resigned herself to the stolid fact that she would never leave this inhospitable world. He recognized the depression in her voice, the distant va-cancy in her eyes, the fear and the anger that resided there, the feeling of impotence and insignificance before the universe around her. He had felt it every day of his life.

"You know how to make God laugh?" he said softly. "Tell Him your plans."

She reacted, surprisingly, by resting her head on his shoulder.

"I know you're trying to make me feel better," she whispered. "But you have to know by now that God doesn't exist."

"A lot of people might disagree with you," he said cautiously, testing the water, preparing for yet another explosion of rage. But the rage had left her.

"Of course they would," she whispered. "People will believe anything as long they don't have to think for themselves."

"That's kind of harsh."

"It's accurate. Simon, people cling to religion because their lives are so unbelievably insignificant that if they put themselves in the proper perspective of the universe the overwhelming futility would drive them mad. Society would break apart. Maybe that's not such a bad thing. It's really not worth saving."

"You can't mean that," he replied.

"I do mean it," she assured him. "There is no point to living, and all the petty bickering people would not be missed by any aspect of Nature. In fact, Nature would be a lot better off without our destructive presence."

"People aren't perfect," Simon defended. "But you can't act as judge and executioner because of a few bad experiences."

"Simon, I'm not going back," she admitted. "I don't want to save the world—and not because my phone is lost. I've seen what people are capable of doing, and I have no sympathy for them. I say let them die."

"What about me?"

"What about you?"

"Do you want me to die?"

"Of course not," she scoffed.

"Why not?"

"You're... different," she said.

"Nothing is stopping you from taking a rock and bashing in my skull right now," he said. "Or better yet, take a knife and plunge it into my heart. I won't argue or protest. Just do it and get it over with."

"Simon, I'm not going to hurt you."

"I'm a person, so I must be a monster. Therefore I must die—and you must kill me."

"That's not what I meant," she argued. "I just don't think I have the ability to go back. That world ended. We can stay here and live out our days, and humanity doesn't have to continue on. I didn't destroy the world; I shouldn't be expected to fix it."

"Maybe God wants us to," he said weakly.

"Simon," she said in her condescending tone, "how can someone of your intelligence put stock in such nonsense?"

"What nonsense?"

"All that God crap," she said. "You know as well as I do that God did not create man in His image; man created God to explain the unknown, to control the actions and loyalty of other people. That's why we have mythology and whole pantheons of gods, as moral lessons for people who can't think on their own. Churches are designed to keep people repeating the same old tired ideas so they can be led like sheep at the whims of their pastors and priests."

"Churches provide stability, both in the community and in one's own life," Simon tried to explain. "Only through devotion to God can we find true inner meaning and strength—"

"It's a damned social club," she snapped, straining the tranquil mood. "Religious zealots spend six days a week disregarding commandments with abandon and then piously judging those who don't show up for the Sunday club meetings. And once they've spent their reverent one hour a week singing silly Jesus songs and dozing through a dull and pointless sermon—that always ends in a plea for money to pay for the enormous and overpriced new sanctuary—they eat in restaurants and then go grocery shopping, all the while condemning those who work on Sunday and don't keep the Sabbath holy. Don't you see the hypocrisy?"

"People aren't perfect," he repeated slowly. "They go to church to worship in whatever way they know how. Maybe it doesn't make a lot of sense. Maybe people don't think things through. Maybe we think too much and that gets in the way of things that are really important."

"Like what?"

"Like watching a sunset," he thought aloud, "enjoying good music, or spending pleasant time in the company of an interesting friend. Interacting with people is what defines us, and those of us who don't practice that find ourselves as outcasts. Maybe that's why we ended up together: maybe God brought His most ridiculous outcasts together just to see if they could find a way to save the world. Maybe it amuses Him."

"Maybe you still think the world is flat," she retorted. "And five thousand years old."

"I don't have the answers," he admitted. "And who cares how old the world is? Five thousand, five billion, it doesn't affect my life in the least. It's all academic. I have bigger concerns."

"Such as?"

"Such as... who is Carista?"

The sudden and unexpected question caught Kasey off guard. She raised her head from his shoulder and looked him in the eyes, a flash of emotion returning life to her defeated soul. For a moment Simon thought she might hit him with that rock he had taunted her with a few minutes ago.

"I don't want to talk about her," she said, her voice softening and the emotion subsiding.

"Was she a friend?" Simon persisted. "Someone you cared about? Your sister?"

Kasey's head jerked toward him as he guessed correctly.

In that moment, as had happened on very few occasions in his life, he understood the universe clearly and completely, if only for an instant.

"You built a time machine to save your sister," he realized. It had been so obvious; it explained a great many things. "That's where you went when you left me in Kansas, and something went horribly wrong."

"Something like that," she admitted, returning her head to his shoulder in defeat.

"Tell me about her," he said softly.

"She was the most beautiful person who ever lived," Kasey said from a dreamy trance. "I adored her, I guess from the moment I was born. We shared a bond like nothing else I can describe."

"She was older?"

"My big sister," Kasey smiled as she remembered Carista's stunningly beautiful face. "My best friend... my mentor... my inspiration... my partner in crime—everything a little girl needed growing up. I loved her."

Simon felt her trembling and sensed she might start crying, something for which he certainly felt unprepared; he had never seen any emotion other than anger emanating from her cold and callous form, and the sudden change shook him.

"I shouldn't be talking like this," she said, sniffling, wiping her nose with the back of her hand and sitting up straight again.

"I think you need to," Simon replied.

"It's a long story."

"We have plenty of time," he replied as he stared out across the dunes; the moon had inched a few degrees lower in the starless sky, but still had a considerable way to go before it completed its nocturnal journey.

Now completely vulnerable and trusting the good intentions of this seemingly weak and cowardly young man who had demonstrated an uncanny propensity for saving her life, Kasey leaned against him in the doorway, her head on his chest, and settled in for a lengthy tale of heartache and disappointment.

Thrilled and a little frightened by her suddenly soft and warm body pressed against his, Simon did his best to pay attention to her every word.

It wasn't easy.

CHAPTER 18

CARISTA

C atalina Carabresa was born into a middle-class family that consisted of a school teacher, a pharmacist, a toddler, two cats, a golden retriever, a parakeet, four guppies, and a yard full of playful squirrels, rabbits, and chipmunks. Named after her paternal grandmother, she got her nickname, Kasey (originally K C), because her older sister Carista found Catalina too difficult to pronounce. It stuck, and for the next nineteen years no one in her family ever called her anything else. Even her school report cards listed her nickname instead of her actual name. But that was fine with her: she loved the fact that her sister had named her.

Kasey's great grandfather, Salvador Carabresa—the family's most revered hero—had emigrated to the United States as a young man in the late 1930s to escape the Mussolini regime in Italy; had married, gotten drafted into World War II, and was shipped back to Italy where he died saving the lives of all the men in his platoon. Kasey didn't know many of the details other than her grandfather had been born shortly after Salvador's death. His wife never remarried. That was how the Carabresas came to America: in a blaze of patriotic glory, fighting for liberty and sacrificing everything for others to be free.

It had always seemed frivolous to her, forfeiting life so that one world leader could win a worldwide chess game against another; and in the end it always boiled down to three things: Power, Money, and Land. No one ever went to war because someone's rights got violated. She cared little about her ancestry other than the fact that her name was Italian, a point that became very important to her sister.

Carista, from an early age, dreamed of returning to the land of her ancestry. She wanted to spend a year exploring the ancient structures, the ruins, the overwhelming museums filled with the world's most important and beautiful works of art; to stroll through Tuscan vineyards, sneak a romantic kiss in a Venetian gondola, stand atop the world's highest dome in the Vatican; she fantasized about living in a Palladian villa, shopping in the exclusive fashion district of Milan, and dining in a quaint restaurant on the shores of Lake Como, with the majestic white Dolomites towering all around. Her enthusiasm infected Kasey, and the sisters spent much of their formative years planning the perfect trip, nagging their parents to let them go, working out every minute detail.

They lived a comfortable life in a rural neighborhood, with trees to climb and a forest to explore; a scattering of other kids to play with after school; a small church to report to every Sunday; and no fear of the dangers that existed in big cities. They rode their bicycles in the streets, chased their dogs through empty lots and strangers' yards, played games wherever they felt the urge. They came to know the residents quite well, spent their summer breaks enjoying cookies and milk in a dozen different homes. Kasey wouldn't have traded her youth for anyone else's in the world.

As a toddler, Carista played with her new baby sister like she was her own little doll, and as the years passed, the toddler Kasey followed her five-year-old sibling everywhere. Carista brought Kasey to Show and Tell in kindergarten, and everyone oohed and aahed at the cutest baby they had ever seen. Later, the big sister eased little Kasey's transition from preschool to elementary school, in the process garnering the admiration of both parents and teachers. Carista felt protective of her baby sister, from the earliest moments of life to the days of bullies in high school.

By the age of two the family sensed something unusual about the spry and inquisitive little Kasey. She developed a fascination for books that bordered on obsession, and no matter where her parents hid them, Kasey found them and devoured them all from beginning to end. Even the top shelf of her closet did not provide a barrier for the determined little girl. One night her parents watched in awe as the fearless toddler carefully climbed up the doorframe, oblivious of gravity, and raked all the books she could reach onto the floor; she then climbed back down and settled into the pile, where she systematically read each and every tome. The greater surprise, more so than the actual acquisition of the volumes, came when her parents figured out that their two-year-old did not just look at the pictures: she read and understood the stories that went along with them. Carista, four and preparing for kindergarten, had taken an interest in picture books; their mother had started her on the basics, teaching her about sounds and letters and words, reading to her at night before bed, completely unaware that Kasey, wanting to be like her sister, paid close attention to everything that transpired. She learned to read before her sister did.

In elementary school, Kasey stayed in trouble for daydreaming. She paid little attention to her teachers, got distracted by the slightest little things—birds outside the classroom windows, unusual cloud formations, the patterns of mineral veins in ceramic floor tiles, even the number of bricks that made up a given wall. Teachers got frustrated and doctors diagnosed her with the fashionable behavioral disorders of the time. But no one considered the real problem until her grades came in. Kasey scored higher than anyone in her class—in her school, in her county, and in her state. By the third grade she read books that adults found intimidating, and in particular she adored fantasy novels. For a while, her brilliance made other students leery of her, until they discovered that she could do their homework for them, a situation that ended poorly for everyone when the grown-ups found out.

More and more, Kasey lost herself in books, preferring the adventurous lives of unreal characters in fantastic realms to the dull people and mundane world into which she had been born. Her grades, though exceptionally high, reflected a lack of interest that kept her from reaching her potential—a word she grew to despise after all the many lectures that revolved around it. But her sister always understood. Carista defended her to parents and teachers, shooed away hurtful bullies, and never tired of listening to Kasey telling her all about the latest book that had captured her imagination. As long as Carista remained on her side, Kasey could endure anything.

Then came high school, which meant a different bus, a different building, a new set of people, and a totally foreign existence—for Carista. Kasey, on the verge of middle school, suddenly felt alone in the world without her sister's constant influence. Carista blossomed into the most beautiful bloom in the garden, vibrantly colorful and radiant, with a scent that attracted everyone. She had no enemies. Her good nature and calm demeanor only emphasized the beauty that emanated from every feature. Kasey, on the other hand, grew too tall, with disproportionately long arms and legs, the occasional blemish that always appeared in the worst place, and a bosom that absolutely refused to assert itself. Loneliness and self-consciousness took their toll, especially in the shadow of her radiant sister; consequently, her talents became forgotten—by her and the people who mattered—with one important exception.

Kasey's first pangs of jealousy began in the ninth grade, when every teacher, teacher's aide, janitor, cafeteria worker, bus driver, principal, visiting school board official—and once even a delegate from a local city council—congratulated her on being Carista's little sister; she must be proud; she must love having her for a sister. Like she had any choice. But Carista always found a way to put such disgraces into a proper perspective for her: all these people knew her already and liked her, because she had spent years developing those relationships and maintaining her positive image. None of them knew Kasey except by association, so it was up to her to make them remember her. Kasey took the advice to heart and poured that effort into her studies, abandoning fantasy novels in favor of text books, which she found dull and boring; she augmented them with the great scientific works of history, from Galileo and Copernicus to the latest volumes on String Theory. By the end of her freshman year she had a perfect GPA, the only one in her class.

Her social life suffered accordingly, and no matter how she tried she could not live up to the standard set by her sister. Teachers tolerated her, and not just because she knew far more than they did about virtually every subject; she developed a cold, scientific edge that made it difficult for anyone to get close.

Few students sat with her in the cafeteria, and those who did generally wanted help with homework—help that Kasey, to her credit, generously gave, though often with an aloof attitude that intimidated them. For her part, Kasey reveled in solitude; she studied and learned and mastered subjects that would have confounded even the brightest college students.

And so she endured the first two years of high school in relative anonymity, safe in the shadows cast by the glowing light of her sister, content to read and study and learn, shunning most human contacts.

Her world changed on Prom Night.

Uninterested in such absurdly promiscuous rituals—and not old enough to attend— Kasey sat home on that Saturday night, studying a book by Hawking, intrigued by curling universes and ways of circumventing time. She tried to explain it to Carista while doing her sister's hair, but her big sister only feigned interest as she thought about the magical time she would have at the dance she had helped to organize. The outer space theme, inspired by Kasey's incessant ramblings and a song she had shared with Carista: Fly Me to the Moon, by Frank Sinatra, promised an out-of-this-world evening.

Kasey took a picture of her insanely beautiful sister in her white sparkling gown that flowed over one shoulder, clung to the most important parts of her physique and left others cloaked in tantalizing mystery; her fiery red hair, done up in a classic Romanesque do with curls hanging loosely about her cheeks, revealed the long and sensuous Carabresa neck, which lofted from between feminine shoulders made for caressing. Carista's eyes, brighter blue than Kasey's, more vibrant and full of joy, revealed a soul more prone to flirt with mischief. Their mother took one last picture of them together before Carista's date arrived in a rented limousine to pick her up.

It was the last picture ever taken of her alive.

Kasey, lost in the pages of her fascinating new book, heard a heart-wrenching scream that echoed from the kitchen downstairs. Vaguely aware of a knock on the door a few moments earlier, she thought nothing of it. But when the shrill, piercing scream of emotional agony penetrated the house and the surrounding neighborhood, Kasey instantly knew that something had happened to her sister. Even before she cautiously crept down the steps and saw the uniformed police officer standing over her parents on the floor she knew Carista had died. She sensed the lost connection, the sudden aloneness, the intense and overwhelming feeling that she would never again experience happiness.

The next few days passed in a foggy blur of tears, half-remembered faces, and cold numbness as people visited the house to comfort the bereaved, to bring food and flowers and cards, to offer meaningless words incapable of mending the ragged hole torn from their lives. She sat in a corner of the funeral home while people pitied her; and then she stood stoically by the casket, her mind pleading with the ghost of her sister for some kind of guidance.

And then it was over.

Soft earth covered the ornate box and life trudged ever onward, but with a persistent and oppressive sorrow that permeated everything associated with Carista: parents, home, school, church. Kasey missed more school, though her grades remained near the top of her class. But she became increasingly introverted, barely speaking for days at a time, moving through life as a shadow that no one noticed until it shifted. Occasionally a brave student tried to offer condolences, but the cold and hardened Catalina Carabresa dismissed such trifles with contempt and withdrew into a fantasy world of her own creation.

She became a problem.

Distant and brooding, friendless and without purpose or motivation, Kasey languished for a year on the fringe of reality, cultivating a dark mood and self-destructive attitude: on those rare occasions when she did interact with people, more often than not they involved heated verbal exchanges, and twice they ended in vicious and spectacular fights that stemmed from only the slightest provocation. She got suspended from school three times her junior year, all the while maintaining high grades, a fact that did not go unnoticed by her teachers, who no longer pitied her. Eventually the students left her alone. Her belligerence faded to apathy as a long and steady depression consumed her within a comfortable cloak of anonymity.

Until one day the spark of an idea reawakened the fire within her soul: In a moment of clarity, an instant of inspiration and understanding, she found her purpose. Spending the last weeks of her junior year studying with fervor unknown even before the tragedy, she achieved the highest GPA in her school's history before applying to colleges the following winter. She decided which schools she could attend based on the criteria of her very specific needs: the tools and equipment necessary to construct a time machine.

With her brilliant mind obsessing on an impossible task that would keep her preoccupied for years, Kasey barely noticed the bickering and fighting at home, the flaring attitudes, the threats and blame that drove a permanent wedge between her once loving and compassionate parents. The death of their favorite daughter shattered them, as individuals and as a couple, and the inevitable divorce occurred during her senior year of high school. But none of that mattered. Only her project interested her, to the exclusion of everything else in her life.

She missed her Senior Prom, and would have worked through graduation if her now much older mother had not badgered her into going. No one applauded when she crossed the stage and accepted her diploma; she kept walking, past chairs, past students and families, until she reached the exit, never knowing if anyone watched her leave—because she never looked back. Her cap and gown landed in a heap on the sidewalk and an hour later she sat at her computer, studying the algorithms for her highly improbable device.

A summer of hard work followed by a year of experimentation had brought her to the first secret trial of her unique invention, a cell phone that could travel through time. She set it to travel one minute into the future in the spring of her first year at college. It vanished from sight in a moment that filled her with satisfaction and triumph.

But it never returned.

Months of careful and meticulous examination eventually resulted in her theory of spatial displacement, which required a massive overhaul, not to mention a new phone, a process that she completed the night before the world ended. The campus rapist had accosted her before she could finish loading the parameters into her new device.

When she and Simon stared down that wall of destruction as the science building crumbled beneath their feet, she had no idea if the thing would work.

CHAPTER 19

FAILURE

"Now you know everything," Kasey said. "I'm not a complicated person, just a miserable one."

Simon stared out at the desert; the moon crept slowly toward the horizon, casting cold shadows across low dunes.

"It must have been awful," he finally whispered. During the tale his arm ended up around her shoulder, a simple and comforting act that she did not reject, particularly as the air had turned chilly and the warmth of his touch felt good to her. Not since the death of her sister had she allowed anyone to get this close; for the first time in years she felt weak, defeated, utterly without hope. She didn't care what happened to her now. Losing her sister twice had taken its toll.

"I believed she would always be with me," Kasey said distantly, "that we would grow old together; the idea of a world without her in it—it never occurred to me."

"What happened to her?" Simon asked cautiously. "How did she—die?"

"A drunk driver," she breathed. "After Prom, Carista and her date stopped at a convenience store, and on her way back to the car a drunk driver entered the parking lot. She never knew what hit her."

Even now, after nearly four years, the recollection brought tears to her eyes—but it wasn't just that. Something else had swirled the emotions closer to the surface, and it had everything to do with her recent visit back in time—or forward, depending on one's perspective.

"He was a little old man," Kasey continued. "His wife of fifty years had just burned to death in a house fire, and he was out of his mind with sorrow. He didn't know what he was doing—he never meant to hurt anyone. I tried to hate him for taking away my sister, but I didn't even have that luxury: I could only pity him and feel as bad for his loss as for my own. They didn't even try him; as far as I know he still lived in a nursing home when the world ended. It was all so meaningless. One instant of grief and bad timing that destroyed so many lives!"

"I know," Simon said comfortingly. "Sometimes things don't make sense."

"I really thought I could save her," Kasey said softly. "I spent years planning every detail. It should have worked."

"Why didn't it?" he asked. "What happened?"

"I failed," she said simply.

"How?"

"It started the morning I left you in Kansas," she began. "I figured that was as good a place as any to leave you—after all, I didn't know you and I didn't want you tagging along, though it probably would have been better if you had—and so I tried to go forward to the day Carista died. You remember how accurate my phone was whenever we used it: I ended up in half a dozen times and places before I finally got close, a week before the incident, which gave me time to fine-tune the program and make changes to the software. But really I just bided my time until that Saturday.

"I guess I had hung around in the shadows too long, because a police officer stopped me about ten o'clock that night and wanted to know what I was doing out so late. It was the same officer who would break the news to my parents in a couple of hours. I couldn't exactly tell him the truth, but he didn't buy my evasive answers. I knew time was getting close and I tried to hint at leaving, but he insisted on driving me home. I declined, which did not set well with him. He threatened to arrest me for truancy.

"I had little recourse but to run away. I have always been fast, so I had no trouble losing him, but it took me longer than I hoped to get back to the convenience store, especially since I had to be careful to avoid getting spotted.

"The store was sort of in the middle of nowhere, with empty lots on both sides. I ran as fast as I could, desperate to get there in time—10:53—and when I arrived I saw Carista standing in the doorway, holding a paper bag and looking over her shoulder, saying something to the clerk behind the counter. I froze when I saw her; I hadn't seen that face, that smile, those beautiful eyes, in almost four years, and somehow she seemed unreal, unchanged since that night when I did her hair and fixed her makeup.

"I guess I froze for a second; but then I saw a light on the street. Simon, it all happened so fast! I started running again, faster than I ever have before, and Carista stepped into the parking lot. The people in the limousine saw what was about to happen and screamed at her; when she finally turned her head it was too late. I was halfway across the parking lot when the car hit her—" Kasey sobbed as she spoke, something Simon had never seen her do, and at first he didn't know how to react; so he held her tighter and hoped for the best. "—She—she flew into the air, into the windshield and across the top of the car, like a ragdoll, and landed in the middle of the lot.

"I was the first one to reach her; she was still alive, barely."

Kasey fought back the tears while Simon held her comfortingly. For a long moment she could not speak, and so the two of them sat in awkward silence in the doorway of the dilapidated old temple in the middle of an ancient desert. The sobs faded as Kasey clung desperately to this previously annoying young freshman, the last remaining hold on her reality. Somehow he now bridged the gap between her tragic past and her unknown future, the anchor that kept her from swaying too far out in the tugging currents of insanity. Simon had become more important to her than she had realized, and that frightened her; she did not want to suffer anymore loss—her heart and her mind could not take it—and so the safe thing was to reject him. But right now she simply lacked the strength. And talking really did relieve the weight from her suffering soul.

"I held her in my arms," Kasey eventually continued. "She recognized me and tried to say something, but she could barely breathe; there was blood everywhere! I thought I would be sick, but I had to stay strong for her. For once, she needed me. But I couldn't save her. No amount of begging and pleading and praying made any difference. Simon, I watched the light fade from her eyes, and the most important part of me died with her. I guess I'm grateful that she didn't die alone this time, that at the very least I was the last thing she ever saw. Maybe that made it easier for her, I don't know. I only know that the most beautiful person who ever lived died in my arms in a convenience store parking lot just as her brilliant life was about to begin—and I, with a time machine, couldn't do a damned thing about it."

"I'm sorry." He didn't know what else to say.

"I left that night and went a few years in the future so I could at least get some ideas about what ended the world. I landed in The Everglades first, at least that's what it looked like. An alligator snapped at me before I could get my bearings. Next came what looked like an African village on the edge of a jungle. After that I went from Manhattan in the 1950s to the French Riviera in the 1920s. Eventually I got close to our campus the summer before my freshman year, and that's where I spent a month redesigning and reconfiguring the device. I broke into the science lab every night, and I had to steal food and water to survive. But I made progress.

"My next jump through time took me close to where I wanted: one year after the end of the world. I tapped into satellites and listened to the last broadcasts of the world's major news outlets. I stayed for a couple of days and appropriated whatever equipment I could find in the ruins of a small city; most of the buildings were either crumbled or abandoned, entire neighborhoods completely derelict. I saw no birds, heard no insects, detected no signs of life whatsoever. Even the trees stood as little more than giant dead sticks jutting out of the ground. It was the eeriest feeling I've ever had.

"I found a television studio downtown, and one of the backup generators still worked. For two days I listened for some kind of signal, from anywhere, but for all I could tell I was the only human being alive on the planet.

"That's when I decided to come back to Kansas. I didn't know why at the time, but I couldn't just leave you to die there, especially after I discovered what had become of you. You were my last link to the world I had lost, and I guess I had the idea that as long as you lived there might still be hope. Like you said, two misfits thrown together to save the world. At least we could still try for that.

"But getting to you was one of the hardest things I've ever done, and it almost killed me."

"I thought your device was working better," Simon remembered.

"It was, but not perfectly," she replied. "It was humanity that was broken."

"I don't understand."

"I landed in Detroit in the 1970s by mistake and got caught in the middle of a gang war," she explained. "I saw three people stabbed and two shot to death before I could get out of there. Then I almost got mugged outside of Phoenix in the 1980s; I hit the guy with my backpack, cracking the screen on my laptop. Which meant I had to go back to our own time, steal another one, and download my work.

"I jumped half a dozen times to get back to when I left you, and each time I encountered violence. Simon, people have been crazy a long time; we think it's so much worse in our own time, but it isn't. People have always been cruel. They've been torturing and maiming and killing each other for as long as they have existed. When I finally got to within a week of when I left, somewhere around St. Louis, I hopped a train and headed to Kansas.

"But a hobo tried to molest me, said no one would hear me scream on a train. He was right. No one heard a thing as he beat me to a pulp. He would have raped and murdered me, but the train stopped and I rolled out in the darkness. He couldn't find me, and so I hopped another train at the last minute. I think I slept for ten or twelve hours, enough to recuperate some of my strength. I walked the last twenty miles, and the rest you know."

No wonder she had given up. He had a better understanding now of why she had abandoned the idea of trying to save the world: she saw no good in it. Outside of her dead sister, he might represent the only positive influence she had ever experienced, and even that had been fleeting and argumentative. But he realized that two things had drawn her back to him: he had not purposely tried to hurt her, and he had not abandoned her. In spite of her tough and frosty façade, this girl needed him more than she probably knew, and now that she had opened up to him he understood that the tumultuous dynamic of their relationship had changed. It scared him.

They sat in silence as the moon inched closer to the horizon. Neither felt like moving. Simon had grown almost comfortable beneath the warm softness of her body leaning against his, and he constantly fought the overwhelming desire to enjoy the sensation; after all, how could he find perverse pleasure in her suffering? He was there to comfort and soothe her in this time of emotional need, not to satisfy his own sophomoric impulses—or freshman, as it were.

Kasey, on the contrary, took refuge in his embrace; the weakness of her mind and body allowed her these few hours of sanctuary without the burden of fear that ruled her every emotion. She became too comfortable to object, and so she let him hold her, lost in the safety of his arms.

They sat in near silence, occasionally conversing about the past.

Eventually, and with great effort, the young time travelers rallied enough strength to regain their feet when the nagging call of Nature insisted on their attention. Opposite sides of the temple sufficed, outside beneath the cold moon, and when they returned to the heavily shadowed interior they stood staring at each other, as if for the first time. She seemed less intimidating to him, and he no longer irritated her. She smiled, and it made his heart flutter.

"There has to be a way out of here," he said, peering into the deep shadows. "Indiana Jones would find a way."

"Who?"

"Indiana Jones," he repeated. The confused look of ignorance on her face startled him. For such a brilliant mind she sure didn't know very much. "When we get back we're going to have to work on your pop culture."

"You seem to forget that I lost all my stuff," she replied.

"It exists, so we'll find it," he assured her. "It's still on your camel, and that caravan shouldn't be hard to find."

"Simon, we're trapped in the middle of nowhere," she insisted, "with no food, no water, no supplies, and no direction. We'll never survive the desert on foot."

"You give up too easily," he said. "We'll find a way. We have to."

She sighed. "It won't be worth the effort," she said coldly, the old frost edging her voice.

"Maybe we'll save the world later, if we have time—pardon the pun," he said with a smirk that surprised and intrigued her.

"Have you always had such a dry sense of humor?"

"Just since we landed in the desert," he replied. "But now we have a more pressing mission to accomplish."

She gazed at him with a mixture of awe and condescension, a look he got an awful lot during his four years working in the grocery store. But he could not mistake the curiosity in her eyes.

"Operation Carista."

CHAPTER 20

TEMPLE

"Simon, you're crazy."

"I get that a lot."

"I tried already, and failed," she insisted. "We can't undo it."

"Kasey, you have a time machine," he emphasized. "But you lack imagination. You went in unprepared, without a plan. Next time we account for every variable."

She scoffed. "Had a time machine," she reminded him. "It marched away into the desert yesterday, remember?"

"I remember," he replied. "A minor detail."

She arched her eyebrows in disbelief. Had he cracked under the strain?

"This is the end of the world for us," she sighed. "We're going to die here."

"No," he said harshly, his voice echoing from the darkness.

Simon reached for his backpack, withdrew an ink pen, and clicked one end of it. A bright LED light flashed to life and he shined it into the temple. Illu-minated columns receded into the darkness, their long shadows moving as he played the light across them. A stone dais rose from the floor at the oth-er end of the chamber, the only visible structure. Mounds of rubble piled along one wall where the ceiling had partially collapsed, allowing sand to pour in; otherwise the chamber remained starkly empty.

"I don't know what you hope to find," Kasey said, instinctively sticking close to him as he moved deep-er into the interior.

"Hopefully not snakes," he muttered.

"Snakes?"

"Never mind." He stopped at the first column and studied it, shining his light all around it. "Fascinat-ing."

"What is it?"

"A column," he replied.

She glared at him in the darkness.

"Not Greek, Roman, or Egyptian," he noted. "But similar to all three."

"How do you know?"

"Art history," he replied. "We just covered this stuff. My favorite class."

"Oh."

"But this I can't explain," he said as he aimed the light at a single rough carving of a two-headed axe the size of his finger, the only decoration on the column. "It's Minoan, but that's impossible."

"Why?"

"Because their civilization existed out in the Mediterranean," Simon explained, "on Crete and Thera, thousands of miles from here. But this looks like one of their symbols."

"If you say so," she sighed, not terribly interested in an archeology lesson. "What good does that do us?"

"Plenty," he lied.

She glared at him again.

"The secret to success is knowledge," he said. "And organization. Okay, that's two secrets. But you get the idea." He moved on to the next column. "The more information you have, the more power you gain over a situation—kind of like looking at a Seurat painting."

Kasey failed to hide the look of bewilderment on her face.

"Georges Seurat," he said as though the name had come down through history as commonplace as Leonardo da Vinci or George Washington or Chef Boyardee. "The famous pointillist."

"Is there some point to this?"

"Nice pun," he smirked.

Again, the confused and now slightly annoyed look.

"Seurat painted enormous canvases using dots of color that up close look like meaningless smudges," he explained. "But as you get further away you start to see the most amazing and complex details, all of which are entirely hidden until you stand far enough back. They are magnificent! It took him sometimes years to complete a single painting and he died young, so his stuff is rare and valuable. Now do you understand?"

"As soon as you explain it to me," she said, followed by a softly muttered "Art Major."

"It means," he said, making a great show of ignoring her remark, "that we need to look at the big picture, which is sometimes made up of all kinds of seemingly useless information. A jigsaw puzzle doesn't look like much until most of the pieces are in place. Right now we only have a few pieces, maybe some of the edge pieces—that's where I like to start. But the point is—"

"I get it," she sighed. "Enough with the metaphors already. I don't see any puzzle pieces or French paintings lying around in the sand. Are you sure you're not going nuts?"

"Hey, good idea," he suddenly said, again partially ignoring her. "I didn't think of that." He dropped to his knees and brushed away some of the sand from the floor, wiping softly with his hands until he found the hard stone beneath. Sure enough, after sweeping a few square feet, he uncovered something that elicited another "fascinating."

Kasey looked over his shoulder and in the glow of the pen light saw the unmistakable carving of a bull, about the size of her foot.

"Definitely Minoan," Simon breathed, feeling rather like Indiana Jones studying the markings of an ancient temple, except without Nazis underfoot. He hoped.

"You keep saying that," she said. "I don't know why it's important."

"That's because it shouldn't be here," he replied. "Unless... maybe he was right after all."

"Who?"

"There's this writer who thinks the Minoans may have had more influence in the Bronze Age than mainstream historians give them credit for; most of the scientific establishment shuns him and his research, sometimes very vocally—as if they have a religious persecution anxiety over his heresy toward their entrenched beliefs. I would have thought truth would be worth investigating, not a continuation of dogma that has to go unchallenged."

"You obviously don't know science very well, or religion for that matter," she sighed.

"I don't know if he's right or wrong, but I can't remember anything about a Minoan temple ever turning up in the Arabian desert."

"Suppose your crackpot is right?" Kasey said. "What good does it do us? No amount of puzzle pieces or colored dots of paint are going to provide us with food or water or passage out of here."

"Now you're using my metaphors against me," he smirked. He wiped away more sand, discovering carvings of bulls, some with people leaping over the horns. "They worshiped bulls, you know."

"I didn't know."

"They might even have a direct influence on the development of bullfighting in Spain," he explained. "Certainly they are closely tied to Greek mythology and stories of the Minotaur."

"Fascinating," she mocked, leaning in casual boredom against a column.

Simon continued his archeological quest to uncover more carvings throughout the chamber. Beautifully painted and preserved beneath the sand, they led him to the dais at the far end of the temple. An oblong stone slab, concave in the middle—no doubt to catch the drippings of offerings—rose waist-high in front of him. A solid affair, it rested atop a table with no discernible legs, smooth walls of rock that connected it to the floor. Weighing at least a ton, the slab jutted out from either end of its monolithic pedestal.

"Maybe they sacrificed virgins here," Kasey mused.

"You're thinking of the Aztecs," he replied.

"My mistake."

"This is odd," Simon said, his eye catching something. "Why do you suppose they would put that here?"

"Maybe to confound snoops like us thousands of years in the future?"

"Or maybe to lead us to an answer," he surmised. "Look at this."

Kasey followed the beam of light as it revealed a double-headed axe carved into one side of the dais. "So?"

"It's not on the other side," he said. "I wonder if that means something?"

"Maybe someone's chisel broke."

"You know, you could be doing something helpful, like looking for more symbols or clues," Simon said with a hint of irritation in his voice.

"No thanks," she smiled wanly. "I'd rather stand here and make fun of you."

Undaunted, Simon searched the chamber, examining every column at length, discovering numerous markings and symbols, mostly variations of the bull and the axe, occasionally accompanied by a form of circular writing that he could not identify. In the end he slumped against the dais, mentally fatigued, temporarily defeated. He had no idea what to do next.

"I hate to say 'I told you so'," she said, "but I could have predicted this." She leaned against the stone altar, opposite Simon, and the thing lurched slightly beneath her weight. "Well, maybe not that," she amended.

"Typical," Simon sighed. "I do all the work and you find the clue...."

She smiled with satisfaction. Having no hope of survival had given her a careless attitude that while better than cold anger still made Simon uncomfortable, especially since as the only other person present he got to be the object of her sarcasm. Still, an improvement.

He hurried to the other side of the dais and examined the floor around it, sweeping away more sand, flashing his light into the tight corners where the pedestal touched the floor. He discovered scratches beneath one side of the altar that extended out to a length equal to that of the slab's base. They existed nowhere else.

"Is this a puzzle piece or a dot of paint?" Kasey asked him.

"Think of it as a thousand-piece puzzle of a Seurat painting," he suggested. "And we just found an edge piece."

He stood and walked to the other side of the altar. Placing both hands on the heavy sacrificial slab of smooth stone he pushed with all his strength. It budged another inch. He heaved and groaned and strained, but that inch represented the extent of his ability. After a long and humiliating minute of futility, which Kasey watched with unabashed amusement, Simon finally collapsed against the edge of the dais, his muscles—what he had of them— taxed beyond relief.

"I thought for a moment you might turn green, rip out of your shirt, and throw the thing through a wall," Kasey said.

"You get that reference but you've never heard of Indiana Jones?"

"Carista liked superheroes," she recalled, her voice softer at the reference of her sister.

"What else did she like?" Simon inquired, panting, wishing he was in better physical shape.

"Lots of things," Kasey said. "Science fiction, seahorses, dragons, cooking, designing clothing—I think that's what she wanted to do: be a fashion designer, or an interior decorator. She was good at creating things."

"Sounds like someone I would like," Simon smiled.

"Everybody liked her," Kasey said softy, her voice more distant now. "You would have had a lot in common, I think."

"We'll find out," Simon replied, "after we find out what's under this rock."

Breathing more easily now, he examined every surface of the stained gray slab and its supporting pedestal, finding only a small drainage hole in the center of the concave surface and carvings of bulls on the sides of the base.

"There has to be a way...," he muttered.

"Maybe it's broken," Kasey said, but the sarcasm had left her voice, replaced with more familiar hopelessness.

"I doubt it," he replied. "I've seen enough movies and TV shows to know that—aha!"

"What?" She followed his gaze and his light toward the wall behind the altar. In it opened a square hole wide enough for a hand, adorned with a double-sided axe. Kasey didn't know what to make of it, until Simon shined his light inside, peering intently into the darkness.

He turned and looked at her, shining the light in her face. "Do you know how much I don't want to put my hand in there?" he asked.

"Don't look at me!"

"When Kate Capshaw did it the hole was filled with bugs," he said. "And in the second Mummy movie the bad guy got his arm dissolved. Dr. McCoy almost got blown up when it happened to him."

"What are you rambling about?" Kasey said, exasperated.

"Just that nothing good ever comes of sticking your arm into a hole," he pointed out. "No matter how innocent it looks."

"Then what do you suggest?"

Without a moment's hesitation he thrust his hand into the hole and pulled a lever he knew he would find there. Somewhere in the darkness behind the wall and under the floor emanated deep clunking sounds of rock scraping rock, a decidedly unnatural and unsettling noise that made their skin crawl. Simon hastily withdrew his arm from the opening, relieved that it remained unscathed.

"What about the movies?" Kasey scoffed, but with the annoyance gone from her voice.

"This is reality, not Hollywood," he said. "Besides, why would the Minoans booby trap their own temple? There's nothing here to steal."

He stepped back to the altar and gave it a push with both hands. It slid gently across the floor on heavy stone rollers, revealing a narrow opening. Simon shined his light into the darkness and discovered a steep stairway descending into the unknown.

Kasey looked at him, obviously apprehensive. "It could be dangerous." But she knew he would insist on investigating the hidden chamber.

"No doubt," he assured her. "Let's get our stuff."

After one last long look at the desert and the moon that now hung low over the horizon, Simon took the first step into spooky blackness, a world of impenetrable darkness that had never seen the light of day, his pen light offering only feeble and mocking illumination that made him fully aware of the insignificance of his fledgling courage. Kasey clung to his trembling body as they descended into the pit. His tiny light played across the walls and steps as they moved in unison, but revealed no clues or surprises. They managed maybe ten steps before Simon's foot sank half an inch into the hard stone, a loose step, that startled him and almost cost them both their balance. In the same instant another deep rumbling shook the stairs as the altar slowly moved back into place overhead, effectively sealing them into the crypt.

"Should have seen that coming," Simon admitted.

"I'll give you that one," she said.

"If there's a way down here, there has to be a way back up," he observed. "I'm not worried."

Clinging to his arm and feeling his body tremble, she knew his words were meant solely for her benefit—a sweet gesture, but unnecessary. "I can take the truth," she assured him.

"These things never end well in the movies," he replied. "Every time Indy got into a temple or a cave he barely got out alive—and a lot of others didn't."

"I wish I understood what you're talking about," she sighed.

"How about The Mummy? Ever see any of those? Plenty of temples and caves."

"How did that go?"

"Let me know if you see any scarabs," he grimaced. "On second thought, don't."

"Do you do anything besides watch movies?"

"I build LEGOs," he replied. "You don't really outgrow those."

"Actually, Carista built up quite a collection," Kasey recalled.

"Nice pun—built up—you're good at that."

"You're so weird."

At the bottom of the stairs they found an uncomfortably dark and creepy chamber the size of a walk-in closet, with a ceiling low enough to scrape their heads when they walked. Simon shined his light all around, finding more carvings, one that unsettled him: a man with the head of a bull.

"That can't be good," he said.

"Isn't that—?"

"Sure looks like it," he answered. "The Minotaur."

You don't suppose this is his labyrinth?"

"Unlikely," he hoped. "That myth would have been centered thousands of miles from here... I think."

"What should we do?"

"We look for a door," he replied. "You know there has to be one."

There was.

They found it beneath the carving of the Minotaur, a stone panel that pushed inward once he pressed a small brick in the wall, unlocking the mechanism. The door, a monolith the size of a dinner tray, required them to crawl on their hands and knees, careful not to bang their heads on the low rock. The opening formed a tunnel not much larger than ductwork, like in the movies, but far more claustrophobic; they crawled interminably, scraping and sliding across hard stone, until finally their worn and frazzled forms emerged into a much larger space.

Simon carefully stood to his full height and reached his hands up into the air, feeling nothing. He played his light around in the darkness, but caught only fleeting images of strangely formed rocks and the shadows they cast. He stood on a broad path that weaved between stalagmites the size of tree trunks, with a craggy ceiling dozens of feet above. Kasey reached out to the closest one, and it felt dry to the touch.

"Do you hear that?" Simon whispered.

"I don't hear anything," she replied.

"Exactly," he confirmed. "This cavern is dead. No dripping water, no erosion, no formation of stalactites and stalagmites. No mold or fungus on the walls, no moisture in the air; I'll bet there are no bats roosting here, either. It's completely dormant."

"I'm okay with that," she said. "It means nothing will try to eat us." "Except the Minotaur."

She punched his arm.

"How do you remember which is which?" she wanted to know.

"Which which is which?" he asked.

"Stalactites and stalagmites," she said. "How do you tell them apart?"

"That's easy," he explained. "Stalactites cling tight to the ceiling, while stalagmites might one day reach up to them."

"That's corny."

"But it works."

The pair of wayward time travelers wended their way through the unexpected cavern far beneath the surface of the desert, covering perhaps miles of terrain free from the harsh glare of the Arabian sun. Large cathedrals of stone opened around them, emphasizing their insignificance, before forcing them into passages barely wide enough to squeeze through. And so the journey progressed, from one enormous chamber to another, connected by often uncomfortably tight conduits that tested their resolve, until eventually they reached a single monumental cavern that made them stop and stare with wide eyes and open mouths. Simon's light barely made a dent in the colossal darkness, but when he played it quickly over a large area they got a sense of the chamber's magnitude: no less than the size of a sports arena, a village could exist in this space and his light might not ever wash across it.

"I'm pretty sure I don't like it here," Kasey whispered, clinging to Simon with no intention of letting go.

"Very spooky," he admitted. "I wonder why no one has ever found it?"

"Some places should remain undiscovered," she pointed out.

"I'll buy that."

They continued along the path through the magnificent chamber, picking their way over broken stalagmites and fallen stalactites, evidence of a disturbance long ago, perhaps an earthquake; in darkness time stood still, so the catastrophic event could have happened last week or ten thousand years ago.

"Someone had to clear this path," Kasey realized. "Where are they?"

"That temple has been buried in the sand for a long time," Simon assured her. "Whoever built it and discovered these caverns must have vanished ages ago. No one could survive here."

"Then how will we?"

"We'll find a way out, just like the Minoans did," he said.

"How can you be so sure they found a way out?"

"No skeletons," he observed. "In this environment, bodies would deteriorate very slowly, probably close to the path, and we would have stumbled over them."

"Sounds pretty flimsy," she said.

"There has to be a way," he repeated, attempting to convince himself as much as her.

"I hope you're right.

He hoped so too. Though he felt no shortage of fear, another much deeper feeling superseded it: courage. Having Kasey with him, clinging to his arm, her soft, warm, vulnerable form so near to his, coaxed from his soul a measure of confidence and nerve—perhaps even manliness—that would not have existed had he traveled the path alone. Her fear gave him strength, perhaps because he subconsciously focused his attention on comforting her instead of concentrating on his own terror. He felt in charge of the situation, in control of his emotions, ready for any circumstance.

The feeling lasted almost five minutes.

"Do you hear something?" Simon asked as they approached the far end of the colossal chamber.

"Sounds like rumbling," Kasey confirmed. "What is it?"

"I don't know," he admitted. "Let's find out."

He led her into a small tunnel that shrank in size after a few yards, forcing them to crawl once again. The passage narrowed to little more than a winding hole barely sufficient to accommodate their tired forms; Simon removed his backpack and pushed it ahead of him as they struggled and wriggled to the end. The rumbling sound grew steadily louder, though still distant enough to not concern him yet. Eventually the tunnel abruptly opened out of a wall, allowing Simon to pull himself into a standing position. Quickly he donned his pack and reached down to grasp Kasey's hands to help her from the passage.

"Where are we?" she asked.

"I don't—" but in that moment he took a fateful step back and careened off the edge of a cliff, leaving Kasey alone in the darkness.

CHAPTER 21

RIVER

"**S**imon!"

The light flashed away from her, followed by the deep, echoing splash of Simon's body plunging into a rush of water: a rapidly flowing subterranean river that would, without her intervention, kill him.

Reacting on pure instinct, Kasey leapt after the light, scarcely considering the possibility of breaking her neck, or bashing in her skull; cool, surging water enveloped her, pulling her with a current faster than anything she had ever felt. Her head bobbed to the surface, engulfed in near total darkness. She spun around until she saw a point of light throwing shadows on the cavern wall a few dozen feet away before it vanished, consumed by the river.

She followed it.

Carista had taught her to swim as a child, and together they had spent much of their youth enjoying the water. Family vacations took them to beaches, water parks, and resorts, where they snorkeled, dived, swam, and floated for endless hours. Kasey developed a knack for holding her breath longer than anyone else, and became a strong swimmer; her sister on the other hand, developed an annoying tendency to attract boys to whatever pool or lake in which her biki-ni-clad body floated. As they grew older, one of their bodies transformed dramatically into that of a beautiful young woman, encouraging Carista to spend far more time flirting with the opposite sex than splashing and playing children's games with her still developing little sister. The last couple of vacations Kasey spent largely alone in the water, ignored by boys who circled Carista like sharks—and wondering why her sister had abandoned her. So she swam and swam, racing and challenging herself, developing skills that soon would lie dormant like so many others in her life.

That skill came back to her the instant she hit the water. Plunging ahead toward the light, her arms and legs pushing in unison with the overwhelming current, Kasey surged forward. Simon, unable to swim, thrashed and tumbled, at the mercy of the swift whorls and eddies, moving slower than her tor-pedo-like form. She pursued intermittent flashes of murky light, distorted by the raging river, hoping Simon still clung to it—because it was the only way she had of finding him in the darkness.

Kasey's head bobbed to the surface for a gasp of air, and in that second she glimpsed the shadowy image of another head close by as the light emerged from the water, waving at the end of a wildly thrashing arm. She redoubled her efforts and darted in his direction, desperate to reach him before the air burst from his lungs.

A flailing arm caught her in the side of the head, stunning her, while in the same instant a knee found her stomach, forcing most of the air from her burning lungs; but the indefatigable young swimmer pressed forward with a burst of strength and thrust through the thrashing tangle of limbs; locating the upper strap of Simon's backpack, Kasey heaved toward the churning surface, her head breaking through ahead of Simon's; one of his flailing legs collided with her kneecap, eliciting an uncharacteristic cry from his rescuer. Irritated, she clubbed him in the face with the heel of her hand, knocking him senseless.

He didn't struggle after that.

He did, however, drop his light.

Repositioning his backpack in order to secure a proper grip on his limp form, she supported him as the rushing current carried them mercilessly downstream, around curves and bends, occasionally brushing them against the cavern wall. The floating pen light traveled with them, but too far out of reach to recover; it rolled and bobbed, casting its light intermittently into the gloom, creating a strobe-like effect that offered fleeting glimpses of the river and the cave that contained it.

The tugging current lessened as the river slowed to a more casual pace, straightening its course and leveling off, relieving the young woman who fought with borrowed strength to keep her companion afloat. The light bobbed twenty feet away.

"Simon, are you okay?" she asked once the roar of rushing water subsided enough for her voice to carry more than a few inches.

"Except for a broken nose," he complained.

"Oh come on, you pansy," she scoffed. "I didn't hit you that hard."

He remained silent.

"You hit me harder than that a few times," she added.

"That wasn't on purpose."

"Oh, okay," she replied. "Next time I'll keep my distance and let you drown."

Her words sank in, forcing him to realize he was being a jerk.

"Sorry," he said. "No one's ever punched me before. Guess I deserved it."

"You almost deserved it again."

"I owe you one," he said.

"I think we're pretty much even on that score," she observed. "You saved me from the desert; I saved you from the river."

"Don't forget, I saved you from the college rapist," he pointed out.

"And then I saved you from the end of the world. Still even."

"Well, we're not out of the river yet," he said, "so technically...."

"Technically... I'm still saving you," she finished. "I can let go any time you give the word."

"That's okay," he said a little too quickly. "I'm fine where I am." He meant that rather more than he indicated: though the sentiment might seem inappropriate, especially to his rescuer, he enjoyed feeling her warm and pleasantly soft body clinging so closely to his; of course, if he even hinted at such a thing she'd likely drop him in the river and watch him drown with disgust. So, for a few minutes of peace, he concentrated on the strong arms wrapped around his torso from behind, the supple hands inadvertently caressing his chest, the sinuous curves pressing against his back, the soft, cool cheek occasionally brushing against his as the now gentle river jostled them together. It was the little things in life that meant so much.

"I wonder where it comes out," Kasey said.

"It could be anywhere," Simon suggested. "Maybe it feeds a spring or an oasis, or maybe it goes all the way to the Nile."

"Do you think it ever reaches the surface?"

"That would be convenient," he said.

"Our luck probably isn't that good, huh?"

"I wouldn't bet on us," Simon admitted. "Still, we did escape from the temple and the desert. I'd say we're doing pretty well."

"Simon, only you would say that."

"We're alive and that's what counts," he said. "We still have hope."

"You put too much stock in hope," she replied. "This is a hopeless situation."

"It's not just hope," he explained. "You have to have faith. I find it hard to believe that God would let us die here in the very bowels of the Earth—the upper intestinal tract, you might say—especially after all that we've been through. It would be pointless."

"Of course it's pointless," she sighed, exasperated. "There is no God, and the only meaning in life is that which we apply to it. No all-powerful force is out there pulling our strings."

"I don't think that's how it works," he argued. "Faith is—"

"Faith is a crutch used by the weak-minded to justify irrational beliefs," she snapped. "You're an intelligent person, even if you are an Art Major, so it baffles me why you fall for such obvious tripe."

"It's not so obvious," he muttered. "I don't claim to have the answers—or to even know most of the questions—and I'm certainly not the best Christian in the world—I get discouraged by hypocrisy as much as the next person—but I do believe in a greater force out there influencing our lives."

"Simon, you're going to have to face it sooner or later," she said sternly, coldness returning to her voice. "We're on our own. We control our destinies, if anyone does, and that's just how it is. Period."

"If you say so," he replied.

"That's it?"

"That's it."

"No arguments?"

"Would it do any good?"

"No."

"Then why argue?"

"Well... we haven't done it in so long...."

"Neither of us is going to influence the other," he told her. "All we'll do is make each other mad, when we need to work together—which we seem to do pretty well when we stop arguing."

"Okay," she agreed. "There is some wisdom floating around in there after all."

"Gee, thanks."

"I guess the first thing we have to consider is how to get out of this river," she said. "I can't keep you afloat indefinitely."

He wouldn't have minded it.

"It could go on for miles," he observed. "Days and days."

"That's not very optimistic," she chided.

"Want me to invoke faith?"

"No thanks. I'll take the river."

They floated in awkward silence, drifting in the quickening and slowing current, until eventually Kasey maneuvered them close enough to the dancing light for Simon to regain his hold on it. Now he could play the bright beam on the ceiling and walls, sometimes with startling results. The river extended as wide as fifty feet, when it slowed to a crawl, and then the cavern narrowed to less than half that, forcing the water to move faster through more confined space.

It passed through larger and smaller chambers, with often cathedral-size ceilings looming away into the darkness, then contracted to a claustrophobic tunnel with a smooth vaulted surface close enough to touch with an outstretched hand. They feared the possibility of the ceiling disappearing altogether, a situation that could not last more than a couple of minutes without them succumbing to a watery grave deep inside the earth.

Long minutes stretched into hours as they floated downstream, constantly peering at the ever-changing landscape of rock and more rock. Nowhere did they see a place to exit the often tumultuous current.

"Kind of reminds me of a TV show my dad and I used to watch when I was little," Simon said as they drifted lazily between high walls that opened into an impossibly immense chasm. "Ever see Land of the Lost?"

"No," Kasey replied. He could tell that she was beyond tired.

"My dad had a huge DVD collection of old TV shows," Simon explained. "Mostly from the sixties and seventies."

"I wasn't born yet."

"Neither was I. But he loved the stuff, was kind of a trivia buff—knew all kinds of facts and information that basically meant nothing to anyone but him, though he thought we were all interested in it."

"Sounds like someone I know," Kasey commented.

"Anyway, Marshall, Will, and Holly, on a routine expedition, encountered the greatest earthquake ever known."

"Are you predicting an earthquake?"

"No, just that in the opening credits you got to see them floating on a raft in a cavern kind of like this one. Just a memory of something when I was a kid."

"Sounds like you had a pretty normal childhood."

"Nothing exciting," he lamented. "Just me and my parents. No drama, no tragedies, no great fortune or poverty. Nothing worth mentioning ever happened to us, or to anybody we knew."

"Sounds boring."

"To say the least," he admitted.

"I think I would appreciate boring," Kasey smiled. "I guess you had a girlfriend in high school?"

"Oh, heavens no!" he exclaimed, taken aback by the unexpected question. "Girls never took to me. And not for a lack of trying on my part."

"I would have thought you'd be one of the popular ones," she said.

He almost swallowed half the river.

"You really must not get out much," he said, coughing and laughing. "I went largely unnoticed by most of the population, and the ones who did notice either made fun of me or scorned me as some kind of a freak. Which I freely admit I was."

"I think I understand that feeling," she said. "It was difficult living in the shadow of my sister. I was pretty awkward in high school."

"I had friends," he said, "but I went kind of nuts when it came to girls."

"How so?"

"I had this notion of the Perfect Girl, and I fantasized about how I would sweep her off her feet and impress her with my courage and wit; somehow she would be drawn to me and like all the things I liked and appreciate the things I obsessed over. And when I did occasionally see a girl who intrigued me, I imposed my notions of moral and intellectual perfections onto her, which never ended well."

"I can imagine."

"One time I got really obsessed," he admitted. "I tried to keep it secret, but someone found out who I liked—somebody way out of my league—and I became the laughingstock of the school and she got made fun of incessantly. It was brutal."

"Sounds pretty bad."

"Her name was Lana, and I obsessed over her for years, even though I knew it was hopeless," he said. "She was the most beautiful girl in the tenth grade—in the history of all tenth grades—and I thought about her night and day. I got real good at daydreaming that year. My friends tormented me. When I wasn't staring at her I hid behind my locker door. The idea of actually speaking to her—well, that was impossible, especially since she always traveled with a mob of squawking girls that never left her side all day. I fantasized that someday I might have the nerve to boldly say something that she would find clever and charming, and then she would trade her friends for me. I know, I was weird.

"One day after school I was alone in the hall—in the eleventh grade—packing up my book bag. I heard footsteps at the other end of the hall, and when I looked up it was Lana— coming right toward me! She was by herself, unprotected by her praetorian guards in skirts and leggings. I'll never forget the way she walked, casually, carrying her book bag over one shoulder, her curly blonde hair cascading down her back. My heart pounded—I thought I might have a stroke. I knew the moment of truth had finally arrived, that God Himself had arranged this seemingly chance encounter in order for me to once and for all win the woman of my dreams."

"What happened? Did you marry her?"

"I stood up as she started to walk past, and when she got close enough she actually said 'hi' to me."

"And then you went in for the kill?"

"Actually, I uttered some kind of low guttural grunt and banged my hand into the locker door when I tried to wave," he said sullenly. "She kept walking and a year later we graduated."

"The Lord giveth and the Lord taketh away," Kasey mocked.

"As you can imagine, I never really dated in high school," he said. "In fact, my effect on women was kind of like a hand grenade thrown into a crowded room: lots of running, ducking for cover, praying, pleading for mercy—general mayhem and pandemonium. And when the shrapnel of my affection did nail someone it became a disfiguring wound that marred her for the remainder of high school."

"Aren't you being hard on yourself?" she laughed involuntarily.

"I lived it," he replied. "Humiliation is one of my best things."

"Maybe you have some qualities better than that," she smiled thinly. "Someday an unsuspecting young freshman might see them."

He chose not to respond.

"What happened to Marshall, Will, and Holly?" she suddenly wanted to know, abruptly and mercifully changing the subject.

"They went over a colossal waterfall, through a rift in the space-time continuum, and landed in the Cretaceous Period," he explained. "Almost got eaten by a dinosaur the moment they landed."

"Did they ever get home?"

"Marshall did, I think...."

The current quickened again, and in the distance they heard the rumble of more rapids. Simon felt Kasey's lithe body tense behind him in anticipation of the difficulties ahead. In the near darkness he saw the strain on her face, the fatigue in her eyes. She tightened her grip on his torso.

"This can't be good," she breathed.

"It would make a good ride at Disney World," he offered.

"A Disney World taken over by demons," she corrected.

"You don't believe in demons," he pointed out.

"I was being metaphorical," she said crossly. "Now's not the time for another argument."

As the freshening current swept them along the narrowing passage, Simon noticed something that had escaped his attention, so gradual had the change taken place: he could see the cavern walls without the aid of his feeble pen light. He clicked it off, and the ambient illumination remained unchanged.

"That's weird," he said.

"What?"

He showed her the light.

"That's weird," she agreed.

"That can only mean one thing," he said, smiling. "Sunlight!"

She returned his smile, a sight that never ceased to entrance him. Face to face, she hugged him tightly, and he returned the surprisingly affectionate gesture. And then her entire demeanor abruptly shifted, startling him. But he hadn't done anything—!

"Good God!" she exclaimed, and he still didn't know what was going on. He only knew that she kicked and thrashed with her arms and legs, tapping a reserve of strength that burst from out of nowhere, pulling him along at a pace no mortal could have achieved—except in a moment of desperation.

Moving futilely against the overwhelming current, Kasey scrambled at the speed of fear, and when Simon chanced a glance downstream he quickly added his arms and legs to the effort. In that split second he saw that the river ended—not in a cave or a turn, but over the edge of a cliff, the height of which he could not begin to guess; but the swirling white mist rising above the sharp chasm indicated a spectacular plunge, reminiscent of his childhood memories of the family vacation to Niagara Falls. Few people ever made it over those and lived to tell about it.

They struggled and flailed, but their strength ebbed after a single burst of power, overwhelmed by the irresistible current. A crashing cacophony of sounds, water surging and thundering in every direction, made speaking impossible during what they knew to be their final moment of life. But it was unnecessary, for each knew the other's heart.

The edge approached almost in slow motion, white water coursing over smooth rocks, pulling with a force that even the most powerful motorboat could not have fought. A multitude of thoughts flashed through Simon's mind, but only one unexpectedly stood out: Carista's beautiful, smiling face in the wrinkled photograph that Kasey had showed him in the temple; he thought how unfair it was for him to be unable to rescue her from destruction—in order to make Kasey happy again.

Clinging to each other, Simon and Kasey plunged over the abyss into the churning unknown.

CHAPTER 22

REFUGE

I t happened in slow motion.

The cavern vomited them from a wide hole high atop a towering cliff, expelling them amidst spraying water that hung like fog before plunging into the depths. Simon glimpsed whirls of rock and mist and sparkling water as his flailing body careened wildly over the precipice; he lost his hold on Kasey, and he might have screamed: he couldn't tell if the sound came from his throat or hers, but it didn't matter as long as one of them did it.

The descent lasted a lifetime as the travelers hung high in the air, engulfed in white roiling froth breaking away from the thunderous fall; their hearts stopped as the world coalesced into a single eternal moment of perfect clarity: the grand glowing chasm into which they had emerged, a churning lake of boiling water a hundred feet below, dozens of similar falls crashing all around, forming a deafening cacophony unlike anything they had ever imagined.

Gravity pulled them at ever increasing speed toward oblivion. Simon inhaled a deep breath in the instant available to him, knowing the futility of the effort, for he could not possibly survive a fall from so great a height. His heart pounded and his body tensed as the bubbling lake approached.

Churning water enveloped him; the enormous pressure of falling water pressed him down, impossible eddies and currents swishing him one way and another; his feet touched solid rock at the bottom of the lake, and he pushed off from it.

Then a familiar hand found his, the grip strong and sure; it pulled and struggled against an impossible vortex, but it did not let go. Simon's burning lungs begged for relief, but he fought the urge for one last long moment, desperate to not die here in this immense subterranean cauldron. Stale breath burst from his chest as his head broke the tumultuous surface, and his instinctive gasp found cool refreshment before the current pulled him back under.

Grasping Simon's helpless form, Kasey kicked and stroked, desperate to escape the boiling, churning tempest. Towering falls, some hundreds of feet high, poured their torrents into the swirling, bubbling lake on every side. She found a larger current near the center and stuck to it until she worked slowly past the falls; only through sheer force of will did she keep Simon's head above the shifting surface, while inadvertently swallowing half the river.

The pulsing, pounding turbulence eased its hold on them as they drifted from the immediate vicinity of the falls, allowing Kasey to guide her trajectory toward the end of the wide channel. They looked back at what they had just survived: quite possibly the single drainage point for every subterranean river on the continent, all converging on a rift in the Earth's crust, pouring untold millions of gallons into one steamy, dark reservoir that probably no human being had ever before encountered.

Simon could have lived quite comfortably for the rest of his life without having discovered it.

Dozens of waterfalls poured from both walls of the chasm, many high enough that he could not see their sources through the swirling mist; he suddenly felt lucky to have emerged where he did; a higher one could easily have proven fatal. He couldn't tell the length of the chasm, but guessed it might have stretched for miles beneath the Arabian Desert—all the water a civilization could ever need, hidden where no one would think to look.

They drifted in silence, Kasey gradually moving them toward the edge of the lake, half a mile from the last of the thundering falls. She aimed for a rock ledge a few inches above the water, narrow but level and curving around the chasm wall. Kasey pushed Simon up over the edge, and then he helped her climb out of the river. Even his backpack, a strap still looped around his leg, survived the ordeal. Someday he would have to thank his grandparents for that particular graduation gift.

Simon and Kasey collapsed in separate heaps at the edge of the water and refused to move for the better part of an hour. They drifted through stages of unconsciousness, their soaking bodies shivering in the cool cavern air. A little discomfort didn't matter after what they had just survived.

"You owe me another one," Kasey said when Simon finally opened his eyes and saw her sitting next to him, leaning casually against the rock wall.

"I'm still counting that as part of the river," he replied. He rolled onto his back and stared into the rocky heavens, discerning a craggy ceiling hundreds of feet overhead. He had hoped to see stars, but realized they remained very far beneath the surface of the Earth.

"That'll set the bar pretty high for when it's your turn again," she said. It made him smile.

"We shouldn't be able to see," he observed.

"The walls are glowing," she informed him. "At least in places. It's not very bright, but down here it doesn't take much."

"What's causing it?"

"I'm not sure," she replied. "Phosphorescent moss or lichen, maybe. We may have made an important scientific discovery."

"It'll be fun bringing the research team down here," he smiled.

"You can lead it."

Simon slowly stood up and stretched, suddenly feeling cold and hungry. "I wish we had some food," he said.

"You're really something," she marveled. "How can you think of food at a time like this?"

"First order of business: survival," he replied, "to quote Jim Kirk, of course."

"Who?"

"James Kirk."

A blank stare.

"Captain James Tiberius Kirk, of the Enterprise?"

Nothing.

"Mr. Spock? Dr. McCoy?"

"Are they historical figures?" Kasey asked with a smirk.

"I thought you said your sister was into science fiction," Simon retorted.

"She was," Kasey said.

"Ever heard of Star Trek?"

"That silly show from the sixties where all the aliens looked human and spoke English every week?"

"Hey, it was one of the most intelligent and innovative science fiction shows of its age," Simon defended. "And it spawned eight more series, fifteen movies, and a loyal fan base like nothing else before it. I'd hardly call that silly."

"If you say so."

"A lot of good stuff came out of Star Trek," Simon sulked.

"Carista thought so," Kasey agreed. "I prefer hard science and reality. Fantasy and I don't really get along so well."

"You could use a little more fantasy in your life," Simon said. "What's wrong with having fun and enjoying some good clean entertainment?"

"Not a thing," she replied. "If you like Star Trek. I think it's cheesy."

"What about Star Wars?"

"Give me a break," she sighed. "Talking droids and magic sages drifting through space like some Japanese melodrama crossed with a western adventure? No thanks!"

Simon's world crumbled, as did his hope for the future of humanity.

"Is there anything you like?"

"Frankenstein," she replied simply.

"Really?"

"My favorite book," she said. "I always felt sympathy for the monster; Victor Frankenstein was the real monster anyway. All his creation wanted was to live in peace, away from the rest of the world, with a mate of his own kind; but Frankenstein, the coward, would have none of it. Typical. He made this monstrous thing without any thought of the consequences, and when it blew up in his face he didn't have the courage or fortitude to set things right. He could only think of his own selfish concerns, and in the end it cost him everything."

He wondered if she realized the frightening parallels between her and the good doctor? Would her perverse creation pursue her to the farthest reaches of oblivion? Suddenly it made sense that Frankenstein was her favorite book.

"Mary Shelley knew her stuff," Simon agreed. "You know it started as a ghost story in a chateau, sort of a contest between Percy Shelly, Mary Shelley, and Lord Byron," he said.

"I know," she replied. "What's your favorite book?"

"The Count of Monte Cristo," he said. "There's nothing like a good tale of revenge, especially when told by Dumas."

"Maybe I'll read it sometime," she said. "If we ever get back to civilization."

"We'll get there," he assured her. "Hey, we got out of the desert and we found water. All we need is some food and we'll be set."

"Does nothing ever discourage your optimism?" she inquired, slowly getting to her feet.

"Sometimes," he admitted. "But I feel like God is watching out for us."

"Let's get moving," she said, "before we have another argument."

They followed the narrow ledge around the curve of the chasm wall until it opened into something quite extraordinary: a vast panorama that caught them completely by surprise, even after what they had already witnessed. A hole in the chasm wall revealed an entirely new world on the other side, a world that stretched immensely beneath the desert inside a massive pocket of space hundreds of feet high and spanning thousands of feet— maybe a mile or more—the far end of which receded out of sight, lost in a glowing haze of atmosphere.

A vast maze of rock formations spread throughout the magnificent chamber, and upon them sprouted millions upon millions of colossal mushrooms, some towering like trees while others grew out of the walls. They varied in color and texture: mottled and dull, vibrant and bright, spots, stripes, elaborate patterns. Some species jutted straight up out of the rock, while others curled and spiraled in unexpected shapes, their mushroom tops ranging from small points to giant umbrella-like spans. A literal forest of fungi extended as far as the eye could see, from tiny 'shrooms the size of a finger to a few specimens rivaling the redwoods of northern California. A cool mist hung in the air, somewhere between the mushroom tops and the distant ceiling, diffusing the greenish-yellowish glow emanating from lichen on the walls, creating an otherworldly effect that unsettled the newcomers.

"Fascinating," Simon said once he was able to form the syllables. He took a step forward on what looked like a recognizable path among the sinuous growths. "I guess Jules Verne was right."

"Who?"

"You don't know Jules Verne? Come on!" Simon exclaimed. "How can you be so smart and know so little?"

"I don't have time for frivolity," she said harshly. "Fiction is nonsense, meaningless diversions from reality that keep us from concentrating on real work."

"Frankenstein is fiction."

"No rule is absolute," she replied.

"Spoken like a true scientist?"

"Simon...."

She followed him along the narrow path, wending among the mushrooms, some the size of small houses, reminding Simon of a Smurf village on steroids. The cavern topography differed from what they had seen in the other chambers, mainly due to its scale; ridges and ravines created small valleys, and in them water collected into ponds teeming with fish, a circumstance Simon had not anticipated. After all, what were the odds of finding fish in the desert? But it made him think of another possibility: what animals lived in this strange wilderness deep inside the Earth? He had seen no bats or birds or bugs, heard nothing to indicate animal life—which relieved him, in a way.

"I wonder if the mushrooms are edible," Simon said after a while. He touched the stem of a treelike mushroom that arced overhead, ending in a wide brim the size of a deck umbrella. It quivered and changed color at his touch, mottled gray and white swirling into an earthy green that gradually faded back to normal.

"That was odd," Kasey said. She placed her palm on a stalk and streaks of blue emanated from her fingertips, deepening until she pulled her hand away.

"Another important discovery," Simon mused. "Who knows? Maybe the cure for cancer is growing down here, hidden for all time."

"Not likely," Kasey scoffed.

Simon shrugged his shoulders. "Maybe God put it here for us to discover."

"Do you have to keep on about that?" she complained. "I've made it pretty clear how I feel."

"I know," he replied. "But that doesn't mean you're right."

"Of course I'm right," she retorted, ire building in her voice. "God cannot exist. It is not rational, it is not logical, and science can easily explain everything primitive people attributed to Him. That is the end of the matter."

"But it isn't," he persisted. "There is more to the world and to humanity than explaining nature. The human soul is more complicated than that. I don't know what God's plan is, but I find it hard to believe that—"

"Jesus Christ, already!" she shouted. "Enough with your goddamned religious crap! God! How can one person be so annoying!"

She stormed through a patch of mushrooms, and Simon let her go, realizing that chasing after her might do more harm than good. It had been an exhausting day, especially for her, and he hadn't made it any easier. He certainly knew how to push her buttons.

But it was more than that. In spite of all they had endured, she only got irrationally angry when he invoked the idea of God; somehow that tapped an unexpected nerve. He smiled as truth dawned on him. God had brought them together for a very real reason: Kasey, as hard and cold as she pretended to be, was no atheist. She spoke harshly and matter-of-factly about religion and God and science, but he now realized that her words served only to convince herself of those evident truths; in reality she felt angry with God for taking her sister, and she could not forgive Him for it. Denying His existence became the easiest and most effective way of dealing with so profound a loss, and the bitterness had eaten away at her soul. Simon, in his bumbling way, forced her to realize the truth of her conflict—and she couldn't handle it.

He followed slowly in the direction she had taken, easily tracking her by the broken stalks and smashed fungi through which she had trod. Her trail meandered into a shallow ravine, along the edge of a long, narrow pond, and among a maze of turns and twists that boggled the mind. But the evidence of her passing remained obvious, even to his untrained eye.

Half an hour crept by without sighting her, causing his Spidey senses to tingle. Even in her current state of mind she must understand the danger of getting separated in this strange and potentially hostile environment. Well, hostile might be too strong a word. After all, what could giant mushrooms do, besides give you indigestion?

When he found her blood-stained shirt strewn across the top of a waist-high mushroom, he realized that once again he had misjudged the situation.

CHAPTER 23

SACRIFICE

H e reached for the torn garment, felt cool blood soaking the fabric, and knew that something had killed her. But he saw no blood on the ground, nothing to indicate catastrophic injury. However, a wide swath of crushed mushrooms presented evidence of a recent struggle; that meant people.

Simon tucked the shirt into his backpack and carefully followed the rough trail hewn by Kasey and her assailants. He kept low, ducking behind large mushrooms whenever he heard, or imagined he heard, the slightest sound. The trail led to a well-worn path— obviously not a naturally occurring phenomenon—similar to the one he and Kasey had followed into the cavern.

Realizing the ease with which the cavern's inhabitants could accost him, he quickly left the path and wended through the dense forest of mushrooms, careful not to leave a trail that anyone could follow. He stepped cautiously but quickly, silently paralleling the path from a higher elevation on the side of a short ridge. His caution paid off when he heard soft footsteps and stopped in his tracks; he knelt behind a flimsy wall of rubbery foliage in time to spot two figures emerge from around a bend in the trail. Wearing only flimsy loin cloths, their ghostly pale bodies practically glowed in the ambient light, and their bulging red eyes revealed a truth that made his blood turn cold. Thin, gaunt, pallid, they lacked musculature he might have expected in natives of any other landscape; shocks of long black hair emphasized the pallor of their smooth, sickly skin. They might have made convincing extras in some bizarre low-budget vampire or zombie film.

One of them spoke, revealing disturbingly sharp teeth, filed to fine points, which urged Simon to shrink further into insignificance. Throughout high school and college he had achieved unwitting anonymity, a circumstance that always discouraged him; he hoped now to put that skill to good use long enough to locate Kasey and get her out of this place.

The natives passed out of sight and Simon started moving again, every sense on alert as adrenaline poured into his veins. He crept deeper into the fungal forest, judging his progress by the positions of rocks on the ceiling and walls. A glance at his watch revealed that he had leapt from the caravan only twelve hours ago. It was still nighttime in the desert, long before dawn, and probably everyone in the caravan—if they survived the sandstorm—still slept in their comfortable tents, probably in an oasis. He wondered if they suspected the fate of the young travelers who had mysteriously vanished from the face of the Earth. Suppose the Arab trader discovered Kasey's backpack and examined the contents? What would an ancient Bedouin make of her bizarre and unearthly materials? Would he destroy them? Hide them? Use them to move through time? He doubted that last one, but he knew they had to get those items away from him and reach a safe haven for Kasey to continue her work.

But first he had to get her away from the clutches of her captors.

"For a girl who claims to be so independent, she sure needs a lot of rescuing," he muttered.

He reached a high ridge from which he could see much of the valley, and the sight that spread out before him startled his already numbed senses. In the center of the valley, nestled alongside a tributary of the river down which he and Kasey had entered this hidden world, stood a small village of strangely constructed houses and buildings, forming a crude arc along the riverbank. Rough hewn stone mingled with the dried timbers of dead mushrooms formed an architectural style never seen in the annals of human history, yet another great discovery for the team of Foxx and Carabresa. Above the village a much larger structure rose up out of the rock, a feebly constructed replica of the desert temple, at the top of which stood a dais similar to the one that had opened up to lead them to this subterranean world. An altar on a platform overlooked a plaza where the people no doubt gathered to worship.

The natives had leveled large tracts of mushroom forest to clear space for the village, leaving bare, gray rock forming natural barriers and passages; but much of the rock they had carved away, crudely landscaping the grounds in patterns that Simon recognized from inside the temple: bulls, double-sided axes, circular writing, and variations that must have evolved over considerable time.

"The Minoans," Simon whispered softly. "What's left of them. They must have taken refuge down here during a sandstorm."

It certainly could explain why no trace of them had ever been found in the Arabian Desert. It also meant they had never found a way out of this cavern.

A dull booming sound, a loud drum, echoed across the cavern, startling him back to reality. It seemed obvious that they had brought Kasey here—fighting and kicking—to turn her over to their leaders. He could not guess how they would treat her, but he doubted it would be pleasant.

The drum's slow, deep rhythm had an extraordinary effect on the mushrooms throughout the chamber: quivering at the sound vibrations, their mottled hues swirled and pulsed in an undulating eruption of color that spread in dynamic waves throughout the subterranean amphitheater. Simon watched the spectacle in awe, his mouth gaped open at the unexpected beauty, and almost failed to notice the dozens of naked inhabitants that poured into the square from every direction, filtering in from trails, the forest, the village, and from across the river. In minutes a few hundred pasty white savages wearing little more than loin cloths—and some not even that—stood jumbled together in a seething mass of sickly white flesh with bright red gums and bulging red eyes that stood out hideously in the starkness of their forms.

But still he saw no sign of Kasey.

The naked savages swayed and rocked to the beat of the drum, chanting in a strange and almost inhuman tongue that made the hairs stand up on the back of Simon's neck. Others joined in, lending their improbably high-pitched shrill calls to a cacophony that pulsed the nearby mushrooms into a maelstrom of swimming colors. They reached a fever pitch, their shaking bodies lurching and bouncing like something out of an old Tarzan film, but far creepier.

Then it all stopped. The natives, perhaps five hundred of them, stood rigid and stared fixedly at the dais atop the temple, fifteen feet above the now terrifyingly silent crowd. They watched in anticipation and Simon watched in horror as a pair of priestesses dressed in long black robes that draped to the floor led a young native woman from the interior of the temple out onto the balcony. The woman between them wore a flimsy white robe tied in the back, a look of fear etched into her hideous face. But she moved steadily with the others and stopped at the edge of the balcony overlooking the crowd.

A man emerged behind her, taller than the other natives, older and wrinkled, his black robe crisp and shimmering; the priest approached the young woman, placed his hands on her shoulders, and spoke to her in soft tones that Simon could not hear—not that hearing would have made any difference. Then he turned his attention to the crowd below and addressed them in a much louder but absurdly high voice that Simon realized must be the norm among these bizarre people. He spoke for several minutes while the crowd stood motionless, transfixed by his words, before walking to the far side of the altar.

The priestesses converged on the trembling young woman, and in a quick motion untied the back of her robe; it fell to the balcony floor, revealing the deathly pale but otherwise flawless naked form of a girl barely out of her youth—probably not a day older than sixteen. Simon stared transfixed at the unexpected sight.

His heart pounded as the priestesses led the girl up onto the stone dais and helped her into a lying position. The priest stood over her, a short golden dagger in his hands, high above his head, his eyes fixed on the smooth valley of white flesh between her heaving breasts. The priestesses pinned her wrists and ankles so that she could not wriggle free as the sharp gleaming point pressed slowly into the pale skin of her chest; brilliant red streams poured forth, trickling down her sides and dripping from her arched back onto the dais. Her pitiful scream split the very fog of the air, echoing from one end of the cavern to the other; she kept on screaming as the priest removed the blade and sank it into another region of her abdomen, continuing until thick foaming blood choked her voice and issued from her lips. She convulsed and collapsed onto the altar while the life force oozed from her corpse and into the drain in the center of the table.

Simon vomited what meager contents his stomach could provide onto a nearby mushroom, turning it a rather nasty shade of pinkish brown.

But it got worse.

The priest reached beneath the altar and retrieved a stone cup dripping with his victim's blood, and drank it; he passed the remainder to the pair of priestesses, who greedily consumed the contents. Satiated, the women picked up the warm body by its arms and legs, dragged it from the dais, and heaved it over the balcony at the now ravenous crowd below. The natives fell upon it like dingoes on an injured calf, ripping and tearing and gouging with teeth, fingers, hands, anything they could use. The young woman, moments ago a terrified and beautiful living being, ended her existence as fodder for depraved animals that only looked minimally human. They tore her to shreds, rending and wrenching, until nothing resembling humanity remained of the bloody heap. They devoured every morsel, fighting and clawing to get a taste, sucking on bones, cracking them open for the marrow. Not a savage stood without splashes of gore covering some part of their naked bodies; Simon saw several licking blood from the bodies of their kin, desperate to taste the sacrificial victim.

Simon retched again. His hands numbed as his blood chilled. Cold sweat covered every inch of his trembling body. These monsters had Kasey, probably inside that damned temple, if she still lived. He had to get her out of there before it became her turn.

Then the drum started beating again.

Simon looked out across the plaza at the dancing, chanting savages, their wet, sticky bodies undulating in unison, long, skinny arms swaying over bobbing heads.

"Multiculturalism my butt," he murmured. "These people need to die."

The ritual resumed, the natives whooping and shrieking, their sinuous forms moving wildly to the beat of the drum, while the priestesses cleaned the altar and prepared it for another sacrifice. Soon they disappeared into the temple's interior while the natives continued their wild heathen frenzy.

Simon studied the temple and the grounds, watching the crowds closely, and started to form a plan in his mind, a way to get close enough to the temple without being seen. Kasey had to be inside, hopefully unaware of what had happened; but of course she could also be in any of the other structures, unconscious, perhaps already dead, and he might not ever find her. If they harmed her he would not hesitate to kill every native in this cavern.

The drums intensified and the priestesses returned to the balcony, accompanying another young victim, who walked calmly between them, also wearing a flimsy white robe. But Simon's heart froze when he saw the golden brown hair, vacant gray eyes, and expressionless features of the woman with whom he had traveled to the very edge of time.

CHAPTER 24

RESCUE

She stood like a zombie, unflinching, as the priest approached her from behind, placed his hands on her shoulders, and spoke in quiet tones. The blood-thirsty crowd stopped their revelry and watched the ceremony, depraved faces ravenous for more flesh.

Simon had seconds in which to act. He needed a weapon. A bazooka would be nice. He got to his feet and raced unseen behind the ridge, circled toward the river, and approached the settlement from behind the temple. Along the way he found a tall, thin mushroom the size of a sign post, which he snapped off at the base. It weighed far less than wood, like most mushrooms containing little solid substance; but it remained sturdy enough.

He had always thought himself a true coward, ready to run at a moment's notice, never ashamed to retreat even when the odds were on his side; the desire to avoid conflict ran deep within his soul, robbing him of self-esteem, which certainly explained his lack of success with women. Guys with the most self-esteem, justified or not, had their pick of beautiful women, and somehow that felt cosmically unfair—until he had realized the kinds of women those guys attracted. Still, he attracted no one and so he felt bitter about it. But as he raced through the empty village toward the demonic temple, carrying a broken mushroom the size of a jousting lance, preparing to attack a pulsating mob of cannibals deep beneath the surface of the Arabian Desert to save the life of a woman who basically despised him—well, he had to seriously reconsider his image as a coward; if he carried through with his half-formed plan he would make cowards everywhere look bad, and they would hate him for it.

Simon forged ahead, listening with bat-like ears enhanced by the invigorating power of adrenaline as the priest gave his shrill speech. He reached the back of the temple unobserved, for no one could have anticipated even one strange visitor, let alone two; the natives all stood at attention on the other side of the structure, leaving no one to guard against intruders.

No one, that is, but a third priestess standing inside the doorway. Her look of surprise matched Simon's, but before she could sound an alarm he punched her so hard in the center of her face that he felt something snap as she reeled backward and dropped to the floor in a heap. His hand throbbed—he had never struck another human being before— but he didn't think he had seriously damaged it; the cracking sound had come from the young woman's brittle nose, the bridge crushed and gushing blood onto her black robe. Probably they would sacrifice her next. He raced up the stairs and stopped at the darkened entrance to the balcony, a few feet behind the priest, who waited on the near side of the altar. The priestesses moved closer to Kasey, who stood motionless between them. The black-clad women reached for the strings on the back of Kasey's robe, tugged them, allowing the flimsy garment to fall at her bare feet. Simon stood in amazement at his helpless companion's naked form, though he could see only her back, cloaked in golden brown hair, everything below her hips concealed by the dais. The crowd below got an eyeful.

Simon swung his giant mushroom at the priest from behind, clubbing him in the side of the head, rendering him instantly unconscious; the sacrificial dagger clattered to the floor. The priestesses, caught by surprise, turned and glared at him with demonic hate, reddened eyes filled with animal rage, pale skin glowing with the dark light of evil. They leapt at him, one across the altar and the other around the side.

Simon ducked and rolled toward the unmoving priest, grasped the dagger, and slashed it at anything that moved. He struck flesh and a wounded hand drew back, accompanied by a shriek of pain. He got to his feet and waved the weapon at the pair of hissing demons, one caressing her oozing hand. They made gestures of attack, but stopped short of the blade's range. Simon waved his broken mushroom to further discourage them. He slid around the edge of dais, where Kasey stood unashamedly naked, inspiring the crowd below. She seemed entirely unaware of what was going on around her.

He maneuvered the priestesses toward Kasey, their backs to the crowd, and took the long mushroom in both hands.

"Kasey," he called over the din of savages below. "Kasey, if you can hear me, I need you to do something, okay?"

She showed no outward sign of comprehension.

"Kasey," he tried again, "I need you to duck! Understand? Do it now!"

To his relief, she quickly dropped to her knees. In the same instant he lurched forward, wielding the mushroom horizontally, and shoved it into the priestesses. Robbed of balance, they staggered backward and careened off the balcony into the waiting talons below. Simon heard the gnashing and rending of teeth on flesh and bone, the chilling screams of living victims as monsters tore them to shreds. He was glad not to have seen it this time.

He rushed over to Kasey, who sat hunched on the floor, arms around her knees, sobbing softly, tears flowing down her cheeks. He quickly covered her with the discarded robe.

"We have to get out of here," he said. "They won't be satisfied for very long. Can you walk?"

He helped her to her feet, but her movement was lethargic, her expression vacant, her eyes glazed with only partial comprehension.

"What have they done to you?" he inquired, more of himself than of her.

Of course, he suddenly realized. Mushrooms! They weren't just for eating on salads. The natives had concocted a drug derived from indigenous fungi, and they no doubt used it liberally in their lives, particularly on those they intended to consume. It prevented the sacrifices from getting too scared to go through with the ritual. He wondered how many people they had devoured, and how often they felt the urge to eat each other.

Simon heaved Kasey's limp form over his shoulder and stepped around the altar as the priest began to stir; a well-placed foot to the face rendered him once more unconscious. No more priestesses blocked the entrance at the bottom of the stairs, but something did catch his eye: wadded up jeans in the corner, along with certain other unmentionables that he would try to remember not to mention. He scooped them up, stuffed them into his backpack, and raced from the building toward the village and the river on the other side.

He didn't make it that far. Swarms of natives poured around the temple, forcing him to change direction, away from the river and into the mushroom forest. Kasey's dead weight slowed him considerably, but adrenaline coursing through his veins leant him strength and speed he would have lacked otherwise; but he knew he could not carry her indefinitely, or the natives would enjoy a third feast.

His jostling gait over uneven rock and occasional slips on crushed mushrooms gradually roused Kasey from her drug-induced trance. He felt her come alive on top of his shoulder, and so he stopped to let her down. She still looked drugged, but her eyes retained the familiar flash of intelligence. Fog clouded her brain, though not enough to keep out the horrors of reality.

"Are you with me?" he asked her.

"Simon…," she managed.

"I need you to run," he told her, speaking slowly and with determination. "Stay with me, okay?"

She nodded.

A pack of angry savages crested the ridge, trampling everything in their path. Shrieks and howls pierced the air when they spotted their quarry, and the beasts doubled their effort in anticipation of fresh blood and meat.

Simon grasped Kasey's hand and raced at the speed of desperation, her long legs easily keeping pace with him, the almost nonexistent gown fluttering out behind her. They kept well ahead of their pursuers, though Simon suspected that could not last for very long.

As was so often the case, he proved correct.

They worked their way toward the river, still their best hope of escaping the madness inside the cavern. He had already decided that he preferred floating into the unknown rather than remaining here surrounded by the known. He could think of better fates than chunks of his body passing through the intestinal tracts of depraved cannibals, the last devolved remnants of a once powerful civilization that might have dominated the Bronze Age for millennia. Menzies had never mentioned this in his book.

Kasey grew stronger as they ran, strenuous activity forcing the drug out of her system, her heart racing and her lungs heaving, blood pulsing through her body with a cleansing effect. By the time they approached the river she appeared almost normal, though still comparatively weak. Simon didn't understand how she continued to hold up after all she had endured on this unexpectedly eventful night—the cavern, the river, the waterfall, and now this. But, as he had gradually come to realize, Catalina Carabresa was no ordinary woman—in any sense of the word.

Minutes of hard running brought them close to the river, its dark, sparkling surface visible through the spindly boles of tree-sized mushrooms. Simon turned and raced for the perceived safety of the wide, calm current, determined to reach it before the natives caught up to them. He might have succeeded, if not for a second wave of demonic creatures that swept in from the other side, moving up the ridge, cutting him off from the river. They circled around in a giant mob, offering no hope of escape, eliminating every avenue of retreat.

Even for a coward, the inability to retreat meant a necessity to fight.

Five hundred to two seemed unfair odds by any standard, especially considering that the two possessed a single inadequate dagger and the five hundred brandished sharp teeth that had already proven more lethal than any implements they could have wielded.

Simon stopped by the thick stem of a mushroom that arced high into the misty air, its massive top leaning out over the river. An absurd plan hastily formed in his mind, the result of desperation and the desire to evade his attackers.

"Come on!" he urged, pulling Kasey behind him as he dug his hands into the soft, rubbery, quivering, color-changing tree. He had chopped enough mushrooms in his time to understand their soft sponginess, the minimal resistance they yielded to pressure. The fungi in this forest offered a variety of textures, the largest ones denser by necessity in order to support the sheer height to which they grew; even so, he found it remarkably easy to dig his hands and feet into the side of the trunk, creating handholds and footholds sufficient for climbing. They easily supported his weight. Kasey followed his example and together they worked their way up the steeply sloping curve of the giant mushroom as hordes converged on their position.

Several natives attempted the climb, unsuccessfully at first, and then with more vigor as they quickly learned how to ascend. The 'shroom vibrated and quivered as naked savages attacked it, scrambling up the trunk with claws and teeth, gouging out gobs of fluffy white matter as they went.

"Simon, they're gaining on us," Kasey said as she looked down at them, a dozen feet below her robe-draped body.

"Keep moving," he urged.

The tree narrowed closer to the top, swaying freely as natives leapt onto the base. Dozens of stout limbs curved out from the thick trunk, varying in size from that of a pencil to something approaching the diameter of Simon's thigh, each topped with a wide umbrella.

Kasey screamed as a savage reached for her ankle, his cold, bony hand scraping her warm flesh, but not deeply enough to draw blood. She kicked him in the face and he tumbled out of the tree, shrieking as his helpless body plummeted sixty feet into the rocky riverbank. A sickening thud ended his life, and the horde of cannibals quickly ended his remains.

"Whatever you do, don't fall!" Simon said unnecessarily. He climbed above the woman he had rescued—again—but she rapidly caught up to him.

"Thanks," she said sarcastically.

"I have an idea," he replied.

Simon snapped off a nearby limb and hurled it at the nearest savage. The weapon weighed little, having no more substance than mushy Styrofoam, but it achieved the desired effect: the unexpected impact startled the native enough to loosen his grip, and he too plunged to his death and consumption.

Kasey tried it and removed two savages with a single shot.

"Show off," Simon frowned.

The tree quivered violently and lurched to one side, shuddering beneath the strain of so much additional weight. Simon and Kasey clung tightly, afraid to move, petrified of falling into the ravenous mouths seventy feet below. Simon looked up into the thin mist and saw the underside of a wide umbrella, easily spanning twenty feet. The trunk narrowed where the two parts of the mushroom connected, and now the entire affair leaned awkwardly over the river.

"Simon, there's no way we're surviving this," Kasey said, clinging desperately to the quavering, vibrating, vacillating stem high in the misty air.

"Have a little faith," he told her. "And follow me."

The mushroom, comparable in size to an old oak tree, leaned dramatically as they neared the top, forcing them to climb on the upward curve, which aided their progress. It also spurred the nearest savages, who surged up the trunk like Old World apes. Simon swung his backpack into a monstrous head, sending the creature reeling out over the river, where it splashed and vanished.

Simon and Kasey reached the underside of the umbrella ahead of the next savage, and together they kicked in unison at his head, achieving the desired effect. But the monsters kept coming.

"We can't keep this up," Kasey cried, exhausted, and embarrassed by the flashes of leg and torso that Simon couldn't help noticing whenever she moved.

"Just hang on," he urged. "Dig in deep."

They plunged their hands into the thick parasol's firm but pliant tissue; to Kasey's utter horror, Simon started shaking and swaying, moving his body in unison with the mushroom's lurching motions, gradually increasing the strain on the structure they now relied on for their lives.

"What the hell are you doing!" Kasey screamed into his ear.

Before he could answer, a loud snapping sound echoed like the report of a gun, startling everyone in the cavern; for an instant all motion and noise ceased. Then the enormous mushroom finally gave beneath the unnatural strain and plunged toward the ground far below. The stem shattered on impact, crushing natives beneath its weight, dislodging those who had clung to it. The giant umbrella popped off the brittle stem as it hit the center of the river; the curved upper surface slid beneath the tranquil current, bobbed, and rose up to float unimpeded downstream.

Simon and Kasey, clinging desperately to the concave surface, flopped onto their new refuge in a pair of terrified heaps, their hearts pounding but entirely undamaged.

They sat up and watched as howling natives screamed and jeered, hurling mushrooms into the river, now helpless and receding into the distance.

The upended mushroom top rounded a bend and the naked savages disappeared from view.

Simon leaned against the broken stem, a satisfied smile on his face. He looked at Kasey, disheveled and distraught, but alive and unharmed, and wondered what she thought of him now after that heroic and epic rescue. Even she could no longer think him cowardly.

"Not a bad piece of rescuing," he finally said, prodding her into saying something— anything—that might acknowledge his valorous act.

She said nothing.

"I got us a boat, too," he boasted.

Kasey turned to face him, fire in her eyes, the familiar hard coldness once more chiseled into her expression. He couldn't help noticing the delicate curve of her bosom as it strained beneath the thin white fabric of her sacrificial gown.

She slapped him hard across the cheek, the sharp sound echoing in his ears. Then she kissed him full on the mouth.

He didn't know which act startled him most.

CHAPTER 25

THE RAFT

K asey reclined into Simon's warm embrace, enjoying the strength of his arms around her waist. She found comfort in his tenseness, knowing that he felt as nervous as she did. Not since Carista's death had she allowed herself to get this close to anyone. Even after her horrible mistreatment of him, her spiteful words and bad attitude, he still risked his life to save her against impossible odds. Who else would have defied a village of cannibals to rescue such a cold, heartless, mean-spirited harpy? Today forced a solid revision of her opinions concerning the stranger who had blundered into her science lab that fateful morning, this time strongly influenced by a factor she never would have expected: her heart.

They sat in dark silence, their boat having long since departed the glowing cavern of savages. Minutes after their escape the river wended into another tunnel, the raft turning in lazy circles as it disappeared into the unknown. Occasionally it scraped against walls, altering the direction of its spin, but the impacts, cushioned by soft mushroom foam, barely disturbed the time travelers who took this rare opportunity to relax after a very eventful night.

Kasey had changed back into her normal clothes, which Simon had also rescued, right down to her socks and shoes; she marveled at his ability, even under stress, to consider such details. Only Simon, his uncanny mind seeing what others overlooked, would have snagged her clothing and kept it for her to put back on after their escape. And he had never doubted their successful escape. She had expected to die, first in the sandstorm, then in the temple, then in the river; but his faith never wavered, and now they floated peacefully in each other's arms, warm and content, hundreds of feet beneath the desert floor.

Simon intrigued her. True, he possessed little physical strength, lacked the rugged good looks most women found attractive, and she stood half an inch taller in bare feet; his awkwardness often got the better of him, but somehow she found that endearing—it reminded her of her own insecurity. In her younger years she imagined dating a tall, dark, handsome man whose deep eyes and mysterious attitude inspired envy among women; a bumbling, inexperienced, social misfit like Simon would never have garnered a second glance.

Even without the distraction of her project for the last four years she would have lived a lonely life of solitude, not because of awkwardness but as a result of her irrational standards. No man would have matched her notion of the ideal, either physically or intellectually, and that would have frustrated her. Dedicating herself to the time machine in a misguided attempt to put right the atrocities of the past had saved her from the disappointments of failed relationships. Not having her sister's guidance would have proven socially catastrophic.

Now she realized the true reward of her labors, the end result of the project that had consumed so much of her life: the meeting of two social outcasts, misfits unnoticed and forgotten by the rest of the world, who had the only real chance of making a difference in the lives of billions.

Simon had achieved the impossible: he had given her hope. And maybe something more.

"I owe you my life," she whispered in the darkness, long after the last of the glowing lichen faded away.

"You don't owe me anything," Simon assured her. "I'm just glad we're out of there in one piece."

"Simon, no one on Earth would have done what you did, especially after the things I said to you."

"You were upset," he replied. "I can't blame you for that."

"I shouldn't have lashed out the way I did," she said softly. "You've done nothing but help me ever since we met, and I have scolded you and made fun of you the whole time."

"I deserved most of it," he admitted.

"You deserved better," she insisted. "I've been monstrous."

"You've had a lot on your mind," he pointed out. "The weight of the world, and that's no exaggeration. You're the strongest person I've ever met."

"Simon, I think I'm probably the weakest person in the world," she said. "You're the strong one—no matter what happens to us, you never lose faith. I wish I could be as strong as you."

Simon sighed.

"You were right about one thing," he admitted, "about faith being a crutch. I talk about God and faith, but deep down I'm just not sure. I want to believe, I convince myself, but then I see the inconsistencies, the hypocrisy, the evil in the world, and wonder how a good and just God can allow such things. And then I see beauty and courage and strength—" he hugged her more tightly, "—and I have to believe that God must be at work in some way, because some things can't be accidental."

Kasey smiled. "Your faith is stronger than you think," she said, nestling closer.

"It takes courage to hold your convictions," Simon replied. "You decided a long time ago that science was right, that God doesn't exist; nothing shakes that belief. But it is still a belief. I think it's a wrong belief, I guess because I'm too afraid of the alternative."

"What do you mean?"

"I mean, suppose I believe and in the end I go to Heaven?" he said. "That's terrific. But what if you're right and in the end I just cease to exist? Not very comforting, but that's that. But if I don't believe and

God does exist the way the Bible says, I spend eternity suffering. At least you're sure of your convictions. I'm not. I want very badly to do what's right, but I think it's out of fear, and probably not for the right reasons."

"It's difficult, the unknowable," Kasey breathed. "I don't know what the truth is. I choose to believe in science, but I grew up in the same kind of church you did. It's funny," she said with a wry chuckle, "I'm the atheist and you're the Christian, and each of us is just as unsure as the other. Our churches didn't make it easy for us to believe much of anything."

"I know you're no atheist," Simon told her. He felt her look up at him in the darkness, though she couldn't see his eyes. "I figured that out in the cavern."

"Oh?"

"You're angry with God. You blame Him for what happened to Carista, and you can't forgive Him for it."

She sat quietly, scarcely breathing. Simon thought she might flip out again, but to his surprise she did not react to his words; he wondered if she had lost consciousness.

"You figured that out?" she finally asked, her voice scarcely a whisper.

"In your fit of anger you invoked God's name three times to add depth to your rage," he explained. "You've been very careful, ever since I've known you, to avoid even mentioning Him, let alone swearing in His name. It might have been different if you swore that way constantly, because it would have lacked any real meaning. But when you lost control of yourself you instinctively drew on God to give weight to your curses. That was when the truth dawned on me. That was when I knew you are just as confused as I am."

"You're really something," she said. "I swear at you and you take it as a sign from God. I try to hurt you, and it only strengthens your resolve to save me. You really defy logic and rationality."

"Art Majors will do that," he smiled.

She kissed him on the cheek.

"When I found your shirt on the mushroom I thought I had lost you," he said. "All that blood...."

"Two of them ambushed me," she explained. "They tore my shirt off, but not before I punched one of them in the nose—that was his blood you found. They bleed pretty easily."

"I noticed that," he recalled.

"One of them hit me on the head and I guess they carried me back to the temple," she explained. "When I woke up I could barely move, and I was dressed in that ridiculous gown. I was aware of what was going on, but it was like I had no will of my own; I could only watch and obey. I've never experienced anything like it."

"I'm pretty sure they drugged you with some kind of mushroom juice," Simon replied. "Some of them were bound to be psychedelic."

"I'm not sure what would have happened if you hadn't been there."

"You didn't see the girl they brought out ahead of you?"

"I saw her go up the steps, but I didn't see her after that."

"Good," he said. "You wouldn't have liked it."

"They ate her, didn't they?"

"Yep."

"I'm really lucky you visited my science lab that day," she said.

"I'm the lucky one," he replied. "Since I've known you I haven't felt alone. For the first time in my life I feel like maybe I'm important to someone. You have no idea how that makes me feel."

"I think I do," she sighed. "I think I might know it better than anyone else. We've both spent too much of our lives alone, clinging to shadows, living in fear. Maybe the light will do us both some good."

"I'll do my best not to annoy you," Simon said. "I guess I've been pretty hard to take lately."

"And I've been totally unreasonable," she admitted. "Besides, I have faith now... in you."

Warmth spread through his body. She felt it as well.

"I don't want to disappoint you or let you down," he told her.

"Simon, you're the only person in my life who hasn't."

Unsurprisingly, the wayward travelers fell asleep. They clung to each other for warmth not only of the body but of the spirit, resulting in the most peaceful and relaxing rest either of them had ever experienced. It had taken a cave of cannibals, a desert sandstorm, and the end of the world, but at long last the two young college students from the future had finally set aside their differences and come to terms not only with each other but with their most devastating inner demons. Only pleasant dreams filled their heads, while hope filled their hearts; Simon rejoiced in the knowledge that Kasey shared his feelings. She seemed genuinely happy now for the first time since he had met her, and the radiant glow of her soul filled him with joy that he had never thought possible.

Plus, he got the impression that for the first time in his life he actually had a girlfriend! What were cannibals and weather and global annihilation compared to that?

Kasey, for her part, lost herself in the comfort of not having to think for a few hours, and simply enjoyed the gentle caress of warm hands on her arms and shoulders, the rapturous heat of his strong body protecting hers from the chilly cave air. She might regret her abandonment in the morning, but right now she felt safe and content for the first time in years.

Simon didn't know how long they slept—minutes or hours—but when he woke to the jostling of the raft and the distant sounds of foreign voices he realized something had changed. First, he could see. He blinked the bleariness from his eyes and sat up. Moist cave walls, smooth along the sides, roughened as they curved upward to form a craggy ceiling twenty feet above, greeting him with sparkling light and deep shadows—not the vague, misty radiance of otherworldly phosphorescence. This light was sharp and clean and natural.

Sunlight.

It radiated from somewhere, though he could not discern a source. Upstream the relatively straight tunnel receded in the distance, disappearing around a gentle curve. Thirty feet across, the trickling current barely moved; he couldn't tell if the river was two feet or twenty feet deep, which made him all the more thankful for the mushy, spongy oddly comfortable raft he had so dramatically acquired.

Simon slowly got to his feet, steadying himself with the broken stem in the center of the upturned umbrella, careful to avoid rousing the beautifully slumbering young woman who had so completely entranced him. She looked peaceful and content, curled up at his feet, nothing at all like the cold, callous, condescending, stone-hearted statue he had met so many weeks ago. He started to turn around to face downstream on the slowly drifting raft, but something solid clubbed him in the back of the head, sending him sprawling face first onto the cushiony mushroom, stumbling over his supine companion.

The impact brought her to consciousness, though not without a moment of disorientation. She rubbed sleep from her eyes and saw Simon struggling on his hands and knees, groaning in pain. Even stranger, she saw beyond him a shaft of warm, golden sunlight piercing the comparative darkness, adding sparkles to the otherwise drab surroundings. A shaking wooden bucket hung unexpectedly down the center of it on a sturdy rope.

Kasey sat up and awkwardly helped Simon do the same, very aware of her hands on his torso as she assisted him; but once the odd sensation passed it felt natural being close to him. She did not regret last night. Not at all.

"What happened?" Simon asked, rubbing his throbbing head.

"I think you just discovered our way out of here," she replied.

He gazed into her steel-gray eyes and saw something in them he had never seen before: warmth. It made him strong.

They turned cautiously from behind the broken mushroom stalk, careful to avoid anymore dangling buckets, and ahead of them, not very far downstream, three more shafts of shimmering warmth formed brilliant columns that connected the outside world with the hidden one beneath the desert. The first pillar of light held a bucket, but it depended from its rope almost at the cave ceiling, far out of reach. They passed directly through the rejuvenating shaft of heat. The second ray contained no bucket, and shined down too far to the left. But the third one inspired hope.

"Do we have everything?" Simon asked as he hastily slung his pack over his shoulders.

"Just your stuff," she replied.

The mushroom raft inched nearer to the golden column, the bucket resting half- submerged in the lethargic current. To Simon's horror, it began to rise. Sloshing water dripped from its wooden surface, sparkling and shimmering as it fell with a trickling splash. Higher it rose as the slow-moving raft drew gradually closer, making excruciatingly languid progress.

"This is going to be close," Simon complained.

"I can't imagine it being any other way," Kasey sighed.

Halfway to the bucket they realized it would ascend out of reach before their raft could get beneath it. They saw no more shafts of light in the distance; either they escaped the cavern now, or they took the chance of following the river to its eventual outlet dozens or hundreds of miles downstream—if it exited the earth at all. It might disappear into the depths, in total oblivion, seeping upward in another part of the world, perhaps as a spring or as quicksand. They could not take that chance.

The bucket rose to shoulder height above the river, and yet the raft still remained too far away for them to reach it. Intermittent voices echoed down from the hole in the ceiling, fragmented sounds: children at play, men talking, women working, animals braying and bleating—inviting, taunting, and oblivious all at once. He had to reach them.

Simon scrambled to the mushroom's leading edge and dropped to his knees.

"Give me your foot," he said to Kasey.

"Simon...."

"Don't miss," he urged.

"Simon, no," she resisted. "I'm not leaving here without you."

"I'll be right behind you," he assured her. "We're only getting one shot at this."

By the time the raft entered the shaft of sunlight the bucket had already ascended out of reach, halfway to the curved ceiling. Kasey placed her foot in Simon's hands as he heaved her upward, and miraculously her long, supple fingers grasped the top edge of the bucket, dumping most of its contents onto her head. But she did not lose her hold. Then she felt a heavy weight on her legs and realized that she now existed as the bridge between Simon and oblivion.

Simon clung with the tenacity of desperation, his mind willing her to not let go. Very slowly the bucket descended to the river, the people above unable to maintain a hold on its suddenly impossible weight. Simon's feet touched the water, his spongy raft now lost in the darkness downstream.

"Kasey, hold tight," Simon called up to her. "I'm going to try to climb up there with you."

"I'm not going anywhere," she assured him.

The daunting climb quickly became awkward as the only handholds—the fabric of her jeans, the waistband at the top, and then her torso and shoulders—proved insufficient, except to get him slapped at such time that she had a free hand with which to chastise him. But he needn't have bothered. By the time he got as high as her thighs it became obvious that the more he climbed the lower the bucket descended, and before long they sank deep into the river, two heads and a rope visible above the placid surface.

"After you?" Simon said.

"Thank you." She smiled awkwardly.

Hand over hand they climbed the taught rope, Kasey leading the way. Simon feared the prospect of his wet hands slipping and losing his grip, the fall depositing him back into the lazy current. He would never catch up to the mushroom again, and for an instant wondered what would eventually become it. But adrenaline flowed quickly and the desperate need to reach safety ensured a tight grip as he inched ever upward along the cord below Kasey's dangling feet. It never occurred to him that she might lose her grip. And, of course, she didn't. In spite of the grueling, exhausting night they had endured, the few hours of rest had done her a world of good, reinvigorating her slender form and replenishing her depleted strength.

"How're you doing up there?" Simon called as she inadvertently kicked him in the top of the head.

"Holding my own," she replied with a wry grin. He thought for a second that maybe he preferred the sarcastic Kasey, not this clever happy version with the twisted sense of humor.

They kept climbing.

"Be careful," Kasey called down to him, her voice slightly muffled. "It gets kind of tricky here."

He looked up and saw that she had entered the narrow shaft through which the warm, energizing sunlight pierced the subterranean darkness. After that he glimpsed only her shadowy movements as she wriggled up the rope above him. He exited the horizontal tube that contained the powerful, life-altering river; he had entered it a cringing coward and left it a hero with a lovely girlfriend—not exactly the way he had pictured the fantasy in the tenth grade, but it would do.

The opening in the ceiling spanned barely two feet, and chunks of rough rock crumbled and fell as he brushed against them, splashing twenty feet below. The echoing water unnerved him. But he continued his ascent, his backpack scraping along as he climbed.

He had never experienced claustrophobia before, but then he had never gotten himself into a position to endure such a paralyzing fear. A wave of panic washed over him as the world—the very ground itself—seemed to close in on him, to crush him like a giant hand squeezing an overripe banana.

"Simon, where are you?" Kasey's voice penetrated through the darkness. He suddenly realized that his eyes had closed and he had stopped moving. Her soft tone brought him back to reality and brushed away the fear as effectively as an eraser cleans a stray line from a drawing.

"I'm here," he replied, his voice sounding stronger than he felt.

Simon heaved and pulled, scraping his body along the impossibly high shaft. Smooth walls roughened into hewn stones, crafted and placed by human hands. He saw movement above, hands and arms reaching into the darkness to aid the young woman who hadn't felt the full warmth of the sun on her pale and dirty face in seemingly days. A commotion broke out as people cried and shouted, the din extending far out of Simon's auditory range.

Moments later he emerged from the top of a stone well in the middle of an oasis, into the rejuvenating heat of the desert sun. Half a dozen hands helped him over the side and his squinting eyes discovered awed and joyous expressions on the faces of men and women alike. Probably none of them had ever seen two people spring up out of the desert in so dramatic a fashion.

Simon climbed down to the packed sand and stood next to Kasey, taking her hand in his—she did not draw away—and together they stared out at their new surroundings: a wide oasis in the middle of the desert, adorned with tall palms and low shrubs and people and animals, tents and caravans by the dozens—a major crossroads in the Arab world. From every direction people rushed toward the magical well that had spat out two strange young foreigners; among them Simon noticed the evidence of long-distance travelers: an array of clothing on a host of meandering people, merchants with their wares clanking on the backs of donkeys and camels, tents of varying quality from those of the simplest traders to the most ostentatious sheiks. He felt Kasey's hand tighten its grip on his.

The crowd grew to hundreds of people, staring and murmuring, jeering and shouting, gesticulating wildly in a manner the young college students could not understand. They couldn't tell if the crowd was hostile or excited, and that scared them. If only someone here spoke their language!

"Does anyone speak English?" Simon suddenly thought to ask. Perhaps in such a major trading center someone might have heard the language. "Or even second-year Spanish?"

"Your Spanish will be about as effective as my Latin," Kasey chided.

"It was worth a shot," he said.

A surge of movement caught his attention, and when he turned his head his jaw nearly dropped to the desert floor. Kasey clung to him, both hands on his arm, her body pressed against his. He definitely liked this new attitude of closeness.

The crowd parted, forming a respectable corridor along which strolled a very familiar Arab trader, his powerful form commanding respect and admiration. Every man shrank from his gaze and made a path as though the force of his will impelled them to do so. He stopped before his missing guests, studied them at great length, and reached out to touch Kasey's hair. He turned to the crowd and spoke a short burst of low guttural syllables, at the end of which everyone erupted into laughter.

The Arab turned around and smiled at the two strange young people, a look of perplexity on his handsome face. He laughed and motioned for his wives to attend them.

Simon and Kasey looked at each other.

"Well, that was easy," Kasey grinned.

Simon certainly enjoyed a healthy dose of irony.

Chapter 26

Moab

The caravan set out late in the day, having delayed its departure on account of the miraculous discovery of the strange young foreigners in the well. Simon and Kasey would have liked to remain in the oasis for a few days to recover from their adventure, but the Arab trader, unable to comprehend their request, paid it little heed. His wives insisted—no doubt at his urging—that Kasey replace her tattered clothing with something more traditional, and to Simon's surprise she acquiesced without argument. Simon couldn't tell if her change in attitude indicated a lack of hope or a return of the good nature that had once dominated her personality before the death of her sister. In either case, both he and the Arab paid closer attention to her.

Arriving at the caravan after her makeover, she stunned Simon with her incomparable beauty: shimmering fabric clung snugly to her body in all the right places, while exposing a long swath above her hips; her luxurious hair crept out from beneath a headpiece that artfully framed her lovely countenance, hinting at the inner defiance that defined her personality. Simon suspected she wore her jeans and sneakers underneath the light folds of fabric.

Simon got new clothing as well, to replace that which had suffered so grievously in the cave and the river. While Kasey sported bold colors—red, blue, and green—his attire remained earthy and drab: white, cream, and brown. He thought the long, draping garments would make him swelter beneath the midday sun, but they had the opposite effect: light, airy layers reflected heat while keeping out the chafing sand. And since his sweat evaporated instantly in the dry air he felt little discomfort in Bedouin garb.

Most importantly, Kasey discovered her backpack still intact. A careful examination revealed every piece of equipment exactly as she had left it, which elicited a sigh of relief. Of course, the situation had not changed from before the sandstorm: she still required power and parts, something that only a Radio Shack could supply, but at least she was no worse off—and perhaps better in light of the hope her new association with Simon afforded.

Kasey smiled inwardly at how readily she had accepted Simon's affections, limited and awkward as they were. Yesterday she had belittled and scoffed at him, unwilling to take him seriously: a nobody without a future, who annoyed her at every encounter. But an unexpected side of him surfaced underground, and it profoundly moved her. It might take time to put her new emotions into proper order, but she could not deny the good feeling she experienced whenever she touched Simon's hand or felt his body close to hers; it gave her strength and confidence. He had shaken her long-held convictions about life and the universe, and about herself, and she didn't know quite what to think of it. So she set to work on her device, ignoring the emotional stress. She looked forward to getting to know this odd young freshman, to open up to him, to learn from the goodness of his nature. She enjoyed the happiness he brought to her, in spite of the confusion that came along with it.

Simon rode astride his camel in the same saddle from which he had leapt a day earlier to save the woman who had utterly dismissed him as useless and irrelevant. He scarcely believed that only a day had gone by, but in that time the quality of his life had changed dramatically. Much of his fear had fallen away, left behind in the cave of cannibals, replaced by newfound courage and determination. Not to mention a girlfriend! The scenes played again and again in his mind, and he thought about what he might have done differently, more heroically, to impress her even more. Nothing had surprised him like that kiss atop the mushroom raft, and he wondered if she had reacted rashly while still under the influence of the native drug; but it had long since worn off and her affection had not. She still held his hand whenever they were together, and she stayed by his side almost all the time, comfortably clinging to his arm, like so many couples he had seen throughout middle and high school. They had shared only the one impulsive kiss, and he had not pressed for another, but that was okay: he would never forget that one. The last thing he wanted was to push her away by demanding more affection than she was willing to give. He understood her fragile emotional state after so many years of shielding herself from the world outside of her own mind; he desired only to be her rock, her anchor, her safe harbor. She had made great progress, but still had some distance to travel; he felt eager to make the journey with her.

Opening his backpack, he retrieved his camera as the magnificent steed gently swayed beneath him, its careful feet plodding through loose sand on a well-established trail over the dunes. The caravan no longer traveled alone in the vast desert, as other individuals and groups labored under the hot sun to reach the same mysterious destination. A second line of traffic plodded in the opposite direction, toward the oasis. He took pictures of caravans along the way and added more sketches to the growing collection in his journal. He spent hours reproducing his vivid memories of the previous night: the cavern, the cannibals, the mushroom forest, the river, and the dramatic sight of light and buckets that represented their harrowing escape from the Underworld. He jotted notes and descriptions along the edges of the pages, which he hoped to find helpful someday when he got around to creating finished works of art.

The day crept by quietly for the well-rested adventurers as they worked and relaxed, refreshed in both mind and body. Then the caravan crested a hill and an unexpectedly magnificent panorama changed everything.

"Kasey, do you see that?" Simon called ahead to her.

"Nice," she said, looking up and then ignoring it again.

"Nice?" he replied. "That's it?"

"Very nice?"

"Kasey, that could be our ticket out of here," he exclaimed. "There's bound to be someone there who can help us, or at least speaks English."

"If you say so," she replied.

Simon stared in fascination at a city positioned on a slight incline a few miles in the distance, on the shore of a substantial body of water, a lake or a sea, the far shore barely visible in the haze of midday heat. A high stone wall encircled this bastion of civilization, which consisted of hundreds if not thousands of small individual structures that melded together to form a complex and bustling city. Columns of travelers entered and exited through at least three gates, the avenues lined with vendors selling everything from vegetables to swords; people swarmed in every sector, a barely organized chaos of sound and motion, reminding Simon of a bustling city street at the peak of tourist season, except with donkeys and camels instead of cars and buses.

Simon sneaked careful pictures from the concealment of his saddle, and then roughed out a sketch that
he hoped to someday turn into a grand work of art.
Drawing from the back of a swaying dromedary was
no easy thing, but if he used quick strokes and moved
in rhythm with the beast he made out fairly well.

Halfway to the city, crowds clogged the road, forcing the caravan to a crawl. Marveling at the elegant
entourage and sensing the Arab's importance, people
cleared out of his way, climbing onto rocks or wading
into fields of grain to let him pass.

The south gate loomed into view, its heavy slabs
of rough hewn stone standing tall and impenetrable. Simon could only imagine the herculean labor
required to build the fortifications of this frontier city.
Ponderous, monolithic slabs stacked to form an opening, rounded at the top, about fifteen feet in width,
through which traffic passed in both directions. Of-
ficials on either side of the gate stopped all travelers, entering and exiting, searching carts and animals,
looking for contraband. Simon sighed as he realized
that nothing had changed even in his own century.

"Simon, where are we?" Kasey called back to him,
her gear safely stowed in her backpack. Too much
noise and jostling motion filled the air for her to con-
centrate on the problems she alone could fix.

"If our host is in fact Arab," Simon replied, "and if
this is Arabia and not North Africa, and since we have
been traveling roughly north by northwest—one of
my favorite movies, by the way—then that body of

water has to be the Dead Sea. Which puts us in the Biblical land of Moab. But that's just a guess."

"How good a guess?"

"This could be Utah ten thousand years in the future and this is what's left of Salt Lake City and The Great Salt Lake," he said. "Or we could be in the middle of the Sahara Desert. I'm just interpreting the clues as I see them."

"Simon, I don't think we're going to find anyone here who can help us," she said. "There are no cars, no telephone or telegraph poles, no electric wires, nothing to indicate the technologies we know."

"This could be a few hundred years in the past," Simon replied. "Maybe we're here in time for one of the Crusades!"

"Somehow I doubt that would do us any good," she chided. "But it would be helpful to know approximately when and where we are so I can program the calculations. It will be crucial if we want to land sometime safer."

"Is that a possibility?" Simon asked. "I mean, are you making progress?"

"Slowly," she sighed. "To save my battery I have to write everything by hand, which takes forever. Once I get the calculations worked out I will be able to put them into the computer pretty quickly; but I can't spare the power to make the work easier. It'll take time."

"I have faith in you."

She smiled and turned away, distracted by the parade converging on either side of the massive city gate, stopping and starting as the guards allowed some people through and halted others.

The wait dragged interminably, but with little effect on the Arab at the head of the caravan, having no doubt experienced this inconvenience many times before; he sat patiently until his turn came. It came sooner than Simon would have guessed. Fully fifty people and half a dozen smaller caravans stood between him and the gate when an official worked his way back to the ornately decorated camels and addressed the powerful and intimidating Arab. The brief exchange involved the passing of several coins from the Arab to the official, which disappeared into the latter's tunic. The discussion resulted in the immediate redirection of the large caravan to a side path, which guards cleared with some alacrity to allow the important trader to pass unhindered. They bypassed the lines of increasingly frustrated travelers and arrived at the gate in front of them, where the official waved the Arab and his entourage through without delay.

Simon smiled. Some things never changed: small bribes provided conveniences the masses could not afford.

The landscape transformed again inside the city. Tables and carts and stalls lined narrow avenues; the shouting of merchants and traders filled the air, their voices rising over the din of rustling people, clanking metal, clopping hooves, and swishing beasts; braying donkeys, whinnying and snorting horses, lowing cattle, bleating sheep, the occasional barking dog—all formed a dizzying cacophony that overwhelmed the young time travelers who had never imagined such chaos.

People mounted on steeds crept along impossibly crowded streets, shoving forward and pressing through the pulsing mass, like a boat slicing through choppy seas. Simon saw people from diverse nationalities and cultures, clothing reflecting their origins, and watched as they bartered and traded, often happily and just as often not. Most stands and carts offered fruits and vegetables for sale, but he observed others that contained fish, cuts of meat, and stacks of bread. Merchants peddled knives and swords, some beautifully bejeweled and deadly, others simple and practical.

The caravan pressed ever forward, twenty camels in single file, their tasseled blankets, intricately detailed leather saddles, and brightly covered tent-like awnings standing above the swarming masses. People stopped and gawked, many waved at the important Arab, who cheerily returned the gesture, and others simply smiled at the ostentatious show of wealth.

The crowds thinned closer to the city's center, for the bulk of activity took place near the gates, where people came from all over to buy and sell their wares. Beyond the outer ring, away from the high protective walls, regular people lived and worked: smiths, coopers, bakers, artisans of all kinds. Here Simon saw inns and bars, liveries and studios, all the elements of an Old West town, but in the narrow confines of an ancient Middle Eastern city on the shore of the Dead Sea. Instead of cowboys and city slickers he observed Arabs, Bedouins, Turks and Jews, all thriving together in the oppressive arid heat on the edge of one of the world's harshest deserts.

The caravan moved more freely, unimpeded by the crush of traffic from the previous avenue, and continued without mishap. People moved about, but in a less hectic manner, more casual, and with a lot less noise. Simon could once again hear himself think. He studied the flat-roofed buildings, constructed from rough clay brick made of mud and straw, one or two stories high, though a few reached four levels. Boasting few decorations, occasional short wooden awnings extended over narrow doorways. Children ran and played among the structures, disappearing in tight alleys between them.

Simon had noted the smell of the ancient city about the time the caravan entered the gate, and it had intensified amid the throng of merchants and traders, but now it hung heavily above the cattle and sheep and chickens that lived in the same spaces as humans throughout the settlement's interior. With no running water or sewer system, waste products landed in the streets, dumped through open windows or deposited by the animals themselves. No one cared—or even knew to care—about cleaning anything. It was

no wonder the ancient world, even into the twentieth century, suffered so much disease. His olfactory
lobes, unaccustomed to such strain, became largely desensitized to the malodorous environment, but
from time to time a new and surprising scent wafted
in to reawaken his disgust.

The Arab led his caravan deep within the city, until a
wide plaza opened up before them, half as expansive
as a football field, ringed by low buildings and covered
in trampled grass and wide stone walkways. Animals
grazed peacefully, oblivious of the people. Vendors
hawked their wares in the shadows of buildings, but
without the frenetic din closer to the city gates. The
environment felt more relaxed, less claustrophobic;
the smell remained, but with less intensity. Simon
wished for a gentle breeze to clear the air.

At the far end of the plaza a small crowd gathered
around a raised platform atop which stood a naked
man in chains, his expression one of utter hopelessness. They called out short deep syllables and raised
their hands, and Simon immediately knew the nature
of their business. The unfortunate young man, glis-
tening with sweat, was led away from the platform
and disappeared into a nearby stall; at the same time
another young man, with jet-black skin—no doubt
taken from the lands south of Egypt—equally un-
clothed, and rippling with powerful muscles, stepped
dejectedly onto the platform, where a trader poked
and prodded him, forced open his mouth to reveal
gleaming white teeth, and slapped him a couple of

times to indicate the sturdiness of his solid musculature. Hands lofted into the air, accompanied by vigorous bidding that resulted in what Simon assumed to
be a substantial price.

He had never seen a slave market before, and it
disgusted him. How could people buy and sell other
people? Men always tried to subjugate other men,
lesser men, and force them to their superior will.
Throughout history one group invariably enslaved another group: from the ancient Egyptian captivity of
the Jews to the Muslim enslavement of Christians to
race-based slavery in the modern era, very little had
changed. It had merely evolved from class to religion
to skin color as a basis. In his own time a new form of
slavery, that of low wages and insurmountable debt,
forced people into lives of poverty disguised as freedom, ruled over by an elite marriage of government
and business—the master and his mistress. Maybe
Kasey was right: it really wasn't worth saving.

He watched as the dark and brooding man in chains
stepped from the platform, his lean and powerful
form towering over the men who had bid on him.
Unchained, he might have fought them all and run to
safety, disappearing into the crowd. But Simon suspected that no one in this part of history would harbor
a fugitive slave; the institution remained too well in-
grained in society, even among the slaves themselves.
Here all men were not equal under the law; that idea
had blossomed late in history, and it had collapsed
kingdoms and empires, replacing them with republics

and democracies. In this era each person knew his place, as ordained by God, and had to be content with it.

Another man climbed atop the platform as the Arab's caravan came to a halt at one end of the wide plaza. The camels stood patiently in the shade while their riders dismounted. Simon suspected they would stay here long enough for the Arab to make arrangements with some inn or livery, and then they would settle in for the night in comfortable quarters. He looked forward to exploring the ancient city with Kasey for a few hours before sunset.

He sat scrutinizing the slave market, a mixture of emotions confusing his mind; the distance of time had made the institution academic, allowing him to avoid the anger of his twenty-first century kin. But here it was real and offensive and there was nothing he could do about it. He felt a tug on his left leg, and when he looked down he saw Kasey gazing up at him, a thin smile enhancing her lovely face.

"You going to sit up there all day?" she asked him. "How about joining me for some lunch?"

"Sounds good to me," he replied, suddenly very cheery. She stepped back while he attempted to dismount from his towering steed, oblivious of the fact that everyone else had done so after their camels had dropped to their knees. In his haste to get close to Kasey he caught his foot in the reins, lost his balance, and toppled over the side. Kasey gasped loudly, drawing the attention of her fellow travelers, who turned their heads in time to see their clumsy companion hanging upside down from his steed, his hair brushing the ground. The camel snorted. A dozen people burst into laughter, gesturing and pointing, shouting sarcastic Bedouin taunts that he felt glad not to understand.

Two heartily laughing Arabs came to his rescue and pulled him free, "accidentally" dropping him on the ground in the process, where he sprawled in the dirt at Kasey's feet. She helped him up as his camel knelt beside him, an absurd look of contempt on its sneering face.

"At least you know how to get on their good side," Kasey chuckled.

"I'm thinking of changing my major to humiliation," he said as he brushed the dust from his clothes. She assisted in the effort, which pleased him.

"It's got to be better than art," she chided. "I mean, isn't that the major for people who can't really decide what they want to do—or maybe don't have the ability to complete a real major? No offense."

"I've heard all that before," he replied as they stepped away from the camels and settled onto a low stone wall within the shadow of a nearby building. Kasey uncovered a loaf of bread and a wedge of cheese, and together they satisfied their ravenous hunger. "Most of the family berated my parents for allowing me to choose art as my major; they said it was a waste of money and that I wouldn't be able to do anything with it."

"Then why did you choose it?" she asked, popping a piece of milky white cheese into her mouth. She sat close to him on the wall, her nearness tantalizing his soul; occasionally she leaned into him or touched his arm, thrilling him almost out of his mind; it took all of his intestinal fortitude to not show his excitement. He really should have dated more growing up.

"It's my passion," he said, choking down a torn piece of bread. "It's what I've always done and hopefully always will do."

"Do companies hire artists?"

He shrugged his shoulders. "Maybe I could teach art."

"I don't see you as the teaching type," she observed. "Students would eat you alive, even in elementary school."

She did have a point.

"I could make a living as a fine artist," he suggested. "Or even as a writer."

"You write as well?"

"My other passion," he smiled.

"I'm guessing you never played football or soccer, huh?"

"I played soccer in the sixth grade," he said, his attitude perking up. "But I wasn't particularly good at it. There was this one time, in a tournament, when the ball landed directly in front of me and all the other players were on the other side of the field; the goal was only twenty feet away and the goalie was on the opposite side. It was the perfect shot. It would make me the hero of the game."

"What happened?"

"I ran up to kick it, missed the ball entirely, and fell flat on my back."

Kasey stifled a laugh.

"Someone from the other team recovered it and kicked it downfield," he finished. "I think we still won, but no thanks to me."

"I kind of wish I could have been there to see it," she smiled, unconsciously holding his arm. He, of course, was very conscious of her touch.

"Hey, with a time machine you may get your wish," he grimaced.

"I'll make that a priority," she laughed.

"Truth is, I never got picked for teams in school," he said, "unless they didn't have a ball and needed something to kick."

She laughed again. He enjoyed that.

"I ran track one year," she recalled. "I was fourteen, too tall and clumsy for my age, but I was fast. I won a few times, when I didn't trip over my feet and skin my knees."

"Guess neither of us is the athletic type," he sighed.

"Guess not," she agreed. "So, what kind of art do you do?"

"Drawings, mainly," he replied, pleased with the sudden change of subject. At least in this area he felt some measure of confidence. He reached into the folds of his desert attire and brought out the small sketchbook, which never left his possession; he kept it either in a pocket or in his backpack, which had protected it from the subterranean river. The black leather cover showed some wear, but the pages inside remained intact. He handed it to Kasey, who carefully opened the small book that revealed the inner passions of his soul.

She thumbed through rough sketches of campus scenes, detailed drawings of leaves, a church steeple, a portrait of his shoes, and then came to something that stopped her cold. He had almost forgotten about the meticulously detailed drawing of her profile in the wheat field of nineteenth century Kansas; he didn't know how she would react to it. For half a minute she didn't. Her eyes moistened, though she pretended otherwise. She turned the page and discovered his recent works, the rough chronicle of their journey, punctuated by sometimes lengthy descriptions that she scanned with the eye of an adoring fan. Then she turned back to her portrait.

"You did this the day we landed in the wheat field," she said softly.

"I had to," he replied. "That moment needed to be captured."

"You barely knew me."

"I knew enough," he said.

"Is this how you really saw me, as hard as I had been on you?"

"It's how I still see you," he explained. "I knew there was more to you than anger. And I was right."

"No one ever had so much patience with me before," she sighed. "Except Carista." She wiped moisture from her eyes. "How about another portrait, right here, except this time include yourself?"

"I've never done a self-portrait before," he replied.

"I have faith in you," she said, smiling warmly. She squeezed his hand and he knew he could not let her down.

"I'll get my pencils," he smiled.

Simon hopped off the wall and stole a quick glance at her, sitting fetchingly on the stone surface, her lovely, softened face exuding happiness he had never thought possible. And to think... he had released that joy from the dark and gloomy dungeon of her heart—he, Simon Foxx, perhaps the most socially inept and ungainly student ever to set foot on a college campus!

He approached his camel and climbed atop the saddle, digging through his backpack for the small satchel that contained his drawing supplies. The effort yielded quick results, and so he took a moment to examine his pencils and sharpeners, blending stumps, gum erasers, and a small brush he used to wipe dust from the paper; his hand would smear the work, and oil from his skin could affect the manner in which the fibers absorbed the graphite or charcoal. Nothing appeared broken or out of order, so he carefully slung the small satchel over his shoulder and prepared to dismount his noble if mocking steed, this time more carefully than before.

But a subtle movement caught his attention, on the side of the camel facing the plaza: a familiar Arab, part of the caravan, crept stealthily along the line of dromedaries, hunching low in the conceal-ment of the great beasts. Another followed, wield-ing a gleaming dagger, and a third near the head of the line looked back and nodded in their direction. They moved slowly past him, taking no notice of the absurdly weak buffoon rummaging through the saddle above. A chill raced along Simon's spine; he discovered the Arab trader a few feet ahead of the first camel, engaged in conversation with a city resident, negotiating a price for the night's lodging, both for his entourage and for his animals; more im-portantly, he stood with his back to the approaching Bedouins, unaware of encroaching danger.

Simon climbed down from his saddle, on the op-posite side from the assailants, and hurried for-ward, unseen by anyone but Kasey. She started to speak, but he held his finger to his lips as he brushed past her, gaining on the assassins. At the first camel, barely six feet behind the unsuspect-ing Arab, Simon slowly and carefully climbed atop the saddle, desperate to be wrong in his assump-tion. But he had seen enough movies and televi-sion shows in his life to know that his eyes did not deceive him—and that the peril to himself was as great as that to the man who had rescued him and Kasey from the desert a week ago. Despite all that had happened, he could not forget that.

The first Bedouin rushed forward from the shadow of the camel, his knife raised high to plunge into the expansive, muscled back of the large, unprotected trader. But an unforeseen circumstance stayed his dark hand: Simon instinctively leapt from the camel's back, for once properly judging his distance, and plowed into the assassin from above and behind, sending him sprawling into the dirt, the knife landing inches from his outstretched fingers.

The great and powerful Arab whirled around in a swirl of robes, saw the young stranger scrambling atop the fallen attacker, the position of the knife telling the story, and immediately realized the truth. The remaining two assassins rushed forward, hoping to disorient him with a full frontal assault, and instantly regretted their rash action. A curved, flashing sword glinted in the sunlight, previously hidden in the folds of the Arab's exquisite attire, and in two quick arcs a disembodied head and a severed hand lay bleeding in the dirt. One man ran away screaming while the other dropped lifelessly to the ground in a heap of gore.

Before Simon could get back on his feet, five more men from the caravan rushed to the scene of carnage, swords drawn, hate in their eyes, voices raised in fury. The giant Arab moved like lightning, swinging and parrying, his enormous blade deflecting every attack and thrusting back his attackers. He twisted and twirled, his long robes swirling around him like a tornado, his feet kicking out at crucial moments to send an assailant reeling, a n occasional massive fist connecting with a jaw or the side of a head. Soon one of the attackers lay sprawled in the dirt, half his skull cleaved cleanly away, and so far not one of them had gotten close enough to the powerful trader to even pose a threat.

Then Simon heard a sound that made his blood run cold.

Kasey screamed. The shrill pitch indicated surprise and fear, a sound he had heard only once from her before. He jumped to his feet and scrambled among the camels to find out what had startled her.

He found three women attacking her. Kasey bounced atop the low wall, kicking and jumping, evading hands and knives, occasionally scoring a solid impact in the center of a face. But before Simon could reach her, one of the Arab's wives grasped Kasey's ankle and pulled her from the wall. They pounced, but the young woman from the future fought back with the strength of desperation, thrashing and kicking, scrambling from beneath them. One wife—the one who had attended Simon the first night—staggered backward into the short wall and toppled over the other side. Kasey, now solidly on her feet and facing two angry women wielding knives in their not-so-dainty hands, finally saw Simon through the dust they had kicked up. Her disheveled hair and dirt-stained face looked no worse for wear, but Simon saw fear in her eyes.

Before he could rush to her aid, a swarthy Arab tackled him to the ground, knocking the breath from his body, and snapping at least one of his pencils. That irritated him. He kicked with all his meager strength, disorienting the attacker long enough to get back onto his feet. He saw the third wife angling toward Kasey, blood trickling from a gash in her forehead. Simon reached into his tunic and removed the small golden dagger he had lifted from the cannibal priest's hand in the temple far beneath the surface of the desert, and tossed it to the young woman that had grown to mean everything to him.

"Kasey, catch!" he shouted as he tossed her the priceless weapon.

She easily caught the dagger by its hilt and slashed it across the nearest attacker's arm, opening a gash that would require immediate attention. The woman drew back, screaming, and disappeared from the fray.

But Simon had bigger fish to fry. His own assailant, none too pleased by his reception, withdrew a long sword from his robe and grinned with satisfaction at the now cringing young victim. This insignificant insect of a man would pay for the interference that had cost them the easy destruction of their hated benefactor. Dark eyes revealed no expression as his wide lips parted to expose large, crooked yellow teeth. Paralyzed with fear, Simon frantically sought some means of escape, a way to reason with the thug, but knew that his back was against a wall—literally. In an act of desperation, he rolled over the wall and fell to the ground on the other side as the heavy blade clanged into the top surface in a shower of sparks.

Simon crawled hastily from the immediate vicinity as the angry Arab climbed over the wall after him.

In the middle distance he observed Kasey fighting off the remaining two wives, using a combination of dagger and fabric to thwart their attacks. She fought gracefully, much more so than Simon did, and moved sinuously among her attackers, intimidating them with her sudden motions and far greater height.

Simon, unfortunately, found himself facing a far more imposing threat, one that had failed twice in his assault and no doubt vowed not to do so a third time. The large Bedouin inched slowly forward, sword raised, fury dripping from his countenance as Simon matched his pace, moving backward, desperate for some respite. His back hit another wall, this one the actual side of a building. A quick glance revealed the futility of escape, and an equally quick examination of his belongings revealed a disturbing lack of weapons—not that he could have competently defended himself.

"Wait!" he called out, holding up his hand, desperate to delay the inevitable, even for a second. To his surprise, the man stopped. Simon reached into a pocket and retrieved his sketchbook, quickly opened it, and showed the man the detailed drawing of Catalina Carabresa.

He seemed genuinely impressed. And then he lost his head. Literally. An unexpected blade from behind separated the ugly head from the swarthy body—the one went flying and the other drooped slowly to the ground—and behind the carnage stood the Arab trader, quite pleased with himself. He smiled and shook his head before moving off to fight yet another of his seemingly endless enemies.

Simon stood alone for the merest instant before remembering Kasey's imminent peril, and then raced to her battle, where now only one wife stood against her, but valiantly so. The other lay squirming on the ground inside a growing dark puddle. A fourth wife—the only ally—fought the one Kasey had injured near the beginning of the fight, and Simon guessed that this new participant had evened the odds.

He ran to Kasey's side, desperate to help her, but a new sound emanated from the plaza, where hundreds of spectators watched the events unfold. Clanking armor indicated rapidly moving soldiers entering the square. When Simon saw them his heart skipped a beat.

The soldiers raced into the fray, slashing and jabbing, until few other people remained standing. They moved with rehearsed precision, the result of endless drilling and training, their short swords making quick work of the more imposing but less skilled Arabs. Soon only the towering trader remained standing, his sword raised, prepared to fight to the death anyone who dared approach him. One soldier did, and in that instant Simon reacted seemingly irrationally.

Waving his arms and yelling at the top of his lungs he quickly positioned himself between the Arab and the guard. Kasey screamed something at him that he could not entirely comprehend. He arrived in time to stop the attack, much to the surprise and annoyance of all present, and when Kasey reached him he saw scorn on her face.

"What are you doing!" she demanded. "We could have escaped!"

"I doubt it," he replied.

But as he spoke, a soldier grasped Kasey's arm and yanked her away, resulting in an unexpected burst of rage from Simon that sent the soldier flailing backward onto the ground. Several more raced forward, weapons drawn, ready for the kill. But before the fight could continue, the powerful Arab trader tossed down his sword and offered surrender. Simon noted the look of wonder on the man's face, and relief on the faces of the soldiers. Kasey could not understand at all what had just happened.

"Simon, you have to be the craziest man on Earth," she scolded. "You're going to get us killed!"

"Actually, I probably just saved our lives," he replied, sweating profusely.

He felt her pressing close to him as the soldiers approached with shackles and chains. The Arab did not resist as they manacled his wrists, but he did not seem at all pleased by the turn of events. Why had this strange young traveler saved him from one group of assassins only to deliver him into the hands of the worst enemy he could ever have imagined?

"Kasey, I think I've narrowed down our place in history," he quickly explained as heavy iron shackles locked tightly about his wrists. "These are Roman centurions, and we would never have escaped them; and they would crucify our friend if he killed one."

Now she understood as clearly as he did the severity of their plight.

They would be lucky indeed to survive the next twenty-four hours.

Chapter 27

Prisoners of the Empire

"You're sure about this?" Kasey asked.

He had rarely felt more certain about anything in his life. He recognized the uniforms, the swords—pugios—the helmets, and the attitudes. It made sense now. They had traveled farther back in time than either of them had realized.

"The Romans didn't have a presence in this part of the world until the first century A.D. So we have to be anywhere from then until the fall of the Empire five hundred years later," he explained. "I can't be any more precise than that."

"It's good enough," she said.

The Roman centurions quickly chained the prisoners together and marched them away from the plaza. The Arab trader, towering above them, suddenly cried out in his native tongue; a soldier threatened to run him through with a sword unless he stopped, or so Simon interpreted the exchange. The Arab smiled broadly and walked in silence behind his foreign companions.

"How are we going to get out of this?" Kasey inquired, wary of speaking too loudly lest she incur the wrath of her captors.

"Maybe if we just try to explain what happened—"

"Simon, our language won't be spoken for fifteen hundred years," she argued. "There's no way we can make them understand where we're from or how we got here. We have no common frame of reference."

She made a valid point. Again.

The line of centurions and prisoners wended through the city streets, crowds parting before them, people stopping to stare at the three unlikely captives, particularly the enormous and exquisitely attired Bedouin. The Romans did not approach the gate, but moved to the other side of the city, where larger public buildings dominated houses and apartments occupied by townspeople and soldiers. A large temple stood near a palace occupied by whatever nobility ruled the city.

They entered through a gate in the palace grounds; Simon expected to see the grand interior, the main court, where he might attempt to plead his case before the magistrate, perhaps using his sketchbook as a medium to convey ideas. In the clarity of desperate hope he considered what pictures to draw in order to influence the understanding of whoever might listen; he could salvage this situation if given half a chance.

He didn't get even a quarter of a chance. The soldiers led them across meticulously landscaped grounds, among lemon, fig, and olive trees; tall palms stood in perfect rows; bright flowers of red and yellow and blue decorated large expanses of the garden, and servants cut the most beautiful specimens for arrangements to brighten the palace interior. Soldiers walked in circuits about the grounds, wary of intruders. The palace, an ornately designed stone structure as old as the Earth itself, rose like a mountain from the center of the gardens, in places six or seven stories high, with large upper windows and balconies that overlooked the nearest quarter of the city and the broader landscape beyond. The occupants might see all the way across the Dead Sea and into Judea on a clear day—or into the vastness of the open and empty expanse of the Arabian Desert on the other side.

The line of Romans and prisoners stopped at a guardhouse behind the palace, where the lead soldier spoke to the guard on duty. They waited until an altogether different kind of man stepped out of the opening in the side of the palace, clad in black, much more muscular, and with a dim light in his dark eyes. He grunted and motioned for the soldiers to follow.

They entered the palace through the back door, which opened into a narrow corridor, barely shoulder-width—a tight fit for the Arab—that led to a dark and winding staircase. The stairs descended deep beneath the palace, illuminated by flickering torchlight on the walls. In the wavering light Simon discerned rows of heavy wooden doors set at regular intervals along either side of the dank passage, small barred openings allowing guards to peek inside. A thin horizontal slot near the bottom of each door allowed a tray of food to enter the cell at random times, the only contact between prisoner and jailor.

Halfway down the corridor the line stopped and the jailor produced a large ring of keys, which he used to unlock one of the heavy doors. The thick panel scraped across the stone floor as it slid inward, revealing a dank and dirty chamber the size of Simon's dorm room, but lacking a window high up on the back wall. Guards unshackled their prisoners and unceremoniously shoved them into the room. Simon suspected that the Arab contemplated escape, but ten armed soldiers proved too much even for his almost superhuman abilities. Had he possessed a sword he might have made the attempt.

The door scraped shut, the key clanked in the lock, and the trio stood helplessly in near darkness, the flickering glow of a torch in the corridor barely penetrating through the bars set into the door, allowing the new residents to see each other's shadowy forms. An ankle-deep layer of straw covered the floor, some of it wet and musty, and Simon got the impression that it was inhabited by creatures far more accustomed to the environment than he was. Their faint rustling movements unsettled him, and they certainly did not make Kasey feel any better. She clung to him more tightly than before.

"We could be here a long time," Simon said grimly.

"How long?" she wanted to know.

"Ever see Ben-Hur?"

"What's that?"

"My favorite movie," he replied. "Maybe they won't keep us here," he said, trying to stay positive for her benefit. "Someone is bound to inquire about us, right?"

"If you say so," she sighed.

The Arab swept a mound of straw into a corner and settled into it, arms crossed and brooding, silently watching every movement made by the unfortunate strangers he had plucked from the desert a week ago.

"I guess we should follow his example," Simon suggested. "May as well get some rest while we can."

"Do you honestly think we'll be able to sleep in this place?" she retorted. "And where is the bathroom?"

"I have a feeling we're standing in it," he grimaced, gesturing toward the straw. "Try not to think about it."

They both thought about it a great deal, until it became quite uncomfortable. A distant corner had to suffice, and with that out of the way they nestled into their own corner. Even under these trying circumstances Simon found comfort in the closeness of Kasey's firm body curled up against his, trembling. He provided what comfort he could by holding her close and gently massaging her shoulders until she lost consciousness; in spite of her words to the contrary, he quickly joined her in slumber.

The Arab watched over them both.

They might have slept for hours or years, occasionally rousing long enough to sense their plight and escape back to the dream world. They remained in the dungeon a single night, holding each other continuously, and woke for good only when the door ground harshly across the rough stone slabs that comprised the floor. The Arab quickly got to his feet as three centurions entered the chamber, swords drawn; more followed, carrying shackles and chains.

The trio found themselves on the move again, and once more Simon felt confident in his ability to argue their case in the palace court. Once they understood what had happened, they would happily let them all go. After all, the other Arabs had initiated the conflict by attempting to assassinate the trader, and would have succeeded if not for his unexpected intervention; once he got that point across, he expected swift justice.

Simon's hope of a quick resolution diminished as a dozen more inmates joined the procession, chained to each other in a single line. Many wore scraggly, matted beards and looked so pale that Simon felt well-tanned by comparison, even though his torso had scarcely seen the light of day in years. They stood draped in filthy rags, those who still had them: some wore little more than loin cloths, their emaciated bodies exposed to the harsh light of the Mediterranean sun.

Simon's hopes evaporated when the Romans led the line of prisoners out of the palace and away from the complex of government buildings, weaving along the bustling city streets an hour after sunrise. Kasey walked ahead of him and the Arab behind, at the end of the line, with three guards in the rear, three in front, and two on either side. Even with a weapon and free hands, escape would have proven futile. Perhaps the Romans had a court of some kind in another section of the city. Faint hope took hold....

... and then dissipated as they approached the west gate. Once outside the wall they followed a well-established path, a road not quite up to Roman standards; it wound through a shallow ravine toward the Dead Sea. The bustling city of Moab receded until only the sounds of chains broke the still desert air. Not even a merciful breeze alleviated the increasing heat of the day.

"Simon, where are we going?" Kasey whispered just loud enough for him to hear. "All of our stuff is back there."

"I know," he replied, worry evident in his voice. "I'm not sure where they are taking us. I hoped we would speak to a magistrate or something."

"This isn't America," she retorted. "You of all people should know they don't do things here the way we do."

"They still have laws and courts and procedures," he protested.

They walked in silence for hours until a vast blue expanse of water spread out before them, the lowest point on the face of the Earth—some 1,300 feet below sea level. Simon had always dreamed of visiting The Dead Sea once in his life, but international turmoil made the journey unrealistic. With terrorist activity erupting seemingly everywhere he usually felt no desire to leave home, let alone venture to remote regions of the planet. Still, he could mark this one off his bucket list—though he doubted anyone would believe him when he got home.

Home.

The further he walked the more he realized he would likely never see home again. Kasey was right, of course: all their stuff had been left behind, packed atop camels, unprotected, at the mercy of whoever found it. He wondered what would become of her phone, her computer, his cameras, the iPad that he almost never used anymore—the screen had cracked in the cavern when he employed his backpack to knock a cannibal from the giant mushroom—and he decided he probably did not want to know. He doubted anyone in this time would figure out how to use the stuff, so he guessed it would just get destroyed. His sketchbook and pencils remained in their small satchel, tucked into his tunic, the only belongings he salvaged. If Kasey had not wanted another portrait he would not have retrieved his small but sturdy bag—and consequently he would not have discovered the plot against their protector. The Arab would lie dead in the plaza and he and Kasey would remain at the mercy of assassins—probably also dead, or worse. He had no doubt of his own demise, but feared Kasey's fate as a forced concubine.

A small village hove into view, an outpost manned by soldiers and the few people who serviced them: innkeepers, liveries, smiths, prostitutes, and servants. A dozen shabby structures leaned over the sandy soil in which nothing grew. Simon realized that a posting here amounted to little better than exile, and he doubted the good nature of the soldiers who ground out their time in this forsaken wasteland.

They entered the small settlement, which boasted neither a wall nor a gate, and stopped in the center of town at a modest structure, a one-room shack the size of a garden shed. A grizzled and fat old guard stepped from the entrance as the dust from the procession settled back onto the ground. Scarred and leathery skin bore testament to a difficult life, and his presence here revealed a career that had gone nowhere—worse than nowhere—and here he must no doubt remain until the end. Simon feared him immediately.

The lead soldier and the old guard exchanged words and then several servants appeared from the remaining shacks, bearing gourds of water and loaves of bread. The first of these went to the Romans, who consumed them with arrogant leisure in front of the prisoners; and once they finished the simple meal the first centurion motioned for the servants to attend the prisoners.

Simon and Kasey shared a gourd of warm but much-needed water, and the stale bread tasted better than anything they could imagine after more than a day of deprivation. Two servants hesitantly approached the towering Arab, but he gracefully accepted the scant meal with no trouble and a slight bow toward the frightened and relieved men. He smiled at the irony of the situation.

The break lasted at most fifteen minutes, during which time the prisoners sat together in the shade of a small hovel, drinking and eating, barely speaking to one another. Most had spent weeks or months in the dungeon beneath the palace, probably without uttering a sound in all that time, and now they felt no desire to say a word. Only Simon and Kasey conversed in soft, hushed tones, their faces close together.

"We have to find a way to escape and get back there," Kasey urged. "It may already be too late."

"How can we get free of these chains?" Simon asked. "And even if we did, they would easily catch us."

"Maybe we can slip away during the night," she suggested. "We could be miles away before they even know we're gone."

"The caravan is probably already gone," he reminded her. "Not to mention that we would never get inside the city at night."

"We could catch up to the caravan," she said. "Simon, we have to get our stuff back!" Her voice started to elevate, drawing the attention of the nearest prisoners, but then she regained control of her emotions. "We will never get out of this time otherwise."

"We'll find a way," he assured her.

"I don't want to spend the rest of my life in Ancient Rome," she stated.

"Neither do I," he agreed. "We just have to reason things out, that's all."

"What do you mean?"

"Well, where are our belongings?"

"I don't know."

"On the camels, right?"

"Right."

"Our friend here still owns them… so it stands to reason that someone is keeping them for him," Simon explained. "Our belongings are with his, probably in storage somewhere. Or, if his wife got away—the one who helped you during the fight—she may have everything tucked safely away."

"So… if we escape, we have to take him with us," she realized.

"Of course."

"I guess all we have to do is figure out how to break these chains and unlock these shackles," she sighed. "Any ideas?"

"Not yet," he replied.

But she recognized the determination on his face, which usually meant trouble for whoever opposed him.

The lead Roman called for the prisoners to stand, which they did grudgingly after the employment of whips against their backs; up they stood, chains clanking and feet rustling, to resume the journey. But to Simon's surprise, they moved toward the sea, not northward along the shore; he discovered a short pier that jutted into the deep blue brine, alongside of which floated a wide, cavernous boat, its single mast supporting a primitive sail that hung at a steep angle against its boom. He would not have called it a ship exactly, for it lacked the features he would have associated with such a vessel: decks, rooms, a bridge, windows. Instead, it consisted of a wide open space crossed with benches for sitting, and plenty of storage. But as no fish existed beneath the Dead Sea he doubted they used the boat for any purpose other than the transport of people—and the storage of prisoners. An image of Charon's ferry crossing the River Styx flashed into his mind. The craft looked rickety and barely seaworthy, and he definitely felt no desire to climb aboard it.

"Simon, I don't like this," Kasey said as they neared the gently swaying vessel that spanned fifteen feet at its widest and thirty-five feet in length.

"I know," he replied. A glance backward revealed a very dark and unhappy expression on their companion's face, and Simon felt bad for causing this grief; but he knew in his bones that if he had not intervened in Moab the Empire would have crucified all three of them. Perhaps literally.

The Arab retained his composure and the three frightened prisoners boarded the leaking old vessel that Simon suspected would carry them anywhere but to freedom.

CHAPTER 28

DEATH MARCH

They settled against the aft hull along the starboard side, beneath a narrow platform upon which a crewmember stood steering the boat with a long tiller attached to the rudder. A short, narrow bench protruding from the hull provided respite for the weary travelers, and the platform produced a sliver of merciful shade. Most prisoners leaned silently against the gunwales, too weak from neglect to make a scene, grateful for the rare ability to rest.

Five men handled the old craft: one at the tiller, three to operate the boom and sail, and one to issue orders. They were not Romans, which made sense to Simon; the Roman presence in this part of the world consisted primarily of military force and government leaders and their families. No citizen in his right mind would choose to live in this barren wilderness full of violence and discomforts, surrounded by hordes of savages who resented them and all they stood for. These men owned the vessel and sold their services to Rome, a comparatively easy trade, crossing this length of narrow sea, transporting goods and personnel from one part of the wilderness to the other. It saved the Romans considerable time and expense, kept the prisoners temporarily satisfied and unwilling to attempt escape—they would die in the lifeless brine even if they did manage to break their bonds— and all for a fair wage, which Simon guessed seemed more reasonable to the Romans than to the seamen.

As the creaking old craft drifted away from the dock and into the open water, and the sailors set to work navigating northward, Kasey settled against Simon and rested her head on his shoulder. He became instantly aware of every point where her body came into contact with his, and he thought he would never get used to this feeling that made his heart beat faster and his blood temperature rise; he enjoyed it, of course, and he certainly would never take her affections for granted—but he wanted desperately to feel comfortable and at ease, not nervous and hyper-conscious of every slight touch or movement. He knew she sensed his tenseness, but it did not seem to bother her. She needed the comfort that only he could provide, and in spite of himself he could not let her down.

"We're never going to get away," she whispered. "It's too far now."

"You have to have faith," he replied. "Whatever happens to us is for a reason; we just have to endure until we find out what that reason is."

"I wish I had your faith," she sighed.

Simon wished he did as well.

They sat in silence, watching the barren landscape through a gap in the planking. Most prisoners slept, but Simon could not force himself to join them—nor could the Arab— Kasey, however, closed her eyes and lost herself in the arms of the man who had broken through her icy exterior and found the scared soul trapped within. Simon wondered if he had done her such a wonderful favor after all. If not for him she probably would not be in this mess. He had to find a way to get her out of it.

The Arab stared at the pair of strangers in wonder, his curiosity trumping his anger at the change in his fortunes. By now Rome would have confiscated his property, an easy task considering that most of what he possessed rested atop the backs of his camels—such was the life of a nomad. But he possessed hidden reserves that he could tap when he got back—if he got back. He studied the face of the young man who had saved his life and could not comprehend why he had done so. Could he not understand his fate? Did he not know why the caravan had set forth across the desert, why they had traveled to Moab in the first place? Certainly no one could possess such naïveté? Something about this brave young coward demanded more attention, but under the circumstances he could only look upon the man with growing curiosity instead of contempt. He had cowered in fear that night of the attempted escape, when his mate had stood strong and defiant; he had suffered insults and humiliations at the hands of nearly everyone, including women and slaves; even the young woman taunted him mercilessly. So why had he risked everything to stop the assassination? And then risk his own freedom—for he and the woman certainly could have escaped in the confusion—to prevent the deaths of a few Roman dogs? This inconsistency made no sense. But he knew he had to find out more, especially considering that he did, in fact, owe the young fool his life.

Simon watched the shore recede as the boat turned northward in the center of the narrow lake, achieving two or three knots in a calm breeze that pressed against the softly flapping sail. He didn't sense much of a current in this dead body, and the landscape beyond appeared equally desolate: dried rocks and crumbling sandy soil that no doubt poisoned anything that attempted to grow in it. No one lived here, and even in his own time he knew from maps that few if any towns or cities existed along its shores; it truly was one of the few places in the world that defied life. No wonder the Romans chose to cross it quickly rather than trudge around it.

Hours crept by while Kasey's sleeping form scarcely moved, and few people aboard the vessel spoke, except for the crew and the Romans who conversed sporadically. Five Romans stood in the center of the boat, occasionally drinking water or eating bread, their attention constantly on the chained prisoners resting in the spotty shade astern. Simon studied them, the sweat dripping from their harsh faces, the obvious intelligence in their eyes, and he wondered if they experienced compassion the way he did—if they even knew the definition of mercy. He suspected that the slightest move of aggression on his part would end in a pugio stuck through his belly, and no one would give it a second thought; they would simply unchain him and dump his squirming body over the side to float painfully in the salty brine until death arrived.

The sun hung low in the west by the time the rickety old vessel slid alongside another dock on the north end of the long sea, the sudden clunking of boards and the jostling of the boat rousing Kasey from her deep slumber.

"It's okay," Simon said softly as she sat up, dazed, her bleary eyes reflecting the orange light of the setting sun. "We're at the other side."

"Oh," she said almost inaudibly.

After securing the boat, the sailors moved out of the way while the Romans cracked whips and shouted orders, which everyone but the young couple from the future understood. But they got the message clearly enough: stand and march. The prisoners followed the Romans out of the ship, down a narrow plank to the dock, along the dock to the shore, and then into an outpost similar to the one at the other end of the lake in the land of Moab. He guessed, based on his memories from church and his studies of maps, that they stood on the outer edge of Judea, with Jerusalem to the west and the River Jordan very close by, emptying its cool waters into the Dead Sea, the only part of which sustained life due to the influx of fresh water.

Fresh Romans greeted them; the leader of the previous group exchanged words with the new commander, and then handed him custody of the prisoners. The officer issued incoherent orders and the line of slaves moved toward the outskirts of the small outpost, and for a moment Simon thought they meant to travel on into the night. But to his relief, they deposited the prisoners into an empty stall previously used by horses, but now unoccupied. The horses slept in a newer structure next door.

"At least it's been a pretty easy day," Simon said in an attempt to comfort Kasey as they settled into matted straw for another night's slumber.

"We have to escape tonight," she insisted. "I still have the dagger—maybe we can use it to kill the guards and unlock our chains."

"Whoa," he replied. "Who said anything about killing?"

She grimaced. "Simon, getting out of here will probably mean getting dirty," she said sternly. "I don't like it either, but we have to do whatever it takes to get free."

"Aside from the moral implications," he replied, "think about the practical considerations."

"What do you mean?"

"Suppose one of these soldiers is a direct ancestor of the Carabresa line?" he offered. "Killing one man might prevent your entire family from ever existing."

"I hadn't thought of that," she said, suddenly appalled by her lack of foresight. "Simon, I never intended for any of this to happen; I just wanted to save my sister. It should have been easy. I never considered the ramifications of altering the past. Our presence here might have irreparably damaged everything already. But we have no way to know."

"There are two schools of thought," Simon replied. "The first is that history will unfold pretty much the same no matter what we do. If Bell didn't invent the phone, someone else would have; if Marconi hadn't developed the wireless another inventor would have done it; people spent decades trying to master powered flight before the Wright brothers—they just succeeded first. Most major innovations will happen whether we intervene or not."

"And the second?"

"That stepping on a blade of grass will trigger minute changes, the rippling effect of which will expand throughout the eons and alter every possible outcome from that point forward," he explained.

"I like the first one better," she said.

"Our best plan is to cause as little trouble as possible while we're here and hope our impact remains minimal," he said. "Otherwise it might not be possible to fix the future once we get back there."

"You still hold out hope?" she said, amazed. "It's all we have left," he replied somberly.

In the morning, the line of prisoners continued northward into the fertile valley of the Jordan. The Romans sat astride sturdy black horses, looking down with superiority at the worthless human chattel strung between them; twenty unfortunate inmates forming two parallel lines marched in time to the clopping of horses' hooves, hope driven from their straining bodies.

The heat became unbearable by midmorning, inspiring the newcomers to shed their clothing, leaving swatches of fabric strewn along the sides of the path. Simon lost much of his Bedouin attire, leaving intact the headpiece and a length of airy cotton that draped over his exposed arms. Following Kasey's example, he had opted to wear his faded jeans and green flannel shirt under his new attire, a decision that cooled him considerably. The Romans had never seen such outlandish garments, but made no issue of them.

Kasey similarly shed most of her desert apparel, revealing her equally faded jeans and gray shirt, keeping the headpiece as Simon had. He thought she looked infinitely better in jeans than he did and for the rest of the day appreciated walking behind her.

They marched among trees and lush fields along the banks of the Jordan. Simon realized that somewhere along this river John the Baptist had Baptized Jesus in these sacred waters—or maybe it hadn't happened yet. Perhaps the nativity would not occur for years, or might have taken place centuries in the past; he wished he could find some clue to narrow his current place in time—not just to help Kasey in her calculations, but to satisfy his curiosity.

Frequently the desert encroached on the path, dry breezes blowing chafing sand into their faces. They climbed over rocks and trudged across towering dunes, then picked their way through low scrub brush, occasionally startling a desert fox or a long, lanky hare. They passed small settlements and lonely homes, the occasional town, and in every instance people stopped their work and stared at the hated Romans and the poor souls they marched mercilessly toward doom. Simon saw compassion in frustrated eyes, an impotent desire to help, and he felt bad for them. Probably they witnessed this procession regularly, and each time it reminded them of what they had lost to the oppressors who had invaded their ancient and sacred lands.

The Romans stopped the procession three times the first day, on each occasion allowing the prisoners to drink their fill of warm water—after the soldiers and the horses had slaked their thirst. In the evening the water ration accompanied a loaf of bread purchased from a local baker; it wasn't much, but it kept the prisoners alive—for the most part.

"They're giving us just the bare minimum," Kasey said at the end of the first day as they settled into a manger on the edge of a small settlement.

"Keeping us alive but weak," Simon agreed.

"To get us to our destination but in no condition to fight," she finished.

"Sound strategy," Simon observed. "I wish I knew where we were going."

"Actually, I might be able to help with that," she said, surprising him.

"Don't tell me you've learned their language already," he groaned. "I know you're smart, but that's pushing it, right?"

"Actually, I already know their language," she replied with a thin smile. "I took four years of Latin in high school."

"I guess that's better than my three years of Spanish," he sighed.

"Their accents and pronunciation take some getting used to," she explained, "but I swear I'm starting to understand at least some of what they're saying. I've forgotten a lot in the last couple of years—it really wasn't my best class and my attention was obviously on something else—but some of it is definitely starting to sound familiar."

"This is good," Simon said, suddenly perking up. "You can talk to them, explain what has happened, make them see the mistake they've made."

"I'm not that good," she admitted. "There's a difference between catching a familiar word and holding a conversation. I need more time."

"Let's hope we have it," he sighed.

The next day they covered as much distance as the previous one, but under a hotter sun and with fewer trees to shade their passage. The desert again crossed their way and the constant climbing through ravines and empty gullies took its toll on the faltering prisoners. The Romans, atop their steeds, suffered nearly as much as their human cargo, but in a different way: heavy armor and weapons weighed them down, and they wore virtually no protection from the harsh sun. But they at least maintained easy access to bags of water draped over their horses.

At midmorning on their second day north of the Dead Sea a prisoner ahead of Kasey lost his footing and fell to his knees. The line stopped and the soldiers shouted, cracking their whips; desperate slaves dragged the unmoving man a few feet, but they lacked the strength to carry him further. Seeing that the man no longer maintained the ability to continue under his own power, the lead Roman dismounted from his horse and walked back to where the man had fallen. Kasey expected the commander to show mercy and carry the wheezing and coughing prisoner atop his horse; at the very least offer him much needed water, a few minutes' rest, an opportunity to recover. Instead the soldier removed a key from his belt and unlocked the slave's shackles, setting him free.

Kasey breathed a sigh of relief—until the Roman, flashing a grim look of hate, withdrew his pugio, the short sword, and thrust it quickly through the prisoner's abdomen. The cringing captive groaned and writhed on the end of the blade before it withdrew from his body; the soldier kicked him and he rolled down the side of the dune, arms and legs flailing in a cloud of sand, before piling up on rocks at the bottom of the ravine; the few creatures eking out a living on the edge of the desert would soon feast well. Simon groaned and Kasey turned white as a ghost. Somehow, some way, they must escape from this cruel and oppressive regime!

The march continued in silence, the jangling of chains and the clopping of hooves on packed sand breaking the monotony of the still desert. The sands receded and the narrow road led back into the valley, where the river's influence comforted the weary travelers with an abundance of trees and shrubs and low grass; an occasional breeze softened the midday sun, and the gently trickling current soothed the souls of those who heard it.

But the journey took a devastating turn by mid-afternoon, when the prisoners still had not eaten and only one break had resulted in a decidedly insufficient ration of water. Simon's heart skipped a beat the first time Kasey faltered, and he quickly reached forward to help steady her; only then did he feel inordinate heat radiating from her skin. He suspected sunburn, but the look on her face indicated something else. She moved unsteadily, feet heavy with effort, head hung low, shoulders slumped—and blood trickled from her left wrist beneath the heavy iron shackle.

"Kasey," he said, his voice dry and weak. "Hang on for just a little while longer; we'll have to stop soon."

She didn't reply, but he thought she nodded her head.

The hours dragged interminably for Kasey, who staggered occasionally and once almost fell. Simon stayed close and supported her, desperate to avoid the fate of the man who had succumbed to the strain. He could not even consider the possibility of that dreaded Roman blade thrusting into her body.

As the sun touched the horizon, the procession arrived in a small town on the west bank of the Jordan, where the Romans once more deposited the slaves in a dirty stall previously occupied by horses. Each prisoner received a loaf of bread and a ration of water, barely a pint by Simon's estimation—enough to keep the strongest of them alive. Everyone ate ravenously, with one exception.

"You have to eat," Simon insisted.

"I need sleep," she rasped, her body trembling with chills, in the grip of a fever that, without medicine or rest, would consume her. The wounds on her wrists, scraped raw by the sharp edges of heavy manacles, had worsened throughout the day, flaying the flesh from her arms. Infection set in, producing unbearable pain that Simon could not imagine.

As she lay shivering in the matted hay Simon placed the remains of his Bedouin attire over her feverish body. He supported her head as he trickled water into her mouth and dabbed his own ration onto her flushed cheeks and forehead. He got her to eat part of the loaf before she drifted into what he hoped was a deep and healing sleep. She tossed and turned during the night, but didn't wake. He knew, because he held her until sunrise.

The Arab watched with a mixture of fascination, compassion, and disappointment. He marveled at the young man's devotion to his beautiful mate, the way he cradled and comforted her, attended to her every need in this decisive moment. The Bedouin had watched the strangely dressed and oddly attractive woman as she weakened and stumbled, her condition deteriorating throughout the afternoon; only the young man's attention had prevented her destruction. The Arab shook his head in sadness and settled back into his heap of straw, disheartened by the unlucky turn of events.

He knew the young woman would not survive the next day's journey.

CHAPTER 29

CAPERNAUM

In the morning some of Kasey's color returned, but she remained weak. Simon had sacrificed his water ration to clean the jagged wounds around her puffy wrists, and then pulled strips of torn cloth between her skin and the shackles, to provide a cushion. She looked up at him with fear in her eyes, knowing as well as he did that she would never see another sunset. Loss of blood, infection, fever, weakness—all meant imminent destruction.

"I saved you some bread," he said, softly brushing hair away from her splotchy red face.

"You need it more than I do," she said weakly.

"Nonsense," he replied with a forced smile. "I'm full already. You have to keep up your strength."

"I have no strength," she said.

"Have some water." He revealed the cup a servant had given him the night before, which still contained half its contents. "Drink this." She tried to stop him from holding it to her lips, but he won the battle of wills and she dutifully swallowed the life-sustaining liquid.

The Romans returned after sunrise, refreshed and ready for another day of grueling and tortuous travel. Simon marveled at their stamina, but had to remember that they slept well, ate well, and rode horses. Plus, they carried ample water to drink along the way, a luxury denied to lowly slaves. They expected weaker prisoners to perish during the journey, saving the Empire the trouble and expense of keeping them alive.

Simon helped Kasey onto her feet and she almost swooned from standing up too quickly; she leaned heavily into his steadying arms, her eyes closed and her head pounding. Soon she recovered enough to walk into the sunlight with the rest of her companions.

Neither Simon nor the Arab ever knew how she did it, but Catalina Carabresa, perhaps the strongest woman either of them had ever encountered, marched in line as the procession turned northward out of the small town. She looked down, concentrating on each step, forcing her feverish body to do the impossible, sore muscles and overwhelming fatigue threatening to topple her at any moment; and yet she endured, step after step, mile after mile, groaning in agony. The soldiers watched her, grimly admiring the will that kept her alive.

At midday, after passing several small towns and homesteads, and crossing increasingly fertile farmland, the procession arrived at another substantial body of water, the source of the Jordan, a freshwater lake of much smaller dimensions than the Dead Sea they had left two days earlier. Simon easily recognized the Sea of Galilee, one of the most important places in the Bible—another checkmark for his bucket list.

The lake spanned ten or fifteen miles in its greatest dimension and he could easily make out the far shore from the slight rise upon which he stood along the southern boundary. Sails from fishing boats dotted the clear blue water on a gloriously sunny day, fluffy white clouds floating lazily overhead. The sight filled him with admiration for nature's exquisite beauty... until clanking shackles and tugging chains returned him to the horror of reality.

By this time Kasey was nearly finished. Her legs still moved, but delirium had overtaken her and Simon supported her wobbling form from behind. He spoke encouraging words, but could not tell if she heard them. A single misstep would prompt the Romans to permanently end her suffering.

"You have to hold on," Simon urged, his arms numb from constantly supporting her weight. He knew she tried with every ounce of determination she possessed, even in her drifting state of semi-consciousness, and he could not help but admire her inner drive. But he also knew it could only last so long.

When the inevitable finally happened, Simon's heart nearly stopped. He lost his grip on Kasey and she stumbled over a rock, dropped to her knees, and sprawled onto the ground, her nearly lifeless form no longer moving, her matted and sweat-soaked hair escaping from the headpiece and spilling across her back and onto the dry soil. The procession staggered to a halt amid the sudden shouting of Romans, who brandished their whips in an attempt to get it moving again; then, upon realizing the cause of the delay, the lead centurion dismounted and strutted to the back of the line, where the strangely dressed young man and the enormous Arab stood over the unconscious woman. The Roman did not smile as he withdrew his short sword, for he admired the strong will and determination of this sick and dying slave. But... he had a job to do.

A second guard arrived with the key to her chains, but before he could get close enough to unlock her shackles and free her from the line, Simon stepped defiantly between him and the suffering woman he had vowed to protect. Angry words issued from the commander, words Simon thankfully could not understand, but he held his ground, crossed his arms, and glared obstinately into the harsh and bewildered face of the stout old soldier who certainly was not accustomed to this kind of behavior in a slave. Scowling, he raised his pugio and threatened Simon with it, but the brave young coward stood firm and resolute, determined to either save Kasey or die with her.

To his surprise—and extreme relief—the Roman backed away and inexplicably sheathed his weapon, his eyes wide, his expression one of surprise mixed with satisfaction. Simon felt a hand on his shoulder, and when he turned he discovered Kasey standing behind him, her lithe body stiffly erect, her breathing irregular; she fought to remain conscious as the color drained from her pale face, fever and pain crippling her. But she hung on, desperate to stay alive. And the Romans, in their way, acknowledged her strength.

"I've never been more proud of anyone in my life," she whispered hoarsely. She kissed him on the cheek before resuming her place in line.

An hour later they stopped to rest in the resort city of Caesarea on the west shore of the Sea of Galilee.

Simon had heard of this city, built by Emperor Tiberius in the first century. The slaves entered through the west gate and arrived at a large and popular well near the center of town, after passing a market similar to the one in Moab. People stopped and jeered and occasionally hurled rotten fruit at them. Simon did his best to shield Kasey from taunts and abuses, but a rotten pomegranate got through and splattered against the side of her head, causing no harm but making a sticky mess that oozed down the length of her tangled and once vibrant tresses. Simon wiped away what he could, and while doing so caught a shower of dates in the back of the head, irritating him more than a little. But it sparked the ire of the soldiers even more, and when they waved their swords and shouted orders into the crowds the abuse immediately stopped. In other towns and settlements the people had looked upon the prisoners with pity, compassion, sorrow; but here, in a city built by the emperor and inhabited by Roman citizens transplanted from the heart of the Empire, the people looked with scorn at anyone who defied their civilization, as these worthless slaves must have done. They deserved contempt, suffering, and slow death in the harshest manner devised by human minds. Simon's good disposition and willingness to understand the other person's point of view took a serious beating in this environment, and he wondered if any Roman existed who shared his values, or who even possessed a conscience.

The taunts ended by the time they stopped at the well, and the instant the line came to a halt Kasey collapsed into Simon's arms. He lowered her to the ground and supported her head in his lap, his hands caressing her fiery cheeks. He had never felt such a fever, her delirious mind no doubt struggling to retain its sanity. Kasey, barely conscious, her chest heaving for every gasp of air, trembled and shivered violently. But the wave of sickness passed as she rallied again, her eyes focusing on Simon's concerned face, the fog lifting from her weary mind. Sweat dripped from every part of her suffering body.

"I'm so cold...," she whispered, a disheartening statement in the middle of the burning wilderness.

"I'll keep you warm," he said, knowing he no longer possessed the ability.

A servant brought bread and water. Simon used most of his ration to mop the sweat from her face in an attempt to alleviate the fever; but when he looked down and saw the blood-soaked bandages he had earlier wrapped around her now impossibly swollen wrists that bulged around her manacles, he knew without a doubt in his heart that she would be dead in a matter of hours, if not minutes. He tried to control his emotions, if only for her sake, but he felt tears welling in his eyes. Turning away to wipe them, he caught a glimpse of the Arab, who looked upon the pitiful scene with obvious sadness.

The powerful Bedouin settled next to Simon and offered his own ration of water and bread, which Simon gratefully accepted; he forced as much of it into Kasey's mouth as she would take, and to his relief she consumed a fair amount, particularly the water, which would do more than anything to sustain her. Simon peered intently into the trader's face and saw the compassion that resided there, the same goodness and curiosity he had observed upon their first meeting; he wished he could understand this enigma of a man, who should harbor feelings of anger and revenge toward him but displayed only kindness and generosity even in the most extreme circumstances.

The Romans lingered in the square for the better part of an hour, far longer than in any of their previous stops, and Simon wondered if they waited for Kasey's benefit; he knew they had grown to admire her, and he suspected they did not want to see her perish. Though none of them approached, the soldiers glanced at her frequently; only when they observed her recovering strength did the commander issue orders to keep moving.

Simon's ministrations had a positive effect on the woman he adored, for her fever abated slightly and some of the pallor left her face; but he had bought her, at most, a few hours—harsh, cruel, difficult, agonizing hours—but she gratefully accepted them. With enormous help she got unsteadily to her feet and moved her legs with an almost inhuman strength of will. She had kept him alive for hours in the subterranean river; now he had to keep her afloat in this equally perilous environment. But she needed days of rest and an antibiotic, which he knew would not arrive for nearly two millennia. Part of him died each time he looked at the struggling form of the woman he had saved—and who had saved him— and as he walked, tears streamed down his face. He desperately did not want to lose her!

The Romans marched their slaves out of the resort city and continued northward along the coast of the Sea of Galilee, climbing to spectacular heights in the surrounding hills, affording breathtaking views of the serene and peaceful lake: fishing boats plied the calm waters, birds arced overhead, quaint and picturesque towns adorned the landscape, rolling green hills contrasted against the deep blue surface. A fresh breeze cooled and relaxed the souls of struggling convicts as they heaved along the sometimes steep and uneven road, their bodies on the verge of collapse, none more than the beautiful young woman staggering only minutes from death.

Wending generally eastward along the northern shore, the road led to a bustling town half the size of the one they had left a few hours earlier. It lacked the monumental structures and decoration of the Roman resort, but retained a local flavor that Simon guessed resulted from countless generations of influence, a place where Rome had little presence. On the outskirts of town shepherds attended flocks of sheep, and here most people walked rather than rode atop horses or camels, which remained conspicuously absent. Numerous paths and roads led toward the settlement, an ancient fishing town that Simon knew existed as a small ruin two thousand years in the future.

They entered Capernaum from the west and passed by traders working in the fish market, the prime commodity in this region. The streets appeared clean, the town open and airy, permeated with a feeling of calm peace. He couldn't explain it: something about the place seemed different, almost cheerful. Simon imagined the inhabitants lived well and happily, accounting for his generally positive impression. Passersby smiled and nodded to each other, and no one threw rocks or rotten vegetables at the prisoners; on the contrary, he saw expressions of compassion and pity that had defined the countenances of people along the Jordan north of the Dead Sea.

In a few minutes the procession reached the well at the center of town and stopped for a much deserved break. Kasey fell in a heap at Simon's feet before he could get into a position to catch her, and she hit her head on the cobblestones below; she barely felt the impact. Simon turned her over and saw the scrape on her temple, a new bruise starting to form, blood seeping from yet another injury. Her breathing, already labored and difficult, became increasingly shallow. The fever had returned, growing to inestimable levels, her once fair cheeks blazing with heat. She could scarcely focus her eyes on him, and speaking occurred only with pain and intense effort. Simon had never seen anyone suffer so miserably and so bravely, and it broke his heart to know that she would never leave this fishing village alive. Her swollen wrists bulged around her shackles, the rags soaked with blood, but she no longer even felt the pain; her arms and legs had long since gone numb.

Simon rested his head on her chest and tried to hold back the sobs, but failed miserably. He felt the Arab's hand on his shoulder, offering comfort, and he appreciated the gesture—though nothing could alleviate the pain and guilt he felt for having brought her to this ignominious destruction.

"I'm sorry," he cried, his tears soaking into her gray blouse, now torn and stained from the long and difficult march. "I wish I knew what to do."

"Just live," she whispered, her voice barely distinguishable from the exhalation of breath. "Save her...."

Even at the last she thought only of her sister, the one true beacon of light in her lonely and disappointing life. Maybe it was best that Kasey's journey ended here, so that now she could join Carista in the Great

Beyond, where they could spend the rest of eternity turning Heaven on its ear.

"God," he whispered. "Please help her...."

The Arab's hand, resting firmly on his shoulder, suddenly gripped it and pulled him back, away from the dying woman who meant everything to him.

"What th—?" he tried to say, but suddenly realized his predicament.

The Arab held him firmly while three Roman soldiers approached, sadness on their faces, one bearing the key to unlock Kasey's shackles. The other had yet to draw his sword, but he hardly needed to: the still form would be dead in minutes, her last gasping breath forcing its way out of her lungs.

"No!" Simon screamed as they freed her from the chains that bound her in life, and dragged her toward the other end of the square, where chains that bound her in death would soon be forged. He could not tell if she still lived, but he writhed and struggled to get free of the overwhelmingly powerful Arab, desperate to reach her side. He kicked and flailed, but to no avail. His strength ebbed as hope drained from his soul; Simon dropped to the dusty ground, sitting at the Arab's feet, tears flowing freely.

He watched as an unusually tall man in a white robe, an undertaker of some kind, knelt over Kasey's body, his hand extended out to touch her face. Simon could only imagine what they would do to her, and he could not watch anymore; he buried his face in his hands and lost himself to the misery and suffering of the most devastating loss he had ever endured.

The Arab sat next to him, moved by his companion's deep emotion; he felt sadness at the loss of so beautiful and vibrant a woman, someone he now would never get to know. Simon thought back to the moment he had first laid eyes on her, struggling beneath the rapist in the science lab, a lifetime ago, and remembered the coldness in her eyes and in her heart. Her entire life had been that same struggle, and only the coldness had kept her alive; he had melted the ice and found the fire within, and now she lay dead on a dusty street in a remote town in an obscure part of history as a result.

He had done her no favors at all.

Simon slumped in the dust, his body quietly convulsing, emotions flowing in torrents he could no longer control; even the Romans stood silent, disappointed by the death of the strong and beautiful young woman they had come to admire. They had given her at least a shadow of a chance, allowing extended rest, larger rations, and no whip, but it had not amounted to enough. At least she had met her end in a town, where people could attend to her corpse with dignity instead of leaving it for the animals to consume. It wasn't much comfort.

Simon didn't know how he would continue on, what he would do, where his own corpse would end up; her dying wish—for him to live, to save her sister—seemed impossible. Only she could operate the device, which needed repair, and he certainly did not possess the mind to attempt it.

A growing commotion emanated from the far end of the square, punctuated by sighs and gasps; several clay containers hit the ground and shattered, spilling their contents into the dry earth. Simon paid it little heed, exhausted from emotional collapse; no doubt Kasey had finally succumbed to the agonies of death and those gathered around had witnessed her last pitiful struggle. He could not bear it.

His head buried in his arms, increasingly oblivious to the world around him, Simon did not hear the approach of footsteps, many of them, and if they did register in his subconscious mind, he regarded them as irrelevant: the passage of pedestrians, the arrival of guards to begin the march yet again. Only when the Arab gripped his shoulder did he retreat from his clouded daze and look up at the scene before him, which had changed dramatically.

Dozens of people stood quietly in the square, soldiers included, all staring at a single lone figure that approached Simon as he slowly got to his feet; hands covering gaping mouths, they cleared a path, and for a long moment the young man from the future could not comprehend the situation. He glimpsed awed expressions, heard quiet murmuring from the crowd, and felt wonder in the air—it was almost electric.

He hardly recognized the lone figure walking toward him along the channel opening in the crowd; his heart pounded as Catalina Carabresa stopped before him, a strange and mysterious look of joy and peace spread across her vibrantly beautiful face. Tears of happiness welled in her gray eyes and streamed down her dirty but healthy cheeks. A glance at her wrists showed no indication of swelling or infection or injury; even the bloody knot on her temple had vanished, as if by a miracle....

Kasey threw her arms around him more tightly and with more passion than ever before, and he melted into her embrace, stress and tension and fear evaporating from his soul. The crowd laughed and applauded and cried out phrases of joy the young people could not comprehend, though they understood the sentiment.

For a long time they held each other, even after the bulk of the crowd dispersed; the soldiers left them alone, scratching their heads in wonder, extending the rest period while they came to terms with what they had witnessed. Simon could not think, did not want to try just now—he only knew that the woman he loved had come back to him, and his heart nearly burst with joy.

The Arab, as stunned by the event as anyone—perhaps even more so—stood behind Simon and watched, wishing he could understand these two strange individuals who had fought so bitterly a week ago and now displayed a love he knew could never be broken. The mystery frustrated him.

Eventually Simon and Kasey parted slightly, still holding each other but with enough distance between them that Simon could get a good look at her. The strength had returned to her weakened body, her color now normal, all signs of death driven away by a force he could not comprehend. Even medical science could not have achieved this end in so short a time.

"It's a miracle," Simon gasped, his eyes red and his face nearly as white as hers had recently been.

"Yes," she agreed with a warm and dreamy smile. "It was...."

Her melodious voice rang out strong and clear; it possessed determination borne by inner peace and a sense of truth that had not existed in her before. She had changed, here in this fishing village along the shores of the Sea of Galilee, and at the moment he could not fathom it. But she was alive and perfect and that was all that mattered. They embraced once more as the Romans made the decision to keep moving, but this time the journey hardly seemed a struggle at all.

The path led them for a short time along the docks, where another commotion broke out as the men on a fishing boat struggled to clear their net of a most remarkable and unprecedented catch: the tattered remains of an enormous, waterlogged mushroom.

CHAPTER 30

FAITH

The procession stopped at a town a dozen miles north of the Sea of Galilee, where the Romans and their prisoners spent the night in relative peace. Everyone stole frequent glances at the remarkable young woman who had miraculously survived death in Capernaum; it gave the slaves hope—and filled their captors with fear. No one could explain her unexpected and sudden recovery, except for Kasey, who walked in peaceful and serene silence for most of the afternoon. The Romans, facing a power they could neither understand nor control, realized that this young woman whom they admired might also prove a serious threat, and so she bore watching.

Simon attempted to get the truth out of her, but she remained frustratingly tight-lipped, lost in meditation, perhaps trying to make sense of the event in her own mind before discussing it with him. So he waited patiently, allowing her time to work things out, without crowding her; she greatly appreciated that.

The grueling trek wound into the hills north of the great lake in the land of Galilee, eventually stopping for the night in a town on the shore of a second, much smaller lake nestled in a shallow valley: a quiet, unremarkable settlement, like so many others they had entered and exited. They never learned its name.

"It really was a miracle," Kasey explained once they had settled in for the night on a bed of hay, next to their Arab companion.

"It does seem that way...," Simon replied skeptically. "But there has to be a rational explanation. Nobody just recovers like th—"

"Simon, you're not hearing me," she said slowly, placing a long, slender finger on his lips; a warm smile of patience and understanding spread across her lovely face. Her eyes practically glowed with new life. "It happened."

"What happened?" he asked, frustrated. "It looked like you died."

"Maybe I did," she said dreamily. "Maybe I had to."

"Kasey...."

"I heard you beg God to save me," she said softly, her bright gray eyes peering deeply into his.

"Yeah," he scoffed. "Then the Romans dragged you away."

She smiled. "It was the best thing they could have done."

"I don't understand."

She took his hands in hers and searched her energized brain for the right words, obviously wanting him to share in her new joy but afraid of scaring him.

"Your prayer, I think, may have saved me," she started. "God is real and watching us and working through us every day."

"You don't believe in God," Simon reminded her.

"Someone very special made me see otherwise," she said. "You were right about me: I was angry at God for taking my sister, and you forced me to accept that truth. It was the first step."

"The first step to what?"

"To the restoration of my faith," she smiled. "Simon, He is here."

Something had certainly rattled her; he knew that near-death experiences often jostled a person's latent religious feelings, which sometimes inspired them to over- compensate for years of spiritual neglect. He wondered how long it would take for her new awareness to fade.

"I know," Simon replied. "God is everywhere."

"And here... specifically," she repeated.

"I still don't follow you."

"He healed me," Kasey said, her face radiating an inner light that startled him, in truth frightened him, but at the same time intrigued his curiosity. "In every way that a person can be healed: mind, body, and soul."

"Kasey, what are you saying...?" But he suspected he already knew her answer, as impossible as he found it to believe.

"The man you saw leaning over me, the undertaker coming for my body," she began, "the one you could not bear to watch...."

"I thought I had failed you," he said.

"But you didn't," she assured him. "It was Him, don't you see?"

It was too much for his weary brain to accept, no matter how she tried to prepare him for the words.

"I saw His face, felt His hands, and for the first time in my life I experienced perfect and total peace," she exclaimed. "He radiated pure love and hope, and in those few seconds I knew the meaning of truth and the purpose of life. Simon, all that we have endured and suffered are nothing compared to what He will sacrifice for us, and all of it is according to His plan. You were right about that. Oh, I wish you could have seen Him, touched Him, heard the sweet sound of His voice—" She broke off very suddenly.

"What is it?" Simon hung on her every word.

"Simon—I understood Him," she gasped. "Either He spoke English or somehow He transmitted His thoughts directly into my brain."

"Was it King James English?"

"No, silly," she laughed. Only she could laugh under these circumstances, chained to a line of slaves in the wilderness of Rome's most backwater province 2,000 years from a home that no longer existed. Either she had snapped, or the joy she felt was the most powerful force ever to enter her life. "He cares for us and loves us and wants us to succeed; He told me that."

"Really?"

"He said our journey would be a long and difficult one, but most worthwhile ones are," she continued. "He told me to be faithful and to trust in the Father and all would be revealed according to His Plan."

"That's... incredible...," Simon said slowly, the gravity of her revelation sinking into his labored mind. But it was impossible, the fever-induced hallucination of a woman on the edge of death, unaware of the difference between dream and reality! He had seen the man, from a distance and from behind, but he could not verify the truth of her words. The whole concept irritated him: Kasey, the devout atheist, who denied even the existence of God, had touched Christ and now believed with a faith infinitely stronger than he could ever have, while he, the professed Christian, felt the doubt and skepticism of a nonbeliever. How could that be? He should have experienced profound joy and happiness at the life-changing event, rejoiced in the miracle that had saved her body and soul, and thanked God for restoring her to him—not only alive and healthy, but filled with inner peace and tranquility that had already altered her personality for the better; instead he felt disbelief, doubt, and even disappointment that she had met the actual real Jesus and he had not. Jealousy encroached on his soul, and though he fought it he could not deny its presence. All those weeks of professing his faith, of annoying Kasey with his blind belief, of wantonly dropping the name of God without any real understanding—had it all been simply to convince himself of that which he truly wanted to believe but could not fully accept? Her recovery and the hope it represented filled him with more happiness than he had ever imagined, but his rational mind needed an explanation more substantial than simply "miracle." Perhaps it was easier for God to work on an angry heart than on a skeptical one.

"You're having a hard time with this," Kasey realized. She nestled close to him, resting her head on his chest as his arms encircled her, preparing for a comfortable night's sleep. "That's okay; I know it's a lot to take."

"I just... I wish... if only I could have met Him," Simon sighed. "There are so many things I could have asked, so many answers He could have given me."

"You want proof that everything you believe is right," she smiled, easily sensing his difficulty. "But you know that's not how faith works. I once told you that faith is a crutch used by the weak-minded to support their irrational beliefs; but the truth is that faith requires strength more powerful than any other force on Earth. A man who has faith can accomplish anything, and even if he fails he can be a source of strength and hope for other men who come after him."

"You're becoming a philosopher," Simon smiled weakly.

"I've become exactly what you have always wanted and needed," she replied, kissing him on the cheek, "and all because of your faith and prayer."

"My faith is not as strong as yours," he admitted. "I have doubts."

"That's because your rational mind is getting in the way of your heart," she smiled. "But I know your faith is stronger than you think it is. C.S. Lewis once wrote that a person's initial reaction to something is often more telling than his later, deliberate response after careful reflection; your instinct, your heart, called on God in your greatest moment of helplessness, and that speaks volumes about the strength of your faith."

"I was desperate not to lose you," he whispered. "Don't most people call on God in moments of stress?"

"Maybe," she replied. "But I know beyond doubt that your faith, whether you accept it or not, has saved us both." She hugged him tightly, her warm body pressed pleasantly against his.

"Why would an atheist read C.S. Lewis?" he suddenly asked.

"I wasn't always an atheist," she said. "I lost my faith for a while… but you helped me find it again. And nothing is ever going to change that."

They lay quietly, until Simon thought Kasey had drifted off to sleep. He massaged the weary muscles of her back and shoulders, whispering, "thank you," in a quiet prayer he thought only God would hear.

Kasey tightened her hold on him, hugging him warmly, and then they both fell into a deep and rejuvenating sleep.

The next morning, shortly after dawn, the Romans roused their slaves and started northward again. Simon could not guess their destination, and he wondered if the soldiers meant to march them all the way to Rome; but he knew such a journey would by necessity require passage on a ship, and their path forged through mountains dozens of miles from the nearest seaport.

Kasey walked with the strident energy of a freshly rejuvenated woman, a smile on her face, a gleam in her eyes, a bounce in her step, and a sense of joy entirely contrary to everyone around her, slave and Roman alike; chained prisoners looked at her in awe and drew strength from her, their own will to survive bolstered by the encouragement that her survival gave them. The Romans rode with a mixture of fear and admiration, pleased to see her alive but afraid of her impact on the other captives. They needed their slaves weak, on the verge of collapse, to prevent breaches of discipline—hence the meager rations and grueling marches through difficult terrain. Kasey's newfound strength could upset that delicate balance.

An hour north of the peaceful town on the lake's tranquil shore, their fortunes changed in a way neither of them could have foreseen. High atop a ridge, above the village in which they had spent their restful night, the procession arrived at a crossroads. Simon had seen many such intersections along the northward journey, leading toward destinations unknown. But at this one they stopped. The soldiers huddled together, making Simon wonder if they had gotten lost in the wilderness without a map or road signs. He doubted even the GPS on his lost phone would be of much use in this remote corner of history.

"What's going on?" Kasey asked. No settlement or village existed in the elevated mountain pass, and so she saw no reason for the procession to stop.

"Not sure," he replied, equally confused. It was not like the Romans to allow extra rest periods. "Maybe they're trying to decide which way to go."

"You think they're lost?" she smiled.

"You know how guys hate to ask for directions," he sighed. "No convenience store in sight."

The lead centurion issued several sharp commands and immediately his subordinates set to work unchaining half the prisoners; they drew their puglios, ready for any man willing to attempt escape. Simon could not guess their intentions, so he and Kasey simply looked at each other, confused by the sudden action. It took only a moment, however, for them to realize the truth, and they both breathed a sigh of relief.

The Romans culled half the slaves to form a new line, which they intended to march westward along the perpendicular road, while everyone else continued north. Simon had initially feared that the soldiers might kill the weakest prisoners and leave them here to rot, but so far no one had shown signs of collapse; Kasey's miracle had rejuvenated them.

"There will be fewer slaves traveling with us," Simon whispered. "And a lot fewer Romans. Maybe we might have a chance of escape after all."

"Do you really think so?"

"At night, if we're quick enough," he replied. "The Arab can easily overpower four or five of them."

"We would need the keys," she pointed out.

"A minor detail," he grimaced. "I'm working on it."

"Work faster," she smiled. "Tonight's a good night to get out of here."

"I'll do my best," he said. "We can be back in Moab in a week if we push ourselves. Then we can pick up the trail of our gear."

"You never give up hope, do you?"

"Sometimes...."

"Never lose that."

Their hands touched and something electric flowed between them, a feeling they both embraced: a sense of goodness, of hope, of warmth. Their souls drew precious life from each other and basked in the glory of mutual joy.

Then two swarthy Romans grasped Kasey by the arms, yanking her away from Simon, while a third unfettered her wrists and ankles.

"Simon...."

He saw sudden fear and confusion spread across her beautiful face as they realized their new predicament.

"No!" he cried out, leaping forward, his chains rattling loudly, tugging at the Arab behind him. He knocked a Roman to the ground and shoved a second one, sending him staggering backward into a third. He grasped onto Kasey and held her as reinforcements rushed to surround them. Hands tugged at his shoulders and arms, but he held tightly as Kasey instinctively pressed her face into his, kissing him with passion and fury; the surprised Romans paused to watch, but their leader shouted a crisp command that shattered the moment.

Six soldiers dragged the young couple away from each other while four others stood by with swords drawn. Simon and Kasey struggled against overwhelming force, until someone punched Simon in the side of the head, eliciting a scream of anger from the young woman and a wave of dizziness from her lover, effectively ending his resistance.

"Simon!" Kasey shouted as four centurions dragged her kicking and flailing toward the new line of slaves, "Don't give up! Promise me you will save her!"

"I promise!" he called back, tears welling in his eyes as the fog lifted from his brain. He struggled, but the

Arab held him back, shaking his head firmly, clearly indicating that they could not win this fight and would only die in the attempt. "I'll find you!" he shouted over the din of chains and shackles and horses and scraping footsteps on the packed road.

The frazzled Romans, some with fresh bruises and at least one sporting a bloody nose, maneuvered the feisty woman into position at the head of the line and secured her to the other slaves. This new procession, consisting of ten prisoners and five centurions, turned northward and resumed the long, grueling, interminable march toward their unknown destination.

Simon and the Arab, at the end of the original line, suddenly found themselves facing west, in the direction of low but treacherous mountains that separated the inner valleys from the Great Sea on the other side.

"Kasey!" he cried, but a soldier slapped him on the back of the head.

The two lines moved away from each other, but through the ringing in his ears he heard four words that would forever change his life, that would see him through the most perilous and hopeless period of his existence, that would etch themselves into his heart and give him the strength and courage to survive every deadly misfortune that blundered into his path:

"Simon, I love you!"

And then she was gone.

CHAPTER 31

TYRE

The fabled city of Tyre emerged from the distance, nestled along the eastern shore of the Great Sea. Built by the Phoenicians and conquered by the Romans, it had grown into one of the most important trading centers of the ancient world, the major crossroads of east and west, north and south. From here goods flowed to and from Rome: everything from purple dye to casks of wine, from governors and centurions to citizens and slaves. Much of the Roman Empire passed through this strategically positioned port along the Lebanese coast, halfway between Egypt and Anatolia. Yesterday, from the hills overlooking the sea, Simon had glimpsed the expansive port hugging a natural bay, buildings spreading inland like a flood of brick and wood. Hundreds of ships floated like toys in the harbor, some displaying enormous striped sails and others barely discernible against the flickering reflections of choppy waves. Competing vessels vied for precious dock space, holds full of fish from the morning catch, or carrying grains and goods from points west. Dwarfing the largest cargo ships, half a dozen imposing Roman galleys loomed like sentinels throughout the harbor; manned by hundreds of slaves chained to their hated oars, the ships of death stood higher and longer and wider than even the most capacious merchant vessels.

Simon had not spoken since his separation from Kasey two days ago—not that anyone could have understood him. His heart felt empty and hollow, his soul half dead; her absence quelled any hope that he would ever find a way out of this ancient world.

The city gate towered overhead as long lines of people waited to pass through it, as they had in Moab so long ago. But these people seemed different somehow, more varied and haggard, desperate in their natures; Simon saw none of the kindness and compassion in their faces that he had observed further south; nor did they curse and mock the prisoners, as had the inhabitants of Caesarea. These people did not notice the human chattel, so accustomed were they to the sight of slaves and the general misery of humanity.

A Roman centurion from the city met the commander, spoke in friendly tones, shook hands with him, and turned to issue sharp commands to someone in the crowd. A path immediately cleared and the slaves marched through the gate and into the city. Simon barely noticed the merchants and vendors lining the inner walls, peddling their wares with loud voices over the humming crowd; swarming, seething, jostling masses of people created a din of disparate sounds, a symphony of chaos that numbed the ears. Obnoxious fumes emanated from fetid and putrid sources that disturbed the eyes and deadened the olfactory lobes; he stepped over and sometimes through them, but his own puny body smelled so disgustingly horrific, covered in a week's worth of sweat and grime, that he neither noticed nor cared. A short beard had sprouted on his strained and weary face, a fact that would have surprised his schoolmates who often derided him for his apparent inability to grow one. None of it mattered as the Romans led him and his companions through the miserable ancient city, chains clanking and feet dragging, shackles digging into their flesh. Simon cared only about the woman he loved, the woman who had despised him a few days earlier and who would have continued to dismiss him if not for their subterranean adventure; he could scarcely believe the sudden change in their relationship, the brief joy they experienced, only to have it ripped asunder by the demented hand of Ancient Rome. That last shocked look of fear on her face would remain burned into his memory for the rest of his life, and her last words to him, her unexpected confession of love, would forever ring in his ears.

Already he hated Rome.

The crowds thinned as the centurions led their slaves deeper toward the interior of Tyre, as they had in other cities, seeking the inevitable square that contained a well. The Romans had not fed or watered their captives all day, and the sun had long since begun its descent toward the western horizon.

As expected, the square soon opened up, filled with men and women and servants patiently waiting their turn at the well; most carried buckets or amphorae to carry back to their homes or their masters. Simon saw Roman citizens and soldiers milling about, and at least two other processions of slaves—swarthy and mean-looking men, powerful beasts barely contained by their shackles and chains. Strained centurion faces betrayed relief at the prospect of relinquishing their charges.

But the lines of slaves did not stop in the square. Simon's companions moaned in pitiful agony, their eyes trained on the precious source of water now denied to them. Simon, distracted by more important considerations, kept walking, his weary brain constantly seeking a solution to his impossible problem.

Only when the procession halted and he inadvertently bumped into the slave in front of him did he finally look up and discover the end that fate had provided for him. Slaves gasped and cried, their once hopeful voices filled with dread and fear, the prospect of survival now entirely stripped from their minds.

Their destination loomed more than two stories above the choppy sea and stretched at least two hundred feet from stem to stern, far larger and more voluminous than Simon had expected. He recalled artists' renditions of galleys in art history books, based on the scant remains of actual ships; descriptions in ancient texts; and primitive mosaics on the dilapidated walls of excavated ruins. None of them matched the grandeur of this colossal warship that dwarfed everything else on the ancient seas. Shipbuilding had developed by necessity after the Punic Wars, and supremacy on the sea would have remained paramount to uninterrupted trade throughout the Mediterranean empire. But never had he imagined that the Romans, as ingenious as their reputations suggested, could have constructed vessels on such a scale.

This trireme, one of the flagships of the fleet—with three banks of oars along either side—had to hold at least one hundred and fifty oarsmen and a powerful complement of sailors and soldiers. The embolus—or battering ram—jutting from the bow and barely discernible at the waterline, was carved with the head of a water god; it showed signs of action, some of the metal covering scraped and at least one chunk of wood broken off. The hull, long and sloping beautifully up and inward from the waterline, excited him with its magnificent lines and imposing decoration: bold tongues of red, orange, and yellow flames, meticulously painted against sky-blue panels, stood out starkly in the early evening light, intended to inspire fear in the heart of the enemy.

The mast rose fifty or sixty feet from the upper deck, supporting a massively furled sail to rival even the great clipper ships of the nineteenth century; simple rigging supported it forward and aft, and ratlines angled up from the gunwales to a small crow's nest at the top, where lookouts remained on duty day and night—a job he certainly did not want to get stuck with. Most of the upper deck remained clear and unobstructed, with the exception of a low structure astern, containing several compartments, atop which stood a primitive version of a poop deck. The captain and the officers lived either in the low structure or beneath it in a series of small chambers at the back of the galley; empty oar holes ended about twenty-five feet from the back of the ship, indicating space for living quarters. Similarly, the front twenty feet at the tapering bow contained either quarters or storage for the supplies necessary to survive a long sea voyage, though Simon knew that voyages on these vessels rarely exceeded a few days or a week. The Romans, fierce and unstoppable on land, retained an almost inhibiting fear of water, forcing them to sail in sight of land, stopping at virtually every major port along their route. This fear had largely dissipated as navigation techniques improved, but Simon would note underlying stress and nervousness at the approach of every storm and unexpected ship.

He watched as lines of slaves carried sacks of food and boxes of supplies on their backs like beasts of burden, disappearing into an opening in the side of the ship, others emerging empty-handed as they crossed rickety planks that connected the massive vessel to the wide dock. Re-provisioning might take hours or days, depending on the expected length of the voyage, and Simon hoped it would give him a chance to rest his weary body.

A different kind of soldier emerged from the ship, similar to a centurion but dressed for naval service, and he met the man at the head of Simon's line of haggard and trembling slaves. The two exchanged words before sharp orders rang out, resulting in what Simon saw as a changing of the guard: naval centurions took the place of their landlubber counterparts, and Simon did not feel that his situation had improved. They looked, if anything, meaner and tougher, more disciplined, battle-hardened, and ready for war. Scars and wounds, some fresh and some very old, indicated action this ship had already seen. Soldiers led the slaves to a plank that angled up to the main deck. Simon gulped audibly as he staggered forward, feeling the strong hand of the Arab on his back to steady him, and stepped onto the quavering wood panel. The ship seemed to stretch to infinity in either direction, encompassing the whole of the universe, an apt description considering the twist of fate that had brought him to this miserable conclusion: very soon nothing would exist for him outside the confining beams and boards of the solidly constructed hull.

He ascended the ramp on numbed legs and might have fallen into the water if not for the supportive hands of his large friend. His feet found the solid and sturdy main deck, which spread out like something from a nightmare. In a single dreamy glance he saw rigging and railings, men tending to their duties, and the imposing structure that occupied the aft quarter. Most unnerving were the square grates spaced in the center of the deck, one forward and one aft of the towering mast, beneath which slumped more than a hundred hopeless slaves, chained to oppressive oars, now withdrawn into the ship for the stay in port. Simon glimpsed their hunched bodies in the dappled sunlight that filtered down to them, saw the wretched faces of zombies barely alive in deprivation, their lives having ended the moment they stepped foot on this ship of doom. He and his companions, most of whom had made the journey from Moab, stood on deck as replacements for those who had perished during the previous voyage. Fifteen men in chains meant at least that many had died, and perhaps that many more would succumb during the next mission.

Simon looked away from the misery below and scanned the horizon, long shadows of boats and ships stretching out to the orange haze of sunset. Under different circumstances he might have recognized the scene's beauty and serenity, but now his lonely heart saw only despair and torment. Pinkish light reflected from white buildings along the docks, a picturesque vista that rivaled anything he had ever observed. He wished Kasey could see it; but that would mean suffering her final days as a galley slave with him, chained to an oar, the brutal strain sapping the life from her body day after day as she fought to stay alive. He had to believe that her path had taken her in a better direction, one that would lead to safety—or at least a means of escape.

The line moved again, toward the back of the ship, where a narrow stairway descended beneath the wide red-painted grate. The slaves in front of him disappeared into the maw, and he held his breath as his turn approached, his heart pounding and sweat soaking his exhausted body. He stole one last glance at the world above before he vanished into the foreboding darkness and gloom of what he now knew to be the end of his journey through time.

Chapter 32

Night Terrors

K asey marched northward for days, but not without incident. She missed Simon more than she would have imagined, the emptiness in her heart rivaling that which she had felt for Carista in those difficult months after her death. But at least Simon still lived, and that provided hope that one of them might escape this nightmare alive. She knew she would never see him again, that Rome would keep them apart for the rest of their lives, imprisoned on opposite ends of the Empire; but her newfound faith intervened as she remembered the calm and peaceful words spoken to her by the most important man who had ever lived, and the hope He inspired allowed her to continue undaunted, confident in the belief that He would guide her through the troubled days ahead.

The procession resumed its previous path, forging through mountain passes and crossing beautiful valleys, stopping once a day for water and bread, and then settling in for the night in a remote village, where she slept alone on a bed of straw, surrounded by slaves too tired to cause her harm.

The first night she barely slept, tossing and turning in discomfort, her chilled body missing the warmth of the man she had so quickly grown to love. Her last words to him had escaped her throat on impulse, but she did not regret them; she felt glad to have gotten the burden off her chest, out in the open, where she could deal with it. Simon had been right about a great many things, particularly her inability to let people into her life for fear of losing them. Simon had become as important to her as Carista, and in the end—she had lost him.

She could not allow him to stay lost.

On the second day the Romans ventured beyond the Holy Lands of the New Testament and into Syria. They entered a wide river valley between imposing ridges of mountains that ran roughly northeast, parallel to the sloping Mediterranean coastline. Small towns and settlements dotted the fertile landscape, teeming with people and animals and wide tracts of farmland.

Fueled by faith and hope, Kasey never faltered as the line of slaves plodded along the narrow road, sometimes climbing slopes that winded everyone around her, even the Romans on their horses; she drew strength from the actions that drained it from every slave and centurion, a fact that did not go unnoticed. On scant measures of bread and water the young woman thrived, displaying indefatigable energy that exhausted everyone who watched her.

On her second night without Simon the Romans stopped in a small village inside the valley along a rapidly flowing river. It consisted of a dozen dwellings, several public buildings, corrals for horses and live-stock, and a low wall to keep out creatures that might otherwise disturb the inhabitants during the night. As the horses utilized the stables, the slaves slept under the stars, along the wall closest to the river. They spaced themselves evenly, their hated chains con-necting them even in slumber. Kasey hadn't noticed how cold the nights had become, because Simon had done his best to keep her warm, and now she shiv-ered; the soldiers did not provide their captives with blankets or straw to trap in heat, and she wondered if that was another way to keep them weak. A person could expend a lot of energy shivering for seven or eight hours, not to mention fatigue from lack of sleep. She suspected that more than one slave would meet the end of a blade by the time the next day ended. She intended to not be among them.

Kasey gazed up at the stars, listening to the sooth-ing rush of the river on the other side of the low wall, contemplating the means for her to escape from this motley band of thugs and crooks. Her favorite constel-lation, Orion, indicated the onset of winter, explaining the chill in the air. Closing her eyes, concentrating on Simon's face, she tried to force warmth into her body. But it didn't work. Opening her eyes she discovered the stars had vanished, replaced by the silhouetted figure of a hideous face with crooked teeth and leering eyes.

He was on her before she could react; a meaty hand clamped over her mouth as his masculine bulk pressed into her squirming body. She writhed and struggled, tried to push him away, but he swept her puny arms aside and straddled her hips. A punch to the stomach rattled her chains and drove the fight from her body as air expelled from her lungs; she gasped and heaved while the vile man released his hold on her mouth, recognizing her inability to sound an alarm. He painfully squeezed the heaving mounds of flesh beneath her shirt, grinned wickedly in the faint starlight, and clumsily reached for her dirty, sweat-soaked jeans.

Straining for breath, unable to voice even a whimper, Kasey lay in shock as the attacker pulled her jeans around her knees. She glared up into his evil eyes as he quickly removed his own lower garment, his masculine region mercifully hidden in shadow, and prepared for the conquest he knew no one would ever discover. This beautiful female prisoner, unprotected and alone under the moonless sky, represented nothing less than a gift from the gods. She could not understand the language and no one could understand her, so she certainly could not explain to anyone what had happened.

Forcing the fear from her panicked brain, Kasey remembered the gift Simon had given her in another tense moment two weeks earlier. The rapist shifted his weight to get a better position, and in that moment Kasey's hand darted between her thighs, where she kept her secret weapon strapped. The tiny golden sacrificial dagger that Simon had lifted from the temple of cannibals deep beneath the earth, and then tossed to her during the fight in Moab, sliced through the air and found a mark somewhere on her attacker's body. She expected a cry of pain, but instead heard only a shocked and labored gurgle as his hands reached up to his throat; his tensed body fell in a heap beside her.

For an eternity she did not move, forgetting the cold air as hot, adrenaline-infused blood coursed through her body; her hands trembled, her heart pounded, and her mind raced at the speed of thought. A wave of nausea accompanied intense fear.

What had she done?

Long silence ensued before she dared to turn her head to see the carnage she had wrought. Her gaze met the dull, open eyes of the Roman centurion lying next to her, a wide, gaping slash across his neck, the ground soaked with his blood. Ghastly muscles contracted his pallid face, eyes staring out from lifeless sockets. His hands clutched his open throat, covered in sticky warm blood.

She had never seen a dead body before, with the exceptions of her sister and the unfortunate slave killed by the Romans on the first leg of the march—and never had she seen one so grisly and close-up as the man she had just murdered in cold blood. She wondered why they called it cold blood; the thick liquid oozing onto her arm felt quite warm.

They would crucify her. Simon had emphasized the danger of harming a Roman soldier, or citizen for that matter, and had risked his life to prevent the Arab from making that dreadful mistake. He also expressed the possible repercussions of killing people so far back in time.

"I hope you're not one of my ancestors," she whispered. "Or one of Simon's."

What would happen? Would he simply cease to exist? It had not wiped her from existence, so that boded well. But what impact would it have on the future two thousand years from now? Would George Washington never be born? Or Adolph Hitler? Or the inventor of Super Glue? Of course, how bad could that be? The only thing it really sticks to is your fingers.

How would the centurions react to what she had done? She understood fragments of the language, but not nearly enough to carry on a conversation or to explain how or why she had defended herself. And perhaps none of that would prove relevant: for all she knew it was perfectly within the rights of soldiers to exercise their depravity on slaves with no standing before the law.

She had to dispose of the body and hide the evidence. It proved less difficult than she would have thought under the circumstances, though it did require some luck and effort. Thankfully, he had arrived unarmed and without armor, which allowed her to work in silence, though her chains rattled softly and she occasionally tugged on a fitfully sleeping slave; even had he awakened, he would not have said a word against her the next day.

Positioned by the wall, a plan formed in her increasingly alert mind as she listened and watched for any indication of discovery. She feared the unwanted arrival of a patrolling guard to catch her in the act of covering up her crime. But if this worked, no one would be the wiser. Kasey heaved the dead centurion onto the low wall and positioned him flat along its length. On the other side, the shimmering black river flowed briskly as it rounded a sharp bend. A steep slope descended from the wall to the wide current. She hoped it was deep enough.

With the strength of fear, desperation, anger, and adrenaline, she heaved the dead weight over the side, heard a dull thump as it hit the ground, and watched it roll unsteadily out of sight. She heard a distinct splash over the steady rush of the current. Hunched low over the stone wall, Kasey peered into the darkness for some indication that her desperate plan had failed. But her attacker had vanished into the night, as if by magic.

Using the dagger and her hands, Kasey hastily dug up a patch of earth and spread it over the blood stains that had soaked in next to her body; with a little luck no one would suspect what had happened during this fateful and disturbing night.

She settled down and peered at the stars, the chill no longer affecting her. Had the man carried the keys to her shackles she would have simply left him behind and followed the river downstream, leaving her captors wondering what she had done and where she had gone—with a head start of at least seven hours. But a thorough search of his tunic had revealed nothing useful. So she remained trapped, but certainly not helpless. She had proven capable of the greatest crime, and though she felt guilty as she justified the necessity of her desperate reaction to his advance, she also felt strangely empowered. Simon and Carista depended on her for their survival, so she could not allow the pawing and violating hands of Rome to stop her from getting back the people she loved—the only two people worthy of her affection. But did that justify taking a human life? Did she have the right to kill another human being, even in self defense? She had not meant to kill him, only to drive him away. A modern jury would find her guilty of involuntary manslaughter, and probably not even that, considering the circumstances. Not speaking the language, she would have a difficult time explaining anything. She made a conscious decision to avoid trouble from this point forward.

But trouble made no such vow in reference to her.

With the small but deadly weapon once more tucked safely between her thighs, hidden by the loosening fabric of her jeans, which no longer fit snugly due to the weight she had lost through illness and starvation, Kasey slept fitfully, her subconscious mind plagued with nightmares from which she escaped only through awakening with a start, covered in cold sweat. Each time she drifted, the phantasms returned, mocking and terrifying her, until she forced herself back to consciousness. Exhausted and trembling, the last time she jolted awake the stars had faded into twilight as the sun announced its arrival from behind the eastern ridge. Kasey thanked God for allowing her to survive the night, with a plea for forgiveness concerning her nocturnal activities—and for the soul of the demented beast who had forced those unfortunate actions.

Shortly after sunrise the Romans appeared, concern on their faces, as they searched the compound for their missing companion. They interrogated the slaves, skipping Kasey because they knew she could not understand them. The situation became particularly tense when they stopped beside her, standing on the churned and patted earth, the only perceivable evidence of what had happened during the night, though they failed to recognize it. To her horror, she spotted blood on the wall, a detail she had not thought to cover up, as she could not have seen it in the near darkness; only a few dry spatters dotted the rough stone surface, thoroughly soaked into the porous rock, but close scrutiny might have revealed the presence of a struggle.

These Romans, despite their fierce reputation, lacked advanced analytical skills, particularly in the area of forensics, and so missed the obvious indications of their friend's fate; to be fair, it never occurred to them that he could have died at the hands of a slave woman during the night, and so they searched not for evidence but for him. Shaking their heads and shrugging their shoulders, baffled by the mystery, they gave up the search with the assumption he had deserted his post—but without any of his scant belongings, which he had mysteriously left behind.

Kasey breathed a sigh of relief as the lead soldier sounded the order to march, and she followed along as before, above suspicion. She knew now that the Romans could be defeated, that they possessed weaknesses like any other men, perhaps more so because they felt emboldened to commit acts of depravity with utter and complete impunity. No one suspected that a delicate, light-haired girl from the future could fight back and survive against the most powerful empire the world had ever known.

They would soon feel the full fury and indomitable will of Catalina Carabresa.

CHAPTER 33

INFERNO

Days turned to weeks and might have dragged into months for all Simon knew. He watched men die, broken under the strain of the oar, sick and diseased, fatigued and fevered; frail and sinewy forms collapsed in heaps of bone and sweat. Ineffective whips flayed soft flesh from nearly dead bodies. All around him lingered the smell of death, the rot of decay, the utter hell of hopelessness.

And yet he did not perish. Kasey's last words kept him alive with a will strong enough that even the Romans had proven unable to break him. On the first day the new captain visited his slaves, spoke harsh but undecipherable words, and singled out Simon as a threat. It stemmed from a wayward glance on Simon's part to a question he could not answer. In response, a guard stung him across the back with a whip and would have continued the beating had not the powerful and intimidating Arab intervened with a few sharp words of his own. The beating abruptly stopped.

At the captain's instructions the hortator, the sturdy, grizzled old man who beat the drum at the front of the rowing chamber, thumped on the tightly stretched skin covering the deep bowl between his knees. In rhythm to the beat, the slaves pushed and pulled their oars, propelling the colossal warship away from the bustling port city of Tyre. Those who could not keep up felt the sharp lash of the whip, inspiring greater effort than many of them could sustain.

After a long and difficult mile the beat increased, forcing more strenuous exertion from the already half-dead slaves. But Simon knew what the Romans intended; he had seen the movie, remembered the defiance in Charlton Heston's eyes, the strength of hope. He was no Charlton Heston—more of an Errol Flynn, perhaps—but he kept pace with the drum, though his chest burned and his lungs begged for fresh air. In response to a command from the captain, the beat increased again, with noticeable results. Oars swung in unison, but a few moved erratically; the weakest slaves failed to respond to lashing whips. One slumped over his oar and another fell sideways onto the deck, grasping his chest and moaning in agony.

The beat increased again. Simon strained and heaved, taxing his muscles, his arms and legs numb from the exertion; more slaves faltered, crying out their last desperate groans as they fell upon their oars. But Simon focused on the stern face of the cruel captain and pressed onward with strength borne by the sheer will of Kasey's faith and his promise to her.

The beat increased.

The hortator pounded his hands into the quivering skin stretched across the drum, sweat pouring from his forehead and dripping down his face. Simon could no longer feel his arms, yet somehow the oar kept moving in time with those around him. A dozen more slaves fell from their seats, in a couple of cases the recoil of their oars colliding with their heads and chests, rendering them mercifully unconscious. The torture continued amid cracking whips, the desperate cries of slaves, the distant splashing of water, the interminable pounding of the hated drum....

The captain issued a command and the activity ceased. One hundred and fifty slaves suddenly slumped over their oars, while another twenty would never again bother with the effort. Simon stared at the captain as he walked past, forgetting his fatigue as he studied the man's harsh face; their gazes met, and through the hatred Simon saw something well hidden: fear, compassion, intelligence, even wonder. He had expected only haughtiness and loathing. The sudden connection of minds startled them both. The captain kept walking, uttering a few low syllables, and disappeared up the steep stairs at the back of the chamber. Guards set to work unchaining the dead and the near dead, preparing them for unceremonious disposal.

That was how a captain weeded out the weak from the strong, allowing him the ability to judge what he could expect in the heat of battle. This one seemed disappointed.

Simon rarely saw the captain in the days after their first encounter, other than the occasional glimpse of his shadowy form standing above the grates, looking down at the miserable human engine strenuously propelling the ship. More importantly, the powerful Arab sat at the oar immediately behind him, occasionally speaking in low tones, though the effort at first baffled Simon.

But soon he realized the importance of the effort: the Arab wanted to communicate, to teach him the language of his fathers, so that Simon could understand the world around him. The lessons began on the first day, shortly after the exhausting test. He learned the name of his friend and companion, the man who had saved his life and proven his loyalty on so many occasions: Achmet Bey. The two would have shaken hands at their introduction if not for the heavy chains securing them to their oars.

Simon gratefully accepted the friendship the powerful man offered. He looked forward to a time when he could actually communicate and explain some of the mysteries that had obviously baffled him. But he knew better than to give away too much information about the future, lest he compromise the development of the entire world—assuming, of course, that he hadn't already.

They had taken away Simon's jeans and tattered shirt on the first day and replaced them with a loincloth that embarrassed him; but as he worked his monotonous oar in the sweat and grime and heat of the rowing chamber, he learned to appreciate the lack of clothing. He might have chafed unbearably inside his jeans, and that was the only thing he could think of that could make life as a galley slave even worse. Kasey certainly would have mocked him for his humiliating new attire and for that he appreciated their separation; but he realized he would rather suffer humiliation with her than respect without her.

He missed her more than anyone he had ever known.

The slaves rowed in twelve hour shifts, overlapping by four hours, which meant that six times a day some of them, in small groups, descended into the depths of the hull for a much-desired rest break. At any given time, thirty or forty lounged in the small space below the rowing chamber, barely high enough for an average person to stand—provided he ducked his head. A few small lamps provided enough illumination in the bilge to keep the slaves from stepping on each other. Bathroom facilities, something Simon decided was a hallmark of civilization, proved rather lacking in the bottom of the ship, comprising as they did of a few buckets shared by nearly two hundred men and changed only when the stench reached the upper deck.

In spite of the obvious hardships, Simon gained immeasurably from his time on the galley. The Arab spent every waking moment drilling words and meanings into Simon's head, starting with the names of familiar objects. Though not as smart as Kasey, Simon learned at a rapid pace, picking up the basics of the language in only a few weeks, making him possibly the only college student in his dorm who could speak English, Spanish, and ancient Arabic—though of the three Spanish represented his weakest effort.

Another consequence of his voyage on the Inferno manifested in a subtle way that he might not have noticed had Achmet Bey not pointed it out after a month of steady rowing: his arms had nearly doubled in girth, along with the musculature across his chest and shoulders. The slight bulge around his middle vanished entirely, revealing solid abs that even he had never seen before. He wondered what Kasey would say about the change in his physique; maybe she preferred his puny form so that she could more easily dominate him.

"Unlikely," Achmet Bey said when Simon posed the question in one of their earliest conversations in which each of them could actually understand the other. "A woman respects strength, of mind and body."

"She fell in love with me before I grew muscles," Simon reminded him.

"She fell in love with the strength of your courage," the Arab explained. "She will be pleased that your body has caught up with your spirit."

It felt good to talk after endless weeks of lonely rowing. They spent their days at the oars learning to communicate, and in the rest periods they had not relented until Simon knew the language. How would he explain this to anyone back home? Even now he thought in terms of getting back there, when deep down he knew the impossibility of it.

"Will I ever see her again?" Simon asked.

"No," Achmet Bey said. His voice sounded like a cross between Morgan Freeman and Barry White, and occasionally he expected the man to break into song—which, thankfully, he didn't.

"Once we get off this ship we'll go back to your oasis, and then we'll find her," Simon assured him.

"For someone who learns quickly, you are not very intelligent," the Bedouin sighed. "You will leave this ship only in death. Besides, we have no reason to return to that oasis."

"Why not?"

"My wives, my servants, and my trusted companions all betrayed me," he lamented. "What the Romans did not confiscate they will have plundered. If I go back they will kill me. And you as well."

"Kasey and I had belongings too," Simon said, "things we have to get back."

"Your packs are lost," the Arab assured him.

"Well, I guess we'll deal with all that when the time comes," Simon replied. "In the meantime, I should thank you for what you did for us."

A puzzled look suddenly crossed his friend's dark face.

"You know, saving us from the desert, feeding us, clothing us, accepting us into your tents," Simon reminded him. "Your hospitality was very generous. You were a good friend to both of us, and I just want to say I appreciate it."

The trader sighed and smiled, then laughed heartily, surprising everyone around them in the rowing chamber.

"What?"

"You truly are a gift from the gods," Achmet Bey said. "It was never my intention to be your friend."

Now Simon displayed the puzzled look.

"I took you to Moab to sell you in the slave market," he laughed. "I intended to keep Kasey as a concubine."

"Oh." Simon said. "Then why help us the way you did?"

"To keep you content," the Arab replied. "I knew I could get a good price for you, and I knew how glorious she would be once she realized her place. That was the extent of my interest in you."

"I don't think so," Simon argued, surprising his friend. "I mean, sure, I guess all that's right, but you were curious about us."

"Certainly. But I would have gotten answers from her… after you were gone."

"Oh."

"Don't feel bad," the Bedouin trader smiled. "I no longer plan to sell you."

"Gee, thanks."

They moved their arms in time to the steady beat, propelling the Inferno at a slow but respectable clip somewhere in the Mediterranean Sea; over the last month or more, Simon had lost track of time as they rowed from port to port, and his beard had filled in thickly.

"What changed your mind?" Simon finally asked. "About helping us, I mean."

"You did," he replied. "I could not fathom why a coward I was preparing to sell would risk his life to save mine. You would have been much better off had you allowed them to assassinate me."

"Yeah, Kasey didn't quite get that either," Simon recalled. "But you did save our lives, regardless of your intentions. I had to do something." It occurred to him that perhaps the Arab was supposed to die treacherously at the behest of his wives, and his intervention had altered the past. What repercussions would result from his hasty actions thousands of years in the future? Of course, if not for his and Kasey's presence in the desert they would never have made that particular journey to Moab in the first place, which would have denied the conspirators the opportunity to carry out their plan. But they had obviously planned it for some time, and might have implemented it on another trip....

Simon closed his eyes and forced the thoughts from his mind. He hated time travel! How did Kasey manage her impossibly complex calculations? She had to be either a super genius or completely insane: it was a fine line.

"I didn't understand the situation," Simon sighed. "Had I known what you intended, I might have slipped out with Kasey and disappeared into the crowd."

"No," Achmet Bey smiled. "Your sense of honor would not have allowed it. You reacted the way you had to, as we all did. Your character is one of strength and honor; you could no more allow a friend—perceived or otherwise—to suffer a fatal blow than the sun could refuse to heat the desert sand. It is your nature. And for it I owe you my life and my loyalty. You are, perhaps, the one true friend I have in this world."

Simon didn't know quite what to say. He had never been good at making friends. Perhaps true friendship required life and death circumstances to test the mettle of those involved, to determine who proved worthy of it. Simon had proven himself to Kasey, and as a result she had allowed herself to fall in love with him; and then he had demonstrated selfless courage to this ancient stranger, earning his loyalty. Perhaps he had truly grown during his adventures after the end of the world.

It gave him the courage and strength to keep moving forward.

Weeks crept by while his mind and body developed at an increasing pace. Only occasionally did a slave succumb to the rigors of the rowing chamber, and as long as Simon gave no indication of trouble the guards left him and Achmet Bey alone to develop their communication. It occurred to him that he would have to learn Latin in order to understand his captors, because at the moment the only person with whom he could converse was his only remaining friend.

In three months, two weeks, and four days chained to his oar Simon Foxx learned ancient Arabic and the very basics of Latin, while Achmet Bey picked up a healthy dose of English; at the same time, his body developed into a powerhouse of strength, rippling cords of muscles bulging across his arms, shoulders, and chest. Body builders of the future would scoff, but for him the improvement remained dramatic.

His fortunes changed the day someone spotted a sail on the horizon, the unmistakable mark of a ship headed directly for the Inferno.

He braced for the inevitable, and hoped that somehow, for Kasey's sake—and with the help of God above—he would survive the encounter.

CHAPTER 34

MARCONIUS

Kasey marched at the end of her slave line, ahead of the mounted soldier that brought up the rear of the procession. No one had discovered the body from the previous night's altercation, nor had any sleeping captives or Romans seen or heard the attack, the defense, or the cover-up. She had gotten away with it, cleanly and neatly. Not that she wanted to make a habit of killing Romans; but if that was what it took to escape, she would not hesitate to butcher them all, one by one. They had waged war against her and Simon by imprisoning them unjustly and torturing them through relentless marching, and in war one killed the enemy.

They led her ever northward while she analyzed the situation. Only four guards remained, too many for her to fight—though the Arab could have easily taken them out. She required more stealth, subtlety, the element of surprise; perhaps another one would attack her in the darkness of night, expecting an easy conquest. But she could not count on that. She had to find some means of escape so that she could locate Simon and get him out of this place.

Of escape she had no doubt. Her mind labored over what to do once she got away. Should she track down the man she loved and break him out during the night? Or should she return south to Moab and search for her cell phone? With it she might prevent their suffering and misery altogether.

The next night passed without incident, as did the one after it. Then the road turned away from the more easterly line of the river, following the contours of low mountains that rose up in the west, separating the widening plain from the Mediterranean Sea on the other side. Eventually a break in the mountains formed a wide pass, with rivers flowing relentlessly toward the sea twenty miles away; when the road climbed a ridge, she glimpsed the hazy blueness far out on the horizon. It gave her hope. For her the water meant relief and sanctuary, a place of comfort where she felt as at home as the average fish; she knew that in the water she could hide and escape and survive longer than anyone else. But it would take a miracle to get her there.

She had no trouble believing in miracles now....

In spite of her hopes, the procession crossed several fast-moving streams, leaving behind the tantalizing pass, once more putting a long ridge of sharp mountains between her and the sea. From time to time she smelled the salt air as it wafted in on an unexpected breeze, keeping her spirit alive, fanning the hope that burned in her soul.

In the town of Hamath, a walled settlement a week out from Galilee, the centurions met up with a fresh garrison of soldiers, newly arrived from Rome, dismayed by the outpost some bureaucrat had chosen for them. Explaining the mysterious disappearance of the soldier and the generally understaffed nature of the expedition, the commander had little difficulty recruiting four more centurions to accompany them to their ultimate destination—with the proviso that they would take on half a dozen more slaves rotting in Hamath's dungeon.

Frustrated by the extra security, Kasey brooded as six more bedraggled men in ragged loincloths fell into line behind her, the stench of death permeating their frail forms. They meant more obstacles in her escape, but she would find a way. Nothing less than the fate of the world depended on it.

She noted the astonished, gaping look of a new soldier as he stared at her in unabashed awe, disbelieving the presence of so beautiful a woman marching in line with worthless slaves. She knew she had seen better days, with tousled hair, no makeup—not that she wore much anyway—dirt on her face, ill-fitting attire torn and stained with everything from blood to sweaty grime, and the strain of the march apparent on her countenance. Nevertheless, to a soldier who had spent weeks on a ship followed by countless days tromping through the outlying wilderness of the Empire's furthest reaches, without so much as a glimpse of a woman, she probably looked pretty appealing. Not exactly much in the way of a compliment, but she suspected that if she played him right she might finally find that avenue of escape.

Waiting for the right moment, she looked quickly away, feigning bashfulness. Younger than most of the career soldiers she had seen, he stood taller, better proportioned, and strangely handsome; curly black hair framed a pleasantly angular face with strong jaws, dimpled chin, and brown eyes set beneath a dark and deeply furrowed brow. Perhaps thirty, he gave the impression of innocence, even naiveté, certainly a sense of compassion that his companions lacked; she imagined that the other soldiers ridiculed him for his softness of character, but she further imagined that he shrugged it off as good-natured ribbing. If she could turn him to her side, perhaps find a way to communicate the circumstances of her capture... might this seemingly intelligent young officer take up her case and assist her in some meaningful way?

The slaves continued north out of Hamath, in the ancient land of Syria, and followed the well-traveled road to their unknown destination. She got the impression that the object of the long march lay relatively close, judging by the increasing numbers of travelers on the road, both coming and going: long caravans of people on horses, camels, and mules, though relatively few that she would have described as Bedouins like the ones she and Simon had encountered far to the south. A major trading center must lie ahead, and she wondered if it meant the end of the line for her. Would they put her in a cell or auction her off in a slave market? Or worse—force her into a harem. That seemed unlikely; at least, she had never heard of Romans operating harems.

A few hours out of Hamath, the handsome young soldier moved his horse close enough to attempt conversation, quickly realizing that she could not understand most of what he said. She had, of course, picked up a fair amount of the language from listening to it for two weeks, and even though what she had learned in high school sounded different from the reality of this ancient world, enough of it overlapped to allow her a general understanding of basic words and phrases; the pronunciation and accent threw her off at first, but she rapidly compensated.

He introduced himself as Marconius and slyly passed her an extra ration of bread when he thought no one else was looking. She smiled and gratefully accepted the precious gift, which accompanied an increased serving of water at their next stop. She spoke to him in English, a language that baffled him, so that he could recognize her foreign nature; he smiled and she saw the wheels turning in his head. Just like the soldier by the river, he wondered whether this woman had the ability to speak out against him if he tried anything....

But Marconius settled on a different approach, inciting the derision of his comrades. At the afternoon stop, he dismounted from his black steed and cautiously approached her, conscious of the eyes both of his fellow soldiers and the nearby slaves, any of whom could pose a threat if he dropped his guard. He spoke to her in kindness, obviously drawn to her unexpected beauty. He saw beyond the dirt and grime and sweat, through the matted light brown hair and torn, stained clothing, and recognized vast potential in her bright gray eyes and shapely feminine curves; her face mesmerized him and she smiled inwardly at his inability to look away from her. She had often noticed Simon doing the same thing, but she did not want this man to get as intimate as the man she had grown to love; only Simon could study her face closely enough to produce a portrait in his own hand, and the memory of his effort warmed her soul.

Marconius gave her water and bread, strengthening her body, an act that he hoped would benefit him later. Other slaves looked on in envy, their dull eyes unable to display any emotion other than sadness. Kasey understood occasional words and phrases, the gist of which amounted to questions concerning how such a beautiful woman had ended up offending Rome grievously enough to land in the wilderness chained to a line of condemned slaves. She could not answer, of course, so she smiled, drawing him in deeper to her purpose. He smiled in return, showing perfect white teeth, and assured her that if she behaved and cooperated he might be inclined to intervene on her behalf. She wondered what he meant by "cooperate". But that would come later. At the moment she had, if not a friend, an ally, someone to protect her and champion her cause.

She hoped she wouldn't hurt herself on this double-edged sword.

The procession stopped for the night at a walled village a few miles from their destination in a wide mountain pass from which she could see a large and bustling city straddling a river by a lake in the distance. Exhausted and hungry, Kasey settled into a bed of hay, still chained to her line of slaves, prepared for a fitful night's sleep. The town afforded them a series of mangers while the horses grazed and slept in a nearby field, so at least they did not have to sleep out in the open.

Servants brought the usual scant rations of stale bread and warm water, but in the process they purposefully skipped Kasey. Her blood started to boil at this obvious punishment until Marconius arrived with a smile on his handsome face and food in his strong, masculine hands. He knelt in the dust beside her and offered a handful of grapes, a small block of goat cheese, fresh bread, and a cup of red wine, which she eyed ravenously. He looked at her with amusement and reached out to smooth back her matted hair, revealing more of the lovely face that mystified him. She did not resist his touch as she carefully consumed the rare and precious food that rejuvenated her body and soul.

He spoke in soft tones while he caressed her cheek and neck, enjoying the happiness his gift had brought her. Kasey knew he intended to seduce her, in spite of disapproving scowls from his comrades, and she wondered how many women in his life had disgraced their honor for a few sour grapes, a hunk of salty cheese, and flat wine. He would, of course, have to do better. When he cupped his hand over her bare shoulder, where a sizeable portion of her shirt had torn away, she recoiled. Marconius spoke again, an imploring quality in his voice, sadness in his deep brown eyes, and a slight quivering of his thick lips.

Kasey smiled and turned back to face him, wiping cheese crumbs from her mouth. His tense body relaxed a little. His hand returned to her shoulder, but she shook her head no. A flash of anger illuminated his features for a shadow of a second and his fingers dug into her soft flesh. And just as quickly the moment subsided and he returned her smile, removing his hand from her body. He got the message, and so did she. This man had every intention of conquering her, and she had every intention of putting up a fight.

Marconius left her alone the remainder of the evening, and Kasey only half-slept that night for fear that he would visit her in the same manner as the other guard a few nights earlier. She did not want to kill this man, nor did she wish to submit to his obvious fantasy. The only answer lay in escape.

By dawn she realized that she had, in fact, drifted into a relatively deep sleep, but remained unmolested. As much as she hated the prospect of another long day's march, she felt glad to have the night behind her again.

Marconius secretly passed her half a loaf of bread and a small canteen of water before the march began, and she worked on them for most of the day. The Romans led their captives through a narrow pass and into a long and beautiful valley that stretched from the upper corner of the Mediterranean Sea to the northeast into Anatolia, what she would know in the twenty-first century as Turkey. Several wide rivers fed a pristine lake in the center of the valley, to the southwest of which sprawled a city the likes of which she had not seen in this remote era of history. Her protector called it Antioch, one of the largest and most important trading centers in this part of the world.

From high up in a mountain pass, Kasey saw thousands of structures teeming with life, spanning both sides of a major river, all contained within massive irregular walls. The place made Moab look like a primitive village full of simple huts. Antioch exuded wealth and progress, wide avenues bisecting the city and arched bridges connecting the two halves across the river; buildings towered over the streets, casting long shadows across neighborhoods; tens of thousands of people swarmed within the walls, trading and living and working, while thousands more cultivated rich farmland in the fertile valley. Long lines of people descended on the city from multiple directions while others moved away, traders and travelers seeking their fortunes.

They arrived late in the afternoon, after a leisurely march along five or six miles of good road—an easy journey after the hardships Kasey had already endured. She fully expected to land in a dank and fetid dungeon for the night, and was therefore surprised when the Romans stopped in a small grass-covered square near the center of the city—a park with trees and squirrels. Sheep and goats grazed obliviously, but they hardly posed a threat. Kasey began to realize that perhaps Antioch was not, in fact, the final destination; where were they taking their slaves?

She noticed a raised platform on the other side of the square and remembered a similar structure in Moab, where Bedouins bought and sold their slaves. Suddenly she understood her fate, and the fate of all the half-dead men chained to her for so long: a lifetime of servitude, probably deep within mines or some other equally dangerous job fit only for the lowest forms of disposable life. Kasey suspected that she had only one more good night with her companions before they all went their separate ways tomorrow, most of them to die horribly in a very short time.

The situation called for desperate measures.

Marconius brought her more food, this time in the form of dried beef, better wine, and a small bowl of dates. Kasey decided to reward him for his efforts, so she did not react when he caressed her shoulder. She inched imperceptibly closer, smiling, suddenly willing to enjoy his company, but with enough reservation to prevent suspicion on his part. She thought about Simon and what he would think of her intentions, whether he would approve of this tactic; but she did it for him, as a means of getting away from this misery and back into his arms—besides, she was at war with Rome and could not feel bad about casualties.

The evening faded into night and Marconius left her alone for a few hours to resume his duties. Kasey rested and watched the stars as they slowly appeared, one by one and then in clusters, starting with Venus in the glowing colors of sunset. Soon Orion watched from high overhead, the hunter looking down at her with apparent approval as she formulated a plan in her head. She knew there would be no going back.

Marconius returned around midnight and he did not disappoint. Unlike the previous soldier, he showed restraint; he brought a blanket rolled up under his arm and a large container of wine, with which he obviously intended to breach her fortifications. Kasey smiled as he settled in next to her, whispering something she could not quite comprehend, though she got the impression that her compulsory cooperation meant assistance on his part. She played along.

Nodding her head in feigned understanding, she allowed him to caress her cheek and shoulder, his strong hands massaging the tension from her tired body. He probed beneath her shirt, smoothing his fingers across her ribs and onto one of her breasts, surprised by the undergarment that thwarted his effort; sports bras would not come into existence for a couple of millennia, and for a moment he didn't know how to combat the unexpected obstacle. Instead he simply held his hand over it while he moved his handsome face closer to hers, pressing her lips in a warm but awkward kiss that left both of them less than satisfied. She desperately did not want to betray Simon, and Marconius easily sensed that her heart was not in it; but that hardly mattered. He would have his pleasure, and if she wanted to live, she would endure it, ultimately growing to accept him and come to terms with her place as his property.

His hands groped along her body, exploring regions no man had ever touched, and while on some level she found his attention stimulating, she felt fear and disgust in equal measures; even Simon did not touch her with impunity. But she had to play her part until the opportunity presented itself.... Marconius eased his solid, muscular body atop hers, both hands groping and fondling her back and shoulders while he persisted in the increasingly uncomfortable kiss that made breathing difficult. Kasey attempted to put her arms around him as a means of reassuring him of her willingness, but her softly rattling chains restricted her movements, allowing only a partial embrace.

Realizing her difficulty and now confident in her submission, Marconius released his hold and sat up, his dark eyes peering into her bright gray ones. He sensed her fear and trepidation, the trembling of her beautiful and desirable body, and knew that she would give herself to him, that this weak woman, with no hope of survival, would do anything to stay alive.

He smiled with satisfaction as he reached into his tunic and removed a single key, the one object in the universe that Kasey would not have hesitated to kill for; her heart skipped a beat as the young Roman fool leaned over and unlocked the shackles on her wrists, freeing her from the bonds of slavery so that she could more easily return his twisted affections. He mistook her grin as one of anticipation, of pleasure at his advances, as she reached her hands across her bare torso, her shirt having opened to reveal her flat stomach and heaving bosom restrained only by the black sports bra that separated her from his ravishing paws. He watched, mesmerized, as Kasey unfastened her loosely fitting jeans, and then he helped her pull them down to her knees. She could almost feel drool dripping from his mouth, hormones raging within his heated body, his mind clouded by the pleasure he would experience as soon as he shifted into the proper position. Her hand reached along the sensuous inner curve of her thigh, and he reached in to feel the warm softness of her flesh....

She moved so quickly and unexpectedly that Marconius had no chance to react. The hidden blade swiped across his cheek before he knew what had hit him, opening a gash that filled with hot, oozing blood and dripped down to his chin and neck. He recoiled in silent fear as Kasey pounced on him, her suddenly powerful form now straddling his stunned body. She drove the blade deep into his heaving chest, but his squirming and convulsing body fouled her aim, lodging the dagger into the soft part of his shoulder. Instinctively she punched him in the face, disorienting him and preventing the cry of pain that would have escaped his lips and alerted everyone in the square.

Dazed and wounded, Marconius writhed as Kasey pressed a torn swatch of fabric into his mouth, tying it securely about his head, effectively eliminating any sounds he might make. She pulled the dagger from his shoulder, causing him intense discomfort, and punched him in the side of the head with the hilt, stunning him into submission. Then she shackled his wrists, chaining him to the line of slaves. Their gazes met and she saw in his eyes fear and surprise; he saw only cold and calculating hatred in the clear gray orbs staring back at him.

Kasey got to her feet and kicked him in the side of the head, rendering him unconscious; she covered him with the blanket on which he had intended to seduce her.

Often a first date didn't go quite the way one planned.

CHAPTER 35

PIRATES

The ship turned out to be Roman, inspiring a collective sigh of relief that spread quickly through the rowing chamber. Every galley slave knew the dangers of battle: if a ship sank, the slaves sank with it; if a ship burned, the slaves roasted alive. No one would save them. Soldiers on deck might survive in the water if another ship picked them up in time... provided ravenous sharks didn't devour them first. Galley slaves existed to propel the ship, and as long as that ship remained afloat they fulfilled their purpose; but once the galley died, no one lamented the loss of its human engine. As condemned men they lived on borrowed time, each day a new gift from the merciful Emperor of Rome.

Simon gazed through the oar port at the bold blue design of the galley's painted hull: a storm of stylized waves and a trident issuing bolts of lightning.

"The Neptune's Fury," Achmet Bey pointed out. "She has seen her share of battles, and always proves victorious."

"How do you know?" Simon inquired.

"The crew talks," the Arab replied. "Once you know the language you will hear much."

"I wonder what they want," Simon said.

"Probably bringing us orders," Achmet Bey guessed. "A new mission."

"Great," Simon sighed. "No rest for the weary. We have to do everything around here!"

The Neptune's Fury came alongside and dropped a launch from astern. The smaller craft, carrying half a dozen men, including two pale and unhappy oarsmen, crawled over the choppy sea in a freshening breeze toward the Inferno. An officer stood in the back of the launch, his absurdly inappropriate hat dripping with light spray blowing off the waves.

"Wish I had my camera," Simon murmured.

"Your what?"

"It's a long story."

The boat disappeared from his limited view, after which he heard occasional sounds from above: a raised voice, a command, the staccato clatter of footsteps on deck planking. He had no idea the importance of the meeting, if any. For all he knew, the captains were old friends having a drink together on the high seas.

Simon, like the other slaves, took the opportunity to rest his head on his oar and relax during this extraordinarily rare and precious moment of inactivity. It might not happen again for months.

The break stretched into the better part of an hour, during which time nearly the entire human engine lost consciousness. Then the sharp crack of whips quickly roused them, and those too groggy to raise their heads in the first seconds felt the stinging lash of leather on their tough hides.

"So much for my beauty sleep," Simon sighed.

The Arab shook his head in wonder.

Drumbeats echoed across the long chamber as slaves scrambled to control their oars, carefully aligning them to move in synchronization. The Inferno inched forward, gradually picking up speed, pulling away from the Neptune's Fury. Simon noticed the other ship moving in a parallel line, the two vessels forming a strike force—or perhaps they sought the same destination, a nearby port. The Inferno stopped in a port every few days, as though afraid to remain at sea. How on Earth had the Romans crossed the Channel to England?

The vessel maintained a steady cruising speed, to which Simon had grown accustomed, his developing muscles more than adequate for the purpose; but since that first day there had been no cause for battle speed, though once they had pushed themselves to avoid a storm looming over the horizon. Simon rowed casually, his mind wandering, giving little thought to the present; he still believed in his escape and how he might yet locate the beautiful young woman who had so movingly professed her love for him. Achmet Bey thought he was crazy.

"You have to have faith," Simon told him many times. "God will show us the way, but we have to seize the opportunities He gives us."

"Yours is a mysterious God," the Arab frequently commented.

"Mysterious, yes," Simon agreed. "And powerful. Not to mention subtle. He put the 'b' in 'subtle' you know."

He recognized the same glazed look that Kasey displayed whenever he tried to be clever.

"It just means He works in ways we can't anticipate," Simon explained.

"The gods of Rome are more prominent," the Arab said. "They cause storms, tidal waves, earthquakes, pestilence, and famine. One can see their influence. What does your God do?"

"He works on men's hearts," Simon replied.

"I put little faith in the whims of gods," his friend said. "We make our own destinies."

He thought about that conversation and a dozen others during the long afternoon of endless, mindless, monotonous rowing, his mind drifting from one scenario to another, a collage of memories and fantasies that passed the time. Kasey remained foremost in his mind as he recalled their many adventures, from their first unlikely meeting to their emotional breakthrough in the mushroom forest deep beneath the Arabian desert; he concocted plan after impossible plan concerning his escape and rescue of the woman he now knew he loved. Sometimes they involved a return to Moab, where he somehow located and used her phone, which suddenly worked properly, to go back in time to snatch her away from the line of slaves before they ever reached the Dead Sea. Other times he encountered her as she journeyed to Moab, freshly escaped, with angry Romans hot on her trail. One of his more prominent fantasies involved Kasey sneaking into his rowing chamber at night with the key to his shackles, whisking him away before anyone knew he was gone.

But that raised the question of where to go once they escaped from Ancient Rome. He gave this considerable thought. It seemed obvious, assuming Kasey got her device working again, that they needed protection during the actual timeshift process; the last few attempts had proven harrowing at best. At the very least they needed pressure suits; but he envisioned a vehicle of some kind to serve as a comfortable base for her device. He pictured an RV that traveled through time—much more practical than Doc Brown's DeLorean—and wondered how to adapt such a thing. Kasey would think he had lost his mind. Granted, it wouldn't do them much good if they traveled to a time before roads, so they would have to limit their activity to very specific periods of history. But since they had only two real objectives—to save Carista and then the rest of the world—his idea retained some merit.

His plan would involve a vast undertaking: laboratory facilities, a manufacturing plant, people to do the work, and years of development—not to mention mountains of money. Of course, with a time machine, such details became academic. As new ideas emerged, he incorporated them into his fantastic plan, which developed nicely over months at sea. By the time of the Neptune's Fury's arrival he had a solid idea of what he and Kasey needed, down to the last detail. She would be impressed. So would he, if it worked.

Shouting from the main deck jolted him back to reality, and when he peered out his oar port he saw something that made his blood run cold: beyond their sister ship, on the horizon a dozen miles away, three sails of foreign origin appeared, their configuration different from the large square canvases that assisted the slaves on Roman ships of war. Triangular sails angled above slender, more maneuverable ships nearly as large as the Roman galleys. A fourth sail emerged over the horizon, and Simon suddenly experienced the terror instilled in the hearts of his fellow slaves. His own heart pounded in anticipation, his palms sweating on his oar, and suddenly all his distant plans faded into obscurity as this moment dominated his existence.

Simon felt more helpless, more powerless, than he ever had before, knowing his fate lay in the decisions made by ancient Romans scrambling on the deck above; they alone controlled direction and speed, the strategy of battle, and the power to carry it out. He could only push and pull his hated oar, trusting the

Romans to fight as well on the sea as they did on land. His dreams and hopes would amount to nothing if he went down with the ship—and Kasey would never know what had become of him.

"God help us," Simon muttered, tightening his grip on the oar.

The drumbeat increased as the Romans scurried above, preparing the Inferno for battle: securing lines, lighting coal scuttles, arming sailors and soldiers, trimming the vessel against the wind. Slaves toiled with increased vigor, afraid of horrific death if they failed in their duties; some welcomed inevitable release from their earthly bonds, but the whips of the overseers and the fury of their shipmates prevented them from slacking in their crucial role as propulsion.

Simon concentrated on his mindless task and pushed away morbid thoughts of death and destruction. He desperately did not want to die here in the middle of nowhere—and nowhen, a term of his own coinage that he suspected Kasey would appreciate—so he sought some means of escape. He could not rely on the Romans to help him; the Arab, powerful as a bear, could not break his bonds; and Simon lacked everything in the way of James Bond gadgets or MacGyver know-how, leaving him at the mercy of Fate.

He lost sight of the enemy as the Inferno came about, and from that point on the battle became an affair of sounds and smells and vibrations. The still air frightened him; anticipation kept him on edge, sweat pouring from his nearly naked body, knowing that at any moment his world might end in sudden violence. Whishing sounds broke the silence, followed by dull thuds peppering the hull. Someone cried out, but Simon could not tell what had happened. Men shouted as soft noises became sharper and more erratic; the ship changed direction.

The drumbeat increased.

Simon chanced a glance out his oar port as a fragment of the battle came into view, and what he discovered amazed him. The Neptune's Fury had already engaged the enemy, cleaving in two a long, narrow pirate vessel, but it had not gone cleanly; most of the enemy's vessel clung to the bows of the Roman warship, flames spreading across both decks as men fought the fire and each other, running about in chaos and terror.

His own ship altered course again, denying him the opportunity to view the outcome of the battle.

The Inferno shuddered violently, wrenching slaves from their seats and hurling them across their oars; only the clinking chains stopped them from flying into the walls. The overseers braced for impact, lacked sufficient strength to save themselves, and flung against the bulkheads, onto the floor, or into the midst of the slaves they had mercilessly whipped for so many long and dreadful months; they landed in heaps throughout the chamber, some with breaks and bruises, others with more serious injuries. One died at the hands of an angry slave who found enough length of chain to do the job.

Shaken and bruised, Simon climbed back onto his seat as Achmet Bey did the same. He scanned the chamber and discovered no indication of hull breaches or water on the floor, a terrific relief; it meant the Inferno remained seaworthy, and as long as it floated, so did its means of propulsion. They must have rammed a second pirate ship, causing considerable damage to both vessels.

The sudden clanking of iron weapons and the occasional shriek of death overhead reinforced his interpretation of events. The Romans had a fight on their hands, and while they occupied themselves with the pirates, he sought a means of escape. Straining at his chains, he struggled to see the condition of the guards as they stirred and moaned. One lay unconscious in the middle of the floor, but he did not carry the key. The captain of the overseers carried it, and he had left the chamber before the battle.

The hortator at the front of the rowing chamber also possessed a key; he glared at the slaves and pounded on his drum, though no one moved an oar—and not one guard possessed the physical ability to crack a whip.

"Nothing has changed," the Arab said. "The chain is still your enemy."

"I have so many it's hard to keep up," Simon sighed. He looked out the oar port and sighted a new enemy that perhaps the Bedouin had overlooked.

"Then this is where we part," the Arab said with morbid resignation. "It is not how I imagined the end of my life, but I will meet it with courage and honor, and in the company of my friend."

"Speak for yourself," Simon cried out, suddenly frantic.

"I did."

A fourth pirate ship, the last to breach the horizon, moved steadily and unwaveringly on a collision course with the Inferno, its long and blunted embolus protruding like a battering ram, occasionally visible above the water as it crested the choppy waves. Simon knew his life would end the moment it hit, that even if the impact did not crush him, the rapid sinking of the ship would pull him to a watery grave.

Other slaves saw it and their moment of rest turned to panic as they strived in vain to pull free of their shackles and chains. Screams of terror elicited from the lips of men who had scarcely uttered a word in months. Only the Arab sat in silence, eyes closed, arms crossed over his chest, waiting for the end with a sense of peace that Simon could not comprehend. He certainly didn't feel it.

The sounds of battle escalated, distracting Simon from his growing anxiety. A loud cracking boom, like the report of a cannon, split the air, and he raised his head in time to watch the ceiling collapse into the rowing chamber. He leapt to avoid a beam that would have crushed his skull like an eggshell. As the dust settled, he discovered that the slave in front of him had not been so lucky: an enormous treelike column, the ship's mast, had splintered free of its base and plunged across the side of the Inferno, gouging a swath of destruction from the center of the deck almost to the waterline, its tapering form running afoul of the oars; shreds of burning sail twisted around it and draped from one deck to the next.

"Jeez!" Simon exclaimed, noting that his friend's wide eyes stared in bewilderment at him and the carnage beyond.

"You are unharmed?" Achmet Bey asked incredulously.

"I think so," Simon replied, searching his body for injuries. "I might have a small splinter in my pinky finger."

He stepped over the debris and made his way back to check on his friend, then turned forward again to examine the destruction. Ten feet of the upper deck had crashed down in front of his seat, mashing and mangling a dozen slaves. The great mast angled from the sea to the main deck, its thick base rending and twisting in a mass of shredded splinters and sputtering flames that attempted to devour it. Beyond it black smoke roiled into the air, obscuring the bright blue sky above. The shouts of warring soldiers and clanking weapons and armor filled the salty air, wafting on the acrid odors of fire, sweat, and death.

"Simon...." The Arab gasped, staring at him in awe.

"What is it? Are you hurt?"

The Bedouin smiled and shook his head, the hope in his dark eyes as evident as the scraggly beard on his face. Simon suddenly realized the truth. He held up his arms, now free of the detestable oar, an eight-foot length of broken chain dangling from the shackle on his right wrist. He smiled, confident that he and his companion might yet survive this disaster; but the joy faded when he realized he could not get to the key.

"Save yourself," the Arab said firmly, resigned to the fate he had already accepted.

The hortator held the other key, but he also possessed a sword and three times Simon's bulk—not to mention uncommon meanness and fighting skill. Also, the flaming carnage wrought by the falling mast entirely cut off the back half of the rowing chamber from the front, rendering any such confrontation moot.

"It can't end this way," Simon said as he peered out the oar port at the pirate ship building speed with every second that crept by. His friend would die in a matter of minutes, along with every person on the Inferno.

"Go!" the Arab urged.

"I'll be back for you," Simon said quickly.

He grasped onto a long shred of burning sail, patting out the flames as he pulled himself up onto the angled mast. The annoying chain hanging down from his wrist got in the way, so he coiled it around his arm, which made climbing difficult; but at least it wouldn't snag on anything. Simon inched up the wide mass of hardwood, three feet thick at its base, avoiding the few remaining patches of flames that had already mostly burned themselves out.

His head poked above the crushed swath of deck and the sickening, brutal, frenzied chaos of battle nearly took his breath away. In the quick scope of a single glance he saw three men run through with swords, another lose an arm below the shoulder, and a fifth plunge over the side screaming as flames consumed his torso. On deck lay the bleeding and convulsing bodies of the dead and dying, many scarcely recognizable as humans. Their moans and screams tore at his soul, but did not drown the ever present clash of m etal on metal, the occasional thumping of spears and arrows, and the all too frequent shrieks of men who met shockingly violent ends.

Fires blazed across portions of the deck where warring combatants had knocked over coal scuttles next to the catapults. He peered forward through thick smoke and flickering flames at the enemy ship, its back broken over the bow of his own vessel, the long decks sloping away from the raised center. He felt sorry for whatever slaves had perished and for those frantic to save their lives, but they were beyond help. He could think only of saving himself and the last friend he had in this horrific world of the ancient past.

He scanned the swarming, seething masses of men as they fought viciously, swords pounding shields, clubs crushing skulls, knives opening bellies, searching for the familiar face of the captain of the overseers, hoping to somehow acquire the key that would set his friend free. But he saw only faceless soldiers pulsing in a cacophony of blurred color that strained the senses. The man he sought might already lay dead, one of the headless mounds of oozing flesh that increasingly littered the bloody deck. Or maybe his armor-laden corpse fell slowly to the bottom of the sea, where aquatic life would feast, leaving iron remnants to slowly dissolve over ensuing eons.

So much for the key.

Simon looked toward the fourth pirate vessel, which had covered half the distance to his own perilously unprotected ship. He had to act, but what could he do in the midst of this carnage? Sights and sounds and smells overwhelmed him, exhausting his weary brain; he closed his eyes and prayed for a miracle.

Shutting off his mind for an instant made a difference as a new and impossible plan formed in his brain.

Searching for a clear path, Simon quickly climbed onto the deck and scrambled to the side of the ship, dodging and ducking as fighting soldiers engaged all around. Combatants avoided the flaming sections of deck, and to those areas Simon forged his winding way. Cutting a section of rope, he swung over a patch of fire, tongues of flame lapping at him as he landed on a comparatively clear section of deck. Half a dozen bodies, some charred by the ravenous conflagration, littered the vicinity but he remained more or less protected by the fires raging on every side.

A dead soldier still gripped his bow, and on a second soldier he found a quiver of arrows. Extricating the weapons from the bodies and slinging the quiver over his shoulder, Simon took up a position by the rail and tested the strength of the bow. A few months ago his puny arms would have proven grossly inadequate for the purpose, a deficiency that had hampered his favorite college P.E. class; he had learned the basics of archery—stance, posture, breathing—but could not get his arrows to fly far enough to hit the targets. But three months of rowing in the bowels of a Roman warship changed all that.

He placed the end of his first arrow into the fire, lighting the dry wood, and pulled the bowstring to his chin. Relaxing his fingers, the shaft arced high across the water and thumped into the mast of the approaching vessel. A small fire caught but quickly petered out. His second shot opened a flaming hole in the sail, less than useful. A third thudded into the deck at the feet of an enemy archer, which did not bode well for the suddenly alarmed college student. The man fired back, barely missing him as the railing intervened, absorbing an impact that otherwise would have pierced his abdomen.

Simon quickly recognized the need for a bigger weapon. He smacked himself on the forehead as he realized the answer, which had loomed before him all the time, hidden in plain sight where his unseeing eyes had overlooked it.

In the vigorous battle that raged across the ship, the Romans had abandoned their primary weapons, the catapults, to fight the more immediate enemies swarming their deck. And as most of the coals had spilled from their scuttles, creating fires that cut them off from the weapons, the catapults remained effectively out of service. The one in front of him appeared intact, except for the loss of the scuttle.

Simon grasped the helmet of a dead centurion, realizing it would no longer do the man any good, and scrambled closer to the fire, carefully scooping up a few burning coals. But when he got to his feet he discovered, standing between him and the weapon, a huge, swarthy pirate with arms as thick as thighs, his massive curved sword already arcing downward to cleave Simon in two.

CHAPTER 36

HEGIRA

Kasey looked around to see if anyone had witnessed her nocturnal action. No one stirred, and in the moonless night they couldn't have seen much anyway. She replaced the small dagger in its home along her thigh, pulled up her torn jeans, and knelt over the unmoving man she had tried to kill. His shoulder bled profusely. Unattended, the wound would kill him before he regained consciousness. Shaking her head in annoyance, Kasey tore long strips of fabric from the blanket, made a compress, and tied it tightly over the wound.

It was all she cared to do, and it delayed her escape by several harrowing minutes that increased her chances of getting discovered. She took his pugio and fastened his belt around her slender waist before slinking into the deep shadows, her careful eyes aware of everything around her.

She raced along a narrow street, now devoid of activity. Few people ventured out this late at night, and so she met no resistance. Moving swiftly and silently, she left no trace of her passage.

Realizing that she could not leave the city through any of its gates, she paused in the cloaking shadow between two buildings near the center of town, far away from the park in which the slaves and centurions slept; she needed time to think of a plan, a direction, some inclination of what to do with her newfound liberation. As much as she hated to admit it, she needed Simon; he would already have dreamed up half a dozen hare-brained schemes that made no rational sense to her but would probably work because of their boldness and audacity. A few weeks ago she wouldn't have given him a second thought, but now she ached for him—had, in a moment of uncharacteristic weakness confessed her love for him— and wished more than anything to feel his comforting and awkward touch. She smiled at how nervous he got when she came into contact with him, how his body tensed and his heartbeat quickened and his face flushed. He tried to hide it, to play it cool, but she saw through his efforts. She found his misery rather endearing, really....

She needed him.

But they had parted ways too long ago for her to follow his trail, which had taken him west across the mountains to the sea. For all she knew the Romans could have put him aboard a ship and carried him to any point in the Empire, from England to Egypt. Returning to Moab seemed equally impossible; that trail had long since run cold. She was on her own. No one would help her, nor could she explain her circumstances. Yet somehow she needed the knowledge and information necessary to locate either Simon or her belongings— preferably both.

First I need to get out of the city, she thought, her back against the cool mud bricks of the wall behind her. It seemed easier in theory than in practice. But then a devious smile crossed her lovely face as the solution to her conundrum presented itself.

Kasey crept toward the center of sleeping Antioch, soon arriving at the wide, slow- moving river that bisected the city. She gazed into the gently flowing blackness, seeing the stars reflecting up at her, and knew that this peaceful current represented her salvation. She would follow its course beyond the city wall and to the coast fifteen miles downstream, from where she could easily locate a road leading south to the port cities. With any luck she might discover Simon along the way. Perhaps he languished in a cell someplace, and she could break him out in the middle of the night. Even if she couldn't find him she would return to Moab and begin the daunting search for her backpack. Maybe Simon had already escaped and right now was on his way there, hoping to encounter her on the road. After all, if she had broken free of her bonds, then certainly he could have found a way....

Her heart pounding in anticipation, Kasey stepped from shadowy concealment into the dim starlight along the edge of the river, near a stone bridge that arched across the wide span.

She covered three steps before someone called out, stopping her cold in her tracks.

A guard cut her off from the river, his heavy armor and iron weapons glinting in the starlight. He left Kasey no time to react, nowhere to run, and no hope of escape. She wondered if the centurions had discovered her missing and sounded an alarm, alerting everyone in the city of her treachery.

He spoke in a harsh tone, his eyes studying her strange attire and shapely form, noting with bewilderment the pugio depending from her left hip. Kasey understood the occasional word, and got the impression that he demanded to know the meaning of her presence here—a reasonable request from his point of view, but damned inconvenient from hers.

She pointed to her throat, indicating her inability to speak. Then she motioned to the bridge, relaying her intention to cross it.

The guard shook his head and uttered more indecipherable words.

Kasey's shoulders slumped, allowing her torn, ill-fitting shirt to slip down her left arm, revealing a smooth curve of perfect white flesh, drawing the soldier's immediate attention. A thin smile curled at the corners of his mouth as his hand reached forward to touch her bare shoulder, to feel the satiny coolness of her soft skin, to experience the pleasure this helpless woman offered, and who could not object to his attention, considering her scant dress and compromising presence long past curfew.

"Don't they have women in this century?" she muttered. The instant his rough hand touched her flesh her leg thrust upward, her shin contacting the inadequately protected region where his legs attached to his torso. As he doubled over in pain she raced across the bridge, hoping to lose him before slipping quietly into the river. The last thing she needed was a whole battalion of soldiers searching the river while she tried in vain to evade them.

But the man reacted more quickly than she anticipated; he followed her to the arching bridge, sword drawn and prepared to cut down the insolent wench who dared to attack a soldier of Rome. Realizing he could not catch her, for she moved as swiftly as any deer he had ever seen, the centurion hurled his short sword, hoping at least to stun her into submission, and at most to lodge the weapon in her back. The blade slapped against her legs, tearing her jeans and tangling between her knees as she tried to run. Kasey stumbled and fell to the stone pavement near the center of the bridge as the iron sword clattered beneath her; she felt fortunate to have survived the attack with only minor scrapes.

Before she could stand up, the man towered over her, holding a short whip designed to flay the desirable flesh from her stunned body. This angry centurion would not allow her to die quickly or easily: on the contrary, the depraved gleam in his dark eyes looked all too familiar, revealing his lascivious desire to steal what pleasure he could before disposing of her corpse in the river. She wondered if all men in this part of history abused women, or if only the Romans felt empowered to dominate them. It didn't matter: she had no intention of allowing him the opportunity to lay a finger on her again.

With the speed a pouncing tigress, Kasey launched herself at the suddenly startled young man, the impact sending them both hurtling off the bridge and out over the softly moving blackness. Kasey gulped a deep breath of air before plunging into the cool darkness and quickly went to work in the silent world beneath. Her opponent writhed and splashed, fighting to reach the surface, but a cold, firm grip on his ankle pulled him into the depths. He panicked and thrashed, desperate to loosen the iron hold.

Kasey squeezed his ankle as she swam to the bottom of the river. Finding a handhold on the base of a stone arch that supported the center of the bridge, she clung to it with all her strength while maintaining a death grip on the man's squirming body. Her mind flashed to the conversation with Simon about the dangers of altering the past by killing or even interacting with people here, and for a moment she considered releasing her hold. Suppose this man's death resulted in Simon's absence in the future? Or hers? But she had to accept the risk, because letting go would prevent her from finding the man she loved and saving the sister she had lost. And in war there were casualties.

The body convulsed and went limp as air exploded from his burning lungs. Kasey removed his belt and used it to tie him to the stone pile so that no one would find his corpse until long after she had vanished.

The job completed, she swam downstream and surfaced fifty feet from the bridge, carefully taking in a long breath of fresh air. In the darkness, bats flitted about, skimming low over the placid river, feasting on flying insects that swarmed in shallow clouds. Satisfied that no one had seen her, Kasey disappeared beneath the black surface and propelled herself with the current before coming up again for air. She worked her way beneath two more bridges and to the outer wall of the city, constantly on edge, fearing that someone might spot her.

Soon the wall loomed overhead, the only remaining barrier to freedom; but she should have realized that her efforts could not bear fruit quite so easily. A metal grate extended downward from the arched opening in the wall, allowing water to escape but effectively preventing anything larger than a rodent from doing so. The grate could be opened, because from the hills the day before she had seen boats passing through the wall.

She eased against the slimy metal slats that crossed in twelve-inch squares, the openings just small enough to prevent her from slipping through. An hour had passed since her escape from the camp, and she knew that at any moment a cry might ring out, or she might hear the rapid clopping of sandaled feet on pavement as a hundred armed men rushed toward her.

But she heard nothing except the gentle sloshing of water against stone.

Using the slats as handholds, Kasey climbed down to the silted riverbed ten feet below the surface. To her relief, the grates did not press all the way into the mud, leaving a gap of several inches. She dug quickly into the soft earth, hollowing out a shallow trench deep enough for her to squeeze through. But the effort took too long, forcing her to return to the surface.

As she gasped for air she saw a dark form atop the wall, a guard making his rounds, and he looked down before she could hide. She held her breath and remained still, not daring to move for fear of drawing his attention. He looked away, and in that instant she disappeared beneath the surface. Wriggling under the grate, she emerged on the other side and swam as fast as her cold limbs could propel her.

The soldier did not sound an alarm. His second glance revealed nothing, and so he chalked it up to shadows and water, oblivious of the escaped slave and the Romans who would scour the countryside for her the next day. He would learn in due time of the slave's dramatic and violent escape, of the mysteriously missing bridge guard, and of the disgraced soldier named Marconius; in light of the anger displayed by everyone involved and the promises of retribution, this particular guard chose not to share what he thought he might have seen, lest he incur wrath for not having sounded an alarm.

After all, what they didn't know couldn't hurt him.

CHAPTER 37

WAR

Terrified, Simon instinctively threw his arm up to shield his helpless body from the deadly blow; to his amazement, the coiled chain wrapped thickly around his forearm deflected the chopping blade, sending it thumping unexpectedly to the deck in a shower of sparks. Simon's eyes met those of his attacker and saw anger and astonishment. He suspected the pirate saw fear and desperation. Before the enemy could react, Simon quickly uncoiled his eight feet of heavy chain and lashed it across the man's back, forcing a moan of agony that neither of them expected.

Fuming with hate, the pirate stood to his full height and glared at Simon, sword raised menacingly, blood dripping from a jagged wound that angled from his right shoulder to his left ribcage. He lurched forward, swiping the blade at Simon's abdomen, intent on spilling the younger man's intestines onto the charred deck; but Simon, naturally clumsy on his best day and hopelessly lacking all sense of coordination on his worst, stumbled backward over a half-burnt corpse and fell flat on his back. The blade missed him by an inch, the unexpected momentum throwing the warrior off balance. Capitalizing on the advantage, Simon slung the chain around the pirate's leg and yanked with unexpected strength; the enemy flopped solidly to the deck. Landing in the fire, the man screamed before scrambling from the licking flames.

As the pirate recovered, Simon quickly retrieved the helmet he had abandoned at the onset of the attack and dumped the smoldering coals into the wide pan at the upper end of the nearest catapult. Sensing imminent danger, he quickly dropped to the ground as the heavy blade swiped across him, again missing by a hair's breadth. But this time the enemy anticipated his opponent's reaction and did not falter. The curved iron sword arced high into the air again and sliced sharply downward.

Simon rolled out of the way and very suddenly ran out of deck.

A missing rail left nothing to prevent the hapless young man from inadvertently flinging himself over the side of the ship. He fell for half an eternity before splashing ungainly between two oars that angled uselessly from the hull; in desperation he reached out to them before his body sank to oblivion—but he bobbed to the surface too far away to grasp anything. His brain clouded with adrenaline-induced anger, he slung his chain toward a detestable oar, wrapping the links around the length of wood, and pulled himself toward it.

Three months ago he could not have made the climb; now, with his new and untested physique, and a determination borne by love and anger in equal measures, he launched himself up the side of the Roman galley, finding handholds and footholds where a more careful person would have hesitated. He gripped the oar and pulled hand over hand until he reached the oar port, oblivious of the man staring back at him from darkness on the other side. Using the port as a foothold, he scrambled up the side of the ship.

The pirate stood with his back to the defeated enemy, seeking other hapless prey, confident that the fire would protect him from the brunt of battle, allowing him to pick and choose his victims at will. Not in ten lifetimes would he have expected to hear the angry cry of the man he had just sent to a watery grave, followed immediately by the sharp, lashing pain of the wet and rusted chain slapping across his shoulder and chest from behind. His eyes grew wide as the furious slave leapt toward him, the young and muscular shoulder colliding with his unprotected abdomen. The impact knocked the air from his lungs and sent him reeling backward, staggering to maintain his balance.

He punched at the young man's sides and back, the sword useless at close range, but Simon continued his charge until the pirate stumbled into something unexpected at the side of the ship. With one mighty heave Simon hefted his enemy into the smoldering coals that filled the pan atop the catapult. For half a heartbeat the man could not conceive of what had happened, as he sat atop the smoldering mass; and then his clothes caught fire, lengthening tongues of flame lapping upward from his seat to his chest. The suddenly terrified man screamed at the top of his lungs, drawing the astonished attention of everyone waging war nearby. Simon pulled the release lever on the catapult and watched in grim satisfaction as his flaming enemy arced across the water, bursting into a fireball halfway to the approaching ship.

The screaming and flailing corpse toppled two enemy catapults, scattering their coal scuttles, sending waves of fire across the foredeck. Flames quickly consumed the portside bow, spreading aft as the breeze of the ship's momentum fed their ravenous hunger. Simon watched in horror as the conflagration exploded like a wildfire in a matchstick forest, consuming decks and spiraling up the dry mast, devouring its sails. The ship slowed as slaves abandoned their oars and the smoking sail ripped from its beams. The action on his own vessel paused as Romans and pirates alike stood in stunned silence. Fire burst from every oar port as men screamed in agony, chained to unimaginably terrifying death. Flaming pirates plunged into the sea, heavy armor dragging them to watery graves. Equally chilling, sharks converged on the carnage and set upon everything that moved in the now churning froth.

Half a ship length from its intended target, the pirate vessel lost momentum and drifted with the current, away from the scene of battle, a massive funeral pyre the likes of which no sailor had seen before—or ever wished to see again.

"Talk about your lucky shot," Simon muttered.

The words had barely left his lips when a sharp pain stabbed his left shoulder, thrusting him backward against the catapult. Looking down, he saw an arrow protruding from his chest, a clean shot that strangely did not hurt. He suspected it would throb like the dickens once the adrenaline of battle dissipated. He ducked for cover before a second shaft could find him, hearing the dull thump as it hit the deck nearby. Grasping the thin wood that had pierced his body, he broke it off near the point of impact, realizing that pulling it out would do more harm than good. Pain surged through his arm at the effort, blinding him for a moment.

"Yeah, that's more like it," he said through gritted teeth.

Locating the bow he had earlier abandoned, he nocked an arrow, drew the string to his chin, and took aim at a pirate through the shimmering light of lapping flames. Blood seeped from his wound and oozed down his chest, but he maintained use of the arm as his left hand firmly grasped the center of the bow. Relaxing his fingers, the arrow flew straight and true, twisting into his target's unprotected neck. He repeated the effort two more times before another arrow thudded into the catapult inches from his head. His observant eye caught the movement of an archer clinging to the rail on the stern of the broken pirate vessel, picking off Roman after Roman from the safety of his hiding place. Simon saw fury on the man's contemptuous face, obviously determined to take out the slave who had just single-handedly destroyed an entire ship and crew.

Simon took careful aim and sent a shaft thumping into the rail in front of his enemy's chest. Another arrow lodged in Simon's catapult, creasing his upper arm an instant before impact. He nocked another arrow and drove it through the enemy railing, narrowly missing his target. His enemy's next shot went wide, flying out over the open sea.

Simon grasped one more arrow, held it into the nearby fire to start a small blaze behind the tip, and took careful aim at his deadly enemy. The pirate understood the grim determination on the young man's face, and scrambled to get in one more good shot; he got his arrow nocked and the string drawn back before the blazing shaft entered his left eye socket. The lifeless body fell backward in a heap, alone on the splintered deck of its dead ship. Breathing a sigh of relief, and now feeling the encroaching pain of his injury, Simon returned his attention to the pirates swarming across the deck of the Inferno. One after another he lodged deadly and well-aimed shafts into the necks, backs, and chests of swarthy pirates, most of whom had no idea what hit them.

He kept up the effort until he ran out of arrows; then, weak from pain and loss of blood, he slumped against his catapult. Pirates approached, recognizing the danger he represented, but the Romans—equally aware of Simon's advantageous presence—intervened and saved the wounded man from destruction.

The tide of war turned in favor of Rome after the destruction of the pirate vessel, thanks in no small part to the efforts of a slave who had miraculously broken his bonds and fought valiantly on the side of those who had unjustly enslaved him in the first place. Simon watched as Roman soldiers, under the direction of their skilled captain, sopped up the mess, sending their enemy to oblivion, capturing or killing everyone remaining on deck.

One ship sped away, opting to avoid the unexpected carnage wrought by the flaming catapult. It soon disappeared over the horizon, abandoning its companions to their fate.

Simon felt unusually weak as the throbbing of his shoulder settled into a numbing ache. He fought to maintain consciousness, afraid that if he dozed the Romans would make a wrong assumption and hurl his corpse to the sharks. The sounds of battle faded. Whether they ceased or his muffled hearing blocked them out he could not tell, but he scarcely discerned the faces of the men who eventually approached him. Gentle masculine hands grasped his arms and legs; the world moved in slow motion, a blur of muffled sound, muted color, and disjointed thoughts. He wondered if the hundreds of people he had killed would alter the timeline in ways he could never imagine. A renewed sense of foreboding washed over him as he realized the destruction he had wrought for the sake of his own survival.

The fog of pain and weakness overwhelmed him as soldiers jostled his insensible body. People stared with wonder and amazement as he passed by them, and he could not tell if they hated him for escaping or admired him for fighting on their side. At the moment he didn't care. The centurions stopped at the end of the deck and Simon expected them to hurl him over the side.

Another man approached, his cold words muffled and indecipherable. Simon looked up to see unabashed astonishment on the hard face of the Inferno's captain in the instant before he finally lost the battle with unconsciousness.

Chapter 38

Flight

K asey remained in the black concealment of the wide, rapidly flowing river almost until it emptied into the Mediterranean Sea a dozen miles downstream of Antioch. Along the way she discerned shadowy images of villages and at least one sizeable settlement, but no indication of people lurking in the night. She wondered how long it would take for someone to discover the bound and wounded form of her foolish paramour, and what punishment he would suffer for his misguided attempts at seduction. How important a property was she, actually? Would they search the surrounding villages and towns, offer a reward, tear up the landscape until they recovered their missing slave? Or would they slap Marconius on the wrist and let the worthless wench go without a second thought? She hoped for the latter.

In the dim light of dawn Kasey crawled from the river where its mouth yawned into the expansive blue emptiness of the Great Sea. She scampered onto the southern bank and stretched in the sand, intending to rest for an hour in the shallow concealment of low bushes before moving on. Instead, when she finally opened her eyes, the sun glared down at her from high in the deep blue sky; she instinctively raised her hand to shield her face.

"Crap," she muttered, rolling onto her side, her muscles stiff from the night's harrowing adventure. At least her clothes had dried out.

The Romans might be anywhere and everywhere, searching high and low for the dangerous, escaped slave woman. She poked her head above the foliage and discovered a comparatively barren landscape filled with patches of scrub brush and not much else. The occasional spindly tree dotted the desolate scene, and when she moved a lizard slinked away across the sand.

Half a mile to the south, a low ridge sloped out of the earth, and snaking along it wound a narrow road. The likelihood of ever seeing either Simon or her backpack again remained virtually nil, but Simon would have told her not to let the odds get in the way; somebody had to win the lottery—just make certain Shirley Jackson had nothing to do with it. She didn't know what he had meant by that, but it had seemed important to him.

Seeing no one in the desert or on the road, Kasey carefully picked her way up the ridge that loomed a few hundred feet above the desolate coast. Some altitude would offer a better chance to get her bearings, something she knew Simon would have said. She had paid closer attention to him than she realized. Her heart longed for him more with each day that passed. Did she really love him? Had she only cried out in the heat of the moment, when she realized she would never see him again? Or had her heart expressed a desperate truth before her rational brain could stop it? She could not deny the fact that she thought of him constantly, and not in the way that teenage girls mooned over boys, satisfying their saccharine egos with silly gossip and flirtatious taunts; she missed his clever wit, his propensity for making her feel good about herself, the way he refused to give up on anything: the salvation of the world, Carista's life, even Kasey's own soul. More than anyone in her life he had stuck by her, supported her, and even risked his own life—on multiple occasions—to protect her. This puny, pathetic, inoffensive little weakling, who once confessed that he would take a good run over a bad stand any day, inspired her to profess her love for him. The self-proclaimed coward turned out not to be such a coward after all, now that he had found something worth fighting for.

Kasey didn't know what to think. Every time she tried to put him out of her mind she saw his sly grin from the corner of her mind's eye, and that image amused her; it comforted her during the worst nights of her life, and gave her hope that the days would turn out better—even though they rarely did.

She followed the road southward, encountering few travelers. Apparently this part of the Empire saw little traffic, allowing her to walk unmolested for much of the afternoon. At first every noise, real or imagined, kept her on edge, her hand constantly on the stolen pugio at her hip; but after a few miles she realized that even if she did encounter someone she doubted they would harm her. Ancient Rome predated all technologies required to disseminate information about her to the rest of the Empire: not even a wanted poster, since paper as she knew it had yet to be invented. The moveable-type printing press would not come about for another millennium and a half. She could hardly imagine a world in which books did not exist, aside from delicate scrolls on parchment or papyrus.

Nevertheless, Kasey knew she had to maintain caution, and part of that meant blending in with the local people. If Marconius did come after her she would stand out like an ostrich in a flock of penguins. Her torn and bloody blouse had certainly seen better days, and did more at this point to entice men than to hide her apparently irresistible figure; and her stained, partly shredded jeans displayed more curves and flashes of leg than prudence allowed in this period of history. Add to that her unusually light brown hair, which few people in the Middle East had ever seen, let alone possessed, she realized that regardless of where she went people would stare at her and wonder where she came from. That would make it easy for inquisitive Romans to locate her.

She had no money, of course. Nor did she speak the language. Yet somehow she needed to acquire new clothing in order to blend in with the populace, not to mention food and water. Her stomach growled and her mouth felt dry, though not as severely as during the long march; her admirer's generosity had satisfied her basic needs, though now that she had gotten used to extra rations her hunger intensified.

All of that left her but one option.

Kasey traveled carefully through the afternoon, hiding in the brush whenever she saw another person on the road in the distance. The further south she ventured the more frequently she had to hide, until a few hours before sunset she discovered a large village straddling a creek that cascaded down from the low mountains and onto the narrow plain before disappearing into the sea. Concealing herself in the shadows high above the settlement, she studied its layout: the primitive, irregular structures; docks that extended over the water, accommodating fishing boats that had long since returned with the day's catch; and the placement of the well in the center of town, surrounded by a broad square in which tradesmen worked their crafts. A couple of hundred people inhabited the village, perhaps half of them still at sea, their wide, shallow boats loaded with fish that they would salt and transport to local markets; dozens of small sails dotted the seascape, casting long shadows over the warm, colorful water as the sun inched closer to the blazing horizon. Simon would have taken the time to capture this scene on paper.

She waited with growing anticipation, and an increasingly cranky stomach, until well after sunset, when most of the town's activity ceased.

"Here goes another commandment," she muttered as she slunk into the village.

An hour later she returned to the road carrying a new wardrobe consisting of robes, head covering, a tunic, and sandals; a satchel large enough to carry her tennis shoes that she certainly did not want to abandon, as well as any other necessary items she found along the way; and enough bread, water, dates, grapes, cheese, figs, and salted fish to keep her going for a week. She tried not to discriminate, stealing from everyone equally, not that it would make much difference if they caught her. But in the quiet of night no one had noticed the presence of a stealthy escaped slave, and part of her wondered if anyone would even miss the few items she had pilfered.

Continuing south along the empty road, she made excellent time in the moonless night, stopping before dawn to rest. Her body ached from the strain and lack of sleep, for she had moved almost constantly for at least eighteen hours. Settling in along the ridge high above the road, using the new clothing as a cushion, she nibbled at her stolen food.

At midmorning, Kasey consumed a small ration of fruits and water while studying the road and the landscape below. People hiked along the narrow path, sometimes singly but more often in pairs or small groups, occasionally on donkeys, covered in the long, draping garments of the day. In the distance, along a slight curve of the coast, a small village beckoned, its fishing boats now well out to sea, their sails fluttering in the morning breeze.

Kasey got to her feet and picked up her now ruffled new clothing: a simple white tunic, a pale blue length of fabric designed to wrap around her body and drape from her shoulders to the ground, and a long brown robe to cover everything. She removed her shirt and jeans, feeling awkward standing out in the open wearing just her underwear—a circumstance that would have annoyed her had Simon been present—and hastily slipped into the tunic, which fit better than expected. It took a few frustrating tries to configure the outer covering, but eventually she managed to make it look almost natural. Next came the robe and the head gear, which after some effort concealed her unusually light hair. She couldn't do anything about her bright steel gray eyes, but hopefully that wouldn't matter.

Emboldened by her new Jedi look, Kasey worked her way down the steep ridge to the winding road, carrying the satchel over her shoulder and the stolen sword under her robe. The journey south followed the contours of the ridge as the road clung to its base, often climbing high above the sea. Occasionally a river or a creek flowed over the rocks or forged through deep channels on its way to the Mediterranean; some she carefully forded, but others required rickety old bridges, constructed long before Roman occupation.

By noon she encountered her first actual travelers on the road, and only through force of will did she not dash into the foliage to hide from them. Two men with long dark beards, tall walking staffs, and expansive robes approached from the direction in which she traveled. They appeared to have covered a great distance, carrying provisions for several days, and she recognized the weary but friendly expressions of men who spent a great deal of time on the road. They looked at her, smiled, and spoke to each other in the local dialect.

Then the oldest, perhaps in his thirties, spoke to her directly.

Not knowing what the guy said, Kasey responded with a blank stare.

The second one tried, this time in Latin, and she understood the occasional phrase, though she got the impression that he had as much trouble with the language as she did. She returned his smile and spoke what she hoped he would take as a greeting. He did.

At the older man's insistence, they moved off the road and settled into a grassy area overlooking the sea to share an early lunch together. Kasey tried to decline the invitation, desperate to put as much distance between her and Antioch as possible, but the older man, in his calm and cordial way, convinced her to take a break from her strenuous travels. Relenting, Kasey decided that at the very least she might learn what lay ahead of her on the road.

Her brunch companions did not disappoint. During a long and pleasant conversation, in which the younger man translated broken Latin back and forth into incomprehensible Aramaic, Kasey learned that three hard days' journey to the south lay one of the most important trading centers of the eastern Roman Empire, where thousands of ships of all sizes and origins came and went from destinations spanning the Mediterranean. Some even journeyed to Rome itself on a regular basis. Kasey explained, as well as possible, the last time she had seen Simon, and the approximate condition of that departure, hoping they would not guess her own status as an escaped slave; if they did suspect her, they did not let on, and instead assured her that if the Romans had taken her friend to the coast they undoubtedly intended to chain him to a galley in Tyre. Thousands of slaves met their end in those hateful ships, and very few ever lived to tell about their experiences.

She learned that her new friends were returning to their village near Antioch, where they intended to spread the word of the miraculous young rabbi they had encountered during their annual visit to Jerusalem. They had seen Him raise a man from the dead, a man who had already begun to decay inside his sealed tomb for three days. Death had not stopped the young teacher from issuing words of faith and healing, affecting everyone fortunate enough to witness the event with their own eyes. These two men, filled with joy and compassion, had decided to make certain that everyone they knew learned of the healer and his powerful words.

Kasey excitedly recounted the story of how this same man, more than a man, had healed her at the most desperate time of her life, filling her soul with hope and peace and joy that it had never experienced before.

They parted as friends, connected in spirit by the one being in the universe who had so profoundly affected their lives and would soon and for all time affect billions of people for the rest of history. The younger man gave Kasey his walking staff, seeing that she was without one, and insisted, against her protests, that she keep it as the heartfelt gift of one fellow traveler to another.

With a lighter mood and the joy of hope and friendship, Kasey continued her solitary journey to the south, now confident that she would somehow find Simon on one of those ships of which her new friends had spoken. Even if his ship was not in port, she suspected that at some point it would be, for they had to return periodically to take on supplies, effect repairs, and replace slaves that perished during the voyages. She would have to bide her time until the right one arrived. Assuming, of course, that she could find a way to determine his presence deep within the bowels of a warship; she had a couple of days at her disposal in which to think of something.

But suppose Simon didn't return to port? Perhaps he had already escaped and at this moment he scoured the lands around Moab searching for her. Or worse... he had succumbed to the unimaginable horrors of the galley. She forced those unproductive thoughts out of her head; she knew in her bones that he still lived, because she would have felt it in her heart otherwise.

The rest of the day passed without event as she drew inevitably closer to her new destination, passing the occasional pedestrian with an affable word of greeting that her friends had taught her. Most people returned her friendly words and moved on in peace, and once in a long while someone tried to ask her a question; but realizing that she did not speak the local language, most confrontations ended quickly with pleasant nods.

And so it went for three long days. Kasey slept fitfully at night on high ground above the road, well beyond sight of other travelers, which became far more frequent the closer she got to Tyre. Several substantial towns and small cities sprung up along the path, offering much in the way of food and lodging, but she kept her distance lest she encounter a Roman or someone equally vile who might jeopardize her mission; besides, she had no money with which to purchase anything, and her own supplies would not run out for days.

On the evening of the third day, as her friends had predicted, Kasey crested a short ridge and looked down on a magnificent port city that sprawled along the seashore, spreading inland like a wave, its far edge wrapping along the coast with dozens of long docks and piers that accommodated hundreds of ships, from fishing boats to cargo vessels to Roman galleys that dominated the bay. Long shadows cloaked the city as the sun sank low upon the horizon, fiery colors splashing against the sea in the west. Lines of people extended along the road that led to the main gate set in the towering stone wall surrounding the port, and she wondered how she would surmount that formidable obstacle. Simon would have found a way.

At sunset the gate would close, barring passage into or out of the city. As no river flowed through its center, as it had in Antioch, she sadly discounted that as an option. The prospect of getting over the twenty-foot barricade unhurt and undetected seemed daunting, but she saw little choice; attempting to enter through the gate the next morning would only get her captured again once the guards discovered her true nature.

And then the solution entered her weary brain, as though it had waited for her to overanalyze the obvious impossibilities before presenting itself. Kasey smiled at its simplicity and remembered another well-known truth Simon had pointed out to her during their brief time together: the best course of action was the simplest one. She didn't need to scale walls or confront Romans.

She waited until well past sunset to descend the slope onto the narrow plain that disappeared into the low waves of the Mediterranean Sea. Under the faint glow of a crescent moon, Kasey hid behind a small, spindly tree and carefully removed her clothing: the headgear, the robe, the wrap, the tunic, everything. She stood boldly in her underwear, the sports bra and matching panties leaving little to the imagination. Kneeling on the ground, she folded her attire and stuffed it into her knapsack. Sealing it tightly, Kasey got to her feet and started to move.

The water felt cool around her ankles as the gentle surf washed in to meet her, a comforting relief after the heat of the day; though the nights got uncomfortably cold, this one maintained enough warmth for the water to feel good. She eased in up to her knees, searching for the bottom with each cautious step, and soon stood waist deep. Once the water came up to her chest she sank in to her neck, holding the parcel above her head. A hundred feet from shore and hidden in the shadows of shallow waves faintly illuminated by the light of the stars and the crescent moon, the slow current gently tugged her toward the city, in the only direction from which she could access her destination without fear of confrontation.

Boats anchored offshore, but as the inhabitants slept or gazed up at the stars, no one noticed her; and even if they had, they would have seen only a bit of debris floating in the darkness, lost from one of the many vessels that plied these well-traveled waters.

Kasey tried to keep her footing on the bottom of the sea, but its uneven surface made the task impossible, and she found herself treading water, carried by the current, her satchel getting wet as a result; she had hoped to prevent her clothes from getting soaked, because she needed to put them back on once she reached the city, but now she would have to let them dry out first.

After an hour of stealthy swimming, the first section of docks drifted into view. At the city's edge, only a few small fishing boats bobbed gently at their moorings, unattended and unnoticed. She considered reaching out to one and climbing onto the dock, but thought better of it when she noticed a guard patrolling near the wall, keeping the city safe from escaped slaves, college students, and other unsavory women.

She floated on, moving to the next dock, and saw several men standing on the wooden pier, laughing and talking, inebriated after an evening of celebration and revelry. One pointed to the satchel drifting in the current and the others jeered at him, but none made a move to retrieve it; Kasey remained far enough out to make the effort too difficult and pointless for their current sensibilities. She breathed a sigh of relief and kept going.

Halfway along the docks, Kasey found an opening and maneuvered toward an uninhabited and inviting pier. It jutted fifty feet into the bay, allowing two cargo ships and a fishing boat berths for the night; she saw no activity, no guards, and no indication that anyone would take notice of a shadowy figure slipping into the city under the concealing cloak of darkness. Sidling up to the corner where the pier connected to the dock, Kasey carefully and silently reached up to a cross-board that supported the juncture; pulling herself half out of the water, she placed her damp satchel onto the edge of the dock.

Sopping wet, shivering, and suddenly very cold, Kasey softly clambered over the edge and lay flat on her stomach, looking around to see if anyone had spotted her. The people in this part of the city—sailors and soldiers, mainly—had already consumed enough grog and beer to make them insensibly drunk, and those who had not passed out were still in the process of achieving that end. Of course, had anyone glimpsed a beautiful young mostly naked woman dripping on the dock, her scanty underwear doing more to enhance than to conceal her exciting figure, they would have sobered immediately.

Discovering that she remained alone on the dock, Kasey got to her feet and hurried toward the deep shadow of an alley between two stone and wood structures. There she intended to don her clothing and disappear into the night.

But an unexpected whistle from a drunken sailor staggering from a nearby doorway stopped her dead in her tracks. Others ventured out to see what had excited him, and they quickly discovered the unmistakable form of a naked woman standing out in the open, begging for some lucky man to show her the ways of the world. They did not, however, expect her to swing a walking staff into the side of his head when he lunged for her, rendering him unconscious. This had the undesirable effect of enraging the other sailors, who swarmed from the building and chased her across the dock.

Frantically, and embarrassingly, Kasey raced as quickly as her long, bare legs could carry her, realizing that she would have to dive back into the sea to escape from these irrationally angry drunkards. She altered course and headed back the way she had come, and very likely would have made a clean getaway, had two Roman centurions not appeared directly in front of her.

Desperate and afraid, she swiped her staff at the closest one, knocking him flat on his back. The second, however, drew his sword and deflected her blunt weapon into the rough planks. Dozens of men, many holding lanterns, poured out to witness the commotion, shrieking, whistling, and jeering at the bare woman who defiantly waged war against the minions of Rome.

Kasey stood poised for another attack, wielding her stick menacingly as the Roman soldier eyed her with amusement. The first centurion slowly got back on his feet, sword in hand, and circled around to one side. Kasey, knowing she could not win this fight, moved sideways in a wide circle that would bring her to the edge of the dock; once she got close enough to the precipice she could escape into the watery depths.

No one warned her of a third centurion creeping up from behind.

She never knew what hit her.

CHAPTER 39

RECOVERY

Simon woke feeling better than he had in months. A deep sleep in a comfortable bed had done him a world of good, more so than any medicine or ministrations by the doctors of the primitive period in which he now lived. The dull ache in his left shoulder became increasingly apparent as consciousness slowly dawned, like a brilliant and colorful sunrise after a starless night of fog and chill. Disoriented, groggy, yet oddly comfortab le, he opened his bleary eyes, unsure of what to expect. Vague, shadowy images of war and death flashed through his memory, the surrealistic visions of waking dreams, real and unreal, like a movie that had affected him deeply. He glimpsed severed limbs, headless corpses, men consumed by fire, arrows protruding from torsos; he heard screaming and groaning, gurgling coughs expelling the last bloody breaths from dying lungs; the lingering acrid odor of death hung sharply in the air, wafted into his nostrils by a gentle breeze that did more to blend the smoke around the scene of carnage than to blow it away.

Looking down, he discovered a thin shaft sticking out of his own body; terror welled inside him, the fear of death taking hold. Kasey's cold, stern, hard face glared at him with those icy steel-colored eyes, her thin lips mouthing the word "coward" as she turned away, her arms crossed and her back fading into ghostly nothingness as he stared ashamedly into the distance.

The images faded to his subconscious mind as he opened his eyes and saw the light of day penetrating the edges of a shuttered window across the room. He gradually became aware of a bed—an actual bed!—beneath him, a thin cotton blanket stretched across his resting body, a soft pillow supporting his head. Beside the bed stood a narrow table on which rested a bowl, a small box, and a miniature altar depicting Latin characters that he could easily identify, though he had no clue as to their meaning; he understood the spoken language to a competent extent, but knew little of the written form.

He had slept for a considerable time, because aside from the wound in his shoulder nothing else hurt. In the distance thumped the muted sound of the hortator's drum, a reminder that whatever had happened during the battle he remained a slave aboard a Roman ship of war. He had botched his one chance of escape, and in the process nearly got his only friend killed—not to mention interfering with a battle that had raged across the burning deck of the aptly named Inferno. He wondered that the crew had not simply tossed him to the sharks.

Simon sat up and regretted the effort. Dizziness and flickering pinpoints of light swirled around the edges of his vision, forcing him back down. He noticed a clean white bandage wrapped around his left shoulder, a small patch of reddish brown blood staining the center of it; his hand and arm functioned normally as he clenched his fist and carefully flexed his limb at the elbow, avoiding too much motion around the shoulder.

He sat up again, leaning against the wall until the wave of uneasiness swept past. How had he gotten here? And why? He remembered the faces of men carrying him from the burning deck in the moments before losing consciousness; he had not expected to ever wake up, let alone in a bed.

He sat staring at the wall, pondering whether he should open the window and let in the light or just watch it strain around the edges; though he would have liked to see what lay on the other side, that required a level of effort well beyond his current capacity.

A shadow fell upon the doorway. Simon turned and discovered the captain standing there, arms crossed, studying him before stepping formally into the room. The two looked at each other without a word for a long moment before one of them finally spoke.

"You must be hungry," the captain said in his characteristically deep, authoritative voice.

"My stomach thinks my throat's been cut," Simon replied, hoping his tenuous grasp of the language did not blunt the intent of his humor.

The captain smiled, though awkwardly. Simon suspected that very little humor found its way aboard Roman ships of war. The man raised his hand and a servant rushed in with a loaf of bread, a bowl of dates, and a cup of wine which he offered to the recuperating young slave.

"You surprised me," the captain said as Simon tore off a piece of bread and stuffed it into his mouth, following it with a long gulp of wine.

"I didn't want to die," Simon admitted, carelessly breaking the age-old rule of talking with his mouth full. "Did we win?"

"Completely." His handsome face lost some of its hard brutality when he smiled again. Simon saw conflict in his eyes. "Thanks in no small part to your unexpected efforts, we carried the day; I find it unlikely that the one remaining pirate will plunder these shipping lanes again."

Simon popped a date into his mouth and savored the sweetness.

The captain shook his head. "Whatever possessed you to fight the way you did? You could have easily escaped to the pirate vessel and joined their crew; it is certain they would have welcomed you as an enemy of Rome."

"I couldn't leave my friend," Simon replied simply, as though that explained everything.

"The Bedouin," the captain spat. "They tell me you speak his language."

"He's taught me his language and yours," Simon explained. "I'm not yet fluent in either, but I'm getting there."

"You're accent is unusual," the Roman admitted. "How did you fall into the company of such a man? Desert nomads are notorious for their treachery—they kill strangers or sell them in the slave markets, when they're not warring against each other for horses and women."

"I guess that's probably true," Simon realized. "He did intend to sell me and keep Kasey as a concubine. But that didn't work out so well for him."

"Kasey?"

"The girl who brought me to this time—uh, place," Simon sighed. "Achmet Bey rescued us from the desert and took us in—I thought because of his generous hospitality and good nature. We didn't speak the language back then, of course."

"Of course."

"By the way, my name's Simon. Simon Foxx." He offered his hand in the friendly gesture he had seen other Romans display during the journey north.

The captain grasped his outstretched hand and said, "Antonius Maxentius."

"Nice to meet you," Simon said. "Were there a lot of casualties?"

"Initially," Antonius replied thoughtfully. "But once you intervened, our forces rallied, both here and on the Neptune."

"Was there a lot of damage to the ship?"

"Simon, my friend, you saved the ship," the captain said boldly. "Not only did you prevent us from getting rammed, you allowed the crew time to put out the fires that otherwise would have consumed us. Next time we engage in battle I intend for you to sit in the crow's nest with the bow of your choice and an unlimited supply of arrows!"

"Didn't the crow's nest end up underwater?"

"A minor detail."

Simon finished his meal and leaned back against the wall, deeply satisfied. The pain in his shoulder subsided, but he didn't test it for fear of aggravating it again. The captain noticed his cautious movements, favoring the injured area.

"Your wound is healing," Antonius Maxentius said, answering the unasked question. "It did not penetrate deeply and missed the bones."

"That's a relief," Simon breathed. "Of course," he held up his right hand, "this is the important one—the one I draw with. The other just holds the paper."

The captain responded with a puzzled look and a deeply furrowed brow. Then a thought entered his mind, a recollection of something important, and Simon watched the transformation spread across his friend's face. Antonius opened the box that rested atop the desk, reached inside, and pulled out a familiar object that nearly took Simon's breath away.

His heart beating rapidly, his mind overcome with emotion, Simon recognized his precious satchel, the one that never left him under any circumstances. He had carried it to class all through high school and college; it had accompanied him to work at the grocery store since he was fourteen; and it had traveled with him two thousand years into the past, beneath the Arabian desert, and into the heart of the Roman Empire. Seeing his small satchel, battered and stained but otherwise in good order, brought a lump to his throat; a part of him—a part of home—had survived after all.

It gave him hope.

"This belongs to you," Antonius said.

"Yes," Simon replied, surprise evident in his eyes and in his voice. "I never thought I would see it again."

"I examined it," Antonius said. He opened the satchel and retrieved the small sketch book that contained Simon's life's work. "I do not claim to understand it, but it intrigues me. Especially this." He opened the book to the page containing Kasey's portrait in the wheat field and showed it to Simon. A flood of emotions overwhelmed him as he fought them back—kind of like trying to plug the hole in the Titanic with a pinky finger.

"Kasey," he whispered. "I have to find her."

"Your companion," the captain realized. "Little wonder that your Arab friend wanted to keep her."

"I drew that a few months ago," Simon said, "right after we—uh, arrived someplace."

"I'm not familiar with your use of the word draw," the captain admitted. "What does it mean?"

"May I?" Simon reached for the sketch book and satchel. Antonius handed him both.

Carefully, with a few twinges of pain from his recovering shoulder, Simon retrieved a 2H pencil, the hard graphite creating ghost lines on a blank page as he quickly roughed in the general shape of the captain's features; once satisfied with the composition, he made bolder strokes with his favorite 2B pencil, the soft, dark lines and heavy shadows quickly defining his friend's face. He employed blending stumps to smooth out harsh lines and soften shadows, creating a lifelike image of the man who wanted to know something about drawing. Simon turned the paper around and showed him the finished work.

Antonius Maxentius briefly thought Simon a sorcerer, able in a few minutes to reproduce the likeness of a person using the mysterious magic of drawing sticks; the surprise on his face amused Simon.

"It's a drawing," he explained. "I use these tools to recreate what I see."

"Fascinating," the captain said, reaching for the book and examining it closely. "I would not have believed it had I not seen it with my own eyes."

"Thanks, uh, I guess."

"Where you are from, do all warriors draw like this?" the captain asked, his eyes lingering on the accurate features of his own face.

"Not exactly," Simon laughed. He could only imagine an entire regiment of artists: the Surrender Battalion, flitting and slapping and hissing their way across the field of battle, with wild hair, tight pants, and the occasional lisp.

Simon learned that he had slept for nearly two days and that the Inferno, though damaged and without a mast, now headed toward the nearest port large enough to accommodate repairs. He had become a hero to the Romans and they talked endlessly about the strange young slave with the foreign accent who had single-handedly saved the ship and turned the tide of battle—with an arrow sticking out of his chest. He heard the rumors firsthand and met many of the officers and crew the next day when Antonius Maxentius escorted him on a tour of the ship.

Fire had ravaged large swaths of the deck, blackening the rough planks, and a gaping hole remained where the mast had toppled over the side and into the sea. His oar no longer existed, nor did those of half a dozen slaves on the starboard side of the ship. Eight men had perished chained to their oars, crushed by the huge beam; only he had escaped injury, the impact snapping his chain instead of his body.

"Yours is a powerful God after all," Achmet Bey said when Simon visited him at the conclusion of the tour. "He saved us all in His effort to save you."

"He works in mysterious ways," Simon agreed. A sling supported his arm, keeping it immobile; he would have given just about anything for a Tylenol, or an Advil, or an Aleve....

"I heard your wound was mortal," the Arab pointed out, noticing the sling.

"You can't always believe rumors," Simon replied.

"But you did destroy an enemy ship," Achmet Bey said matter-of-factly. "I saw that with my own eyes. Everyone saw it."

"I got lucky, I guess."

"Luck has little to do with it," the Arab surmised. He saw weakness on his friend's drawn face and decided not to continue the interview. "What will you do now, in the absence of your oar?"

"The captain has allowed me to recover in his quarters," Simon said. "They're all treating me pretty well."

"As they should," Achmet Bey observed. "Slave or no slave, the Romans recognize a hero when they see one."

"I'm no hero," Simon defended. "I just didn't want either of us to die. Anybody else would have done the same."

The Bedouin trader laughed. "My friend, no one would have done the same, under any circumstances. You are unique in this miserable world, and that is why they will keep you alive—until you become a threat. I suggest you get some rest and recover your strength, because you will need it before this voyage is over."

Simon took his friend's advice and went back on deck, but instead of returning to bed he found a quiet corner near the bow and began to draw, the unconscious effort taking his mind off his pain and troubles as he concentrated on the lines and shapes and spaces he created with his collection of pencils and blending stumps. He couldn't believe that the Romans had preserved his belongings—the centurion in charge of the slave line had given it to the captain upon turning the slaves over to him on the docks of Tyre—but the very fact that they had recognized its significance and its importance filled him with hope he had not expected. Perhaps these Romans were not simply the mindless, soulless, efficient killing machines of the ancient world that he had always assumed them to be, the Nazis of the distant past bent on world domination. These men lived and breathed as he did; experienced love and joy and sadness, fear and excitement and hope; had families that longed for their return and dreaded news of their destruction. At first he had hated all Romans for their callous and cruel treatment of prisoners, but honestly he could not recall a time during his captivity when any Roman had acted unprofessionally.

He would have to reevaluate his opinion of the people populating this era of history and think of them in an entirely different context—the context of familiarity.

Simon spent three days recuperating all over the ship, drawing everyday scenes of galley life, complet-

ing portraits of the officers and men as they request-
ed. He captured them working, patching and repairing
battle damage, and on occasion he went below to
record images of the slaves hunched miserably over
their oars. Simon filled page after therapeutic page in
his small sketch book, some with quick lines that he intended to turn into much larger and more expressive
works, and some with detailed and intimate scenes
that warmed and impressed all who viewed them.

When the familiar port city of Tyre appeared on the
horizon, with the masts and sails of a thousand ships
stretching across the broad expanse of sea between
the Inferno and the coast, Simon filled pages with
mesmerizing images, his hands and eyes laboring to
reproduce a fraction of the beauty he saw all around.
He drew fishing boats, galleys, small pleasure craft,
at least two yachts, and several panoramic views of
the bustling port from different perspectives as the
Inferno drew nearer, allowing him greater access to
detail.

People everywhere stopped what they were doing
and stared in awe, jaws gaped open, as the formidable
Roman warship slipped into port, its battle-damaged
hull and missing mast creating a sensation among
the throngs of people who saw it. Rumors spread of
a devastating ambush from which the Roman vessel had narrowly escaped; how Neptune himself had
fought on behalf of the Empire to assure an unlikely victory at sea. The truth would shock people and
sound like the most unbelievable rumor of all, and yet

it would spread throughout the Empire, forming the basis of a local legend, perhaps even reaching the ear of Tiberius himself.

Simon could not know the impact he would have on Ancient Rome.

Chapter 40

The Cell

Kasey languished in her dank, miserable cell for three months. She counted the days, each one, scraping a small mark on the stone wall with a pebble at every sunrise. She could not exactly see the sun, or the window high up on the wall that allowed in the only breathable air and the dim light of day; the opening remained obscured by a complex of walls and cells that made any effort to locate the source of light an exercise in frustration. She only knew that every morning the muted light appeared, lasted all day, and then faded in the evening.

It was an expansive cell, twice the size of her college dorm room; damp straw littered wide patches of floor and often rustled with the shallow movements of tiny creatures that almost never showed themselves. Occasionally she felt one crawling across her legs in the middle of the night, and so she almost never slept then; she dozed during the day and kept silent vigil against hidden nocturnal terrors.

In the first weeks of her captivity she sought a way out: a hidden passage, a loose stone, a careless guard. But her efforts proved frustratingly useless. She saw no guards after the first day; her door never opened and no other human spoke to her. At random, irregular intervals a small panel in the bottom of the door slid open and a tray of nasty food slid through onto the floor; most days she found it inedible: soggy bread, leathery strips of meat, the occasional shriveled fruit or vegetable, a cup of water with tiny things swimming in it. Kasey went days without eating, until she had to consume what they gave her in order to stay alive. It made her sick and she writhed in her cell, moaning and clutching her stomach until the evil passed from her body. Some days the stench of vomit and diarrhea overwhelmed her and she sobbed like a little girl curled up in the fetal position in a corner.

But she never lost count of the days.

After a month her stomach grew accustomed to the sparse diet and the sickness subsided, though occasional bouts of intestinal distress caused unbearable suffering. When she regained the capacity for rational thought she resolved to survive, for the specific purpose of locating Simon and getting away from the Roman Empire. To that end, she embarked on a physical and mental quest to strengthen her mind and body, keeping her fit and prepared for the escape opportunity she knew would present itself. Kasey walked around the perimeter of her cell, a distance of twenty normal paces, fewer if she jogged or ran, and counted the laps. By her reckoning, one hundred and five circuits constituted a mile, a distance she easily covered in fifteen minutes at a good stroll—ten minutes at a brisk walk, and six minutes at a decent run. In two months she journeyed from New York to San Francisco, stopping at scenic points along the way: Chicago, Mount Rushmore, Yellowstone, and Lake Tahoe. She imagined every stretch of road, the weather—sunshine, rain, wind—and the people and towns she would have encountered along the way. Sometimes she pretended to stop at a diner for a cheeseburger and a chocolate milkshake, while other times she slept out under the stars and stared up at the brilliant swath of lights that made up the Milky Way.

As she journeyed across the great country that currently did not—and eventually would not—exist, she grew strong, her already shapely legs filling out with a layer of musculature that enhanced her beauty in ways she could not yet imagine. Her stamina increased such that a brisk walk or an all-out run for hours at a time barely winded her. When not walking, she did push-ups and sit-ups, building her upper body and toning her stomach until scarcely an ounce of fat remained anywhere on her slender form. The strenuous efforts required more food, which meant forcing down her horrid daily rations instead of leaving them for the rats. Sometimes the moldy food left her incapacitated for days at a stretch, but more often it sustained her.

In all that time she never lost count of her steps, her laps, and the days that came and went on the other side of her cell wall.

And during that time she set to work fashioning, from a length of stone pried from the wall, a rudimentary knife that, while not as pretty as the one she had lost upon entering this miserable abyss, might someday make the difference between eternal captivity and glorious freedom.

A reckoning began three months to the day of her capture on the docks of Tyre. She barely remembered that distant event, assuming someone had hit her on the head, which would explain the massive headaches plaguing her first week of captivity. Her captors had taken away her leather bag, her clothing, and her staff, so for three months she had worn only her black sports bra and matching panties; sometimes the nights got unbearably cold, but her attire felt comfortable during the hottest parts of the day. To preserve the life of her garments, she removed them during the intense hours of her workouts, confident that no one could see her; they would have attempted to molest her by now. To her knowledge, no one had tried anything during her long state of unconsciousness, and while that surprised her, given soldiers' propensity for taking what they wanted, she felt relieved that maybe even they maintained rules of decorum. Or perhaps they feared what she would do to them.

Three months after she awoke in the nightmarish hell beneath the city of Tyre, Kasey's luck changed. The cell door opened, and for a moment she believed her captors had finally come to get her, perhaps having realized the error of her imprisonment. She longed for bright rays of sunlight to warm her bare, pale flesh, rejuvenate her soul, breathe life back into her withering body. She smiled at the possibility of seeing the world again....

And then the guards shoved a new prisoner into the cell, clanking the door closed behind him.

The man did not see her as he staggered into the darkness, scuffing the matted straw, stirring up a cloud of dust and wispy fibers. He bellowed at the top of his lungs, spat obscenities at his captors, and flung himself at the door. But Kasey knew the frustrating impenetrability of that hated obstacle. She stood quietly in the corner and watched him rage against the hard wood, pounding his meaty fists into it, screaming like a madman. A dark scraggly beard obscured his probably ugly face, merging with unkempt hair, making a distinction between the two impossible; dark, deep-set eyes blinked through the wild disarray, above a crooked, broken nose that seemed glued onto the thick, bushy fur of his hidden face.

The man gave up his rant and stomped around in the near darkness, mumbling indecipherable words, occasionally raising his voice in case some distant centurion might take notice of his insults. Kasey doubted anyone cared; once they dropped you into the forgotten pit of hell they didn't come back to ask your opinion on matters of State. He circled the room haphazardly, absent mindedly, disgusted by the fate Rome had handed him, until eventually he became gradually aware of someone else sharing his abominable plight. He might have heard her soft breathing, or the hard thumping of her heart against her breastbone; or perhaps he smelled her scent, distinct from his own, though probably just as rancid after three months of imprisonment; maybe the odor of dried vomit and waste assailed his nostrils; or, more likely, he simply sensed the presence of another living creature, as everyone who has ever been alone in a house at night knows when someone else is in the room with them. Whatever the case, he suddenly stopped his irregular pacing and stared directly at her, his small black eyes penetrating through the cloak of darkness and the scant barricade of her underwear.

A creepy smile formed on his narrow lips, revealing broken and yellow teeth, between which a sickening tongue flicked like that of a serpent. Kasey recognized the look; she had seen it too many times and knew exactly what to expect. No one would protect her in the basement of a darkened prison two thousand years from home.

He spoke in a sleazy, condescending whine that made her skin crawl; she only understood the occasional word, but got the message clearly enough.

Her cellmate approached boldly, his eyes adjusted to the dim light, and scoured every inch of her flawless and nearly bare figure, no doubt deciding that captivity had its merits after all. Nowhere in the outside world would a woman of such beauty give herself to his perverse carnal desires, nor did he expect this one to do so willingly; but the outside world obviously did not care what became of her, and so he knew he could implement with impunity any means of persuasion necessary for her to accept the situation on his terms.

The smile broadened into a wicked grin as his calloused and dirty hand reached for the bare curve of her smooth shoulder, his long fingernails scraping across her pale flesh. Kasey stood rigid and trembling against the stone wall, desperate to get away not only from his vile touch but from the swirling atmosphere of stench that assailed her nostrils. Both his knotty hands probed her hardened flesh, discovering first her shoulders and stomach, then reaching up to fondle her breasts, mercifully protected by the suddenly inadequate garment that had served her for so long. As he gripped the side of her sports bra to tear it from her torso, Kasey slid her hand into the waistband at the back of her lower undergarment, where she had placed the prison shank she had spent so much time honing to sharpened perfection.

Her assailant's expression of perverse pleasure froze into something akin to terror, though it was difficult to tell through all the dark and matted hair. His small eyes bulged from their sockets as the unexpected weapon slashed sharply upward in an arc that sliced across his face, from his chin to his forehead, opening jagged slits through his cheek and brow. Staggering backward in sudden shock, blood oozing from half a dozen deep gashes, the man screamed in agony, his desperate cry ringing through the prison and beyond, echoing along the busy streets of Tyre.

Kasey pounced on her now frantic would-be rapist, his arms raised in desperate defense; he fell backward beneath the considerable force of her impact and collided with the wall on the other side of the room. She whirled around and kicked him in the stomach, Chuck Norris-style, suddenly remembering the moves her sister had taught her as a child in their short-lived experimentation with karate classes—which had, of course, ended after the unfortunate incident with the pair of living room end tables.

Shrill screams and desperate pleas boomed from the darkened cell as the wretched, miserable excuse of a man crumpled to the floor and scrambled to get away from the tigress someone had loosed on him; Kasey plunged her deadly homemade blade deep into his torso, resulting in an intensity of agonized moans, now choked and gurgling with internal hemorrhaging.

His death was messy and violent; he thrashed and convulsed as darkness expanded beneath him; she could not get close enough to deal the final blow, and had to wait in mortifying horror while the life gradually drained from his twitching form. But in a few tortuous minutes It was over.

Kasey leaned against the wall and tried not to think about what she had done. Blood covered her hands and stains splattered her torso from her hip to her shoulder; the sickening smell overpowered everything else in the dingy cell. Her heart pounded and sweat poured from every inch of her flesh, soaking her in coldness; she could barely feel her hands and feet.

But what else could she have done? The man had tried to molest her, and in so doing would have crushed her will to survive; he would have dominated her and then killed her when she could no longer satisfy him. If one of them had to die, she would rather sacrifice him. Simon needed her, and so did Carista. She could not let them down.

A new sound echoed in the corridor: feet pounding rapidly on stone. They were coming to kill her. She pressed her back to the wall beside the door, gripping the primitive, dripping, crudely sharpened shank, and waited; controlling her breathing by sheer force of will, Kasey stood perfectly still as heavy movement drew inexorably nearer.

The cell door flung carelessly open and four armed guards rushed into the room, swords drawn, one carrying a blazing torch. They swept past her in a flurry, seeing the dead man on the floor, and hastened in to investigate. No one noticed the young woman, naked and dripping with blood and sweat, waiting for them when they entered; as the last man stopped, his back inches from her, Kasey slashed at his neck with the tip of her shank, eliciting a cry of stunned surprise; in the same instant she grasped the pugio from his belt and kicked him into his companions. The torch he held flew from his hand and landed in the dry straw, smoldered for a handful of seconds, and blazed to life.

Kasey paused for most of a heartbeat as the terrified Romans suddenly realized the fate she had dealt them; they could not act swiftly enough to stop the prisoner from darting into the corridor and pulling the door shut behind her.

The conflagration spread quickly.

Kasey raced along the corridor, carrying her new weapon, tears streaming down her face as she tried to block out the agonized screams echoing along with her; hands and feet pounded on the door with intensifying fury as hungry flames consumed everything within the hellish prison cell.

Soldiers descended into the depths to ascertain the nature of the commotion, oblivious of their comrades roasting alive at the end of the corridor. Hiding in an alcove, Kasey avoided the flickering torchlight, and in their haste to get to the scene of carnage they failed to notice her shadowed form as they filed quickly past.

Her strong legs carried her up an unattended flight of stairs and into a ground-level corridor, at the end of which she discovered the door to freedom, guarded by a man who stood fortuitously distracted; in one hand he held a very familiar golden sacrificial dagger, his appreciative eye admiring his newest acquisition, no doubt won from another soldier in a lucrative game of dice.

His body crumpled silently to the floor as Kasey disappeared into the shadows of early evening.

CHAPTER 41

THE PLAN

Simon stood on the bow of the Inferno as the great ship of war slid into its berth along a lengthy pier, greeted by centurions, dock workers, and citizens, many holding hands to their mouths in expressions of awe. Few had ever witnessed the fresh damage of battle, the scars of war that expert hands would soon obscure with fresh paint and new construction. Feeling stronger, his arm remained in its sling a week out from battle; he expected it to heal completely in the time it took skilled craftsmen to repair the injured Inferno. He wondered how much damage the arrow might have caused had he not spent three months chained to that damnable oar building up muscles and stamina.

The city looked different from this perspective, standing on deck looking out from a dozen feet above the water; he had last seen it as a slave trudging between the struggling forms of desperate and dejected men, the demoralizing and intimidating shape of the galley looming over him, a mobile prison from which no man ever escaped except through slow and tortuous death. And yet... he had escaped, in a manner of speaking. Antonius Maxentius, perceiving his young prisoner's surprising lack of animosity toward those who had probably unjustly imprisoned him, had shown him as much hospitality as possible on a damaged ship filled with men who desired to be anywhere else. He had assured Simon that he would pursue the matter of his arrest and imprisonment with the highest authorities, and once they heard the plea of a victorious galley captain, they could not fail to release him.

But Antonius recognized the impatient look on Simon's face, the determination in his bright blue eyes, and knew that his friend contemplated something rash.

"They will hunt you down and destroy you," the captain said as he stopped next to Simon along the battered rail.

"I have to find her," he replied simply.

"Let me investigate," Antonius said. "I have friends in ports around the Empire. They can contact jailors; we will find her together, and I will use my influence to secure her release. From what you have told me, the two of you did nothing wrong. I am certain that the new governor will hear me; we were friends as children in Rome; he attended my wedding celebration, and sent me an expensive gift when I achieved the rank of captain; I returned the favor when he was appointed governor of Judea. He would not turn me away or refuse to hear my argument on your behalf."

"Is his name Pontius Pliate?" Simon inquired.

"You know him?" The captain's stunned expression amused Simon, forcing an ironic grin.

"Let's just say that where I come from he has a reputation for cruelty," Simon replied. "I have little hope of justice where he is concerned."

"I do not know how you could judge him," the captain sighed, "But the friend I know is compassionate and fair, and he is your best hope of freedom."

"I'll take my chances," Simon said, refuting his friend's wisdom. "I can escape so that no one will blame you. All I ask is to take Achmet Bey with me."

"Rome will hunt me down as well as you," the captain said sternly, both hands on the rail as he leaned over the side, peering down at the narrow strip of water separating the ship from the dock. "If you leave, you will go alone. He cannot accompany you."

"But he didn't do anything wrong either," Simon insisted. "I was there; his own people tried to assassinate him, and then the Romans tried to kill him. It wasn't his fault."

Antonius Maxentius sighed deeply and significantly.

"Rome has a long memory," he said carefully. "As do the Bedouins. Your Arab friend has neglected to inform you of his past—the deeds of his youth that made the incident at Moab more significant than you understand."

"What did he do?"

"I advise you to ask him," the captain replied, "or you will think I am attempting to color your perception of the man you admire."

Simon silently studied the nearby buildings while the captain attended to the duties of mooring the ship and arranging for a host of repairs. Then he turned and descended the steep stairs that led into the rowing chamber.

Achmet Bey rested against his immobile oar, taking advantage of rare downtime to recuperate from the exertions of the day. Even for the strongest and most powerful man on the ship, the constant strain of monotonous rowing took its toll. His bones and muscles ached without relief.

"You have come to set me free," the Arab half-joked as his friend stood by his side. Simon's own oar and bench had vanished, torn away from him when the mast had crushed this portion of the ship.

"Actually, I tried that," he replied. "But we're both trapped here, although I think one of us is more trapped than the other."

"You no longer wear the chains of a slave."

"We both wear the chains of deception," Simon said. "You've been a good friend—I never would have survived here without you—but I need to know what I'm in for if I set you free. Why did Rome send you here to die?"

"You've been talking to the captain again." The Bedouin frowned, shaking his massive, hairy face, unkempt and unshaved for three months. "He's willing to let you "escape" but only if you go alone; you wanted to liberate me, but he will not allow it."

"Something like that."

"What did he tell you about me?"

"Only that I should hear it from you."

"A wise man," Achmet Bey mused. "From him you would think it a lie, but from me...."

"What did you do?"

"Nothing as bad as you imagine," the Arab replied distantly as he recalled the impetuosity of youth. "Before I amassed my wealth I was a warrior defending tribal lands against the invasion forces of an Empire bent on conquering every innocent realm."

"Rome."

"They do not take kindly to any man who defends his home when they desire to take it from him, and for that they sentence me to death here in this bottomless hole of despair."

"There must be more to the story," Simon insisted. "Or else they would have arrested you the first time your caravan entered Moab."

"Of course there is," the Arab replied. "Romans killed Bedouins, Bedouins killed Romans, and each side maintains animosity toward the other. Some of us are more proficient at killing than others, and we are labeled enemies of the Empire. So I disappeared for ten years, became rich through trade, powerful through reputation, and anonymous through the distance of time. I changed, but the world did not; my own people grew treacherous."

"Why did they try to kill you?" Simon asked.

"I should have recognized the signs," Achmet Bey sighed. "One of my wives got too close to my most trusted advisor and they poisoned the others against me. When you and Kasey arrived and I became intrigued by her, they used that as an excuse to act. My rash decision to return to Moab so soon after my previous trip gave them the opportunity they needed. You know the rest."

"That doesn't explain the involvement of Rome."

"Rome does not forget its enemies," the Arab replied somberly. "My advisor—before I beheaded him—contacted the local centurions and informed them of my identity before the assassination attempt. My friends were to kill me, saving Rome the trouble, in exchange for immunity and reward."

"Guess it didn't go the way they planned," Simon recalled.

"One of my wives remained loyal," Achmet Bey said heavily. "I fear for her."

"She's the one who helped Kasey...," Simon realized, remembering the woman who had intervened during the conflict and saved her from the mismatched fight.

"I will never see her again in this life."

"Never say never," Simon replied. "Anything can happen. This isn't the end of the world; trust me, I know a thing or two about that."

"My friend, I sometimes do not understand you."

"So Rome wants you dead," Simon said, "as do your own people. But maybe it doesn't have to be that way."

"What are you saying?"

"I have a plan." And strangely, the hastily forming scheme made more sense than any his oddly creative brain had contemplated since that first fateful encounter with the woman who had so completely changed his life. She would resist the idea, to be sure, but he could not fail to convince her once he made the case that now presented itself so forcefully and logically inside his head. Once she saw the rationality—and understood the consequences—she would leap for the same conclusion.

All he had to do was defy the most powerful empire in the history of the world, locate a single woman somewhere from England to Judea, and help her to create a new time machine using only the materials available in the ancient past. Piece of cake.

The hard part would be explaining to the Arab how he would fit into his new role as a time traveler.

CHAPTER 42

THE SEARCH FOR SIMON FOXX

For a week Kasey hid in the back alleys and deep shadows of ancient Tyre. The Romans conducted an exhaustive search of the port, scouring every building, barn, and boat before realizing that she had either stowed away aboard a ship or secretly joined a caravan heading in any of a dozen directions. She saw frustration on their faces, but also smug determination, patient understanding that she could not hide indefinitely in a world dominated by Rome. She would make a mistake and they would find her.

The sun had crept below the horizon before her frantic departure, providing long, intense shadows in which to hide; nearly naked, pale as a ghost, smeared with sweat and blood, and stinking from three months of horrid underground confinement, it would not have taken much for someone to sound an alarm. But no one had noticed, and she vanished without a sound.

Her heart ached over the carnage she had wrought in that hated prison, the suffering and terror inflicted during her desperate escape. What would Simon think of her? What would God think? Had He healed her and given her hope and purpose so she could mete out death and destruction with impunity wherever she went? He was a wrathful God, as the Old Testament clearly demonstrated, but she found it difficult to believe that He would utilize her as a weapon in His Plan to save His Chosen People from the tyranny of Rome. God leveled the cities of the wicked while Jesus loved His enemies; both were the same and yet different and none of it made any sense. Religion was more complicated than time travel and it made her brain want to explode.

She could only trust that the path she traveled was the one God had laid out for her, convoluted and dismal as it often appeared.

Washing the filth from her body in the sea near a deserted dock, she contemplated drifting with the current and taking her chances along the road the next day, but quickly thought better of it. She had come here to look for Simon, and if Rome had made him a galley slave—as her friends on the road had suggested—his ship would ultimately return here for repairs and provisions. Besides, she could not travel in her underwear.

After her glorious bath she had crept through the night and stolen the supplies necessary to survive and remain hidden. A cloth bag, pilfered from one sleeping tradesman, soon held bread, cheese, olives, and dates filched from another; she acquired clothing to cover her body from head to foot, including a dark cloak that obscured her disheveled face from the prying light of day. Sandals protected her feet from the rocks and dust of the streets, and the occasional unpleasantness that resided there, while a newly stolen walking staff completed her ensemble.

Many people dressed similarly in the city, and so after days of hiding in places where the Romans could not find her—hay lofts, attics, cellars, closets, never in any one place for more than a few hours—she became emboldened enough to mingle with the crowds. No one paid attention to her.

As the days plodded inexorably on and she gained confidence, Kasey visited the great galleys as they rowed into port—half a dozen in a week's time, each painted in bold schemes: red fire with blazing eyes on the bow; deep blue with expansive, feathery wings along the sides; black with cyclonic storms and bolts of lightning covering the hull; and deep green emblazoned with fantastic monsters of the sea. She studied the colossal warships from as close as she dared without drawing attention to herself, but could not tell if the man she desired slumped over an oar deep within any of them; the oar ports remained too small and cloaked in shadow to see within. Calling his name risked bringing the might of Rome down on her, for she could not simply disguise her voice.

She needed a more effective way of getting his attention, a way that only he would understand, a means of communication to which he could easily respond, even from the bowels of his mobile prison.

The answer arrived by way of divine inspiration, and for it she offered a quick prayer of thanks.

Strolling past the first galley, Kasey whistled a tune she knew Simon would recognize: Darth Vader's Theme. Her sister's obsession with those movies bordered on mania; she could quote virtually all the dialogue and frequently discussed—at dismaying length—minutia that bored Kasey to tears. Kasey had suffered through them more times than she could count and knew that Simon, with his extensive cinematic experience— resulting from his lack of dating experience—would hear the tune and respond in kind. She needed only to keep trying until she located the right ship.

As with all desperate and hastily conceived plans, she relied on good luck—and on three assumptions: he still lived, he was in fact enslaved on a ship of war, and the ship would eventually return to this port. The plan also required her to stay hidden in plain sight, away from prying eyes curious about the mysterious stranger and the foreboding tune that issued from hidden lips.

Kasey waited until evening on the day of her first attempt to get Simon's attention. The noises of the dock subsided but people lingered. Most sailors and dockhands retired to pubs, inns, and brothels to wile away the warm night in the amorous arms of drunkenness, leaving few people to notice the stranger in the shadows. Kasey remembered all too well her first appearance in this part of town, when a mob of angry people had nearly lynched her; months of recollection led her to realize that the two guards she had attacked—and the unseen third one who had clubbed her on the back of the head—had saved her life by removing her from the increasingly vicious throng of ruffians. The guards had ushered her immediately to jail, where they had left her largely forgotten for three months. They paid the price for that oversight on the evening of her escape.

Kasey scanned every direction, and when she felt safe enough she whistled a few bars from one of John Williams' most recognizable works, projecting the bold, imperial sounds toward the galley—the one painted red and looking back at her with dark eyes on the bow. Heads turned as people stared into the darkness at the origin of the strange and catchy tune, and then she abruptly stopped. Kasey clung to the shadows further along the dock and made a second attempt. Three more times she tried it, but no one responded.

Feeling foolish, she left the docks and located a place to spend the night, finding some comfort in the fact that no one had accosted her. The first attempt had failed, as she suspected it would, but other galleys would enter the port and she would rule them out one by one.

Day after day, for most of a week, vessels came and went, and when the magnificent ships of war drew her attention she whistled her tune, each time straining to hear an answer from within.

One day a blue ship painted to look like a furious storm at sea limped into port with charred and crumbled planks scorched from one side to the other; the bow suffered extensive damage, probably from ramming another ship in battle, and she got the impression that the war had not gone well for the Romans.

What a shame, she thought. Poor Romans.

Poor Simon! Suppose he had served unwillingly on that very ship and suffered grievously during battle! What if the enemy had killed him? Or taken him as their slave? She could not bear such thoughts. He had to live, or none of this would have any meaning.

Kasey inched closer to the dock, ambled along the wide pier, and found an alcove near its juncture with the main avenue. There she sat in silence during the hottest part of the day, watching and listening, struggling to decipher the few words and phrases she understood from people passing by.

A battle had raged a hundred miles out to sea, involving two Roman galleys and four much swifter Phoenician pirate vessels. Two pirates had gotten rammed, effectively incapacitating the galleys, while the others attempted to ram the Romans. But something had gone horribly wrong for the pirates, according to witnesses on the newly arrived Neptune's Fury. From what Kasey gathered, a rogue slave, after smashing his chains, had single-handedly destroyed an entire pirate vessel by launching a flaming enemy soldier into its upper decks, initiating a conflagration that consumed the ship before it could ram the galley.

According to tales already spinning around the docks, the man had fought alone against half the Phoenician Navy, overwhelmed them with his extraordinary size and strength, and thrashed them mercilessly—with half a dozen arrows sticking out of his chest and back. No one knew if he had survived the battle, but he had certainly saved the day for the Empire.

Kasey hoped Simon never encountered that malicious warrior and that his own ship had not ventured anywhere near the scene of carnage. But if it had, he would have found a suitable place in which to hide until the danger passed. When sunset arrived, she ventured close to the Neptune's Fury and whistled Darth Vader's Theme. Changing positions, she tried half a dozen times, but with no effect. Simon either was not aboard, or was in no condition to reply.

Suppose he heard her but lay wounded and unable to answer her call? What if he had already left port frustrated at his inability to respond?

She could only keep trying until something forced her to stop—or until she found him.

The next day everything changed.

The whole city of Tyre turned out for the anticipated arrival of a familiar galley, the Inferno, which appeared in the distance at midmorning and gradually eased toward the docks by the hottest part of the afternoon. Kasey watched from the safety of a rooftop a few blocks from the pier, as mesmerized by the scene as anyone else in the city.

The ship had suffered more than anyone imagined, with a partially crushed bow, one side caved in almost to the waterline, and the scorched scars of fires that had consumed the forward half of the vessel. Most noticeably, even from a distance, the entire mast, and the expanse of red and white striped sail that had dominated the ship, no longer existed, ripped away during battle, exposing the bare decks like a beautiful woman whose dress had suddenly torn free. Thousands of people stood in awe, pointing and gasping as the great battleship slid longingly toward its berth.

More than the battle-scarred ship brought out the multitudes on that hot afternoon: throngs of curious onlookers scanned the decks, hands shielding wide eyes from the sun, for a glimpse of the now famous slave who had overnight become a local legend owing to his deadly prowess in battle. They looked for a towering giant of a man, his bronze flesh stretched tight over rippling sinews of muscle, broken chains still dangling from his wrists. Instead they saw soldiers and sailors attending to their duties, a man who looked like the captain discussing something with a young officer who wore his arm in a sling, and the shadowy movements of slaves rowing in their chamber, glimpsed through the gaping hole in the side of the Inferno. Kasey, from her lofty vantage, noticed all the same things, and wondered how she would navigate the sea of onlookers to get close enough for her tune to penetrate the broken hull of this battered galley. If Simon did reside aboard the Inferno he would have seen plenty of action, judging from the condition of the ship; and with that hole in the side, in the midst of the rowing chamber, she suddenly realized that he could have been crushed to death.

Her careful eye returned to the deck, studying the figures by the rail. She had initially discounted them, for both were Roman... at least they dressed that way. The captain stood talking to an injured man, whose arm rested in a makeshift sling, his bandaged upper torso largely bare, revealing a muscular frame that surprised her—not the shape of a body builder or a giant, like the crowds expected, but that of a solid, well-formed young man... who looked oddly familiar. His thick, scraggly beard threw her off for a moment, as did the wild, unkempt hair, but those bright blue eyes that shined in the light of the mid-afternoon sun were unmistakable.

"Simon...," she whispered breathlessly. Her heart raced with excitement and her blood boiled in her veins as joy the likes of which she had never known spread through her arms and legs and burst from her fingertips and toes. A smile of pure and unadulterated love animated her beautiful face, her steel gray eyes glowing, her pale cheeks flushing with rosy warmth.

Her quest was over. She had but to attract his attention and they would find a way to survive this harsh world together and escape back to their own time, or somewhere thereabouts.

Kasey left her hiding place and scampered down the steps to the street, in her haste failing to take her usual precautions. Drawn like a fuzzy-winged moth to the glowing blue light of a bug lamp, or a ruby-throated hummingbird to an innocuous feeder hanging too close to a back porch and the house cat that resided there, Kasey quickly threaded her way onto the wide expanse of docks, now filled with throngs of people staring at the great damaged hulk.

She had taken maybe three steps when she collided with the unexpected form of a Roman centurion. Kasey gasped when the man's scarred face turned to her with a leering and hate-filled glare that suddenly made her blood run cold. A wicked and knowing smile bared perfect white teeth, sneering at her like a wild animal preparing for the kill.

"Marconius!"

Kasey turned to run, but a pair of centurions flanked her; emerging from the crowd, their muscular bulk indicated the futility of a fight. She could not comprehend how he had found her, though a moment of thought would have put the obvious pieces together.

Reacting on instinct, Kasey swung her walking staff toward the vile man's head, which he easily deflected with his arm; but the distraction allowed her to break free of the trap and sprint across the dock toward the great charred mass of the Inferno and the man she loved. The crowd slowed her; though as the chase ensued, people moved out of the way, clearing an uneasy path for the cloaked stranger who had not gone unnoticed on the docks for the last week. The three centurions pursued their desperate quarry, swords raised, armor clanking as their feet pounded heavily on the wooden docks.

Simon returned to the rail to watch the crowds as the Inferno rested in its berth. The crew had secured the great vessel to the dock and arranged for a long, rickety plank to connect the one with the other. He knew he could simply walk off the galley and disappear into the crowd and no one onboard his ship would stop him; they admired and respected him enough that every man would assist—secretly, of course—in whatever he intended to do. But not so for the Arab. Achmet Bey, a despised criminal, had gained no such popularity; the men took satisfaction in his suffering and looked forward to watching him die of fatigue. But the indefatigable Bedouin seemed unbreakable.

"I can't leave without him," Simon muttered as he scanned the city and the multitudes of people glaring up at him. The captain had given him a Roman uniform: a tunic, belt, sandals, and underclothes, though they required alteration to accommodate the bandage encasing his left shoulder and the sling that still supported his arm; most of his chest remained bare, allowing the Mediterranean sun to bring back his color, leaving him feeling better than he had in months. He could not have known that the inhabitants of Tyre studied him with disappointment, hoping for a glimpse of the powerfully defiant slave who had single-handedly altered the tide of battle.

His mind and his heart in turmoil, Simon stared blankly out at the panoramic scene, torn by conflicting duties. Kasey needed him and he could not let her down; but so did his friend. How could he abandon Achmet Bey to the slow death of the galley? He sensed the return of the captain by his side.

"He told you the truth?" Antonius Maxentius inquired in a solemn tone.

"He told me he fought against Rome in his youth, when Rome invaded his land," Simon replied. "But that he is no longer the man he once was."

"You must know that nomads have no land," the captain said, "no country to fight for and no government to direct their actions. What he and his desert dwellers did they did of their own accord."

"It was war," Simon insisted, understanding now what could happen under extreme circumstances. "People do things in war that they would never imagine in peace."

"Perhaps," the captain sighed. "But few men kill as swiftly and as abundantly as your friend. He did not boast of his exploits?"

"Only that Romans killed Arabs and Arabs killed Romans."

"It took considerable sacrifice to subdue that uprising," Antonius Maxentius explained. "Our legions hunted down the leaders, but some escaped. The man whom you claim saved your life is a valuable prisoner, one whose fate is closely guarded by the forces of Rome; my superiors, and theirs, want him to suffer at length before he perishes."

"You know I won't let that happen."

"I don't see that you have much choice."

"If God wills it, Rome will have little to say about it."

"I have heard of your God," Antonius smiled. "Rather an unassuming and unimportant God, weak and powerless."

"He's a lot more subtle than we give Him credit for," Simon replied. "He works on people in ways we don't realize, and then—"

Simon broke off as a disturbance in the crowd drew his attention. People scattered as a cloaked figure emerged, racing desperately toward the Inferno, pursued by three much larger and more powerful men.

"Someone has cornered a thief," the captain mused.

Long pale legs flashed beneath dark robes as the figure sprinted across the docks, and something clicked in Simon's head; he knew those legs, that gait, the long and careful stride of a cross-country runner. His heart pounded and his blood ran cold, his hands turning white as he gripped the wooden rail on the side of the ship.

"No...," he whispered, staring intently into the darkness of the hood that covered the mysterious face. "It can't be...."

Wind pushed back the hood as she ran through the parting crowd, revealing a ghostly pale face, steel-gray eyes, and golden brown hair that trailed behind her in a tangled mass of matted curls. Simon's heart stopped and the color drained from his face.

"Kasey!" he yelled at the top of his lungs. "Kasey!"

"Simon!" she called out as their gazes met for the first time since that awful separation more than three months ago—the day she had spoken the most important words anyone had ever said to him. He lunged toward the ramp the sailor had just positioned, but the captain placed a hand on his arm.

"I cannot protect you once you leave the ship," he warned. "Get her aboard and I will treat her as I treat you."

"I understand."

Simon took another step and then froze in his tracks. An unseen guard, hidden by the crowd, tackled the running figure, slamming her onto the dock. The three pursuing men quickly caught up and surrounded her; the one with an ugly scar on his cheek kicked her in the side, and the others joined him, reveling in the violence. Kasey howled with pain.

"No!" Simon bellowed as he raced with renewed energy, rage welling within him. Antonius Maxentius followed closely behind, prepared to accompany his friend into the midst of angry centurions.

But before Simon reached the top of the gangway the man with the scar withdrew his short sword, flashed it high over his head, and plunged it into the struggling young woman at his feet.

Simon's body went numb. He barely felt his captain's restraining arms. He struggled, tears pouring from his eyes, desperate to do something, anything, to avoid this catastrophe.

His last thought before someone clubbed him over the head was that in spite of his hopes and promises, contrary to the faith he professed, God had at long last abandoned them.

More importantly, Simon Foxx had failed the woman he loved.

Author's Note

If I didn't have to work for a living, I could write a first draft in about a month, give or take a week; but in the case of Edge of Time, I spent the better part of thirty years getting it just the way I wanted. But, with time travel, thirty seconds and thirty years amount to pretty much the same thing, depending on your perspective. Along the way I found inspiration in some of the most absurd places: I encountered at least one character name from an engraved name plaque when I worked for a sign engraving company; another character was inspired by one of my favorite cinematic villains, though he will ultimately become one of the most powerful good guys of the series; and my favorite movie of all time certainly played a role in some of the settings, as well as the fate of at least one character. And I cannot emphasize enough the impetus that got this sprawling work started during my sophomore year of college sometime in the previous century: one of the most intense nightmares of my life, involving a massive flood and a wall of water that entirely inundated the campus and everything in it! I remember waking up in a cold sweat in the middle of the night and writing down every detail I could remember of the dream before it faded into nothingness—a practice that I encourage everyone to explore!

My eighth grade teacher once told the class that you could remember your dreams simply by telling yourself before bed to remember your dreams—and it actually works! (On those rare occasions when I remember to tell myself to remember them.... Sigh). Another teacher, I can't remember which one this far removed, suggested keeping a dream journal by the bed, for recording the wanderings of the mind upon waking; some of them can be quite exciting, extraordinarily terrifying, or just plain bizarre. But often, more than the visual images that sometimes don't make sense, it is the underlying feelings associated with the dreams that make the most impact. It's difficult to put such things into words, to adequately describe how a dream makes you feel, but you know you feel it and sometimes it can be overpowering. That intense underlying emotion led me to escape the nightmare of my submerged campus the only way I knew how: by writing about it.

I'm sure there are deeper psychological implications involved with that much water and helplessness, but the important thing is that I survived college more or less intact, though less dramatically than Simon Foxx or Catalina Carabresa. The original story, handwritten in 3,173 pages across 16 notebooks over 15 months represented my first real obsession as I merged from student to adult; there would be other obsessions, but there is nothing quite like the first one! Over the course of decades I rewrote and tweaked and cut and added until the final book you have just read bears little resemblance to the wild ramblings of a wide-eyed youth whose only experience with literature involved Edgar Rice Burroughs and Piers Anthony (both of whom I recommend as brilliant fuel for imagination!). Eventually my friend Tim introduced me to one of my literary heroes, Alexandre Dumas, and I have never been the same since; his books are remarkable, but even more than the stories and the characters, his words are a joy to read. I am frequently aware of a feeling of euphoria just by the way he constructs his sentences and the words he employs, the ways in which he weaves his tales, and the masterful manner in which he draws all the strings together to form a tapestry of such beauty and intricacy that in a lot of ways you never see it coming. I never want his books to end because the joy of reading them is so great that I want them to continue as long as possible. So many times, reading other authors, I have simply plowed forward just to see how it ends so that I can move on to the next thing—often wishing for a shorter book so that I can get it over with sooner. I sincerely hope that Edge of Time lands closer to the Dumas end of the scale!

I got my first computer for Christmas in 1999, so naturally I put it to work starting in January of 2000 on Edge of Time Book VII (yes, you have plenty to look forward to!), a vast sprawling timescape that encompassed more than 1,300 pages of adventure, from here to there and back again! I discovered that writing on a computer takes considerably less time than writing by hand (even though my typing skills are laughable) and involves far less pain (believe it or not, my hand resting on the paper for so many hours became a terrible source of aggravation: the paper draws the moisture out of the skin and creates a chapped, cracked, bloody mess that only clears up when you stop writing; who could ever imagine a writer being allergic to paper? That was maddening!) But I digress. Even working two jobs, which take up the first sixty hours of my week, I can still write books at a decent pace, thanks to the miracles of modern technology—like these magical computer thingys and that internet sorcery. Even though I'm still baffled by electricity and intrigued by magnetism (and don't get me started on wireless technology—pure magic!) I am perfectly comfortable traveling through time with a cell phone and a sketch book, so there will be plenty more Edge of Time volumes to come. There have to be, because we're all still here, so Simon must have figured something out—or maybe that's next week? If the world suddenly ends next October, it's not my fault!

Before the world does come to an end, I should take the time to acknowledge some of the people who helped to make this work possible. First, Mrs. Nielson, my fifth grade teacher who taught me how to physically make a book, from design to binding—I still have it on my book shelf; Mrs. Sowers, my high school English teacher who never minded my 50+ page journal entries that often involved alien invasions of the school, and who taught me about semicolons; Prof. Kirkwood, my college freshman English teacher who was a master of intense storytelling; and Prof. Huffstetler, my college creative writing teacher who encouraged me even after the rest of the class either gave up on my rambling tales or with misplaced malevolence hacked them to pieces (along with their author, on occasion).

My first real fan, and perhaps the only person to read all of my works over the years, Crystal has been my steadfast friend and guiding light for more than two decades; she has inspired me in so many ways I cannot recount them all. In fact, she is directly responsible for an entire book series, all because of the way she drives....

Olivia has devoured everything I have written in a very short span of time, and she knows how this trilogy is going to end; her influence has helped me to see in a way I never imagined before, and I am grateful for her friendship.

Tim has long been a source of encouragement, ever since our early days of battling the insanity of working nights in a grocery store; he introduced me to Dumas, Dostoevsky, and de Balzac, not to mention the importance of reading non-fiction as a way to inform and shape fiction. He also knows more about everything than I ever will, and so I always get more out of our conversations than he does—though every once in a while I think I surprise him with an unanticipated insight!

Brad is the personification of quiet strength and stability, a stalwart and dedicated traveler in life's long and sometimes monotonous journey; his insights and encouragement and extraordinary good nature, often in the face of insanity, have been truly inspiring.

Christon's encouragement and friendship helped awaken my desire to complete this project, and for that I will always be grateful; plus, I look forward to hearing him voice the characters if I ever get around to an audio version!

Grace became one of my earliest and youngest fans, and now she is my boss, sort of; without her tireless efforts and brilliant creativity, this project would never have gotten beyond my own desktop computer. It would be impossible to overstate her influence, and one underestimates her abilities at one's own peril!

Sarah has been a true delight and is an author's dream copy editor! She knows her stuff and doesn't miss anything; in fact, I have to fight for every comma and semicolon, and usually I lose because (I hate to admit this) she's usually right! Fortunately she's extraordinarily good-natured about it, so her insights are always welcomed!

Mr. Webb, my friend and mentor for more than 30 years, sadly and inexplicably passed away five years ago; he was a timeless source of wisdom and kept me grounded when life seemed impossible; for decades, the stresses of life dissipated over wine and cheese, along with conversations that lasted into the middle of the night. He would have been overjoyed by the release of this work. He is still greatly missed.

My parents never ceased to encourage me in any creative endeavor, even when they didn't really know what I was doing until I presented the final work; sure, the teenage boy locked in his room for endless hours at a stretch, day after day after day, might have worried any other parents. But I always emerged days or weeks later with some intricate or insanely ambitious art project, so they always supported my work and tolerated my moods. For that I am truly grateful.

Though my brother Jeremy lives farther away than I would like, he is always as close as a text message or a phone call; his encouragement and support have never wavered. The same is true for my sister-in-law Cheri and my wonderfully talented niece and nephew, Olivia and Noah.

I also would like to thank all the people who have offered feedback and encouragement on this project: friends, friends of friends, in many cases people I have never met. Bless you and thank you for helping to make this project a reality.

And to the readers out there, I hope you will enjoy a long and satisfying relationship with not only the characters who feel increasingly real to me, but with the author who has had the privilege of bringing them to life on the page. There are writers I have grown up with and consider friends, even though they have no idea who I am. There is no greater or more effective mode of time travel than the written word, the ability to cross vast epochs of time simply by reading a page and absorbing the ideas set down by another person in a faraway time and place, just for you. It's a conversation between minds that remains timeless.

ABOUT THE AUTHOR

Jeff Mills is a lot of things: artist, writer, photographer, world traveler, daydreamer, Scottish Lord, Purveyor of Pathetic Puns, LEGO enthusiast, collector of oddities, Martian Ambassador to Earth (unofficial), and grocery clerk. He divides his time between working, working, and working, and when he does have a free moment (every other Thursday between 11:45 and noon), he stops to smell the LEGO flowers—though, admittedly, the scent is fairly faint. Born and raised in the Blue Ridge Mountains near Roanoke, VA, he earned a degree from Bridgewater College sometime in the late 1900s before turning his attention to the exciting world of groceries, where even now he can be seen carefully placing items on shelves, when he's not banished to the Sweat Box to engage in his Alec Guinness impersonation.

When the world does finally end, he will be the guy with the folding lawn chair sitting atop the highest mountain, cracking jokes until the meteor hits; those within earshot will side with the rock.

www.ingramcontent.com/pod-product-compliance
Lightning Source LLC
Chambersburg PA
CBHW070540030726
47505CB00001B/102